ALSO BY MELISSA GOOD

Dar and Kerry Series
Tropical Storm
Hurricane Watch
Eye of the Storm
Red Sky At Morning
Thicker Than Water
Terrors of the High Seas
Tropical Convergence
Stormy Waters
Moving Target
Storm Surge: Book One
Storm Surge: Book Two
Winds of Change: Book One
Winds of Change: Book Two
Southern Stars

Partners Series
Partners: Book One
Partners: Book Two
Of Sea and Stars

Southern Stars

Melissa Good

Yellow Rose Books
by Regal Crest

Copyright © 2017 by Melissa Good

All rights reserved. No part of this publication may be reproduced, transmitted in any form or by any means, electronic or mechanical, including photocopy, recording, or any information storage and retrieval system, without permission in writing from the publisher. The characters, incidents and dialogue herein are fictional and any resemblance to actual events or persons, living or dead, is purely coincidental.

ISBN 978-1-61929-348-9

First Printing 2016

9 8 7 6 5 4 3 2 1

Cover design by Acorn Graphics

Published by:

Regal Crest Enterprises

Find us on the World Wide Web at
http://www.regalcrest.biz

Printed in the United States of America

Chapter One

THE LONG TWO lane road was sprinkled with rocks and bits of debris, all a faint crunching under the wheels of the RV making its steady way along it. The RV was light and dark blue in swirls, and on the back of the roof was perched a satellite dish dome near a skylight that could open fully.

It crested the last bit of elevation and then went along levelly toward a set of stone and wood buildings, surrounded by smaller cabins, and alongside a large parking lot that already had a few similar RVs parked in it.

The RV pulled into the lot, and into a spot near one end.

"Here we are." Kerry turned off the engine of the vehicle, leaning forward to peer out the front windshield. "Cute," she said, taking in the cozy cuddle of rustic looking cabins that bordered a lodge shaped building lit in the late afternoon sun. "Nice place to spend a few days before we start off on our great river adventure."

Behind her, a tall, dark haired figure levered itself up off a plush leather couch and came forward through the small kitchen area of the RV to the front to join the shorter, fair haired driver.

"Whatcha think?" Kerry leaned back in the captain's chair.

Dar removed her sunglasses and inspected their destination. "I think I see a hot tub." She pointed past the lodge. "Wanna go check in and look around? See what trouble we can get into?"

"Aaabsolutely." Kerry opened the driver's side door, letting in a rush of cool, dry air. "This is going to be fun." She hopped out. "Too bad we couldn't take the kids with us down the river."

Dar opened the passenger door of the RV and followed. "They're fine in their puppy palace. I think they had a hot tub too." She paused to look around. "And a spa."

"Did you book them pedicures?" Kerry stretched and bounced a little on the balls of her feet. "I bet Chi would love painted toenails."

Dar chortled. "Bet she wouldn't. But I booked them both for baths and swimming in the pool, and the platinum toy package." She looked around at their surroundings, and the canyon walls they could see past the line of trees beyond. "It's pretty here. Whole drive's been amazing."

The lodge was perched on the edge of a canyon wall, and Kerry drew in a contented breath as they walked across the sandy ground, taking in the endless array of reds and ochres, and the vivid blue of the sky. She could smell a wood fire on the breeze, and there were two couples crossing from the lodge to the cabins, carrying bags.

Dar whistled softly under her breath, her dark hair pulled back into a ponytail. She put her sunglasses back on as they walked across the parking lot and onto a rock lined path. "Hey. Look there." She pointed behind the lodge. "Horses."

"Hey, look there." Kerry pointed in a second direction. "ATVs. Vroom vroom."

Dar chuckled.

"We can do both." Kerry hooked her elbow through Dar's. "It's just nice being on vacation, even if we had to work like idiots up to the last minute."

"Yup."

"It really has been a nice drive too," Kerry said. "Especially since we crossed into New Mexico."

"Your camera got a workout," Dar said, "and the dogs liked the campgrounds."

"I liked campground we brought with us," Kerry said, "a small, air conditioned apartment with a kitchen; that also has a shower and Internet access."

"Microsoft Rustic," Dar said. "All the pretty sights and none of the bugs and sand."

They mounted the steps to the lodge and Dar opened the door, standing back for Kerry to enter. The front of the lodge was decorated with what she thought of as typical southwestern, a cow skull on the wall and a long front box full of nicely tended cactus.

A lot of striped carpeting, a lot of what appeared to be Indian inspired patterns. She followed Kerry inside, nodding at the huge, natural rock fireplace and the preponderance of weathered wood furniture. "Nice." She observed the rocking chairs near the fireplace, and the presence of a cat on a pillow nearby.

Kerry went to the front desk. "We have a reservation, name is Roberts." She told the young woman behind the counter. "We're doing the river trip on Sunday."

The woman nodded. "Yes, we have it right here. You have an RV?"

Dar caught up. "Yep. Parked it over there with the rest of em."

"It's a full-service campground. All the hookups you need," the woman said. "But you know, we've got some really nice cabins if you're interested in upgrading," she fished delicately, watching them with faint anticipation.

Kerry smiled at her and leaned on the counter. "Talk me into it. We're staying two days after we get back."

"And you've booked the premier package." The woman smiled back at her. "Want to look at our Silver Rim suite? I can walk you over."

Dar reasonably assumed she was going to end somewhere other than the RV. "I'm gonna get a drink." She patted Kerry on the back. "Let me know when you want me to move the baggage, hon."

Kerry looked at the brochure the girl handed her. "This looks really nice. Let's go." She watched her guide pick up a heavy, old-fashioned key and twirl it around her finger as she stepped around the counter and started for the door.

"Have you done any white-water rafting?" The woman asked, as they walked out a side entrance and headed across the dusty ground. "I'm Tamara, by the way."

"Kerry, and no, this is a first."

"Oh, you're going to love it. Glad you started off with us." Tamara led the way between two lines of smaller cabins, to a large one on the very edge of the canyon. "A lot of the ops here are bare bones. They get a lot more customers, but we like to think we're giving a select experience."

"That's why we booked with you." Kerry eyed the tidy building they were climbing the steps up to. "We don't go on vacation much, so we want the ones we go on to be good."

Tamara opened the door and pushed it open. Inside was a space Kerry had to admit was charming. They walked forward into a bedroom area that had a huge king size bed, a rock lined Jacuzzi bubbling gently in the corner, and a wraparound window that showed Grand Canyon to the horizon.

"It's so close to the edge, we know no one can see in the window, so it's private, but you get a fantastic view from the bed," Tamara said, in a practical tone. "The sunset is spectacular."

"Sold," Kerry responded. She walked to the window and looked out and down into the canyon, whose walls in all shades of yellow and orange and red collected and spread the light. Below she could see the river. "Is that where we go in?"

Tamara came over. "Yep, that's our launch. We carry you all down in our helicopter." She pointed. "Landing pad there, and at the other end you get a ride back here on our plane from a ranch that has a strip. You'll get lunch at the ranch before you come back, and then we usually have the group have a big dinner here if enough of the crowd is staying over."

"Awesome," Kerry said. "Sounds like a plan." She turned. "Let's get signed up." She followed Tamara out the door and they started across the grounds again. "I think we're going to really enjoy this."

"For sure," Tamara said. "Almost everyone does. I mean," She glanced sideways at Kerry, "there's always one or two people who book and don't realize what a white-water rafting trip is with the boat, and the water and getting wet and all."

"Not a problem," Kerry assured her. "We like water. Generally, it's salt water, though. We live in Miami." She followed Tamara back into the main lodge, and they approached the desk again, where another agent was speaking to a man and woman who were apparently also checking in.

"Nice." Tamara eyed her. "Are you....um..."

"Family?" Kerry suppressed a smile. "Partners? More than friends?"

Tamara smiled back. "Something like that, yeah." She went behind the desk and tapped something into her computer. "Okay, here we go."

"Is that a problem?" Kerry asked after a pause.

"Not for me," Tamara responded cheerfully. "We just like to let the river guys know so they don't say something silly, you know what I mean? Just trying to be funny?"

"Absolutely I do." Kerry removed her credit card from her wallet and slid it across the desk. "Like, are you sisters?" She leaned on the counter. "Or, hey, you want to go out?"

"Exactly." Tamara swiped her card and handed it back. "Okay, I see the trip is prepaid, so it's just for the cabin and incidentals, that all right?"

"Yup." Kerry put her card away. "Now let me go find Dar and whatever drink it is she's gotten me." She took the key Tamara handed her. "Let's get this party started."

Tamara grinned and waved, then turned to greet another customer.

Kerry went around toward the fireplace and paused to give the cat a scratch behind the ears before she proceeded farther into the lodge.

DAR GLANCED AT the lodge restaurant menu, before she

set down the two cups in her hands on a small table on the porch. She took a seat and extended her legs out along the terra cotta tile.

Nice. She took a sip of her beverage, and licked her lips. There was a group of people around her age at a nearby table, laughing, and a couple in the corner, studying some brochures.

To one side of the porch she could see the barn with the horses, and smell them a little. Across the way a rabbit scooted across the ground. The air had a dry, clean taste, and there were high, white contrails across the solid blue sky. She made a mental note to retrieve the lip balm they'd gotten going through New Mexico.

It felt good to see new things. Dar smiled to herself and thought about the past few days of driving; crossing areas she'd never seen and experiencing living in the RV. What had Kerry called it? Condo on wheels? She chuckled under her breath.

It had been fun, just driving along and stopping wherever they wanted. At pretty areas or just roadside tourist traps and little restaurants. No rush, no stress. Dar let her head rest against the chair back. It was nice to just relax.

The group at the next table were going down the river and were really excited about it. Dar listened to them talk about their previous white water experience, and found herself looking forward to doing something she'd never done before.

"There you are." Kerry walked up behind Dar and put both hands on her shoulders. "We're all signed up." She put a kiss on Dar's head as she moved past, and then sat on the chair next to hers. "And we triggered gaydar, but apparently, that's okay."

Dar pushed a cup over to her. "I see."

Kerry took a sip, then started laughing. "What is this?" She looked at the contents. "Is that a piece of cactus?" She fished it out and examined it. "It is."

"It's a Grand Canyon welcome special," Dar said. "I think it has tequila in it."

"It does." Kerry sat back with her drink and regarded the view. "This is nice." She took a sip. "We can go to our posh cabin and take a shower, and then have some dinner in the lodge. Sound good?"

"Whatever you want, hon." Dar rested her elbows on the chair arms, watching the sun splash across the floor. "I'm not the one who's been cooking the last few days."

"Hey, that built in grill's pretty nice."

"One of the group at the next table stood up. "Let's go check our gear." He was a red headed man with freckles and an athletic physique. "We better weigh it. They said no more than twenty for each of us." He glanced aside at Kerry and Dar and grinned. "You going down the river too?"

"We are." Kerry said.

"Cool! First time?"

Both Dar and Kerry nodded.

"River virgins!" The man chortled. "Nah just kidding, you'll love it. It's so much fun!" He rocked the chair he'd been sitting in and the rest of the group got up, grumbling a little good naturedly. "I've been down five times. This is the earliest in the year for me though, first run."

One of his companions looked tolerantly at him. "That's a good thing, just a small group usually." He held a hand out to Kerry. "Hi, I'm Dave, and that's Richard. He'll settle down once we start, I promise."

Kerry took the hand. "No problem. I'm Kerry, and this is Dar."

Two of the women from the group came over. "Sally and Trisha. We're from Montana. You?" Both were tall and spare, with pale blond hair in braids.

"Miami" Kerry responded.

"Oh cool!" Sally said. "My grandmother moved down there. She loves it."

Kerry grinned. "We do too. Sounds like you're all veterans of this kind of thing."

"We are." Dave sat down. "Rich has done the most, but this is my third trip. First down the Colorado though." He grinned. "I can't wait. I've seen the pictures he brought back last time and wow, we jumped on it."

Rich beamed.

"The slot canyons are gorgeous." Trisha took the seat next to Dar. "And this op seems to have its act together. I went with one that didn't, and that was a mess."

"A mess," Sally said. "Dumped one of the rafts midway and lost everything. We got real tired of protein bars, let me tell you."

"No, these guys are good," Rich said. "They got good boats and good guides."

"And good chow," Dave reminded him. "Did we make sure they had Sally's rabbit food?"

"Absolutely." Rich sounded indignant. "C'mon! Would I do that to Sal?" He looked at the table. "Are you ladies' vegetarian?"

"No." Dar spoke up for the first time.

"According to the brochure they have a pretty good selection," Kerry said. "I think we'll be fine."

The group stood up. "We'll see you all later," Dave said. "Hey, want to join us for dinner? One of the cool things about these trips is getting to know people, you know?" He smiled in an engaging way at Kerry. "We make friends every single time."

Kerry gave Dar a quick glance, and then nodded. "Sure. Here at the lodge? In the restaurant?" She asked. "How about an hour from now?"

Rich gave her thumbs up. "Right on." He backed away then, turned and trotted toward the door. The rest of them followed, half turning to wave at Dar and Kerry as they disappeared.

Dar swirled her drink in her cup and took a sip of it. "Seems like a nice bunch," she said, after a pause. "I think they said we'd only have a dozen on the trip."

"Are you okay with joining them for dinner?" Kerry asked. "I couldn't really tell with those sunglasses on."

Dar chuckled and removed them, turning to look at Kerry. "It's fine. We can get some intel about the trip. I like to know what I'm in for." She glanced up as another couple entered, walked over to one of the far tables and took a seat.

Unlike the group that had just left, these two looked rather glum. They waved off the waitress who came over to see if they wanted anything.

Kerry extended her hand. "Let's go get our stuff settled." She waited for Dar to take hold and then squeezed her fingers. "Want to go over and say hi to the horses?"

Dar grinned.

"And I think they have llamas," Kerry whispered, bending closer. "I want a picture of you with a llama."

"MY GOSH THAT'S beautiful." Kerry paused, her finger resting on the camera shutter. She watched the shift of light as the dawn light painted the canyon. "I can't wait to see what the river's going to be like."

"Mm." Dar edged in behind her on the small patio and set a tray down on the even smaller table. "Coffee?"

"Heck yeah." Kerry was dressed in a pair of worn jeans and a hoodie, with a pair of brand new llama slippers on her feet. "Anyone else up?"

"Not that I saw." Dar herself had heavy sweatpants and sneakers on, and a pullover. "I ran all the way down the road where that fence was and didn't see anyone until I went into the lodge to get this." She finished sorting the coffee out and offered Kerry a cup.

Kerry sat on the second chair and pulled her coffee over. "Horseback riding in the morning, then ATV in the afternoon?" She extended her slippered feet out and crossed her legs at the ankles. "Then we should figure out what to pack. Did they really mean twenty pounds?"

"Uh huh." Dar watched a bird circle above the striated rock levels of the canyon. "Glad I'm not bringing a laptop. That would take most of mine." She hiked one sneaker up and put it on its opposing knee. "But I saw they had light thermal stuff in the shop there."

Kerry gave her a wry grin. "At a premium."

"Sure. Marketing opportunity. But I'd rather pack that and have room for peanut butter crackers after all that talk about healthy meals on the ride."

Kerry laughed and put her cup down hastily to avoid spilling it. "Dar."

"I'm serious," Dar grumbled. "You know I can't deal with salad and granola." She tapped her thumb against the bone of her ankle under its clean white sock. "It's not like there's Publix down there to grab fried chicken at."

"I'm sure it's going to be fine." Kerry gave her an affectionate look. "I'll save some space for snacks for you in my bag too, hon. If they have a chunk of protein at dinner at least there's that."

"Grab me a fish and have homemade sushi." Dar eyed her. "Can't you see that? Blood spurting everywhere when I bite into the damn thing?"

Kerry covered her eyes in mock horror.

Dar chuckled. "Hell, it's only seven days." She sighed. "I'm sure I'll survive." She propped her elbows on the chair arms and sucked at the coffee. "And you're right about the scenery. It's gorgeous."

It was. Kerry settled back contentedly. "They know we won't have any signal once we go down into the canyon, right? Mark and Maria, I mean?"

"They know," Dar replied. "Everything's on track, all the projects are on schedule, even the government's, and we delivered Dade County before we left. They shouldn't need us for anything."

"Mm."

"Shouldn't." Dar repeated. "We've got a good team there,

Ker. We can trust them."

"I'm not saying we can't," Kerry said. "It's just weird stuff happens, you know? We could have a Martian spaceship drop down into the central court at the office. Do they know what to do about that?"

"Do we?"

"Well, that's a point"

Dar drained her coffee and stood up. "I'm gonna change. You up for breakfast?"

"Yup." Kerry put her cup down and picked up her camera, as the sun came up over the cabin and splashed beautifully past it. "Just going to get a few more shots while you do that."

Dar crossed behind her, giving the back of her neck a little scratch as she ducked inside the door and left Kerry to her snapshots.

SO FAR THE morning ride was fun. Dar and Kerry were joined by two of their new friends, Dave and Sally, who both had ridden before and appeared to love horses.

Kerry was content enough to be riding a good-natured piebald, with hazel eyes and a sedate walk. He was happy to follow along where his equine buddies led, and she felt comfortable enough to tuck her reins under one knee and lift her camera up as they ambled along.

Dar was just ahead of her, riding a tall, dark gray horse with a black mane and tail. Her head swept back and forth as they moved through thick, fragrant trees with the faint hint of wood smoke on the breeze. They were following a clearly marked path that would wind up the next ridge and back down.

Nothing crazy exciting. Kerry was okay with that, remembering the last time she'd ridden horseback and ended up falling off her bee stung steed, scaring Dar half to death.

She tapped her horse gently on the ribs and he stepped along faster, bringing her even with Dar, allowing her to snap a profile shot of her partner.

Dar eyed her wryly. Then she smiled and winked.

Kerry took advantage of this, then put the camera down and picked up her reins again as they started down the slope toward a small gully. "This is nice."

"We're not galloping." Dar sighed mournfully.

"That's what I meant." Kerry patted her knee. "We'll have a wild enough ride starting tomorrow, hon. I don't want to get my ass thrown off like the last time."

"Wasn't your fault."

Kerry noticed the other two riders stop ahead and point at something. "What do you figure, squirrel?"

"Bobcat."

Kerry stared. "Really?"

"No, I have no idea." Dar flexed her hands, then rested them on her thighs. "I just want to see a bobcat. I think they're cool and I saw they had them here." She drummed her fingers against the denim surface. "And coyotes."

They rode up next to the other two horses and stopped. Kerry leaned forward and asked, "What's up?"

"It's a Mexican spotted owl," Dave whispered, pointing into the trees nearby. "Isn't it cool? See it?"

"It's brown," Sally added helpfully. "Right there on the branch."

"See it." Kerry lifted her camera and focused, zooming in a little and getting a decent shot of the bird. "It's pretty, with those yellow markings."

The horses took advantage of this by nibbling at the scrub grass. Dar casually reached over to take hold of Kerry's reins as she got another shot of the owl.

It was a nice-looking bird, she acknowledged, watching it rotate it's head a little. "Aren't they supposed to be nocturnal?"

"Yes!" Sally whispered. "I've never seen one in the morning before. It's cool!"

Unexpectedly, the owl took off from the branch, apparently bored with its spectators. A moment later it landed on Dar's hastily thrown up arm as she saw it coming at her. "What the hell!"

It was heavier than she'd expected, and she was glad she had a long sleeve shirt on as she felt its claws grab her arm as she stared at it in wide-eyed surprise.

It sidestepped along, opening and closing its beak with a small hissing squeaking sound.

"Wow!" Sally's eyes were almost as wide.

"Oh, nice." Kerry was busy snapping away, ducking when the owl took off again, this time to soar across the wooded area and land in another tree much farther away. "It's that animal magnetism." She let the camera drop and took her reins. "Never fails."

Dave stared at Dar. "That was amazing! Are you an animal trainer or something?"

"Or Native American?" Sally suggested. "I've heard a lot of

the myths around here about that."

Dar looked up from inspecting her sleeve. "Computer programmer," she replied. "From Miami. Let's get moving before some bear decides to try that and I end up flat on my ass with this horse breakdancing." She put her reins against her horse's neck and guided him from the trees and back up onto the path.

"That was amazing," Dave repeated. "Really amazing."

"Really cool; I got a picture too." Sally slid her point and shoot camera back into her pocket. "I can't wait to see what kind of wildlife we're going to see on the river."

They prodded their mounts to follow Dar. "Did I see you going to that blue RV last night?"

"Yep," Kerry said. "We drove from Florida."

"That's a long drive." Dave settled into his saddle. "I drove to Seattle once. That was long enough for me. "

"It was all right. We had our dogs with us, and nice weather." Kerry slid her camera into the pack she had attached to the saddle. "I've never driven a lot cross country. I'm from Michigan."

They started downhill and the horses picked up the pace a little. They caught up to Dar and broke into a gentle canter, coming into a more open slope.

It was pleasant. Kerry could see Dar was enjoying the motion and she briefly envied that relaxed and natural posture as her partner moved almost as a part of the animal.

A little crazy, since she knew Dar really didn't have that much experience with horses, especially not recently. She herself felt a little unsure, a little on the edge of control riding this unfamiliar animal at any type of speed, but they were almost at the bottom of the slope and she figured it would slow down any minute.

Alas, no. The horses could sense their comfortable barn ahead and sped up, thundering through the grassy tufts in the sandy ground. "Oh boy."

She leaned forward a little, and concentrated on keeping her balance as Sally and Dave whooped in excitement as they chased after Dar's tall form.

Scary. But after a minute of nothing catastrophic happening, Kerry relaxed a little and enjoyed the experience, seeing Dar's horse already slowing down as they met the dirt road that lead off into the trees where the ATV's were.

She was sort of in the rhythm now, and almost regretted it when her mounts pace slacked and became bouncier and jarring before they reached the edge of the grass.

Dar turned her horse and came cantering back as the rest of them arrived and joined them. "That was fun." She grinned as she ended up next to Kerry. "You okay?"

"Yup, me and old Paint here had a great ride." Kerry patted her horse on the shoulder. "No bees this time." She ran her fingers through her now thoroughly disordered hair. "But I have to be honest and tell you I like it better when I'm driving."

Dar chuckled. "Yeah, I know." She glanced up at the bright sunlight, and pushed the sleeves of her shirt up a little as their horses ambled side by side down the track toward the corral that was half shaded by trees. "Ah. Owl tracks."

Kerry leaned over to look at the red marks. "Just a few scratches."

Loud voices suddenly attracted their attention and they looked up to see the couple that had come in late the evening before standing with Tamara near the rustic pole fence that bordered the corral.

Kerry watched them from the corner of her eye as they got to the gate and one of the staff opened it for them, waving them inside. "Wonder what their issue is?"

Dar glanced behind her, then dismounted and handed her reins over, turning at once to take hold of the gray's bridle as Kerry got herself down off it's back.

They dusted each other off. Dave and Sally joined them and they all stood for a moment.

The yelling got louder. The man waved his hands, and pointed at Tamara. The woman was clearly upset. Tamara had both hands out in a calming gesture.

Kerry stretched her legs out. "Should we..."

"No." Dar put her arm around Kerry's shoulders and steered her toward the lodge. "I learned my lesson with Kristie. I'm done. No sticking my nose in other people's business anymore." She turned her back on the argument. "Grab some lunch before we ATV?"

Kerry was momentarily silent, then she nodded. "Yep." She put her arm around Dar's back. Behind them she could still hear the yelling, but she also understood where Dar was coming from.

At least, she thought she did.

"Don't get me wrong," Dar said, as though listening to her internal dialog. "For you, for my family, for our friends I'd step in front of a bus."

"Mm."

"But not for strangers. Not anymore."

And Kerry really couldn't blame her. Twice in a row, once for a company, once for a worker on the island they lived on Dar had stood up, and taken it on the chin in return. Literally. They were in the process of searching for a new place to live due to the fallout from the last scene.

She got it. "I hear ya, hon." Kerry gave her a little squeeze. "Totally understand."

The voices faded behind them and as they mounted the steps into the lodge Tamara came trotting behind them, shaking her head as she opened the door and let them enter ahead of her. "Did you enjoy the ride folks?"

"We did."

Sally and Dave had been oblivious to the drama. "We saw a spotted owl! It landed on her arm!" She pointed at Dar. "It was amazing!"

"Really?" Tamara gathered herself together and shook off the recently ended disagreement. "That's a first!" She craned her neck to see the digital display Kerry held out. "Oh, my gosh!" She looked up at Dar. "It just flew onto your arm?"

Dar had her hands in her pockets now and she nodded mutely, as they all filed into the lodge and started to spread out inside.

"Really cool," Tamara said, firmly. "Can you send me a copy of it? Do you mind if we put it on the website?" She crossed ahead of them, talking half over her shoulder. "We'll crop it so you can't see who it is if you want, just the owl."

"Sure," Kerry said. "Give me an email address and I will, no problem."

Rich appeared from the patio area. "Hey, glad you guys are back; they're putting lunch out. I think they've got snake sushi!"

Both Dar and Kerry, and, in fact Tamara, pulled up short and looked at him, nonplussed.

Sally rolled her eyes. "Get out."

Rich grinned at them. "Just kidding. Cream of asparagus soup and chicken salad sandwiches with fruit." He waved them forward. "C'mon."

"Two out of three ain't bad," Sally said. "I'm going to go wash my hands. Meet you in there."

Kerry put her camera back in her backpack and followed, Dar whistling softly under her breath at her heels. They all entered the ladies room and went to the sinks, which had baskets between them with fragrant potpourri and clean white hand towels.

"That was pretty cool," Sally said, as she scrubbed her hands. "I really like horses. Do you have—I mean, do you live on a ranch?" She looked sideways at Dar. "You're a good rider."

Kerry chuckled, but remained silent.

Dar cleared her throat. "No, we live in a development near downtown Miami. I got to ride a little growing up." She wiped her hands on one of the towels. "I've always liked horses though."

Sally smiled at her. "Obviously, animals like you." She paused, as one of the stalls opened and the woman who had been arguing with Tamara came out. She walked past them without a word, shoved the door open and then slammed it shut.

Kerry wiped her hands down and put the damp towel in the basin.

"That's going to be a downer," Sally said, wryly. "She and her boyfriend bought a private raft trip, and these guys couldn't deliver it. The guide team that was supposed to take them got sick at the last minute and didn't make the flight out here from Toronto."

"Ah."

"I mean, I get they're pissed, but they offered them a full refund, and their travel and everything."

"Well." Kerry went to the door and opened it. "Maybe they were really looking forward to it? If they're not going to go, why are they still around?"

Sally paused near the door. "That's the bad news for us. They're going to be on our trip."

"Maybe they'll cheer up after we're on the way," Kerry suggested, as they exited and started for the patio, where the sounds of silverware and the soft strains of new age music were drifting from. "After they get over the disappointment. This place is so gorgeous, how could you stay pissed?"

Sally nodded in agreement. "Exactly."

They entered the patio and were greeted by Rich and the rest of their gang, seated already at a larger table that could accommodate all of them. As they sat down a waitress came over to take their drink order.

Dar rested her elbows on the chair arms as Kerry ordered for them. She smiled briefly at the excited, interested faces around her, everyone exchanging stories of the day and clamoring to see Kerry's pictures.

Different than the people she was usually surrounded by. They were open and friendly. That was kind of nice, and what was more, she and Kerry were just accepted and included.

Behind them, four women were at a table listening, and after a moment, they too got up and came over. "Hey, there," one said. "So, you all are part of the raft group too, right?" She had hazel eyes and a deep tan that went with the Southern drawl. "We're on break from school." She pointed around. "Carla, PJ, Jan and I'm Terry."

"Take a seat," Rich said. "The more the merrier."

An older couple had been standing in the doorway, and now joined them as well. "We're Donald and Marcia. I think we round out the lot." Donald smiled at them. "This is our first time on a raft."

"Us too." Kerry indicated herself and Dar. "Glad we're not the only ones."

The waitress came back and stopped. "Whoops, I'm gonna need a bigger tray." She delivered the drinks and rambled off, as everyone pushed back their chairs to make room for all the new comers. "Be right back."

DAR ZIPPED UP her duffel bag and straightened. "You ready, Ker?"

"Yes, ma'am." Kerry pulled a hoodie over her head, as she emerged from the bathroom, her own duffel already packed near the door. "Holy crap, Dar. Do you know how long it's been since I played actual cards?" She ran her fingers through her hair, freeing it from the hood. "That was kinda fun."

"It was," Dar readily said. "Fun bunch." She slung her bag over her shoulder and put her hands in the front pockets of her own hoodie. "I think Donald may be ex-Navy."

"Some kind of veteran, yeah." Kerry picked up her bag and opened the door. "Let's go rafting, Dardar."

They left the comfort of the cabin and went into a faintly smoke scented early dawn light, heading across the center of the complex toward a helicopter pad behind the lodge.

It was quiet, and ethereal, the air dry and clean. A faint breeze stirred their hair as they came around the side of the lodge to where the rest of the team was assembling, stifling yawns and stretching as the light slowly grew around them.

"Hey, morning!" Dave said as they arrived, and added their bags to the pile waiting for the helicopter. "We ready for this?"

The college girls were all seated on the ground near their duffels, half asleep, but they waved faintly. "Shh," the dark skinned and dark haired PJ added. "We had to finish the tequila we brought last night."

Kerry chuckled a little under her breath. "Oh, I remember those days." She leaned against the post rail fence surrounding the pad.

"Me too." Marcia leaned next to her. She and Donald were in their mid-fifties, rough and weathered and dressed in matching lined and waterproof jackets. "Now I stick to a glass of white wine."

"Beer," Kerry said.

"Milk," Dar chimed in drolly. "Chocolate milk when I really get wild."

"Please don't say chocolate milk," PJ begged. "My stomach could barely handle the oatmeal this morning."

A young man, wearing a blue jacket with the name of the lodge on it, came over and opened the side of the helicopter. "Okay, folks. We go six at a time, and I'm Jimbo, your pilot." He started loading the bags in, then paused as Tamara came up next to him with a clipboard. "Hey, Tam."

She leaned close and whispered to him, displaying the clipboard.

"Oh." Jimbo paused in his loading. "Okay, let me do that first then." He ducked around the side of the helicopter and motioned at two people standing off to one side. "C'mon, then, let me get you down, okay?"

Sally folded her arms. "Ah. The grumbles."

The two disgruntled customers got into the helicopter, refusing to look at anyone as Jimbo got their bags loaded and then closed the door.

"Man, that's going to be a drag," Rich said. "It only takes one sourpuss, you know? Everything's gonna be wrong for them. The weather, the seat, the river, the food."

"Well, you never know," Kerry said. "Let's give it a chance."

Dar had her sunglasses on, as the sun was now splashing over the plateau. She leaned next to Kerry against the fence and watched the helicopter spool up. The blast from the rotors fluttered her jacket against her skin, and seeing the profiles inside the window she privately considered that Rich was probably closer to the truth than Kerry was.

Tamara watched the craft take off, then came over to them, looking more than a little apologetic. "We have two late additions,"she said. "They were supposed to have a different guide, but we had a conflict."

"They look kinda pissed off," Dave said.

"Well, it's our fault," Tamara said. "We'll try to make it up to them, and hopefully it won't bother the rest of you because you've all got such a great attitude. Anyway, sorry about that." She turned and headed toward the lodge, breaking into a run as she went past the fence.

"Into everyone's lives a few assholes must fall," Dar intoned, pushing her sunglasses up on her nose a little.

Rich heard her, and laughed. Sally's sister, Trisha, did as well. "Yeah." Rich mock sighed. "There's always that one guy. Or gal. Or both."

The sound of the helicopter returning got them all stirring around and a moment later Tamara and one of her colleagues returned with a tray with cups on it. "Hey, guys, here's some hot chocolate to start the day off. With a little bit of extra."

PJ took a cup and sipped it. "Kahlua, nice."

"Hair of the dog," Jan said. "Just what we needed."

Kerry took a sip, tasting the rich creamy beverage, and noted a hint of cinnamon along with the Kahlua. "That's good."

"It is," Dar said. "They can serve this for dinner every day far as I'm concerned." She straightened up and drained the chocolate, setting the cup on the tray as Tamara came around to collect them. "Thanks."

"You're welcome." Tamara smiled at her. "Have a great trip, ladies. Take lots of good pictures." She winked at Kerry. "Already had six or seven comments on that owl."

Six of them boarded the helicopter, including Dar and Kerry, and a moment later they were airborne, lifting into the morning sun to tip over the edge of the canyon and down into it. The sound of the rotors echoed off the striated walls, and the colors spread with the sun as it chased them downward.

Below they could see the green blue of the river, with splats of brown through it. On one side was a landing with sturdy wooden posts bracketing a set of heavy well-built raft boats.

They were odd looking, square in parts and pontoon in parts, like no other boat she'd ever seen. Dar watched with interest as the river guides bounced all over them, loading gear.

The chopper landed on a pad on a little rise and Jimbo jumped out and popped the side door open to let them out. "Here we go, peeps. Don't worry about your bags. We'll handle them."

They scrambled down out of the craft and Dar smelled the distinct scent of the water, and now, closer, they could see the current rippling past.

Rich, Dave, Sally and Trisha were with them, and they moved away from the landing pad and toward a set of picnic tables under a sturdy tarp that shaded them from the sun, as the helicopter lifted again to pick up the rest of the group.

The other couple was already there, seated at one of the tables. As the rest of them wandered in and started to settle, Rich went over to them. "Hi!" He sat down at the table. "I'm Rich. I guess we'll be spending the next week with each other."

The two of them stared at him, but after a moment the woman unfroze a little and cleared her throat. "Hi," she said. "I'm Amy, and this is Todd, my fiancé."

"Hi," Todd added, briefly.

He had a crew cut, and a squared face with a muscular jaw and very pale hazel eyes. Amy was pert and pretty, with long blond hair, a creamy complexion, and gray eyes. She was dressed in what Kerry considered haut outdoorsman.

They looked like they were in their early twenties.

Dar took a seat next to her and leaned on the table, tipping forward her sunglasses a little as she regarded their surroundings. The boat team was busy loading all their gear into deck boxes, calling to each other and paying more attention to their tasks than their passengers.

Sally and Trisha joined them at their table, while Dave wandered over to join Rich at the next one.

"Nice day," Trisha said. "Going to be great weather for rafting." She and her sister had their hair pulled back into identical pony tails and they were wearing similar waterproof rain jackets and multi pocketed cargo pants.

Dar and Kerry were also wearing cargo pants with tank tops under their hoodies. Dar was glad since she could already feel the air warming down at river level in the canyon. She left Kerry to continue the casual chatter and looked around at the striated walls, their craggy outlines and shades of color appealing to her eye.

"I'm looking forward to seeing those slot canyons you told us about," Kerry said. "They sound amazing."

Sally immediately smiled. "Oh, they are! I mean, the river's nice and I like the rapids, but the hikes into those slots for me, that's the best part."

"Hope we don't get flash floods," Trisha added. "I got caught in one once, and that was no fun, let me tell you. Do you guys swim? I think you said you did."

"We're divers," Kerry said, then they fell silent as two of the boat crew came over, a guy and a gal with clipboards.

The rest of the group had now joined them and they had twelve passengers, who turned looks of various levels of attentiveness toward them.

"Hi there, folks," The woman said. "My name is Janet Wilson and I'll be your trip coordinator for our first run down the river this year. Everyone excited?"

"Yes," the group answered back.

"This is Douglas. He's the raft captain. So, he's in charge of everything that moves and I'm in charge of everything else. Okay?" Janet had a confident, no nonsense attitude and looked as though she expected everyone to be okay with that.

"So, we're going to go through the safety basics, even though I know some of you have not only done this before, but done this before with us," Janet said. "Because we really want everyone to have a great time, and really enjoy themselves, but what the most important thing to all of us is, that we all do that in a safe way."

Dar nodded.

"How many of you have rafted or done whitewater?" She scanned the raised hands. "Okay great, about half of you. That's awesome." She half turned. "Doug, you want to go over the safety features of our custom made, cool looking rafts?"

Doug smiled. "Sure." He had a backpack on his back, and a sparse beard and was probably in his mid-thirties. "Let's get this party started," He said. "C'mon over to the boat."

They went as a group along a rough rock lined path down to the river's edge. The raft was pulled up to a wooden pier, and Dar could see the current tugging at it, rippling past at a good clip. The craft was cross tied against it, with a walkway set from the pier to allow them access.

"So, you can see we have lots of seats," Doug said. "We can take a total capacity of twenty people on one of these, so you all are going to have lots of space and you can move around to different seats depending on how you feel that day. "He stepped onto the surface. "These seats up here, on the front pontoons are the action stations. You feel every bump."

Rich grinned. "My kinda ride."

"Behind them, that row, you get plenty wet, but it's more stable. Behind them, more stable again. There in the middle, and in the rear of the raft where I stand, it's the Barcaloungers," Doug said. "You can walk around while we're between rapids, but we do recommend you sit down to go through em."

The group chuckled.

"Now let's talk about water safety." He looked across at them. "I don't have any mariners this trip, do I?"

After a brief pause, the older man, Donald, raised his hand, and a moment later, Dar did also, and then they looked at each other. "Navy?" Dar hazarded a guess.

Donald grinned. "Coast Guard. You're Navy, right?"

"Only by proxy," Dar said. "But I have a captain's license."

Doug regarded her with interest. "OUPV?"

"Masters," Dar replied in casual tone.

"Nice." He grinned at her. "Not useful on the river, though."

"Not in the slightest," Dar said. "Since you're driving and I'm used to salt water."

"But I don't have to explain port and starboard to ya." He looked around at the rest of the group. "For the rest of you, the boat does have two sides, port and starboard. Easy to remember that port has four letters, and so does left. So, left is portside, and right is starboard. Got it?"

Dar saw some rolling eyeballs. She put her hands in her pockets and watched the group, as Todd walked past where Doug was talking and started inspecting the boat on his own.

Doug swung around to watch him, and drew a breath. Then Janet touched his arm and shook her head. He glanced at her, then shrugged and went back to his briefing. "So, anyway the most important thing to know is what to do if you fall off."

"Oh, yeah," Kerry muttered. "There aren't any seat belts on that thing."

Dar regarded the craft. "No. You don't want to be strapped down if it flips." She glanced at Kerry, whose eyebrows were lifted. "Well think about it, hon. We carry those seat belt cutters in the car for a reason, right? Besides you can swim."

"So, if you go into the water, the most critical thing is not to freak out," Doug said. "You'll be wearing safety jackets that have enough lift to keep you at the surface, and we've got enough horsepower to come after you. Don't worry." He grinned. "When it's calm, you don't have to wear the jackets but we'll let you know when you do."

"Mm," Kerry rumbled under her breath. "I hate when someone says that."

Dar rocked up and down on her heels. She could see the rest of the group was getting restless. "Let's get this moving. Want to see new things."

Chapter Two

RICH CLAIMED ONE of the pontoon seats on the front. So did Trish and PJ. Donald and Marcia settled in the middle, with the rest of the collegians in their row. Amy and Todd took seats in the back, near Doug.

Dar, Kerry, Sally and Dave decided to take the front row and settled there, arranging their dry bags that clipped onto the relatively sturdy seats. Dar stood up and took off her hoodie, stuffing it in the dry bag along with a handful of peanut butter crackers and a bottle of water.

The air was still cool, but the sun slanted down over them and it felt good on her bare shoulders. She left her lurid orange life vest on the back of the chair and strolled around the decking that bordered the seats. In the middle of them were long, large lockers where their gear was stowed, and near the back of the raft, two of the crew were loading beer and wine into floating coolers that they then pushed into the water.

"Natural refrigeration." One of them smiled at Dar. "Next one has the margaritas in it." He pointed at the gear lockers. "We put the chow in the lower level of those, keeps everything nice and chilled."

Janet saw her standing there and came over. "And it's eco-friendlier. Which is cool."

"It's cool," Dar said.

"You're...ah, Dar, right?" Janet said. "Roberts?"

She nodded. "That's me. First time on white water."

"A lot of first timers," Janet said, "and that's really cool for me. I love sharing the Colorado with new people. Just seeing the faces." She grinned and her serious demeanor eased.

"I feel the same way about diving," Dar responded agreeably. She noticed Todd come back to his seat and slump into it, a can of beer in his hand. His safety jacket was on the floor and as she watched, he put his military booted feet on it and popped the top on the can.

Janet saw it also, and frowned. Then she just shook her head and focused on Dar. "What kind of work do you do?"

"Computers," Dar said. "I co-own a small private tech company."

Janet regarded her with a faintly puzzled expression. "And

you're a boat captain too?"

Dar put her hands in her pockets and nodded. "I've been on the water since I could walk, so when I inherited a boat, I figured I should learn how to drive it."

Doug was fiddling with his station, and looked up with a grin. "Good idea. How many screws?"

"Twin diesels," Dar said. "Eight hundred horsepower."

Doug stopped in mid motion, and looked at her. After a minute he laughed, and Dar did too. "So now I know who I can ask to spell me, right? I thought you were just messing with me with the license."

"Totally different type of driving," Dar said. She half turned as one of the crew came over with two plastic tubes of liquid and offered her one. "Thanks."

"Raspberry lemonade," the crewman said. "We're ready, Janet."

"Excuse me." The woman smiled at Dar and edged past. "Okay, Doug, let's line off, and get going."

Dar took her tube of lemonade back to her seat and settled into her end seat next to Kerry. She opened it and took sip, then offered it to Kerry. "Ready?"

Kerry had taken off her hoodie as well, but sat with her safety jacket on, snugged firmly around her body. She took the tube and sucked in a swallow, swishing it around a little. "Mm." She licked her lips. "That's good." She closed the tube and clipped it to her vest with the small plastic ring on its top. "Ready, Dardar."

The lines came off and the crew boarded. The staff onshore pulled the gangway free and waved as the raft backed out into the current. With a brief gun on the engine, the raft turned and started downstream.

It was sunny and breezy. The river before them was relatively placid and calm and Dar drew in a breath of contented well-being as she relaxed in her seat, and absorbed the new scenery.

Ahead of them, she could see what looked like eagles circling, and the cliffs that rose on either side were strange and craggy. It was an odd juxtaposition between a desert like environment and the river, which burbled and splashed all around them.

In front of them, straddling the pontoons, Rich raised both hands and let out a whoop, that echoed back to them from the walls as the launch point disappeared behind them.

DAR REALIZED RATHER quickly that just sitting on a raft, going down a river didn't really do that much for her. Kerry at least had her camera to entertain herself with, and was busy taking shots of the moving scenery, and her raft mates, while she waited for something to happen.

When booking, Dar briefly considered signing them up for one of the paddling trips, but after some mental tug-of-war decided on the posh run, given they'd never done anything like it before. Seven days was a long time if you found out you really didn't like paddling a canoe.

Ah well. She draped her arm over the back of Kerry's seat. Just then Kerry swiveled and tilted backward to lean against Dar's body so she could take a picture of a bird.

Dar rested her cheek against Kerry's pale hair and listened to the little sounds of the shutter and the low chuckle of achievement, deliberately refusing to think about what was going on back in Miami.

It was at least easier now, with the projects their company was working on. None of the accounts so far required the kind of attentive support she'd been used to in her previous job. She was confident that once out of the canyon their phones would not contain multiple increasingly agitated voice mails.

"What does that piece of rock look like to you, Dar?"

"A piece of rock," Dar amiably supplied. "Are you suggesting it's something else?"

"It looks like a hatchet, doesn't it?"

Dar tilted her head. "Sort of," she admitted, briefly glancing around at their raft mates. Most were pointing and gesturing to the various scenes to either side. Marcia, though, was knitting. No one was giving them one of "those" looks, or even a second glance.

Nice. Not that either of them would care if there had been, but there was something oddly comforting at the anonymous perspective of it all, not being the center of attention as they often were at work.

Dar regarded the flowing river with a smile. Nice to just be a couple of people on a raft.

"Okay, folks," Janet said, making her rounds. "In about five minutes we'd like you to all get your vests on because we're going to start rocking and rolling a little before we meet our first challenge, Badger Creek rapids."

Kerry already had hers on, but she sat up and swiveled around to let Dar lean forward and pull hers out from the back of her seat and slide it onto her shoulders. She put her camera down and let it hang around her neck as she adjusted the straps and snapped the connectors together. "There."

Dar wriggled a little and tightened the restraints. The garment was reasonably comfortable and not inclined to hike up and hit her chin. She folded her bare arms over her chest and regarded the increasing pace of the water with approval. "Vroom."

The canyon walls narrowed slightly and the pitch of the water now had small whitecaps ruffling it's green-brown edges. All round them the rest of the raft party was getting ready, and now Marcia put her knitting into a dry bag and faced forward with an expression of excited pleasure.

"We're about to get drenched, aren't we?" Kerry said. She tucked her camera into its waterproof housing. "I never figured I'd use this above the surface. She indicated the dive case. "How cold do you figure the water is?"

"They're chilling your beer in it," Dar responded dryly. "How cold is our refrigerator?"

"Oh boy."

Dar chuckled."Sun's nice. We'll dry out." She heard the motor behind her gun a little and the raft slewed sideways in the current, as they approached a bend in the river. She could hear beyond it the flutter and rush of rapidly moving water.

"Okay!" Doug yelled. "We're going to take it straight front, to the left!"

Kerry wrapped her legs around the base of her seat, and hesitated. "Wonder what that means? I probably should put this down and hold on."

Dar took hold of the back of Kerry's jacket and clamped a hand through one of the belts. "G'wan. I got ya," she said, confidently "You aren't going anywhere without me attached."

Kerry lifted her camera and grinned, starting the video recording as the raft headed into the white water, flexing and bucking under them. She took a breath and then her eyes widened as she felt the raft slam sideways and plunge into a cleft in the water, a wall of green and white froth crashing over the pontoons and completely covering the three people riding up there.

Then they came up and bucked sideways. She was glad Dar was hanging onto her as she saw the water coming at them. It rolled over them with a shocking chill and she fought to keep the camera steady.

"Booah," Dar barked, as she got hit in the face with the cold liquid. She had one hand clenched in Kerry's jacket, the other latched onto the railing alongside the seats. The shock of the water made her inhale sharply. She shook her head and blinked, catching a little bit of the water in her mouth. It was sweet and minerally, so different than the ocean water she was used to.

Kerry let out a yell as they plunged to the left, and the raft tipped up halfway on its side. She almost ended up in Dar's lap, barely keeping control of the camera as they came up and over a ridge in the water and then went down into a gap with a stomach wrenching motion.

The raft went half under again and then popped up and over and they were out of the rapids and into a wider part of the river. The current still moved, but with no rough disruptions.

Kerry triggered the stop on the video and shook her head to scatter water everywhere. "Oh, that was fun! I want to do it again!"

Janet was at their side. "Oh, you will." she assured her with a big grin. She handed Dar a small towel and extended one to Kerry, before moving past them. "You three will need more than this." she called down to the three on the pontoons, who were completely soaked and laughing.

"That was cool," Dar said. "Literally and figuratively." She released Kerry, who then leaned back in her seat.

"It was," Kerry said. She wiped down the camera case and then ran back to footage. "Oh, Dar, look." She extended the camera. "Like being in a washing machine!"

The sun had come through the water, just as it was washing over them, in a blast of color. "That's cool." Dar leaned back in her seat herself and took a swig of their tube of lemonade. "This is going to be fun. And the sun's nice." She appreciated the warmth of it, and ran her fingers through her hair, escaped from its ponytail, to push it out of her face. "I liked that."

"Me too." Kerry smiled in contentment, half turning in her seat to take a picture of Dar, sunlight glistening through the remaining droplets of water on her face. Then she swiveled and prepared the camera for their next bit of adventure.

Janet walked back and forth, giving them tidbits about the area they were passing through and the lands beyond it. Dar relaxed and listened, fishing in her dry bag for one of her packets of crackers. In her peripheral vision, she saw Dave getting up to remove the sweatshirt he'd had on under his jacket, and Sally was wringing her hair out, half standing in her seat.

She loosened the straps on her water jacket and munched her

snack, offering Kerry one of the peanut butter crackers and putting it between her partner's teeth when she nodded in agreement.

Dave wandered over. "Hey, Rich, want to swap places for the next one?"

"No!" Rich shot back. "We flipped a coin. You lost. Wait for tomorrow."

"That did look fun," Kerry mused. "Those front seats."

"By the end of a day or two, he'll swap with you," Dave confided. "You get chafed. Know what I mean?" He ruffled his hair dry with the towel. "Got some good flow on the river. That was deeper and twistier than I expected."

Rich scrambled up from his seat on the pontoon, and come climbing along the ropes to the upper level. "Woo hoo!" He accepted a tube of lemonade from one of the crew, who was passing them out from an over the shoulder leather bag. "Nice! House Rock's gonna be awesome. I bet we come close to vertical on that left hand turn!"

He shivered a little, the tube shaking in his hands. "Gotta get a dry off, That water's cold, but I'm used to being here a little later in the summer."

Sally came over and handed him a towel. "Here, before you start chattering." She resumed her seat, casually looking behind her, then at them. "Got some problems back there I guess."

Dar leaned on the back of her seat and looked, spotting Todd back facing off against Doug in a truculent stance. There was far too much noise, between the water and the engine, to hear what they were saying, but she saw two more of the male crew drifting over, heads cocked.

With a shake of her head she faced forward again, glad for once it wasn't her issue.

"This is so gorgeous," Dave said, as he also turned back around. "Why would anyone want to be a jerk instead of enjoying it? I don't get it."

Sally patted his arm. "Some people are just natural grumps. Ignore it."

Kerry fluffed her hair out and wiped off the plastic housing of the camera. She lifted it up and focused, then paused and pulled her head back a little, watching the reflection that showed her what was going on behind her back. The girl Amy sat with her arms wrapped around her, back to the argument going on in the rear, a look of wistful longing on her face as she watched the rest of the group. There was something very lost in that look. It made Kerry wonder.

"Okay, folks," Janet said, "one more bit of excitement, and we're going to stop at a nice beach for a lunch break, and to stretch our legs. There's a nice little hike up the wall a bit, and you get a great shot of the river."

Janet walked across the boat, zipping up her waterproof jacket. The motion broke the scene, and Amy glanced aside as Todd rejoined her, folding his brawny arms over his chest, a look of satisfaction on his face. She leaned over and asked him something, and he just laughed, making a brushing away gesture at her.

Kerry glanced to her left, where her solicitous spouse handed her another cracker and reminded her once again how freaking lucky she was in the lottery of life. "Thank you, honey." She took the cracker and nibbled it." Have I told you today how much I love you?"

Dar smiled her sweet, and usually just between them smile. "I never get tired of hearing it." She settled her arm back around Kerry's shoulders. "Back at you."

"Aw, you guys are cute," Sally said, casually. "I have a cousin that's gay, and she and her partner act like absolute jerks most of the time." She accepted one of Dar's crackers."Thanks."

"Thanks for being cool about us," Dar responded, with a wry grin. "A lot of straight folks act like absolute jerks about us most of the time." Her eyes twinkled a little. "How old is your cousin?"

"Twenty-one."

"Ah a baby dyke." Kerry grinned. "But Dar's right. It's nice when people don't react in a bad way to us. Your cousin will probably grow out of the...um..."She looked over at Dar. "Drama phase?"

Dar nodded.

"That's a relief. I'll let my aunt know." Sally munched her cracker. "I'm Bi." she added unexpectedly.

Kerry blinked, somewhat nonplussed, then shrugged. "Well I'm Republican," she answered, feeling Dar start to shake with laughter. "Takes all kinds, right?"

Sally winked and went past, heading over to where the drink coolers were.

"DAR, THIS IS gorgeous." Kerry focused her camera on the spears of sunlight penetrating down the sides of the small slot canyon they were hiking in. "Oh, my God."

Dar looked around in somewhat awed appreciation. They had hiked up a small slope from the gentle white beach the raft was pulled up to at a curve in the river that gave them a fantastic view of the canyon they were going to head into next.

Lunch had been turkey wraps and they had been acceptably tasty. Dar relaxed a little, now that it seemed she wasn't going to have to live on her stash of crackers.

The air was cool and dry and this far from the river had a faint dusty taste to it, the sand and dirt they were walking over already gathering to coat their hiking boots.

Ahead of them was a rock wall and Dar went over and put her hand on it, leaning closer to examine the layers and layers running through it.

"It's amazing, isn't it?" Dave said from a nearby vantage point. "This whole canyon is so amazing."

Dar turned and looked out over the gap, with its winding river at the bottom. "Amazing that this whole thing was made by that." She pointed at the river. "All those years of it just doing what it does."

Amy stood close by while Todd explored a cleft a little farther down the wall. She glanced at him, then edged a few steps over. "It's kind of a parable for life, you know?" she said quietly. "So, like, if you keep at something long enough it will change anything."

She had a faint lilt in her voice, an almost accent Dar couldn't quite place. As she turned to regard her, the woman didn't quite meet her eyes.

Dave dove right in. "Well, it had help from this being limestone and sandstone," he said. "It would've taken a hell of a lot longer if it had been granite, but yeah." He nodded. "I did a whole semester in geology on this place."

Dar wondered if she'd ever even taken geology. "We don't have much geology in Florida," she said. "It's just limestone. One good kick and it dissolves."

"Have you been in the aquifer?" Dave asked. "I've seen pictures, that's cool."

Dar shook her head. "Not my thing to squirm down a hole in the ground."

Amy moved a little closer. "I've been spelunking in Pennsylvania," she said. "I love caves." She peeked over her shoulder. "That's why I wanted...I mean we wanted to come here, to see the caverns and rocks."

"Hey," Todd called, seeing them standing together. "Come

see this." He jerked his head at Amy.

"Excuse me." Amy gave them a brief smile and climbed up toward him, using a hiking pole she handled with skill. She got up to the level he was standing at and they moved along past an outcropping and out of immediate view.

"Don't like that guy," Dave said.

"Me either," Dar responded. "As my father would say, he makes the toe of mah boot itch." She allowed her drawl to emerge, keeping Kerry's scrambling form in her peripheral vision as her partner moved around to get the striated color in the rocks focused.

Dave laughed. "Are you from the south?"

"I'm from Miami," Dar said. "It's not the south. But my dad's from Alabama, which is." She saw a small cascade of rocks tumble down and stepped away from the wall to see where they'd come from. "Hey what's that?"

"Dar! Look!" Kerry hopped up the slope sideways, moving from bright sunlight into the shade of the wall as she brought her camera up. "A..." she focused. "Sheep?"

"Yeah!" Rich came bouncing over. "A big horn! Check it out!"

Dar climbed up the slope until she was at Kerry's side. She looked up to see a rock shelf about thirty feet over their heads with an animal standing on it. It looked down at them. It was large, and had brush brown shaggy fur with long curving horns over the top of its head. "Big horn," she said, as she shaded her eyes. "Got it."

Kerry chuckled softly. "It's sticking it's tongue out at us." She zoomed the camera in and took a shot.

There was a rush on the rocks as the whole group scrambled up to get a look. The sheep remained standing there, as though content to pose for them.

"Hey!" Dave suddenly called out. "Don't climb up there!"

Todd was scaling the cliff side, fingers caught in small cracks in the rock, feet feeling for ledges. His muscular body was taut under the long sleeve t-shirt and camo pants he wore and he paid no attention to Dave's warning. He had obvious skill and was moving at some speed, angling up toward where the sheep was standing.

Sally came over. "Hey be careful!"

Amy turned and waved them off. "It's okay. He's a solo climber."

Kerry turned her camera sideways and took a careful,

considered shot of the rock face, Todd, and the sheep. "That animal might not ask for his references," she commented in a mutter to Dar. They watched the man make his way up the face like a spider.

"My hope is that it turns around and poops on his head," Dar responded, half turning as Janet arrived at a near run at their side. "Make sure you get a shot of that, Ker."

"Don't worry I will."

"Oh, for God's sake." Janet expelled an exasperated breath.

"He's really good," Amy objected.

"If he falls is that going to matter?" Dar asked, in a mild tone. "Sucky way to end a trip, on the first day."

"He won't fall. He does this all the time." Amy looked briefly uncomfortable, but she moved away and went to the wall, peering up at the still climbing Todd, who was now nearing the shelf the sheep was standing on, watching him with a bemused expression on its face.

Amy pulled a point and shoot camera out of her pocket and took a picture.

Janet sighed. "That's why they wanted a private trip down the river," she said. "They wanted to do all the caverns and some climbs. The guy who was supposed to lead them is a climbing expert. Has ropes and stuff for safety. We don't."

"Ah." Kerry nodded. "Got it."

Dave shrugged. "He signed the release. If he falls doing this it's on him. But I hope this doesn't mean we have to deal with this crap every time we stop." He shook his head and turned around, pointedly turning his back on the drama and heading for one of the under hangs where Rich was kneeling examining something.

Janet sighed again, and Kerry gave her a sympathetic look. "Hard to make everyone happy." She looked around for something else to focus on and spotted a lizard, basking in the sun. "Will you pose for me too, Mr. lizard?" She eased closer, also turning her back on the wall.

Todd reached the level of the ledge and gripped firmly with one hand, then released the other and extended it out toward the sheep. After a puzzled pause, the animal sniffed his fingers and then nibbled them, before turning and leaping away up the cliff farther past and out of sight.

"Dja get that!" Todd yelled down. "Amy! Didja?"

"Yes!" She called up. "I got it."

Todd pulled himself up onto the ledge the sheep had been standing on and stood up, extending both arms up in triumph. "Yes!" he shouted out over the ground, his voice echoing back from the walls opposite. "I am a rock star!"

Dar shook her head and went to join Kerry. They moved past the lizard and went closer to a shallow cave in the rock wall that had glinting bits of stone in it. "Dogs," she said, briefly. "I'll pass on having kids."

"Yep." Kerry switched her lens for a macro, and adjusted her focus. "Dogs."

THE LIGHT MUTED into a gentle haze as the raft steered its way into an alcove, a deep cleft in the canyon that featured a long, white beach that was a well-known landing point to the crew.

Kerry stood on the raft deck near her seat, wringing out her shirt. She was dressed in her cargo pants and a sports bra, a towel draped over her. "That last rapid was fun. Wasn't expecting the wave over our heads though."

"Uh huh." Dar hadn't bothered taking off her wet tank top. She relaxed in her seat and watched the crew tie up the raft. "Glad they mix the floating and the stopping stuff," she said. "Either one could get boring."

Kerry eyed her affectionately. "I know. Typical type A nerd ADD."

Dar twiddled her thumbs. "Is what it is."

"You are what you are." Kerry reached over and smoothed the wet hair out of Dar's eyes. "And I love what you are."

Dar tilted her head a little, the words producing a gentle smile.

A cool breeze blew over them, and Janet circled the deck with a tray of mugs, holding what smelled like mulled cider.

Dar took two cups as she came past and offered one to Kerry, once she'd gotten her now only damp shirt back on. "This smells good."

Kerry sipped it. "Oh, that is good."

It was some kind of fruit cider with nutmeg and a shot of liquor, and it took the chill off. "Do I wonder how they got this hot?" Dar mused. "Or just enjoy it?"

Kerry chuckled.

"Okay, folks," Doug said. "This is where we're stopping for the night. So, the drill is you all get off and find a spot you like onshore, and stake a claim to it. Then we'll bring over the cots and tents."

Todd and Amy hopped off the front of the raft and started up the slight slope into the camping area.

Doug watched them, then shook his head a little. "Since its going to be cool tonight we suggest a tent. But if you want, you can just sleep under the stars. Your choice."

Kerry got up and hefted her dry sack. "Tent?"

"Uh huh." Dar said. "Back in the day, in Florida, sleeping without a tent regardless of the weather was an invitation to wake up with a palmetto bug on your pillow."

Kerry paused and stared at her, jaw slightly dropped.

Dar wiggled her fingers up near her temple and snickered. "Don't worry. They're tropical."

"You better hope so." Kerry shouldered her sack with some dignity. "Or you're going to find me on your pillow."

"Mm." Dar got behind her and leaned in to nibble the skin on the back of her neck. "Lucky me."

Cool skin, warm lips. Kerry almost tripped on the edge of the seating area. "Oh."

They made their way off the raft along with the rest, and paused on the beach. Dar pointed to the left, and started in that direction, as the rest of the crowd split up in their small groups and wandered off.

The small beach curved around a little, and they walked along its edge until they came to a small slope upwards. The ground was mostly rock and sand, with a few tufts of hardy grass. They had to lean forward as they climbed up, moving around two large boulders before they found a small, relatively level spot near the cliff wall.

It was quiet, and they turned and looked behind them. The raft was just out of sight, but the sun was slanting against the far wall of the canyon, painting it in a hundred shades of desert colors. They could see the river rushing past, and with a satisfied grunt, Dar dropped her dry bag in the sand. "This works."

"Nice," Kerry said.

They heard the others in the near distance, voices echoing softly against the rock, but there was no one else within view. Kerry took out her camera, getting a few shots of the view before she went and sat on a table height rock that had an almost flat top.

"I'll go tell em where we are," Dar said. "Be right back."

Kerry lifted one hand in assent, then leaned back on the rock and let the breeze flutter over her, its dryness already sucking the damp out of her clothes and ruffling her short cut blond hair. She was looking forward to the dinner, and relaxing, and she felt a sense of letting go.

When they'd started driving she hadn't felt that, since they were in the range of their phones and e-mail and talked about work almost the whole way.

Now, she felt the constant churn of ideas fading. They'd left their phones back in the RV, sending one last message to everyone that they would see them on the other side.

She didn't even feel anxious about it now. It was getting easier to just live in the moment and let the future wait. This was odd and strange and a little intimidating, but it brought a sense of tentative peace to her that had been hard to find in the recent past.

She braced her hands on the rock, feeling the residual sun warmth against her palms. She drummed the heels of her hiking boots against the stone in idle rhythm and watched the light's progress across the canyon walls until she heard footsteps approaching again.

"Hey, good spot." It was Pete, one of the mates, who accompanied Dar with a sizable sack carried on his back. He put the sack down and straightened up. "We've got some drinks going down by the raft, why don't you all take part while I get this set up for you?"

Kerry took the hint and got up, moving past him to collect Dar, who looked like she might want to take over the tent making process. "C'mon, hon. Let's go watch the fun." She hooked her arm through Dar's and kept going, encouraging Dar to turn and move with her. "Pete doesn't need anyone telling him how to set up a tent."

She winked at Pete, who broke into a grin and gave her thumbs up.

They walked down the slope to the river and over to where the rest of the group was clustered around the landing point where some quickly assembled bar height tables were set up with mugs and dishes of trail mix on them.

Sally and Dave were near the edge of the river, pointing across. Marcia was perched in one of the tall directors' chairs that had been set up facing the west. She had a sketch pad out, and was drawing on it.

"Your mother would love this place," Kerry said, observing her. "So many colors."

"She would," Dar readily said. "I bet when they see the pictures they'll decide to do a trip."

Kerry considered that, as they went to the tables to collect their beverages. "Your dad would make these people nuts, hon."

"No doubt." Dar started strolling down the edge of the water, and after a moment Kerry caught up with her. "Not with these guys, I mean just in general. Don't think Dad's ever been out here." She watched a bird coast overhead, coming to roost on a small ledge in the cliffs.

They moved around a small bend and paused. Doug knelt by a pile of gear in an alcove that had obviously been used many times for a camp. Doug stood, turned, and paused as well on seeing them. "Oh. Hi."

"Hi," Kerry returned the greeting.

"This where you all camp?" Dar asked, noting the well-worn look to the gear.

Doug nodded and stuck his hands in his pockets. "Gotta have a little down time." He gestured upward. "We let the clients pick the nice spots, and we usually take this area. Doesn't really have a view and that."

Dar regarded the river moving past. Then she looked up the slope, which was full of rubble and tufted grass. "You guys make the other side nicer? Did it look like this before?"

Doug came over and regarded her.

"I don't care," Dar said, in a gentler tone. "I grew up on a Navy base in the scrublands of far south Florida. I've camped a lot rougher."

He nodded, and shrugged a little. "You know, people pay for a nice experience. If we charge what we charge, we need to put skin in the game and make it worth it," he said, frankly. "So, sure, we found nice spots to camp so they can take pictures, and go home and show everyone and it's wow."

"Nothing wrong with that," Kerry said. 'It's a business. We get it. We run our own."

Doug relaxed a little. "Yeah, you guys seem cool," he said. "Some people aren't." He glanced past as his name was called. "Sorry. Got to go start cooking." He gave them a brief grin, and then followed them as they retreated along the shore toward the main camp.

The crew was setting up an outdoor kitchen, and some of them were carrying tent gear and large square boxes up and into the brush.

"The necessary," Rich said and indicated the latter group with his mug as they arrived.

Janet was busy with a checklist, and she looked up with a smile. "Necessaries," she corrected. "One for the ladies, and one for the gentlemen." She shifted her eyes, and her lips twitched. "So to speak."

Todd and Amy approached, and as they did, Dar felt that internal twitch, that silent, unseen prickling of her hackles that Kerry always kindly called her crusader instinct flaring.

But no, she'd decided she wasn't going to do that, hadn't she?

"Hey," Todd said. "How long is it going to take to get that tent up? We need to change." He indicated himself and Amy, who was shivering in the breeze. "Can you get it moving?"

Rich was quick to sidle up. "Maybe you shouldn't have picked that way out spot," he said. "Cause our stuff's already up. Takes them a while to get the tent gear up to your area."

"Shut the fuck up," Todd told him. "No one asked you."

Janet visibly counted silently to ten. "Okay, let's see if we can speed it up." She put her clipboard down and motioned to Doug, who put down the table he was setting up and trudged after her.

"That's it," Todd said, "get your asses up there." He stared at the rest of them. "These guys screwed up our whole vacation. Damn right I want service from them. You got something to say about that?" He looked at Dar, who regarded him steadily.

"Yeah, I do," Dar said. "If your SO is cold you should give her your shirt." With a shake of her head she moved past and went over to the bar top tables to investigate the trail mix.

Todd took a breath, then released it, visibly nonplussed. "Uh."

Kerry scratched the bridge of her nose, and stifled a laugh as she followed Dar, leaving the discontented pair behind. Rich scrambled to join them. "He wasn't expecting you to say that."

Dar had sorted out the mix and gotten a handful of cashews, which she offered to share. "I mean, c'mon." She took a sip of what was apparently rum punch. "How about some common sense?"

Rich laughed and took a handful of the mix and tossed them into his mouth. "That was funny. But I think you pissed him off."

Dar sighed "Wouldn't be the first. Won't be the last. I'm waiting for the words—don't you know who I am—to come out of his mouth."

"Yeah, me too," Rich said. "He is someone, by the way. Sally googled him before we left. His dad's the owner of some big company."

Dar rolled her eyes. "Even better."

Kerry had seated herself so she could see behind them.

"Mm...but he gave his shirt to her, so there's that." She took a swallow of her grog. "And he won't be the last to take advice from you, hon." She gently poked her elbow into Dar's side. "His father was probably one of our old customers."

"Meh."

Sally and PJ came over. "We get veggie fajitas," Sally announced, with some satisfaction. "And yellow squash soup." She took a handful of the mix. "I think you guys are stuck with either steak or chicken."

"Moo," Dar responded. "Too bad they didn't bring milk."

IT WAS DARK when they left the dining area, the sounds of harmonicas and guitars having faded into the night silence that was now broken by the sound of the river, and their footsteps against the sand as they climbed.

"That wasn't bad," Kerry said, as they got up to the level where their tent was pitched, and approached it. "I really liked that soup."

"I like your cooking better," Dar said. "You use better spices."

"Thank you, sweetheart." Kerry had her arm around Dar's waist and she unwound her hold now as they got to the tent. She undid the ties and drew aside the flaps, exposing the neatly made interior. "Ah."

Dar entered and removed the flashlight from her pocket and moved the beam around the inside. There were two folding bunks made up, with a foam pad on them, covered with a sleeping bag, and at the head an inflatable pillow covered in a cotton pillow cloth.

A small battery lantern was hung at the apogee, and she switched it on, turning off her flash as Kerry came in and knelt next to one bunk and pulled over the duffel bag she'd last seen getting on the helicopter.

It was nice. Dar sat on her bunk and opened her duffel. Along with those, the raft team had delivered a six pack of water for each of them and a kit for the toilets, including hand sanitizer.

It was good to get her hiking boots and socks off, "I think those water boots were a better idea. Like what Rich has on," she said. "They dry faster."

"And no socks," Kerry said. "Next time." She set her boots and Dar's near the doorway. "Glad we brought spares." She paused to poke her head out. "Turn that light off, would you Dar?"

"Sure."

Behind her, the light went out and then she was able to look up at the night sky, full of stars. The distinctive swath of the Milky Way splashed across the center of it. "Oh wow."

Dar poked her head out. "What. Oh." She studied the view. "Yeah that's nice. You want to change and then sit outside for a while?" She indicated the two director's chairs planted in the sandy ground.

"Yes, I do."

They ducked back inside and changed, and Dar took the time to open the three screened in window panels, to allow the breeze to enter.

Then they took a bottle of water each and emerged into the night, taking seats and settling in to enjoy the stars and the residual warmth of the sun in the sand under their feet.

"So," Dar said, after a few minutes of compatible silence. "What do you think so far?" She reached over and took Kerry's hand in hers. "What you expected?"

Kerry leaned back and tipped her head up so she could study the stars. They were dense and beautiful, and so much more plentiful than she was used to back at home. "I'm not sure what I was expecting," she answered. "I just mostly wanted to be with you, and not be dealing with work for a week. So, in that case, it's definitely met my expectations."

"Mm."

"And the views are pretty, like I thought they'd be," Kerry added, after a pause. "You?"

What did she think about it? Dar considered that for a while. "I like the rapids. Those are fun," she said. "I like the hiking. The views are really different. But I don't know that I enjoy hanging out on the boat getting from point A to point B."

"Mm." Kerry regarded her with a sideways glance. "Why not see if Marcia has another sketch pad? I could see you were getting bored. I have my camera."

"Nah. I can read a book," Dar said, wiggling her toes. "I've got a few with me. I'll put one in my dry bag tomorrow."

"What is it?"

"*Lord of the Rings* trilogy."

Kerry started laughing. "You really did come prepared."

Dar chuckled along with her. Then they both paused and sat up as a shrill scream broke the silence of the camp. After a moment, there was the sound of running and the moving spears of flashlights, and another scream.

"Hope it's nothing serious," Kerry said, gathering herself to stand. "And it isn't a palmetto bug."

THE SCREAMS WERE coming, it seemed, from the outhouse. Kerry was a step ahead of Dar as they joined a group of others, the combined light of their flashlights illuminating the tarp covered structures.

Janet arrived and moved decisively forward. "Hey! What's wrong!" She tapped on the outside of the tarp. "What's all the screaming about?"

"Snake," Dave suggested.

"Scorpion," Rich disagreed.

"No toilet paper," Dar dryly supplied, and chuckles rose around them.

"Hey. That'd make me scream," Marcia said. "My age? You betcha."

Janet had apparently received permission to enter as she'd unlatched the tarp and stepped inside, with two of the raft crew standing hesitantly behind her. A moment later she emerged holding PJ's arm, who was limping, tears visible on her face.

"Huh." Kerry folded her arms over her chest. "Wonder what happened?" The two other crew members ducked inside, and she could see flashlights moving around.

Janet guided PJ over to one of the camp chairs. "Sit down." After the girl was seated, Janet shone her light on her foot. Janet's eyes widened as blood was immediately visible. "Oh, crap. Doug! Get the kit!"

"It looks like a cut," Marcia said, in a low voice.

"Janet, here it is." One of the crew had emerged and came over, holding something in his hand. "Someone must have broken a beer bottle. It's a big piece of glass."

Dar got a brief glimpse of the item, which was long and curved, and a pale gold in color. "Ouch," She muttered.

Janet briefly glanced at it, her lips tightening. "Get the rake, and make sure that's the only one," she said, sternly. "And go through the checklist and see that nothing else was missed."

The crew member gave her a glum look, but carefully put the shard into one of his cargo shorts pockets and moved away, the other crew trotting off to get some tools.

"Oh, my God it hurts," PJ moaned.

Janet stood and faced the crowd. "Okay, folks. Show's over. Please go back to your tents and give PJ some space." She made shooing motions with her hands. "We'll get her fixed up."

"That's bad luck," Kerry said, as they moved through the darkness toward their little camp. "She was saying how much she was looking forward to hiking."

Dar glanced casually around, then tipped her head back a little, looking up at the small escarpment where Todd and Amy had put their gear. She saw a shadow against the pale rocks past it, and as she watched the shadow moved and disappeared.

They walked back to their tent and settled back into their chairs. Dar put her elbows on the chair arms and steepled her fingers, brow slightly creased. "That was a big piece of glass to miss," She commented, after a moment. "But I'm not sure I'd be walking around here without shoes either."

"No, that's true. Though you go barefoot all the time at home."

"I've paid for that." Dar removed one of her sandals and directed her light to the bottom of her foot. "Still have marks where that damn fish bit me. I remember how much that hurt, so yeah, it sucks to be her."

"Hm." Kerry glanced at her bottle of water as the steadily cooling breeze brushed over her skin. "You feel like some tea? They had a jug of hot green tea down by the kitchen." She stood up. "Be right back."

"Sure." Dar slid her sandal on and leaned back in her chair. She watched Kerry disappear, then tipped her head back to regard the canopy of stars, and the dark outline of the canyon walls against it.

"YOU KNOW WHAT, Dar?"

Dar sealed the zipper on her duffel bag and straightened up. "You like your bathrooms to be bathrooms," she said.

"Mm."

"I'm not crazy for the whole water in a canvas basin either," Dar said with a grin. "When we used to camp back in the day we'd just dive into the nearest water and consider it done." She lifted their duffels and moved outside the tent, setting them on the dry, cool ground.

Kerry followed her, and regarded the beautiful pink and gray dawn around them, with the ever-present sound of the river, and the clatter and clamor of the group getting ready to go down to the kitchen for breakfast. "Does that make me a sissy? I feel like it."

"Why?"

"I don't know why. Everyone else seems so naturfied."

"Ker." Dar draped an arm over her shoulders. "We're not from the country. No sense in pretending we are. Even if I did some camping rough in the past, I've been a well-off city gal long enough to want my comforts and conveniences."

Something about that made Kerry smile. Maybe because though she knew it was true, and she knew Dar believed it was true, it wasn't the whole truth. There was a rough surface under Dar's techie façade that she herself did not possess

Dar put her hands in her hoodie pockets. "C'mon let's go get some granola." She had traded her boots for the thick-soled sandals she'd worn the previous night and she flexed her toes in them. "Better than wearing wet leather all day."

"For sure," Kerry said, and they walked down the slope together.

They joined the rest of the party at the tables neatly set for breakfast, and the small group clustered around PJ. She had her foot up on a second chair, and it was wrapped very well, and had a plastic protection around it.

"How are you feeling?" Kerry asked.

"Bummed!" PJ's face shifted into a pout. "I can't believe I was so stupid, not to wear shoes into the loo."

Todd and Amy were at a nearby table, and he turned to look at her. "Their fault." He indicated the crew. "They're supposed to make sure no shit is dangerous like that. Lots of people walk barefoot in camp." He indicated his own feet, which were bare. "Lucky as crap it wasn't me."

Dar had detoured to the buffet and now she took two plates and moved methodically along, plunking bits of fruit and a half bagel each onto the plate. She paused at the offering of yogurt and granola and sighed, then took a cup of each and added it to the platters.

One of the crew had been watching her, alert to assist if needed. "What's your usual morning fare, Ms. Roberts?" he asked, in a quiet voice. "I kind of get the feeling it's not this."

Ah, their tent assembler, Pete, from the previous night. "Coffee and pastalitos," Dar responded readily. "Cuban pastries that have cheese, or meat, or coconut in them."

He considered that. "I think that sounds yummy. Where I live there's a doughnut shop and I sometimes start with a maple bacon one." He edged closer, and was randomly sorting the yogurt cups. "Or sometimes sushi."

"I like sushi." Dar finished her selection and glanced casually around. "All work out last night?"

Pete sighed. "We got yelled at," he said. "Someone must have missed that piece of bottle. Big no-no." He went to the end of the table. "Want some chilled OJ?"

"Sure." Dar had both plates gripped in one hand. "Be right back." She turned and went to one of the high-top tables, setting the plates down and regarding the back of Kerry's head as her partner stood talking to PJ. After a moment of that, Kerry looked around and made eye contact, then smiled when Dar pointed to the plates.

Dar made a little satisfied grunting sound, and went back for the juice. Marcia was standing chatting with Pete, and she moved aside a little to make way for her. "Good morning."

"Good morning," Marcia responded at once. "We saw a coyote just before dawn." She picked up a cup of the yogurt. "We got a picture. It was wonderful. We were walking up near the bushes there." She pointed with a spoon.

"Really?" Pete asked. "Wow, we haven't seen one along the river in a while." He gave Dar two glasses of juice. "Wish I'd seen it."

"Me too," Dar said. "I want to see a bobcat."

"Oh! So, do I!" Marcia responded. "I hope we do!"

"I'll do my best to find one for you, ladies." Pete gave them both a little bow. "They're nocturnal, so keep those flashes handy."

"Absolutely." Marcia beamed at him. "Thank you so much."

Dar brought the juice to the table and they both perched on the foldable stools. Sally and Rich came over and plunked their plates down on the small table with them. "Morning," Kerry greeted.

"And a nice one it is," Sally said. "Except for poor PJ. Bummer."

"Bummer." Rich said. "She's lucky it was glass and not rusty metal." He vigorously stirred his granola into the yogurt. "I put a rusty spike through my hand a couple trips back and holy cow was that a mess." He lifted one large, muscular hand and exposed the palm. "See?"

Kerry grimaced at the knotted scar. "Ouch."

"Got infected, ugh. I was miserable."

"So, this sort of thing happens out here sometimes?" Dar asked.

"Hey, they try their best," Rich answered immediately. "But

you know, it's like the wilderness out here, and you can't catch everything. Real fault belongs to whatever moron left broken glass around instead of packing it out."

Todd had been passing and now he pointed at Rich. "You go on believing that. Like I said, lucky it wasn't me." He went past to deposit his plate on the table, tossing the silverware onto it before heading up to where they'd made camp.

They watched him retreat, then Kerry shook her head and went back to her bagel.

"Hey." Rich lowered his voice, and glanced around to where Amy was still seated. She had a small leather bound book with her and was scribbling into it. "So, the big company his dad works for? It's a law firm."

Sally rolled her eyes. "Figures. Probably threatening the op with lawsuits every time the sun changes inclination." She sectioned a piece of fruit neatly in her plate, eating it. "No wonder they're running so scared."

Dar was sucking on her spoon, and from the corner of her eye she saw Kerry's jaw tighten, and her eyes narrow. "Yeah that makes sense," she said. "Who wants trouble with a big ass legal firm."

"Right. Not me," Rich said. "Not that I don't wish he didn't fall on his ass so we could all laugh at him, but there's no way I want that kind of complication in my life. I'm leaving them alone. Taking his advice and shutting the hell up from now on."

"Right on. But I told you that yesterday," Sally said. "No one wants any trouble."

Kerry cleared her throat a little. "Did you like that?" She indicated the yogurt.

"Not really," Dar said. "But it's the closest thing to milk they have." She rested her chin on her fist and gave Kerry a mournful look.

"Aw." Kerry finished up her bagel and took both of their plates. "It's just a week, hon." She gently bumped Dar's shoulder, then leaned over and put a kiss on the back of it. "I promise I had the dispenser filled before we left."

"Mmmmoooo," Dar rumbled softly, as she got up and went to the river's edge, hopping up and down and shadow boxing as the water burbled past.

Kerry walked over to where the crew was washing up and sorted the silverware and crockery into the bins they were working from. "Thanks, guys."

The two workers glanced up at her in some surprise, and

gave her smiles.

Kerry smiled back and went over to pick up both her and Dar's dry bags, slinging them over her shoulder as she joined the struggle of people starting to climb up onto the raft as the crew worked to stow all the camping gear and the staff onshore rushed to finish packing.

Not an easy job. She fastened the bags to their chosen seats from the previous day, no one seeming to want to trade them, at least for the moment, though some of the other chairs were in the midst of being swapped.

Dave and Rich, for example, with Dave now straddling the pontoon, his dry bag strapped across his chest, the dark orange safety vest under it.

Rich took a seat next to Kerry, and Sally swapped with her sister.

"Should we pick another spot?" Kerry asked, as Dar crossed over from the gangway and joined her.

"Not unless you want to. I liked the front row seat." Dar eyed the pontoons. "Might want to see if I can do that one time."

"Brr." Kerry rubbed her arms through the hoodie sleeves. "Maybe in the afternoon."

Dar chuckled. "Polar bear. You can stay up here and only be mostly drenched."

"True." Kerry twisted her body around in both directions to loosen up. "We're going to see that waterfall today, Dar. I can't wait."

They watched as Doug and Pete linked arms, and made a living chair to lift PJ up and carry her onto the raft, a situation not at all unpleasing to the college student, followed by her three friends, all laughing. She was settled into one of the second-row seats, and then was joined a moment later by the older couple.

Don came over to where Dar was standing and offered her a sack of throat lozenges. "Gets dry here."

Dar took one. "It does. Thanks." She watched from the corner of her eye as Todd made his way onboard, going over to where Amy was getting herself settled. He took a seat in the plush, comfortable space alongside.

Don was doing the same. "Peculiar fella," He commented.

"Asshole," Dar said. "Determined to get every bit of his dissatisfaction out on the team there."

"True, and funnily enough, seems I remember him being up around those WCs before that gal did." Don rolled the lozenge around in his mouth. "Not that it means anything, necessarily."

Dar remained silent for a bit, thinking. "Suspicious old salts, aren't we?" Her eyes twinkled a little. "Comes from being around a while."

"Comes from," Don said. "Most of these kids haven't seen much." He amiably changed the subject as Doug and Janet walked up. "So, what did your dad do in the service?"

Dar went along with it, noting the furrowed brows on the two in charge. "Special forces."

"Ah hah." Don chortled. "Now that's a different breed of fella, too. But in a good way." He paused a moment. "Hold on. You said your name was Roberts?"

Dar nodded.

He stepped back and looked at Dar intently. "Your dad isn't Andrew Roberts, is he?"

Dar nodded again, with a smile this time.

Don nodded back. "I thought you looked a little bit familiar. He did a tour on my ship in the Gulf, way back. Stand up guy."

"He is," Dar said.

"Okay, folks, we're ready to go. Can you take your seats for the launch? It can get a little wobbly." Doug waved them back. "Don't want anyone to get an unexpected bath."

"Talk to you later." Don obeyed the shooing and went over to where Marcia was getting her knitting out. He leaned over and said something to her, and she looked up in some mild surprise at Dar, but then the raft started to move and everyone settled in.

"He knows Dad?" Kerry asked, looking up from getting her camera sorted.

Dar shrugged. "Apparently. Guess we'll find out more later." She faced forward in her chair as the raft was released from its mooring and shoved off from the beach, the crew scrambling onboard as they moved into the current and were caught up in it.

"Got your book?"

Dar patted the dry bag, but she left it closed for the moment. The walls started to move past them with some speed and the breeze brushed over her. "There's another sheep." She pointed to it. "Up there on that ledge."

Kerry smiled. "Got it."

Overhead the sky was a deepening blue, with no clouds anywhere to be seen. The sun was just slanting in and painting the top of the canyon wall with sunrise, and as they passed a slightly narrower part of the river, with a bump of speed and slight roar it was setting up to be a beautiful day.

Chapter Three

IT WAS A fairly short drift until they came around a bend, and then everyone drew breath as the red canyon walls suddenly burst into vivid green as multiple waterfalls came gushing out of the stone and down a stepped series of ledges to the river below.

"Oh, wow." Kerry was already focusing her camera, as the sun splashed into the canyon and lit the wall up, exposing flashes of brilliance in the rock.

Dar put her book away and sat up, regarding the wall they were now approaching.

"Vesey's Paradise," Janet said, with some satisfaction in her tone. "That's all fresh water, being drawn out of the rock. We'll pull in to the left there so you all can get a good look."

Doug piloted the raft into a cleft in the rocks at the shore and everyone climbed down, splashing through some shallow water and carefully evading the tumbled rubble at the base of the falls.

"Be careful of your footing, folks, and stay clear of the foliage," Janet said. "I'll be glad to take pictures of anyone who wants the falls as a background."

Kerry availed herself of the offer, and handed off her camera as she moved to one side and put her arm around Dar. "Feel that mist?"

"I do." Dar amiably draped one long arm over Kerry's shoulders as Janet knelt and got an angle that included both them and the falls. Dar waited for Janet to finish then turned around and faced the cliff wall.

The rest of the group was scattering to explore, Sally and her sister climbing around the edge of some rocks to a small cave behind it, and Marcia and Don strolling down and around the bend where the whole river could be seen.

"Stay clear of that foliage!" Janet called out, as Amy and Todd started climbing up the face of the falls. "Be careful!"

Dar put her hands in her pockets.

Amy half turned and waved at them, then they continued, picking their way up the stepped rocks, into the mist of the falls and through the heavy shrubbery.

Janet came up to stand next to Dar. "Why can't they all be like you, Ms. Roberts?" She sighed. "If they slip and fall it's going to be a really long day."

"Going to be long anyway," Dar said. "That's poison ivy they're climbing through."

"Holy crap, are you kidding?" Kerry shaded her eyes. "You sure?"

"Oh shit." Janet started running, moving after them.

"Yup." Dar rocked up and down on her heels. "C'mon, let's go see those shiny rocks." She turned her back on the climbers and pointed where Sally and her sister had gone. "Think we can drink the water?"

Kerry tore her eyes from the climbers and rejoined Dar as they walked through the shallow water and into a crevice, where some of the others were examining a layer of intensely sparkling rock, as the sun plunged into the canyon and lit it up. "That's not going to end well."

"Nope. But it's not my problem." Dar drew in a deep breath of the cool air. She put her hand on the rock wall and leaned close to inspect it, the striated layers drawing her interest. "A lot of history here."

They heard a yell behind them.

Kerry slipped a macro lens on and focused, taking a shot of a piece of the wall that was half in shadow, half in sunlight, with all its layers in all their uneven patterning.

Another yell.

Kerry took another shot, then glanced at Dar, who stood there, hands clasped behind her back, regarding a knot in the stone. After a moment, Dar looked back at her.

They both sighed.

Don made his way over to them. "Hey what's going on back there? You hear that?" He had a backpack on his back, and a walking stick that had a neatly carved head.

"Amy and Todd decided to climb the wall," Kerry said. "Probably has something to do with that."

Don sighed. "What is wrong with those kids?" He headed around the rock that blocked the view of the wall and disappeared around it.

"What's wrong with them right about now is that they're breaking out into big itchy lumps," Dar said. Then she started climbing up a short slope to the small cavern, where Sally and Dave were already exploring. The path up had worn hand holds, and she pulled herself up readily.

Kerry felt a certain level of sympathy despite the grumpiness of the pair, having once experienced the poison plant herself. But she ignored the yelling behind her and changed lenses again, this time to capture Dar's progress up the rock, the tank top exposing her supple back and the inky black panther tattoo on her shoulder.

She took another shot, then turned and moved around the edge of the rock to get a better angle. That let her get a view of the argument and she paused for a moment as she saw Amy sitting on a rock, rubbing her legs, tears in her eyes.

She felt bad, at that. Don was standing nearby, thumbs hooked in the straps of his backpack and Doug was just coming back from the raft with a first aid box in his hand. Todd was arguing with Janet, who had both hands out in a pacifying gesture.

Don stepped forward and said something. Todd turned around and shoved him, and the older man stumbled back and lost his balance, falling onto the rocks. Kerry surrendered to instinct, shoved her camera into her pack and started toward him, reaching him just as Todd returned to his argument.

"Hey, easy." Kerry extended a hand to Don. "You okay?"

"Leave him the fuck where he is I'm not done with him!" Todd yelled at her.

Kerry turned and pinned him with a stare. "Go to hell," she said. "I'll help anyone I want, you piece of pig shit."

He stared back. "You have no idea who you're dealing with you little bitch."

"Likewise." Kerry smiled coolly at him, aware from the corner of her eye that Dar was leaping down the rocks like a demented antelope heading her way. She turned and offered Don a hand up again, confident her back was covered. "You okay, Don?"

"Yeah." He looked disgusted, and rolled over onto his knees to rise. "Just a jerk." He got up and brushed himself off, grimacing a little as he touched the back of his hip. "Hit something."

Dar arrived at that moment, sliding a little on the wet rocks near the shore. "What happened?" she asked. "You okay?"

Don made a face. "Can't stay out of other people's mix ups," he admitted, in a low tone, glancing past her to where Todd had gone back to arguing with Janet. "I'm too old for this crap."

Janet walked past them toward the raft, her cheeks flushed and red. Todd came over to them and pointed at Kerry. "And you stay out of my business."

Dar reached out and took hold of his hand, pushing it aside. "Don't do that," she said, in a quiet, even tone. "You're the idiot who went climbing up into poison ivy after they told you not to. It's not their fault." She released him.

Don stepped up next to Dar, instinctively standing shoulder to shoulder with her. A moment later, Doug joined them, but Todd just laughed and backed off. "The more the merrier for the lawsuit. No problem, jackasses."

"No problem," Dar responded, still in that mild tone. But he turned his back and went over to Amy, who was drying her tears as she inspected her calamine tainted skin.

"Jerk," Don muttered.

"Rich jerk whose father's a lawyer," Doug said with a sigh. "And really, folks, not that I don't appreciate you all standing up for us, stay out of it. No sense in getting yourselves mixed up in this. We have liability insurance." He looked meaningfully at Don. "Please."

Don lifted his hands. "Sorry."

Doug smiled briefly and walked back to the aid kit, kneeling beside it.

Kerry sighed. "Dudley Douchebag." She shook her head. "Why does it always have be Dudley Douchebag, Dar?" She looked up to see Dar's profile as her partner watched the scene at her back, and saw that narrowing at the corners of those blue eyes.

Then Dar put her sunglasses back on and dusted her hands off. "I thought," she said, "I could bring back a handful or so of those rocks. I think my mother'd like em."

Kerry went with the subject change as they carefully maneuvered back across the slippery rocks to the slope. "The ones with all those colors? I bet she would." She joined Dar in examining the specimens near the water's edge, which were shaped and rounded by the river. "What would Dad like?"

"A bobcat."

Kerry chuckled softly under her breath.

THEY WERE BACK on the boat, on the river, heading for another rapid when the sky overhead started to gather a few clouds. The sun rippled through them, making large, dark splotches against the water's surface. Kerry caught Janet turn her head and watch them as she balanced along one side of the raft.

"Okay, everyone, get ready!" Doug yelled, from the back. "We're going to the wall, and then down that side channel! Hang on!"

The river ahead split in two, one side turning into a thick churn of white whirlpools, and the other a faster rush between a huge boulder and the wall. The water seemed smoother, but ahead of that Kerry could see a drop. Not a huge one, but a plunge anyway and that was where Doug was aiming them.

She reached down and got her camera ready, feeling the powerful tug as Dar took hold of her safety jacket and the rest of the crew edged down the sides of the raft, holding onto the support ropes.

Rich was already whooping like a cowboy, holding on with one hand and waving the other one as they lurched hard to the right and came up against the rock wall, sliding up partly sideways against it and throwing them all against their respective restraints.

"Holy crap." Dar squirmed out of her seat and got behind Kerry's, trading her one-handed hold with both arms clasping herself to the seat back and around Kerry's body in a tight squeeze, bracing both long legs against the deck.

For a long moment, the raft tipped up sideways and Kerry was sure they were going over. She started breathing harder, but kept the record button down on her camera as the front right side of the raft came up and scraped against the wall.

Then, just as she was sure they were going to end up overturning, the river slammed them around and the front of the raft plunged down again into the gap between the rock and the wall. They were moving fast, heading right into a froth of churning water that exploded up around them in a wash of sun splashed brilliant green.

A blob came right up and whacked Kerry in the face, obscuring her vision as she felt Dar press up behind her. The raft bucked under them as it turned and plunged down a definite slope and a wave came up and wet them all through and through.

"Oh yeah!" Rich yelled in excitement.

The water drained off the raft and they were through the rapids and emerged into a wider, slower stretch. "That was fun," Kerry said as she reached up to wipe the water out of her eyes. "I thought we were going in for a minute."

"Me too." Dar released her and licked her lips. "I was all ready to start swimming."

"Fun, huh?" Janet was next to them. "I love that rapid."

Don wiped his face with a towel. "It was great," He said. "Did you get that on your camera, Kerry?"

"I did." Kerry said. "The best part was when the front of the raft came down there, and all the sun? It was great."

PJ came over and peered past Kerry's shoulder. "Rock star."

She bumped Kerry's shoulder with her fist. "I was hoping someone on this thing could use a camera better than I could. Everything I shoot is out of focus. I don't have a clue why."

"Yeah, I already know who's going to be featured on the screen at the end of ride dinner." Janet smiled and glanced around. "Hey, folks, listen up?" She raised her voice. "We're going to run it a little later today so we get to a camp where we've got some hard shelter overhead. I think we're in for a rare event, a rainstorm on the river."

She pointed overhead, where the scattered clouds were becoming less scattered and dark. A brisk wind ruffled across the water, fluttering the clothing they all were wearing. "Sleeping out in that is no fun, and cooking isn't either. So, we're going to stop at a place where there's a nice big cave to set up camp in."

"Indian cave?" Don asked with interest. "Read about those."

"Yes," Janet said. "We have permission," she added, seeing some raised eyebrows. "They know we treat the place with respect, and always leave it in pristine condition."

Todd and Amy were huddled in the plush seats at the back center, and merely listened. They were covered with waterproof ponchos, and Amy was visibly shivering. "How much longer?" Todd asked, brusquely.

"About two hours." Janet didn't even check her watch. "So, I'm going to hand out some snacks, and we'll move along so we can get undercover before the weather breaks." She moved along to the storage bins and opened one, and two other crew members went with her.

"Hm." Kerry accepted a towel Dar offered. "Have you ever slept in a cave?"

Dar was momentarily silent then she grinned briefly. "Yeah." She sat down and ruffled her hair dry. "Wasn't much fun. Me and some of the guys were caught out up in the Polypody jungle, mid state. They have limestone formations there and...well, anyway."

"Polypody jungle?"

"Long story."

Kerry squinted at her. "Is this the kind of story that ends up with mud and worms?"

Dar cleared her throat. "A cow, actually. Tell you later."

It was near sundown when they started to pull over toward an inlet. The sky was already darkened overhead and they could hear thunder in the distance. There was a faint sense of urgency in the crew and they hurried the passengers off the raft. Doug jogged in the lead, taking a moment to stick glow sticks in the ground to lead them as the purple light was rapidly starting to fade.

The river had a distinct smell, but over that Kerry could smell rain coming, that odd, almost musty scent she had become used to over her time spent in Florida, which had more than its share of it. She followed Dar off the raft, almost the last of the group to step down onto a red sand covered beach they'd pulled the boat up onto.

The wind was whistling around them, coursing in and out of the rock walls and she felt it buffet her between the shoulder blades, pushing her forward a little as the climbed up the slope to a level area full of random rocky debris.

"Careful," Dar said, as she stepped between several larger rocks.

Kerry had her personal bag over her shoulder and she shifted it from one side to the other as she followed in Dar's footsteps. She turned her head to look behind her, and saw the outline of the cliff face still distinct against the darkening sky.

She heard falling rocks and looked up, stopping abruptly as her vision was occluded by Dar's back. "Oh."

Above them on the wall a large bird was just landing, folding its wings as it came to perch on a ledge full of random sticks and debris. "Is that a nest?"

"I think it was a hawk." Dar peered at it. "Too dark to get a shot?"

"Hold this." Kerry handed over her bag and lifted her camera in its case up, adjusting the controls for a moment before she looked through the viewfinder and zoomed in. The light wasn't great, but just as she snapped the picture a flash of far off lightning, as though accommodating her, lit up the sky.

"Folks, please let's get under cover." Janet's voice chided them. "It's going to start pouring rain and we need the path clear to get all the gear inside."

"Sorry." Kerry turned the camera off and followed Dar around a huge boulder to find the entrance to the promised cave ahead of them. "Oh."

It was larger than she'd thought it would be. An irregularly shaped dark gap in the wall, higher on one side than the other, but tall enough to allow them to enter upright with ease.

Inside, the crew already had some lanterns lit, and as Dar and Kerry entered they all trotted purposefully outside to get more gear. The cave itself was extremely large, and her momentary anxiety that she was going to end up cheek by jowl to the rest of the crowd was eased.

The rest of the group was clustered near a central, now darkened, fire pit and they joined them to wait for whatever was going to come next.

Dar put down both of their bags, then she put her hands on her hips, one eyebrow edging up. After a moment of silent pondering, she drew in a breath, then released it. "This'll go faster if we help," she said. "C'mon." She turned and started for the entrance, not watching to see who followed her.

Kerry suppressed a smile, then followed, and as she did she caught movement out of the corner of her eye and was surrounded by a cluster of bodies who joined them as they walked back out, into a wind already tinged with moisture.

"Good idea," Don commented as they evaded the shooing hands of the crew and grabbed the gear bags lining the shoreline. "C'mon, kids, none of us are cripples. Move aside."

Dar picked up a tent and put it on her shoulder and the college gals picked up one of the two big kitchen kits, and they started back toward the cave as Rich and Sally grabbed another sealed bin and Kerry lifted a large duffel bag.

"Choo." Rich waved Janet out of the way. "C'mon, we're gonna get wet."

The rest of the crew looked unabashedly relieved, and two of them broke off moving gear to go over to where Doug was standing, sorting out ropes to tie the raft down with.

"Thanks," Janet said. She lifted a box and joined them. "I really do appreciate the help. They want to get the boat secured in case we get a surge of downstream."

"Exactly," Rich said. "Last thing we need is to lose that."

The first spattering of raindrops just caught them as they marched inside the cave, depositing their burdens and turning around for another trip. "Hey," Dar addressed the few lingerers. "Start sorting that out while we get the rest of it."

Todd and Amy, especially stared at her.

"Aren't you hungry?" Dar asked. "C'mon!"

There was a moment of silence, then grudging movement. Dar shook her head and grumbled under her breath, as they emerged back into the weather.

"Sure you weren't in the navy?" Don asked, as he caught up to her, chuckling a little. "Coulda fooled me."

KERRY HUNG HER shirt up to dry on the line she'd strung

from their tent and sat down on one of the two folding chairs the staff had placed nearby. She ran her fingers through her damp hair and exhaled, watching the crew set up their cook stove inside the old fire pit as Janet picked up a tray and started circulating with drinks.

Their tent was on a slight rise to one side of the pit and Kerry was the first to be offered. "Thanks." She took two of the cups and put them down on the small camp table.

"Thank you for helping out," Janet replied. "I know I said that before, but I wanted you to know I really meant it."

Kerry smiled. "Hey, it was to our advantage. Glad we made it here before the storm really let loose. It's raining sideways out there."

Janet looked over her shoulder. "It is. But I'm not worried, really, about what it's doing here. I'm worried about what it's doing upstream." She confided. "Let's hope it just moves over us and goes west."

Kerry considered that as she watched the woman make her way along the rocks, going clockwise around the large chamber that now had a somewhat incongruous set of colored tents scattered around its large interior.

There were torches planted randomly and lanterns, and they gave the large space a sense of curious mystery. There were markings on the walls, but the light was too dim to make them out, and the surface above the cook pit was darkened visibly from smoke.

Above where they had the tents set up there was a higher level, but this was blocked off by a chain and post fence, and there were signs positioned along it. Behind that the darkness obscured her vision, but she made a mental note to wander up in the morning and see what was past it.

The next tents over were the college kids. PJ was seated with her foot up on a box, with Doug and Don tending her foot. Past them Sally was wandering around taking pictures.

Todd and Amy, predictably, had set up their tent near the fence. One of the crew was carrying a first aid kit up to where they were seated.

Dar emerged from the temporary bathroom, which had been set up as far away as possible from everyone else, near the other side of the cavern. She paused at the entrance to the cave to look out, the wind blowing her dark hair back as she studied the storm.

Then she continued across the front of the cave, past the busy crew, stopping to watch two of the crew hauling out what they were going to make for dinner.

SALLY CAME OVER and sat down next to Kerry. "Hope this storm doesn't last long," she said, with a sigh. "Starting to get the sense this trip's kinda...um..."

"Cursed?" Kerry supplied.

"Sort of." The lanky woman said. "First we pick up the douches, then PJ's foot, then the poison ivy...I mean I'm used to little things happening, but wow. Now the rain?"

Kerry hiked up one foot and put it on her knee, clasping her hands around her knee. "Well," she mused. "At least two of those things are related."

"Mm."

Kerry caught sight of Dar straightening up to her full height and craning her neck to observe the contents of a tray being moved toward the cook stove. She chuckled under her breath as a relatively content expression appeared and Dar continued on her way up to the tent.

"You're so funny," Sally said.

"Sometimes." Kerry reached out a hand as Dar got up to where they were. She smiled as it was clasped and lifted, and a kiss planted on the back of her knuckles in a gentle, absent gesture. "So, you satisfied with dinner, hon?"

Dar sat down on the ground, reaching over to pick up the mug. "I think so. Looks like salmon."

"Oh." Sally seemed surprised. "Hey, something I eat. Hot damn." She rested her elbows on the chair arms. "I didn't think they brought fish with them." She got up from the chair. "I'm going to scope it out. See you guys at dinner."

"Sally was just wondering if we were cursed," Kerry said, after Sally had walked out of earshot. "You think? Or is it just one of our typical vacations?"

Dar smiled. "Our one?" She said. "I think we're fine. Better than if we'd gotten caught out in the storm. They did a good job getting us to cover." She took a sip from the mug. "Can I be honest?"

Kerry reached out and riffled her fingers through her partner's dark hair. "You're bored with this. I can tell." She watched as Dar looked up at her, eyes shaded almost sand color from the dim light. "Sorry, hon."

"Why? We both decided on this." Dar said. "I just think...I just want to do more." She looked a touch embarrassed. "I feel bad about just sitting around letting these guys take us from spot to spot. Too..."

"Touristy?"

Dar shrugged. "Maybe."

Kerry considered that, "Ah well. It's only a couple more days. Then we can get back in our camper, pick up our dogs and go find some adventure on the way back to Vegas." She gently brushed her thumb over Dar's cheekbone. "I'll get some decent pictures out of it at least."

Dar nodded. "It's fine," She said. "We're supposed to go to that swimming hole tomorrow. That sounds fun. I think there's a ledge you can dive off." She sounded more enthusiastic. "And there's more rapids."

"And you have your book."

"And I have my book." Dar grinned at her, standing up and offering her hand. "Let's go sit around the campfire. Maybe those kids will drag out that trivia game again."

They walked down to where the crowd was starting to gather, sitting around the two large tables that had been set up by the crew. PJ had just hopped down and Rich brought out his deck of cards and was starting a game of fish.

Don and Marcia came over and sat down next to them, and a moment later Pete came over with a tray of drinks and a dish of cut fruits and vegetables with a few bowls of things to dip them in. He put them down and smiled and everyone reached over to sample.

The celery was crisp, and tasted fresh. Kerry crunched it contentedly as Rich dealt everyone a hand.

PJ inspected her cards. "Hey, Kerry. You're in IT, right?"

"We both are." Kerry indicated herself and then Dar. "We own an IT company."

"That's cool." PJ put a card down. "My boyfriend...well, my ex-boyfriend." She gave her companions a droll look as they sniggered. "He was majoring in IT. But all the people he hung out with were just..." She eyed Kerry.

"Nerds?" Kerry put down a pair of cards.

"Yeah, just really geeky."

Dar had her chin resting on her fists, watching Kerry's hand. "We're really geeky."

"You don't seem geeky," PJ said. "So that's what I was going to ask, is it different because you aren't guys? Is it just the guys who are so weird and freaky?"

"Well." Kerry was aware of Todd and Amy wandering down, staring at the two tables with distaste, then going over to sit on the far side away from the rest of them. "Dar programs in her head and I run operations."

"I have a copy of *Lord of the Rings* in my backpack," Dar said. "Not sure what you consider nerd cred."

Everyone chuckled.

"We have a lot of nerds working for us. They never seemed really weird," Kerry said. "Just smart guys and some gals, with a good work ethic." She put down another pair. "Go fish."

Rich picked up a card. "My uncle works for Microsoft. He's kinda weird. He has glasses and wears those pocket protector things. Hates the outdoors." He took a sip of his drink. "I'd rather hang with people who do outdoors things."

Outside the rain started coming down harder, and thunder rumbled overhead, sounding close and intense as the mouth of the cave lit up with a flash of silver.

One of the crew jumped, then picked up a tray of plates and came, circling the table and putting the plates down. "Wow that's loud," he said. "Sure glad we're in here."

They put aside the cards for the moment. Kerry pulled the plate over and found chilled vegetables on it, string beans and radishes, with curls of lettuce. "Sorry, hon." She bumped her head against Dar's shoulder, as her partner took a long-suffering breath and released it. "Try a bean."

Dar studied one of the items. Then she reached over and dipped it into the dill cream dip for the celery and tried a bite of that. "Hm." She pulled the bowl of dip over and started consuming the vegetables.

"I'm gonna have to get that recipe," Kerry said, and bit into a piece of radish. "PJ, what are you majoring in again?"

"Marketing," PJ said. "It's all rainbows and unicorns. You get to go into rooms with a bunch of other people, all of whom are talking bullshit, and have a contest to find out who can lie the best and they get the best grade."

"Sounds like marketing," Kerry said. "I rue the day when we're going to have to hire a marketer."

"Or a sales department."

Rich looked at them. "You have a company without sales and marketing? Where is this? Miami? Can I come work for you?"

"Can't be much of a business," Todd said.

"Ah, we do all right," Dar said, and continued munching steadily through the string beans.

"How many people in your company, Dar?" Don asked. "Is it consulting?"

"A little of everything," Kerry said, with a smile. "I think we're...what is it now, Dar, eighty-eight?"

"Hundred."

"We started off with five, including us." Kerry put down a pair of sixes, and picked up a card. "It's nice to own your own business."

Two of the crew came over with a trivet, and a small cast iron pot. They put the trivet down and set the pot on it, and a third crew member handed around small bowls.

Janet followed them over with a ladle. "Soup is good on a night like tonight. It's vegetable barley. We're going to fire up the weather radio, so we can see what the prognosis is."

Don took the ladle from her and started to serve the soup, glancing over his shoulder at the cave entrance. The darkness outside obscured the view, but they could hear the rain coming down and the thunder was getting more frequent.

Rich put the cards away as he received his bowl of soup, sniffing it appreciatively. "Mmm."

They all jumped a moment later as a blast of lightning hit outside, and Doug left his position at the cook stove and went to the entrance to look outside.

Todd also got up and went to the opening. Amy watched him go, but remained seated. The dim light hid the rash on her hands, and it was obscured as well by the medication they'd painted her with. After a moment, she looked up at the rest of them and smiled briefly.

"How's the itch?" Sally asked.

"It's okay," Amy said. "They gave me an antihistamine and I'm going to take that after dinner. I think it will make me sleepy."

"Hardly expected to see something like that out here," Don said. "Sorry you fell into it."

Amy smiled a little more naturally. "We didn't expect it either. I'm glad I had long sleeves on. I turned that shirt right inside out and put it in a bag." She looked around and then back at her companions. "This is a cool cave."

"It is," Kerry said. "I'm glad we're in here, and not outside." They all nodded in agreement. "We have storms like that back in Miami. No fun."

"No fun," Rich said. "But it's gonna make tomorrow all that more exciting." He grinned in anticipation. "The surge down the river's gonna be awesome."

"Really?" Amy asked, pausing.

"Oh sure." Sally reached out to take a roll from the basket that had just been deposited. "If they take a lot of rain up above the dam, they'll released it down the river and we'll be in for a hella ride."

Dar visibly perked up. "More rapids?"

"Big big." Rich was almost bouncing in his seat. "Can take those class fours and fives and take them up past that. Hope you all can swim!"

Kerry felt a bit intimidated by that, but she could see the idea interested Dar. "I think I need a bungee cord." She took a roll herself and a spoon of soup. The broth was tasty, and the vegetables and barley were plump and thick.

"They won't release the water with us in here, will they?" Marcia asked, after a moment of silence. "Couldn't it come right up into the cave? You can see the waterline up there." She pointed at the wall. "That would be a mess."

Todd returned and dropped into his seat. "Keeps raining, I'm going to spend the time walking this cave." he said, then grabbed a roll and ripped it in half. "That fence wont' keep me out."

No one answered him. The smell of grilling salmon wafted over, and the cavern reverberated with thunder, and Kerry chewed on a mouthful of the barley, suddenly wishing she was home. She glanced aside and found Dar watching her, a look of wry understanding on her face.

She smiled and felt Dar's knee bump hers under the table.

THE THUNDER KEPT up. Kerry was glad to duck inside their tent, where the folding bunks were set up nicely, pillows ready and light sleeping bags all tucked into their place. The mesh covered windows had all been rolled down and tied and a breeze was wafting through, tinged on its edges with a faint hint of the grilled fish and the sweeter overtones of the warmed brownies they'd been given for dessert.

Dar was already sprawled on her bunk, a small battery powered lamp clamped near her head as she read from the thick paperback held in one hand. "I heard that moron go over the fence about five minutes ago," Dar commented as Kerry sat down. "He's going to end up getting his ass either killed or arrested."

"His girlfriend didn't go," Kerry said, as she took off her sandals. "She was down by the fire, having some hot chocolate with the rest of us."

"Maybe getting a clue."

"Maybe." Kerry listened to the storm. "Should we tell Janet?"

"No," Dar said, firmly. "Better for us if he gets hauled off to Indian jail."

Kerry chuckled. "Or gets the crap scared out of him by an Indian spirit. That's what this cave's known for, ya know."

Dar made a mild, groaning noise.

"Hon, they know better than to come here and bother you. I'm pretty sure there's an Internet message board somewhere for spooks, and after New Orleans they opened a thread on that crazy Florida person who stands off ghosts bare assed naked."

Dar chortled under her breath softly.

They heard some bangs and thunks, and Kerry got back up and went to the door of the tent, peering out. "They're moving everything away from the entrance."

Dar joined her and they both watched as the crew worked quickly, moving the boxes with the food stores up onto the rise that led to where they were, frequently turning their heads to look back at the entrance. "Hm." She took a step outside the tent. "Water's coming up."

Kerry could see the line of the river now even with the entrance, and a moment later Sally appeared, coming over from the nearby spot where she and her sister had settled.

"What's up?" Sally asked.

"The river, apparently." Kerry pointed. "They're bringing all the gear up."

"Wow," Sally said, after a pause. "Guess they just want to make sure nothing gets wet."

The crew finished their work and now, apparently more relaxed, gathered together in a clump to listen to whatever it was Janet and Doug were telling them.

"Yeah. Wet granola's no fun," Dar said.

"I just hope it's stopped by the morning." Sally stifled a yawn. "I don't' mind getting wet in the rapids, but I don't like doing that with rain all day long. I caught the worst cold last time that happened on a trip." She started down the slope. "Night you two."

They watched the crew disperse toward the area they had set up for themselves, as Doug went alone to the edge of the cave, swinging a rain poncho over his shoulders as he settled on the small beach chair perched on the rocky verge, his bare feet splayed out on the red stone.

"Not sure I want to ride all day in the rain either," Kerry commented.

Dar draped her arm over Kerry's shoulders. "Want to try skiing next time? Less group, more Jacuzzis."

Kerry sighed. "I don't know why I had such high hopes for this vacation. They never go like you expect them to, do they?"

"Not ours." Dar laughed briefly. "Ah, it's not that bad, Ker."

They retreated inside the tent and then stood there regarding each other. "Well," Kerry said, with a faint shrug. "You never know if you don't try stuff, right?" She eyed Dar, who was unbuttoning the shirt she was wearing.

Dar produced a faint but sexy grin as she bared her upper body and moved closer. "Ever try kissing in a cave?" She traced Kerry's pulse point with her fingertip, feeling it strengthen.

"Never done anything in a cave," Kerry said, stepping closer, throwing a quick glance to either side of the tent, where the screen windows were open to the outer air. "Or a tent. Should we close the windows?"

"Nah." Dar circled her with both arms and tilted her head down, engaging Kerry's lips with her own. They ignored the rumbling outside and let their bodies press against each other in a moment of slowly escalating sensuality. "I like the breeze."

Kerry eased her shirt off over her head and tossed it aside. "I kinda do too." She felt the faint brush of the air against her shoulder blades as she stepped forward again and her bare skin touched Dar's and their lips met again. The combination between the heat and the cool made her nape hairs prickle and she felt goose bumps rising.

After a little while they paused, and Dar touched the tip of her nose to Kerry's, watching her eyes close rather than cross trying to meet hers. "Let's try to make the tent rock. How about that?"

"They said we had to bring our entertainment with us." Kerry unbuttoned Dar's jeans and bumped her backwards. "Entertain me."

"Anytime." Dar stepped out of her jeans and half turned, regarding the separated cots. "Anytime after I re-engineer this."

Kerry chuckled.

"Not going to get black and blue butts."

Chapter Four

IT WAS DARK when Kerry opened her eyes, and though she could hear the river's rush outside, the sound of thunder was conspicuous by its absence. She carefully lifted herself up and checked her watch, then she returned her body to its former position and exhaled a little.

She looked over at the dark figure next to her, and after a moment, Dar opened her eyes and looked back.

Barely visible in the dim light coming from the lanterns parked outside, but even so she could see the faint shift of skin as Dar smiled at her.

They were on the ground. Cots stacked up against the wall of the tent leaving them with their mattress pads and sleeping bags snuggled up in the center. Kerry reached out her hand and tangled her fingers with Dar, aware of a sense of contentment that only intensified as they curled up in each other's arms.

They had plenty of time to relax. It was at least an hour to dawn, and there wasn't a sound outside that could be the crew starting to get things going for the day.

It was nice to just relax there together. "Stopped raining," Kerry murmured.

"Good." Dar closed her eyes again.

"What is today, Wednesday?"

Dar opened one eye halfway, regarding her in silence for a moment. "Tuesday," she finally decided. "It's weird to think we haven't communicated with anyone for that long."

"Mm."

"Should I think about all the possible disasters that could be happening?"

"No." Kerry rubbed the edge of her thumb against Dar's knuckle. "What's the point? You can't do anything about it."

"True." Dar exhaled and let the one eye close.

They were both quiet for a while, then Dar opened her eye again and found Kerry looking back at her.

They sighed at the same time, and sat up, untangling themselves from the covers and sitting cross-legged. "Want to go for a walk?" Kerry suggested. "Maybe the clouds are gone and we can see the stars."

Dar looked interested. "Sure." She levered herself up to her feet and slid a shirt and jeans on, holding her hand down to offer Kerry a boost up. "I suck at sleeping in."

"I know." Kerry gave her a good-humored smile. "I live with you." She dressed and got her sandals on and they emerged into the cavern, where the cool breeze from outside blew against them. The gentle slope down to the entrance was a little damp and as they emerged into the cooking area, they noted a cooler left out with cups.

The seat by the edge of the cavern was empty, and against the wall saw a figure rolled up in a sleeping bag sound asleep.

Outside the sky was, in fact, clear. Kerry sucked in a breath of awe, as she paused and looked up, finding a thick ribbon of stars past the outline of the cliffs. "Oh wow."

The air outside was chilly, but it made the sky seem even crisper, and Kerry took a deep breath as she turned slowly in a circle, staring up.

Dar stood next to her, hands in the pockets of her jeans, a gentle fog marking her breath. She studied the swath of stars visible overhead. "That's cool." She pointed. "The milky way. Look at all those suckers."

"That is cool," Kerry said. "I'm glad we got up."

"Me too." Nearby Dar heard an owl and studied the scrubby trees growing up the cliff, seeing a pair of yellow eyes watching them. She took a few steps down the shore, to where the raft was securely tied and sat down on one of the rocks.

The sound of the river was almost hypnotic. It burbled and rushed along, a never-ending cascade of sound and this moment of pre-dawn quiet seemed a little magical.

Kerry came over and sat next to her, tasting the scent of the water on the back of her tongue. "So pretty."

Dar cleared her throat, then quietly started to sing.

Twinkle, twinkle, little star
How I wonder what you are
Up above the world so high
Like a diamond in the sky
Twinkle, twinkle little star
How I wonder what you are

When the blazing sun is gone
When the nothing shines upon
Then you show your little light
Twinkle, twinkle, all the night

Twinkle, twinkle, little star
How I wonder what you are

Kerry smiled in delight, humming along to the nursery song, enjoying the sound of Dar's clear voice and the grin she could hear in the words.

Then, as she leaned against Dar's body and glanced past her, she gasped, causing Dar to stop abruptly and stare at her. "Look!" She pointed to the right, past the raft. "There's something watching us!"

Dar slowly turned her head, spotting the outline of an animal on the shore past where the craft was tied. "Oh!" She bounced a little in excitement. "Kerry, it's a bobcat!"

"Are you sure?" Kerry whispered back, squinting in that direction. "I can hardly see it!"

"I can see the whiskers!" Dar stared in fascination at the animal, who agreeably sat down and lifted a paw to lick it. "Wow."

Kerry was explicitly glad. If the trip itself was being something of a disappointment at least Dar had gotten to see her bobcat. "Wish I had my camera," she lamented. "I know if I go get it the thing will be gone."

Just then, the owl lifted off its branch and winged away and in the east a faint glow was appearing, making the edge of the cliffs etch sharply. They sat still and watched as the bobcat paced toward the raft, then jumped up onto it, swaggering across the seats and sniffing the storage boxes.

In the faint lantern glow from the cavern, Kerry could now see it more clearly, it's compact body, the fluffy fur on its face, and it's small stubby tail. "Oh wow."

"Cool," Dar said, leaning forward to watch the animal as it turned it's head and looked right into her eyes, it's own a tawny yellow.

It bared it's fangs at them with a touch of insolence, then it jumped down and headed off, down the riverside with a twitch of its tail.

Kerry squeezed Dar's arm, grinning with excitement. "Really glad we got up now!"

"Nice," Dar rumbled. "Really nice."

"Now I know why they lock all that stuff up." Kerry whispered, bumping shoulders with her. "Bet that cat would have eaten anything it found."

"Bet it would." Dar half turned as they heard footsteps behind them, to find Don and Marcia coming out of the cave. "Morning."

"Morning you two," Marcia greeted. "You missed the kerfuffle last night. That little gal came running out half past midnight and all upset because her fellow didn't come back."

"Meh." Dar snorted. "Glad I slept through it."

"Me too," Kerry said. "So, what happened?"

"Well, I don't know," Don said. "Some of the crew went off, and we went to bed. Don't have to tell me twice, I wasn't getting involved in it. Silly kid."

"Jerk went off into the cave around nine or ten," Dar said. "I heard him jumping over that fence."

Marcia clucked her tongue. "Want some coffee? They left a thermos out and I heard noises from the crew area." She looked up at the sky, where the stars were starting to get washed out by the glow in the east. She sighed. "Aren't those pretty?"

Rich came out with Sally trailing behind him. At their heels one of the crew had a tray with cups on it. He stifled a yawn with one wrist. "Late night, Chris?" Don asked him.

"We were hunting in the cave," the young man said. "Took us five hours to find the guy who jumped the fence. I'm toast." He offered them cups and then wandered back toward the cave. "Morning." He offered the tray to a few other wanderers.

Don frowned. "That's a shame." He walked over to the raft and examined the ground. "These kids work hard enough without having to work all that much harder." He peered out over the river. "Got some water coming down today, we do."

Marcia sat down on one of the storage boxes that had been left near the raft, ropes fastening it to the rigging. "It's pretty this morning, isn't it?" she said. "So clear."

Dar got up and wandered along the riverside. She paused where they'd seen the bobcat and crouched down to look at the ground.

Kerry sipped at the freshly made, artisanal tasting coffee. "Guess what we just saw? A bobcat."

"No, really?" Marcia said.

"Really. Walked down the edge of the river and right up onto our raft." Kerry watched Dar reach down and touch the ground, putting her fingers into what she could only assume were the tracks from the cat. "Dar's so happy. She really wanted to see one." She looked up as they heard a motor approaching and watched as a powerboat came maneuvering into the small bay the cave was in.

"Ah hah," Don said. "I figured we'd get a visit from the native patrol."

The sky was now a coral pink edged with gilt as the sun got ready to appear over the rocks. Janet emerged from the cave, with Doug behind her, at the sound of the motorboat's roar.

Kerry got up and headed away from the river. She went through the entrance as more of the crew came out, noting the apprehensive looks on their faces.

Meant nothing good. She went quickly to the tent and got her camera, then paused and knelt to stuff their gear into the duffle bags and zip them shut. Then she carried them out of the tent so the crew could strike it if they needed to.

PJ was limping carefully down the slope and paused when she saw Kerry. "Hey, Kerry. What's going on?"

"Hard to say." Kerry joined her on the route outside. "There was some issue last night and a boat just showed up with some officials or something."

PJ frowned. "Oh, that's not good. Tribal police?"

"Not sure."

They reached the entrance to the cave, passing the four or five crew who were preparing breakfast. Outside the four people from the boat were standing on the river's edge, facing Doug and Janet. "Yep," PJ said. "Was it that dude?"

Kerry regarded the scene. "That's what I heard." She shook her head, and turned right, heading back over to where Dar was seated, watching the sunrise.

When she got near her, Dar pointed at a bighorn sheep that was making its way up the side of the cliff across from them.

Kerry quickly got her camera ready and took a shot. "Did that cat leave tracks? I was going to take a picture of it for you."

Dar circled her arm around Kerry's leg, and leaned her head against her hip. "Thanks." She indicated the ground. "I was hoping you'd do that. I put a circle of rocks around it so we could find it again." Dar leaned forward and looked past Kerry's kneecap. "They in trouble?"

Kerry took her focus off the sheep and put it on the ground. She untangled herself from Dar's grip and knelt, as a bit of the sun splashed the rocks and brought out their striated colors. "Oo."

There were several paw prints but Dar, typically, had found the most perfect one, with the toes and the pad well defined. The sun made the shot even more interesting and she spent a few minutes taking several pictures of it from a few different angles.

Dar watched with an indulgent and pleased smile, glad this bit of their adventure was being captured. She could easily picture a copy of that ending up in a frame on the wall and it made her happy. She whistled softly under her breath, then glanced up and over as voices started to rise.

The four people who had arrived were in weathered jackets and jeans. They were tall and had similar builds. She could see the placating body posture in Janet. Doug had his hands in his pockets and listened in silence.

Almost without thought, she slowly started making her way toward the group. "Be right back, hon."

Kerry looked up, and a moment later she stood up and followed. When they neared the group the voices became clear.

"Look, you people know the rules." The tallest of the men said. "We let you use this place on those conditions."

"We know," Janet said. "We didn't know anyone had breached the fence until someone told us one of the passengers was gone and they couldn't find them." She glanced aside as Dar approached and turned to her. "Oh, hey, I think breakfast is ready. We'll be done here in a moment."

Dar kept walking until she was standing next to Janet. She paused, regarding the four men over Janet's head. "I heard him go over the fence around ten," she said. "We were told not to go near the back, he didn't give a crap."

The tallest of the men regarded her back with a solemn expression. He had a heavy, rugged face, and lined eyes, with dark, straight hair pulled back in a ponytail and Dar figured he was mostly native. His eyes were dark brown and they met hers in a stolid kind of way.

She stopped speaking and waited.

"About ten, you say?" the man said, after a long pause.

"Right, so we didn't know he was missing until after midnight," Janet said, hastily. "Because you didn't say anything to anyone, did you Ms. Roberts?"

"I didn't say anything to anyone," Dar said.

"Why not?" the man asked. "Seems like a good camper would want to tell someone that."

"Because he's an idiot." Dar said. "I was hoping he'd get bitten by something that would require him to be airlifted out of here and leave us the hell alone." Dar held out a hand. "Sorry, Dar Roberts."

A corner of the man's lip twitched, and then he returned the gesture and took her hand in his. "Jonny Redhawk," he said. "So, this guy's a troublemaker?" His body posture relaxed a little and he folded his arms over his chest.

"He's a pain in our ass," Dar said. "Got a chip on his shoulder and wants us all to pay for it."

Janet took a breath, then she paused and released it, remaining silent. Doug put his hands behind his back and rocked back and forth a little. "He has a beef with us." He admitted. "We were supposed to take him on a private trip, and our team didn't make the flight out."

"Ah." Redhawk grunted.

"Any chance he's broken enough laws for you to haul his ass off?" Dar asked in a hopeful tone, noting the faint grins on the faces of the other natives. "Seriously, they didn't know." She said. "Guys just a punk with a rich dad."

Redhawk nodded a little. "Seen a few of those. This outfit don't cater to the blue collar I reckon." He regarded her with a brief smile. "Let's go talk to this guy." He indicated the cavern. "Then we'll talk to you all."

Janet nodded. "Okay, sure." She hesitated, looking at Dar.

"We're going to have breakfast," Dar reassured her. "We're done here." She held a hand out to Kerry and they walked past the group, heading for the table they could see the rest of the company clustered around. "Not sure if that was a good thing to do or not."

"It was a you thing to do." Kerry smiled, patting her on the back. "Crusader Dar, even when you decide not to be."

"Mm."

"Hey, hon, I think they have bacon."

THEY DID, IN fact, have bacon, and biscuits. Dar considered her morning pretty well a good one as she sat on the pontoon of the raft and waited for the rest of the company to get packed up and moving. She had her bathing suit on under her shorts and was looking forward to them getting underway.

She kicked her sandals against the pontoon and drew in a breath of the cool air, keeping her ears cocked for Kerry's approach, as her partner had remained behind collecting some fruit to take onboard the raft for their morning's trip.

She was looking forward to the swimming, and seeing some of the waterfalls they were scheduled to look at, along with the natural slides the pictures had promised and it all seemed to offer a more active participation in their little trip.

Rich came over and sat down on the pontoon next to her. "Hey."

"Hey," Dar responded amiably.

"So, you're a computer person, right?"

"Right." Dar said. "You're not going to ask me how to clean your mouse balls are you?"

In the middle of taking a breath, Rich paused and gave her a look. "Uh what?"

"Never mind. Did you have a question?"

"Oh, okay, well yeah, my nephew is just getting out of college and he was wondering if it was a good idea to get into computers."

Dar regarded him. "What did he go to college for?"

"He was a Tibetan history major."

"Does he want to make a living?"

Rich grinned sheepishly. "Yeah, it's a joke, right? Something like that, all you can do is either write books, teach history, or keep going to school."

Dar pondered a moment. "Does he like computers?"

Rich nodded. "He really does. He's got like, four of them and he's always doing stuff with them on the Internet, in these chat things. You know," he said. "But how do you get started for real with them? How did you start?"

"I started by programming the integrated circuits in nuclear submarines."

Rich squinted at her. "I thought you said you weren't in the service?"

"I wasn't. I was ten," Dar said almost apologetically. "But seriously if he wants to get into computers he started the right way. Just use the hell out of them. Learn a programming language. Do some small stuff. Get a job in tech support."

Rich put his hands in his pockets and studied her in silence for a minute. "You were ten?"

"Nine and a half." Dar's eyes twinkled a little.

Two of the crew moved past them, carrying gear. Both were shaking their heads.

"Yeeo. Guess it's time to get going." Rich got up and climbed up onto the raft, chuckling a little under his breath as he went to his favorite perch on the front of the middle pontoon.

Dar chuckled a little herself, remembering being that precocious brat, earning Hershey bars tweaking sensors for her father's skipper and him telling her father his kid was some kind of genius.

That had gotten her ice cream to go with the Hershey. It all had seemed a little silly to her, doing these things that were so basic and common sense to her, and magic to everyone else.

But then they'd taken her in for some tests, two days of what she remembered as being a bit boring, and then her parents discussing the results which had numbers and statistics that hadn't meant anything to her at the time.

Only later on, when she'd gotten to high school and all of those advanced placement classes and the academic attention, did she realize there was something different in her head. Things that came so easily to her didn't always do the same for her classmates.

Certainly hadn't helped her cocky antisocial self much. Dar grinned briefly. What an absolute jerk she'd been.

She got up and went to the two seats she and Kerry had claimed, arranging the day bags she'd taken out, positioning Kerry's so her camera would be handy on the right hand side. Then she took a seat and hooked her feet on the rungs of the steel supports, removing her sunglasses from her bag and sliding them into place over her eyes as she watched the entrance to the cave.

The four natives emerged, and Janet walked them down to their boat. Amy and Todd came out behind them. Todd looked both sleepy and disgruntled, his head half turned watching the visitors get into their boat. After a moment, he lifted his middle finger in their direction, then shifted his duffel on one shoulder and headed for the raft.

"Nice." Dar kept her eyes forward as the two mounted the raft and crossed behind her, hearing Todd drop the duffel onto his seat and then detecting the scuff and creek of footsteps approaching her. She kept her hands relaxed on her knees, but was aware of a tension coming into her body, and a faint increase in her breathing.

Todd stopped next to her. "Hey."

"Hey," Dar responded.

"You tell those fuckers I jumped the fence?"

"Yep." Dar turned her head slightly and regarded him through her sunglasses.

"Why?"

"Because I felt like it." She dropped her head a little, letting the glassed slide forward enough for her to look over the top. They stared at each other for a long moment in silence. "No sense in letting these guys get in trouble for your idiocy."

He took a step forward and Dar stood up in response, her hands coming to rest at her sides half curled into fists. After what seemed like a long, breathless pause he just moved back and went to the drink cooler, flipping it open and removing a can from it. "Asshole," he tossed back over his shoulder.

"Pipsqueak," Dar responded, with a chuckle. She resumed her seat and pushed her sunglasses back up, then realized that Rich had seen it. He stood up in place and walked across the pontoon and came to her side.

"What was that?" Kerry asked, arriving from the other direction at the same time.

"A moron." Dar inspected the selection of fruit Kerry was carrying and removing a pear from her grasp.

"That guy was going to hit you," Rich said in a serious tone.

"He thought about it," Dar said. She took a bite of the pear. "He might have taken a swing at Ker," she added. "But I'm six foot four and not a little girl pushover."

Kerry eyed her. "Hey, who's the registered gun owner in our family?"

"Neither are you a pushover, slugger," Dar said. "But he doesn't know that." She wiggled her toes in contentment. "Bullies pick targets they figure they can roll right over." She nibbled around the seeds. "But we better check around our tent from now on, hon."

"Ugh." Kerry stuffed the rest of the fruit into her pack and sat down. "Jerkity Jerk Jerk Jerk."

Dar got up and put the pear in between her teeth, miming a drink and moving off toward the cooler, as the rest of the party got settled.

"That guy is trouble," Rich told Kerry. "She should be careful."

"Yeah." Kerry grinned wryly. "We both should be careful. But we're not. Problem is, Dar really doesn't have a careful gene."

Rich started laughing.

"Seriously. She's got no fear in her," Kerry said. "And, though we really prefer to be mild mannered derfy nerds, we honestly don't take any crap from people, so hopefully the moron back there will just chill out and start enjoying the ride."

"Not sure he's going to," Rich said. "So watch out."

Kerry leaned on the arm of the chair. "We will. But honestly?" Her eyes twinkled a little. "We're more trouble than he is. I know that sounds sketch. But it's true."

Rich looked dubiously at her. "Hope you know what you're doing. Anyway I'll keep an eye out on him just on general principals. He could be trouble for anyone." He moved off back to his pontoon, pulling off his over shirt and putting it away before settling down.

Kerry watched him. "Nice guy." She got her camera out, and inserted it into her waterproof casing. "Looks like a beautiful day."

KERRY MUNCHED ON an apple, one foot propped up against the aluminum frame, enjoying the sunlight as they coasted along between the walls of the canyon, the raft rocking back and forth a bit.

Ahead she saw a bend, and the crew was starting to prepare the lines as they traveled toward the promised water playground that was supposed to be just past it. Dar had both feet up against the frame, reading a book she was holding in one hand.

The pontoons were empty, their residents back near the supply area, picking up cups of hot apple cider. Kerry was pondering doing the same thing herself as they reached the bend and started around it.

"So here we get to relax for a couple of hours, and then have lunch," Janet announced, as the raft coasted through a ripple of white ruffled waters, and they emerged into an area full of sculpted rock. "Look at those natural slides!"

Rain and erosion had modeled the sandstone into loops and whirls, with water surging through them making a natural playground. Dar stood up as they approached the rustic landing. She put her book away in her day bag and bounced up and down a little on the balls of her feet.

"Water's high from that storm," Sally said, from her seat next to Kerry. "Should be fun!"

It looked it. Kerry grinned. The breeze had picked up a little, and it ruffled her hair, as she got her daypack settled on her shoulder and prepared to follow Dar off the raft.

They docked and everyone scrambled off, walking down the driftwood landing and up onto a flat space where the crew was already offloading the tables and gear to prepare for lunch.

"You can put your stuff up here." Janet indicated a rock shelf just above that. "And go have fun!"

With a pout, PJ settled herself to watch on a flat rock, putting her bandaged foot up and spreading tanning lotion out along her skin. She looked up with a smile as one of the crew offered to help, and handed over the bottle. "Kerry, you want me to take some pictures of you guys? Since I can't swim?"

"Sure." Kerry handed over the camera.

"Hot damn." Dar glanced over her shoulder at them. "Now

I'll get some pictures with you in them." She grinned as she stripped out of her long sleeve t-shirt and shorts.

"Hah hah." Kerry good naturedly joined her, giving her a poke in the hip as she removed her own shirt. They were both in one-piece suits and as she half turned the sun splashed over her chest picking out the colors of her tattoo, the infinity snake and its multicolor scales bright and distinct.

Then the golden light touched the vivid eyes and claws of Dar's, there on the cap of her shoulder and Kerry impulsively leaned over and gave the cat a kiss.

Dar glanced at her and smiled, then reached out and tickled Kerry's snake with the tip of her finger. "Let's go have some fun."

"Go on, I'll be right there." Kerry started to remove her shorts. "Wow, that water looks nice."

"Yep." Dar put her sunglasses and clothes inside her pack and went to the edge of the water. The landing was at the outer end of a long, deep curve in the river, and there was a set of lines that blocked off the bay, making a protected swimming area.

It looked cool and fresh, and without hesitation she went to a flat rock at its edge and dove into it, judging the depth sufficient.

It was. She opened her eyes and saw the whiteness of the rocks and a few startled fish splurting out of her way as she reached the bottom of the dive and started up again. It was just as refreshing as she'd figured it would be, and as she surfaced she heard the muted screams of the others jumping in.

She could feel the current, milder than in the main part of the river, but still a bit of a tugging at her as she turned and started swimming back and the exertion felt good. She switched her stroke to a butterfly and stretched her body out as she angled her motion toward where Kerry was making her more casual entry into the water.

"Oh, chilly," Marcia said as she eased into the water up to her knees.

Kerry took a breath and steeled herself, then waded up to her hips into the water before she just threw herself forward, stifling a reflexive inhale at the temperature.

Halfway across the lagoon she saw Dar's head as she swam steadily toward them, her long arms coming up and out of the water as she moved against the current that Kerry felt pushing against her shoulder blades.

Still, after a moment of adjustment it felt good and she relaxed, rolling over onto her back and letting the current take her briefly into deeper water. Then turned over and started pushing against the flow.

Half of the crew were also in the water in shorty wet suits, several of them with float bullets, obviously keeping an eye on their clients.

Kerry found she could make progress, but it took some effort. But after the last week of just spectating it felt good and she only wished she had her dive fins on to get a little more leg action into it.

She made it back to the shallows just as Dar caught up to her and they both stood together, leaning against the current as the rest of the party got wet. "Nice." She ran a hand over her hair to move it out of her eyes.

"Very," Dar said. "Want to go do the slides?" she asked, pointing to the climb up to the curve of the waterfront that allowed access to the irregular natural formations. "I think they're setting up for some water volleyball."

"Can I sit on your shoulders for it?" Kerry joked ruefully, as they started in the direction of the shore.

"Heh." Dar chuckled. "Remember that game at the party?"

Kerry thought a moment, then smiled at the memory. "I do." She followed Dar as they started up the slope, walking carefully on the slippery sandstone. "Mariana told me she knew for sure that night," she said. "About us, I mean."

"Why, because I showed up for a party half naked and played volleyball with you?" Dar inquired with mock surprise. "What a sleuth!"

"Mm." Kerry chuckled under her breath. "I was standing next to Maria when you came in, and while my hormones were busy crawling out my ears, she was just like, oh isn't that a nice outfit Jefa has on. Kerry, you should go tell her that."

"She knew." Dar picked a path up the slope, appreciating the sun now hitting her skin. "She's known me a long time."

"I liked her from the start." Kerry climbed up next to her and they went to the top of the first slide area. "Meet you at the bottom?"

"Booyah." Dar picked a slope and stepped into the wash of the water cascading down it, sitting down and letting the force of the current take her forward.

The slope was mild, but the rush of the water gave it at least an illusion of speed. She slide down the winding curves of the stone, ending in an abrupt plunge in a falling surge of water as she came out and went into the water at the end of it.

It was deep enough to be over her head, but she arrested her motion and kicked upward, breaking the surface and turning to see Kerry shoot out the end and tumble in midair, laughing.

"Woo!" Rich and Sally scrambled up the slope to follow them. Even Amy and Todd grudgingly headed in that direction.

Kerry came up next to Dar. "Let's go again. That was fun."

More than willing, Dar started for the shore, clearing the landing area for the next sliders. Faint strains of music emerging from a solar powered radio caught her ear and she looked to the other shore where the crew was setting up a little canopy and putting chairs out.

Then she spotted Rich climb up onto a shelf a respectable distance from the surface. He leaped off, and she grinned.

"Oh boy." Kerry covered her eyes.

IT WAS LATE afternoon and the sun was turning to a burnished gold as it headed west, the music still chiming over the water as everyone relaxed after hours of water play.

Dar was stretched out along one of the pontoons drying off, pleasantly tired and enjoying the warmth of the sun after several hours of being in the cold water. Nearby, Kerry sat in one of the forward seats, talking to Sally and PJ.

Dar felt the raft undulating beneath her and turned her head to see the edge of the water now higher against the rocks. Then the motion settled down and she half shrugged, closing her eyes again.

"No, I used to only shoot film." Kerry shifted a little in her seat, keeping an eye on Dar out there on the pontoon. "I just switched to digital."

"My roommate still uses film, and develops his own negatives," PJ said. "Holy bleep that stinks."

Kerry laughed. "That I never did."

"He shot things you'd get arrested for trying to get developed these days," PJ said, matter-of-factly. "So, there's that."

Kerry grimaced.

"Yeah, it was gross," PJ said. "He was selling the pictures but he finally got busted and they showed up at the apartment one morning last month and dragged his ass off to jail." She took a last bite of her banana, pausing to fold the skin up in a neat bundle. "I was glad he'd paid the rent at least."

Sally was laying on the platform in front of the seats, her face half obscured by a hat. "This was a blast today," she said. "Especially that platform diving. I love it."

"I think I liked the slides better, Kerry said. "I'm not really fond of heights. But it was fun watching, and I got some good shots of Dar with her acrobatics." She gave her partner a fond look, aware of the one, sharp blue eye open now and watching her. "We're going to have to add a few walls, hon, for all these pictures."

Dar stuck her tongue out, then relaxed again on the pontoon, the reddish light gilding her skin.

Janet appeared, with a tray. "Everyone have a good time?" She offered the tray. "Got some lemonade here before we pack up and take off."

"I'm fine, thanks." Kerry leaned back to let PJ take a mug. "Today was great, Janet. I think everyone had a good time." She put a slight emphasis on the word.

Janet smiled. "Yeah, it didn't start so great, but I agree." She stepped between them and started for the other side of the raft. "Ms. Roberts? Want some lemonade?"

Dar waved her hand negatively. "All good." She sat up, then got to her feet and made her way over to where Kerry was. She pulled her shirt back on and sat down in her seat, resting her elbows on the chair arms.

Rich came over, ruffling his hair dry. "Tomorrow's full of rapids. It's the biggest rapids day. All white water, all the time." He grinned. "Literally nonstop."

"And we've got two hikes when we do stop," Sally said. "Sorry PJ."

PJ stuck her tongue out.

Doug jumped up onto the raft and went back to the pilot's seat, as everyone started to wander back onboard. He blew the raft's horn gently twice, then started to prepare the craft to leave.

"And there's a lot of water coming down," Rich said, looking out over the river they were preparing to pull back out onto. "We're in for a big ride."

THE CAMPING SPOT that night was a picturesque side canyon that held a winding creek split off from the Colorado. On the shore was a big sandy beach that fronted the cliffs rising high over them.

The tents were all set up along the beach, with tiki torches between them. The crew gathered driftwood and built a fire to grill dinner over instead of using their camp stove.

Dar sprawled in her chair in front of their tent and drew in a breath of whatever was being grilled, which smelled like meat and peppers. Overhead was a blanket of stars, only slightly washed out by the fire and she watched with a benign expression as Kerry approached carrying two bottles of beer.

Kerry was barefoot and in shorts and a long-sleeved shirt with the sleeves rolled up. She put the bottles down on their little camp table and sat down next to Dar with a contented sigh. "This is kinda more like it."

"Yup."

"And tomorrow sounds really fun."

"Vroom vroom," Dar said. "Seventy-five miles they said of rapids? Twenty-five? Something like that, but it sounds like a nice rollercoaster."

"Rich is stoked."

The fire snapped a little as they turned the meat on the grill, sending a wafting of sparks up into the dark night sky. One of the crew brought out a guitar and was tuning it, a companion sitting down with a long, wooden flute.

A little way off they heard the rush of the river, a reminder of what they had in store tomorrow. Kerry tipped her head back to watch the stars, a smile on her face.

Midway down the beach, someone had pulled out a Frisbee and the younger members of the party were racing up and down the sand, playing catch. "Hope that doesn't land in the fire." Kerry said, idly.

"Better a fire than the teeth of a barracuda," Dar responded. "Though the plastic burning will ruin those nice steaks."

"I think we're going to have some fajitas. I saw them unpacking the tortillas," Kerry said. "And I thought I saw them frying up green tomatoes." She took a sip of her beer and hiked up her ankle on one knee. "And, danger boy has been quiet the whole damn day. Maybe you scared him."

Dar chuckled. "I doubt it."

They heard a loud whistle to the left near the water, and spotted Doug outlined against the glow of the fire, pulling back on a fishing line.

Kerry smiled. "Maybe fish tacos, too."

"Won't be as good as yours," Dar said.

"My catcher of fish is cuter." Kerry winked at her. "So naturally the tacos taste better." She reached over and tickled Dar's ear. "You got some sunburn."

"I did," Dar said. "I had a really good time today. I liked those slides."

"You liked jumping off that rock."

Dar grinned.

"I got some great pictures of you diving."

"Oh no, not more bathroom art."

They clinked their beers together and took swallows of the cold beverage, falling silent as the guitar player started to pluck out a melody. It was Spanish sounding, and quite beautiful. After a moment the flute player joined in with a reedy counterpoint.

"Pretty," Kerry said. Then she half turned her head to regard her companion. "Were you ever into music when you were a kid? I was forced to have piano lessons that were never really successful."

"No," Dar admitted. "I mean, aside from singing Christmas hymns with Dad." She listened to the music. "I kinda wanted to play the guitar, but just never got around to it."

Behind the players, the rest of the crew were bringing platters to the tables and they got up to walk over, strolling across the sand along the waterside.

Today they had set up the tables in a line rather than scattered them. Dar and Kerry took seats a little way from one end and relaxed as the rest of the party joined them.

The platters held, as Kerry had suspected, fajitas and fixings, and were served family style with everyone sharing. They had toasted the tortillas a little, giving them a bit of a smoky flavor and Kerry contentedly piled hers up with roasted veggies and some strips of grilled chicken, along with a dusting of cheese.

"What a great day," Marcia said. "I managed to get a nice sketch in of that cove. How lovely that was."

Todd and Amy took seats in the end of the table, and pulled one of the platters over to their plates. Amy stood up and was assembling dishes for both, the fading marks of poison ivy still visible on her arms and hands.

PJ, with an air of taking one for the team, leaned closer to them. "Hey, you guys want some lemonade?"

"Yes, please," Amy answered before Todd could. He sat calmly in his chair, picking up the folded tortilla and chewing it.

PJ handed over the pitcher. "Here ya go." She turned back to face Kerry across the table. "You want to take some sunrise shots tomorrow? From this angle, it's going to be awesome if it's clear out."

"Sure." Kerry enjoyed the earthy taste of the grilled peppers, and leaned back in her chair, extending her legs out under the table and crossing them at the ankles. "You mean over the ridge there?"

Behind them Dar saw the crew working on the raft, stringing out more guide ropes and tightening down the lashings. She studied them for a few minutes, but they didn't seem worried. They were laughing and relaxed as they worked so she returned her attention to the table.

Her peripheral vision caught Todd watching what was going on behind them as well, and a faint smirk appeared on his face that immediately made her hackles stand up and she chewed more slowly, listening to Kerry's banter while keeping him in view.

What's the little bastard done? She pondered. Poisoned the food? She stopped chewing and sucked in a little air over her tongue, but tasted nothing unusual and she could see he was focusing on the crew busy at work.

Could he have done something to the raft? Something to the crew? Did the little jerk put a snake into one of the boxes? Dar was unsettled enough to get up out of her chair, and put down her half-eaten fajita. "Be right back."

Kerry watched her alertly, her pale eyebrows hiking in question.

Dar gave her a pat on the shoulder, then moved away from the table and around the fire pit, feeling the heat of the campfire against her skin. She spotted Janet walking around the other side and aimed for her, holding a hand up slightly to catch her attention.

Janet spotted the motion and paused, squaring her shoulders visibly as she waited for Dar to approach.

That was not an attitude Dar was unfamiliar with, and she muffled a wry smile as she slowed to a halt next to the woman. "Just want to let you know something."

"Okay," Janet responded agreeably.

"That jackass likely did something unpleasant to some piece of your business," Dar said. "Just keep an eye out."

Janet studied her in pensive silence for a moment. "How do you know that?" she asked. "Don't get me wrong, Ms. Roberts, I really do appreciate you wanting to look out for us, but we've done this before, you know?"

"I know," Dar said. "Let's just say I've had a lot of experience in my lifetime of jackasses. Maybe because I'm in IT? Maybe because I am one?" Her eyes twinkled wryly. "He's the kind that won't rest until he gets the last laugh."

Janet cocked her head and her brow puckered a little. "He's not a stupid guy," She finally said. "He's just a kid, you know?"

She exhaled. "I'll have the guys check things twice, but really, I don't think he'd do something to cause that kind of trouble."

"Okay," Dar said. "Had to say it."

Janet smiled. "And believe me, I appreciate it. Go on and enjoy your dinner. We're almost done rigging and we're going to join for the music." She waved her hand, and watched as Dar retreated to the table, resuming her seat.

"What was that?" Doug paused and asked her.

"Gypsy warning." Janet sighed. "Thinks climber boy is going to screw with us." She shook her head. "I mean, c'mon."

Doug frowned thoughtfully. "They had some words this morning," he said. "He knows she told the tribals about his little trip over the fence." He shifted a rope over his shoulder. "She could be right, Jan. He's a vindictive little jockstrap. I still think he put the glass in the loo."

"That makes no sense, Doug. I told you that. PJ didn't do anything to him, that's psychotic." Janet shook her head. "C'mon."

He shrugged. "Well, let me tell you this, I'm going to check everything twice anyway, because I get the feeling that lady is kinda clue full." He moved on toward the raft, leaving Janet to stand on the other side of the fire, hands in her pockets, frowning.

She regarded the table of clients through the fire and judged the relative satisfaction, seeing most plates emptied and sighing in a bit of relief at the smiles and laughter. She could see Todd and Amy at the end of the table, but even they looked okay and she dismissed the thought of them doing damage as somewhat overcautious speculation on their fellow travelers' part.

With a faint shrug of her own, she continued around the fire and went over to the cooking area. "What do we have for dessert tonight, Chris?"

"S'mores." Chris grinned. "Including roasted marshmallows." He indicated a container. "Want to help assemble them?"

"Sure." Janet opened a box of graham crackers. "That should cap the night off okay."

"Yup, and tomorrow should be fun." Chris grinned. "Looking forward to it."

Chapter Five

KERRY LAY FLAT on the ground on her stomach, getting her camera about as even with the surface of the water as she could. She focused on the slanted red spear of light coming over the escarpment on the east side of the main river, catching dust motes and insects outlined in crimson.

A few feet away, PJ sat on a rock with her bandaged foot propped up, taking pictures of the sun as it started to come up over the ridge. "Nice."

Kerry felt a bit of damp coolness through her shirt, and the pressure of some rocks but she remained where she was as the light changed, then rolled over onto her side and got a nice shot of the canyon they were in and the river beyond it. "It's so beautiful here."

"Right," PJ said. "Like, all dramatic."

It was dramatic. Kerry put the camera aside and just watched for a moment, as the shifting light caught on the rocks, trees, and the moving water.

Past them to the rear the crew was getting the raft ready to go, packing on the gear and getting ready to tear down the cook pit as soon as everyone had gotten their breakfast.

Kerry had finished hers, and Dar was wandering down the narrow strip of land between the creek and the cliff walls. She strolled casually and looked around at the beginning to glow canyon they didn't see much of the previous day.

Down the coast the creek meandered and turned to the left, and Kerry saw, at the edge of her vision, a waterfall tumbling down the rock face. She sat up and let her elbows rest on her knees, composing a shot that included the dawn light, the water, the cliffs, a tiny bit of the waterfall and Dar's profile as she stood quietly watching with her hands in her pockets.

There was a calm to the scene that almost made her hold her breath.

Then the air around her filled with chatter, and several of her fellow passengers clustered around the fire as the crew moved past carrying the folded tents. Kerry stood up and dusted herself off, letting her camera hang around her neck as Marcia came up to her.

The older woman was finishing up a breakfast wrap and she

had a cup of tea in one hand. "Good morning." She took a sip. "Sleep well? There must have been some kind of critter near our tent, kept waking us up."

"Didn't hear a thing," Kerry said. "We were on the end there." She turned and pointed to the far side of the landing. "Maybe the sound of the river washed it out."

"White noise," Marcia said, stifling a yawn. "Oh well, I hear it's going to be exciting on the water today so it'll keep us awake." She moved past and climbed up onto the raft, going to the middle seats she and Don had selected.

Kerry went over to the cook fire and picked up a cup of coffee, and took a wrap with her as she joined them up on the raft.

The rising sun splashed over her and she fished her sunglasses out and put them on, enjoying the beauty of the scene and the moment. Her enjoyment intensified when Dar returned from her stroll, leaned over the back of the chair, and kissed her on the back of her neck. "Mmm."

"Mmm," Dar echoed her, as she came around and sat down next to her. "Pretty."

The raft rocked as more people joined them. Todd and Amy climbed on, holding hands, and went back to their far aft seats in silence.

Dar looked ahead of them and saw the whitecaps in the river. She smiled in anticipation, glancing over as Kerry handed her half of her wrap. She could smell the water, and as the sun dappled over it reflected rainbows popped into view.

"Okay, everyone, get your jackets on please, and make sure you all have your things tied down." Doug came up the center of the raft. "We're in for a wild ride. Look at those rapids just ahead of us." He watched the passengers all rummaging for their protective floating vests. "Please hang on tight today, unless I tell ya not to."

Several of the crew chuckled a little as they walked around securing the tie downs. They all wore their own jackets themselves.

"So, let's just say this," Doug said. "If we do tip, or if you fall off, please, please, please, just relax. The vests will float you. If you stay loose, and relaxed, you'll come through the rapids just fine."

"He's right," Rich said. "I fell off the last time. If you tense up you'll bounce off the rocks. If you relax, you slide over them. Sliding is lots less painful. Trust me."

The crew all nodded, and so did Doug. "I've got a motor, I

know how to use it, and every single one of the crew is certified in water rescue. Soon as we're clear of the rapids all of us will come after you, it won't be a problem. You won't end up at the Hoover Dam. I promise."

Kerry fit her camera into its case and sealed it, then settled back in her chair and wrapped her legs around the supports. "Woo."

Janet went around counting heads, then sat down in the small jump seat in the third row and buckled up her own jacket as they pushed off from the shore, and moved out into the narrow creek that flowed back into the main river.

As soon as they pulled out into the river Kerry felt the difference. The turn almost tipped them to one side, and PJ screamed a little in surprise. Sally lunged after her coffee cup that went flying. Once Doug straightened them out they moved at a rapid clip, and the raft flexed under them in a powerful, restless way.

"Woah." Dar re-settled her sunglasses on her nose.

They were in a long straight stretch, and it was full of whirlpools and ruffles, thick rushing plumes showing where the walls narrowed a little.

The sun lit the top of one wall, but the level they were at was still in shadow. As a blast of white ruffled green surged over them it was a shocking and breath taking chill. Kerry felt the water soak into the fabric of her shirt and she shoved herself back against the back of the chair and tightened her hold.

Rich was already soaked and he yelled in excitement as the raft plunged down and sideways a bit, and a green wall of water washed right over him, and the two others on either side of him. It came up and over the front row of seats and then through the rest of the craft at about knee level.

Kerry grimaced a little as the cold water hit her kneecaps.

They plunged through another ripple, past a side canyon that let a blast of sunlight through and it felt warm and wonderful, but only lasted a moment and then they were pitching up again and sideways.

The raft unexpectedly spun in a circle. In reflex Dar reached over to grab Kerry's arm as they were thrown sideways, and the raft was then going backwards down the river.

"Hang on!" Doug yelled, from his position now in the front. "Hang on!"

A wall of water came up over him as the back of the raft plunged downwards. He ducked, as the water lifted over his head and crashed down on top of the back row of chairs. Then he gunned the motor and it bucked and thrummed as the raft went sideways through another whirlpool and then was going straight again.

"Fuck!" Todd let out a yell.

Sally and Marcia laughed in delight, and behind her, Dar heard Janet chuckling as they came straight again and sped up, heading for a narrow whose roar they could hear clearly.

Kerry put her camera down and shook her the wet hair out of her eyes. "That was fun."

"Here we go! Hang on!" Doug sang out. "We're gonna pop off the top there!"

They were at the narrows, and the speed increased as they approached what they could now see as a dip and then a rise that then dropped down sharply. Rich let out a howl as he scrambled to take hold of the ropes on the pontoon as they dropped and then surged upward.

Kerry's eyes widened. "Oh crap."

The raft came up out of the water and then shot off the top of the underwater ridge, going momentarily airborne as screams rang out. Then the front of the raft dropped sharply and went under water, thrusting back up and bucking like a bronco as wave after wave came up over the top of the raft, soaking everyone and everything with a frothy green thoroughness.

"That's just the start!" One of the crew yelled. "It gets better now!"

KERRY RUBBED HER arms. "Brr. Wish we'd brought our rubber."

"No sense in drying off." Dar braced herself as they moved through a slightly calmer stretch of water, with at least the comfort of sun overhead now warming them. She finished wringing out her wet t-shirt and put it back on, then raked her fingers through her hair and exhaled.

They were drenched, the raft was drenched, the crew was drenched, water was sloshing back and forth between the seats. Kerry took the opportunity of some calm to swap out the digital card in her camera, tucking it into the waterproof bag before putting the camera back into its case.

Then she sat down and got herself arranged, tugging the straps on her vest a little tighter.

It was too rough for mugs, but one of the crew was scurrying around with sealed tubes that were warm to the touch and smelled of hazelnut. Dar tentatively sipped at hers and grunted approval, resuming her seat and wrapping her legs around the chair supports again.

Behind her, she heard Todd griping, but she resolutely remained facing forward as they moved over a rippling surface at a good clip.

"Once we get past the next set of big rapids, we'll find a place to tie up for lunch," Janet said as she walked between the seats. "There are a few slot canyons we can climb up into."

PJ pouted.

"But there are lots more rapids after that," Janet assured her. "We'll be stopping late tonight and I can guarantee you everyone's going to get a good sleep."

A soft chiming sounded, and she turned, with a surprised look. "What the what?" She went over to the lock box on the side of the raft and unlatched it, throwing it open and pulling out a satellite phone. "Hello?"

She listened, then turned away and shielded her mouth with her hand, facing out along the port side of the raft.

Kerry was leaning back in her chair watching. "Hm."

"Hm," Dar said. "Sat phone calls are probably not good."

Sally came up between them. "Probably not. Or could just need a supply drop or something." She smiled. "Sometimes a carrot is just a carrot, you know?"

Janet put the phone back in the box and secured it, then made her way along the port side of the raft back to where Doug was leaning against the big rear storage chests. He leaned closer as she came up next to him and listened as she spoke.

Doug looked sharply behind him, then he waved Janet forward and called over two of the mates.

"Not good," Kerry said.

They both felt nervous energy suddenly surround them as Janet moved to a spot in the middle of the raft and they turned to watch her.

"Okay, folks," Janet said. "We just got word they had to release water from the dam. A lot of it is coming up behind us so we're going to get past this stretch and see if we can duck into one of the slot canyons to let it pass."

"What do we need to do?" Sally asked.

"Get up off the pontoons." Janet said. "You three? Come on back up here and stand between the lockers."

Rich and the other two scrambled up off their perches and climbed up past the first row of seats, coming to stand behind them.

Kerry eyed the roughly frothing water and took her camera off, keeping it in its case but putting it into her day bag as Dar slipped off her seat and stood between it and Kerry's, taking hold of the back rail.

They were in between two tall canyon walls and on a straightaway. Dar could see a fair way behind them and though she hadn't much experience she thought she could detect the water behind them coming up into a boil.

"Shit," Rich muttered. "That's not funny."

"What did they do?" Kerry asked.

"I guess the storm dumped too much water down," he said. Rich was just behind Dar, and he was watching the same direction. "So, they open the gates, you know? Let the run off just come down the river."

Kerry sensed the nervousness in his voice and she also got up, finding comfort in pressing her body against Dar's as the raft started moving faster, and dipping from side to side as they lunged unexpectedly toward one wall.

Doug called over one of the crew and they stood together, fighting the surge of the water while the rest of the crew scrambled over the raft tightening the ropes.

Todd got up and watched them, for once without a sneer. He picked up a rope lying nearby and tied it off in front of the seats he and Amy were sitting in, bracing himself against the locker and tightening the straps on his vest he'd only been casually wearing before.

The raft slid sideways and they were all thrown roughly to one side and the next moment it felt like something big was shoving them from behind. They slammed against the rock walls and the raft spun.

"Oh boy." Kerry grabbed the back of the seat as Dar spread her legs out a little, bracing herself and Kerry. The raft tilted to the right and they were thrown together.

"Hang on!" Doug yelled out suddenly. "Oh shit!"

The raft tilted, and then hit some rocks and the front of it went under water. Before they had a chance to react the craft tipped over and they went with it, in a painful thrash of equipment and water.

It was so sudden. So violent.

Kerry barely had time to suck in a breath before she was in the water and the raft was riding over her, aware that the back of her vest was gripped. She felt the shock of the cold and then she was under. She held her breath and tucked her arms and legs into her body as the raft slammed into her back and drove her far down under the surface.

She opened her eyes and saw rocks and branches as she bumped upward and was hit again by something. She felt the pressure in her chest to breathe start to mount.

Then she got the sense whatever was over her was gone and she was rising in the water, her arms tangling with boxes and supplies banging against her as her head broke the surface and she sucked in a relieved breath.

Dar's arms went around her and they were swirling in the water together as the current pulled them quickly through the rapids, turning them around and around in the white froth, tumbling repeatedly.

She heard screams. The water was taking her in a spiral and she kept going under repeatedly until she was pulled over onto her back and she could take a breath again and see the sky.

So, blue. So calm looking against the roar of the river exploded into presence around her as the water drained from her ears and she could hear clearly.

Wow.

She coughed a little, then turned her head to see Dar next to her in the rushing flood, one arm wrapped around her body, the other outstretched to ward off rocks, calm and self-possessed as always, a little blood on her skin from a scrape just under her cheekbone.

A second later Dar turned her head and met Kerry's eyes, shaking her head a little and sticking her tongue out.

"Thanks, hon!" Kerry turned over and kept herself upright, her vest keeping her afloat. She looked around and saw the raft, still upside down, careening ahead of them. Behind them were bobbing figures amidst the white water, along with floating boxes and crates.

"That sucked," Dar said. "We lost the whole damn raft."

"And all our stuff." Kerry said. "Unless we can find it and grab it."

They saw Doug heading after the raft, swimming strongly in the current along with several of the crew, while the others were grabbing the trailing ropes and tie downs. Janet took hold of a kayak they hadn't realized they were carrying and got into it.

"Looks like they're on the ball," Kerry said.

The progress through the water was cold, but less rough when you were in it than when you were on it and Dar found by twisting her body around she could avoid the boulders in the center of the river and let the current take them without too much thumping.

"Shit!" Rich tumbled by, gripping a line that had a box attached to it that was slamming into him.

The water was rising rapidly and though it caused a thunderous roar, they realized that the greater volume of water let them avoid most of the rocks, but that had also made the raft disappear into the distance, around a curve they could just see ahead of them.

"Are you all right?" Janet paddled with an expert's touch back and forth and now she neared them.

"We're okay," Dar answered. "We got a plan?"

Janet shook her head and paddled past. "Just stay together and stay on top!" she yelled over her shoulder, moving on to the next clump of passengers, four together that were holding onto each other, and a second group of six ahead of them.

Dar swiveled so she was facing forward and had her legs out, with her sandals bumping them off rocks slick with algae as they moved quickly downstream. She kept one arm around Kerry and Kerry had taken hold of the back of her jacket.

"This is going to be a mess," Dar said.

"Mm." Kerry wiped the hair out of her eyes. "But it's not as bad as I thought it might be if we tipped over," she admitted.

"It's gonna get worse if they can't catch that raft," Dar said. "We're gonna have to walk out of here."

"Or just float." Kerry took a breath as they went between two sets of rocks and a wash of water swamped them as they whirled in a circle then came out the other side. "Pppffpfpbut."

PJ and Sally both waved at them. "Hey, catch up to us guys!" PJ called out. "Let's stick together!"

Rich joined them and just past Kerry saw Don and Marcia in a clump that included Amy and Todd. "Better the kids." She nudged Dar. "I can only imagine what crap is coming out of his mouth." She pointed at Todd, who was in fact flapping his jaws.

Dar pulled them in a circle then shoved off an underground rock as they neared the small group and joined them. "That wasn't fun," she said, as they fit into the circle of floaters.

"No, it wasn't," Rich said, in a serious tone. "We could have really gotten hurt. I think Janet head counted everyone though."

"So, what happens now?" PJ asked. "I mean...like, to us?"

They swirled through a gap in the rocks and went in a circle as the water level increased again. "Janet caught up to Doug," Rich said, after they could hear again. "So, they'll paddle down and get the raft. I'm sure it'll catch up on something."

"What if it gets wrecked?" PJ said. She lifted her foot up out of the water and looked at it. "Not looking forward to hiking."

Everyone looked at each other a little awkwardly. "Let's wait to see what the situation is." Dar finally concluded. "Maybe we'll get lucky."

Kerry had been looking up at the sky. "Let's hope they don't get bit by our vacation curse." She muttered low enough for just Dar to hear her. "At least there aren't any pirates on the river."

Dar eyed her.

"We hope."

KERRY WAS COLD. Despite the sun lighting the surface of the river she felt shivers in her core.

They were close to the bend now, though, and she hoped to see something that would let them at least take a break and get out of the water. She could see that PJ, and Sally were also looking uncomfortable. "Brr," she said, giving them a wry look.

"Yeah," Rich said. "Hope we can catch a break out of here soon. Slot canyon or something."

Janet and Doug had disappeared around the bend about ten minutes previously and just as Kerry was about to comment on that she felt a warm pressure against her back and glanced aside to where Dar had just pulled her closer.

Dar winked at her.

Now, how did Dar do that? Kerry studied her partner who was still watching the river with some interest, seemingly at ease in the rush of the water. "You really are part marine mammal, aren't you?"

Dar chuckled.

"What's that?" PJ asked.

"Dar is warm," Kerry said, simply. "I have no idea on earth how she manages that, but even when we dive in the ocean she never gets cold."

"Really?" Rich asked.

Dar extended a hand to him and watched his eyes widen as he reached over to touch it. They had used a rope to link them all together using their jacket clips. "Probably because I've spent time in the water since birth, pretty much." She shrugged off the anomaly.

"Nice. Kind of like a seal," Rich said. "Right?"

Both Dar and Kerry laughed. "Your dad would agree," Kerry

said. "Oh, hey I can see...oh." She made a face as the rest of them turned. "Wow."

"Crap," Dar said.

They were halfway through the bend and they could see the raft ahead, tilted up and caught on two large rocks where water was gushing in all directions. The gear containers were cracked and many were open, tops hanging with bags and supplies dangling.

"Oh boy," Rich said. "That sure doesn't look good."

"No, it doesn't," Sally said.

The kayak was tied off nearby, and Janet and Doug were climbing carefully over the rocks toward the craft, while several of the crew had just finished running a rope across the open cataracts and were waving at the oncoming floaters.

"Grab the rope!" Doug yelled at them, seeing the approach. "Grab it and hang on! We'll get a tow on you!"

Two of the crew were working to set a lower rope and one leaped across from one rock to another and slipped, falling hard and then tumbling into the water.

Dar was the closest to the top rope and she reached up to grab it as Rich lunged to do the same next to her. The surge of the water nearly ripped the line out of her hand but she got her other one up to take hold and tensed her body as it came up out of the water.

The rest of the group tried to help, but the current grabbed them and it was just Dar and Rich for a minute until one of the crewmen, Toby, got hold of Rich's jacket and snapped a climbing ring to it and to the rope to take the pressure off.

Another crew member was hand over handing down the line to where Dar was grimly hanging on. A moment later he had her hooked in. "See if you can pull over!"

Dar ducked to the other side of the line and pulled as hard as she could, allowing the crewman to move past her and get a ring into the jacket straps on Kerry's jacket.

That gave her a moment to just hang there, half in and half out of the water, and watch as two of the crew fought to pull the man who had fallen in back to the rocks. She felt the surge of the water against her legs and knew a new sense of respect for it.

Kerry was next to Dar, one foot braced against the rocks, her hands holding the rope. "Holy crap."

"Watch out!" Sally suddenly yelled. "Doug!"

Doug scrambled across the rocks as a clump of the passengers rushed toward the rope. Don was trying to get into position to grab it. His wife was hanging on to the straps with a frightened look on her face and one hand clasped with Amy's, who looked equally scared.

Todd reached out as they got to the rocks and grabbed a hold on them, curling his fingertips into some cracks and shoving one big foot out to hold them in place. His shoe slipped on the algae after a second and he twisted around as Don grabbed the rope.

They all slammed against the rocks but Todd kept his grip, his jaw smacking the stone as the muscles stood out under his wet shirt. Amy let out a shout and reached for him, as Toby lunged and got hold of Don's vest.

Doug had a large carabiner snapped to the rope and he released his hands off it to grab Don's arm. He reached down to snap a hook around the straps as Todd's swinging on the rope pulled him off the rocks and he plunged into the water up to his waist.

Toby turned around and pulled another carabiner from his belt and snapped it onto Todd's vest just as the crew member being hauled in reached them. The crew member braced himself against the rocks to catch his breath. Toby got the rope from his hands and squirmed across the rocks to a fallen trunk lodged midstream to tie it off.

"Okay start working your way to the shore!" Doug yelled. "Use the lower rope!" He gave a tug on it as Toby yelled something the wind ripped past them. "C'mon! Hurry before the rest of them get here. We need space to catch them!"

Don was the closest and he turned to help Marcia get to the rope, and they started to inch their way toward the shore. Todd reluctantly released the rock and rubbed the visible bump on his jaw, before he grabbed the straps on Amy's jacket and pulled her up behind him.

Toby grabbed PJ around the waist with one arm. "Got you. Take it slow."

Rich and Sally were right behind him, with Dar and Kerry waiting to bring up the rear. They fought their way through the white water toward the shore, just past the upended raft.

BY THE TIME they got to the shore Kerry was shivering again. She was glad to slide off the last rock and climb up the short slope into the small crevice. She gratefully put her back against the sun-warmed stone. "Ugh."

Her legs shook a little. The water had been ferocious and the rest of the passengers looked equally shaken. Even Todd was hunkered down on a small ledge, his eyes a little wide. Amy sat next to him, hugging herself.

Rich's feisty enthusiasm was absent. He sat down on the ground on the other side of Dar, with Sally and her sister next to him. Both Don and Marcia looked exhausted.

"Don't want to have to do that again," Don said. "Didn't mind the floating that much, but those rocks were slippery."

Marcia dabbed at scrape on her leg. "I'm so tired!"

Dar leaned on the stone next to Kerry, ankles crossed, and arms folded, a serious expression on her face. She watched the crew try to right the raft, and from this angle the damage to it was far more obvious.

The supports between the pontoons had been ruptured, and most of the gear boxes were bent. Some had lost their tops as the raft had tumbled end over end in the water in a motion it wasn't designed to deal with. The mechanics of the craft seemed intact, but it was hard to say how salvageable it was.

Not good.

Kerry folded her arms and leaned against Dar's shoulder. "Y'know–"

"I know," Dar responded with a little grimace. She pointed briefly at something. "That was the box the phone was in." It was shattered, and hanging loose, very obviously empty.

Kerry sighed. "Of course it was. The only way it wouldn't have gotten munched with us around is if there'd been a puppy in there with it."

Dar chuckled wryly.

Janet came over to them wringing her hands together a little. "Okay, folks," she said. "We've obviously gotten into a little pickle here."

Todd looked up. "A little?"

"Well, we collected everyone. No one got lost, and there were only a few scuffs and bruises, so yeah." Janet looked a touch truculent. "Just a little pickle because this is the wild, and it could have been a lot worse."

"You could have croaked," Rich said, "so, shut the fuck up."

Todd just rolled his eyes.

The crew behind her was dragging everything they'd salvaged up onto the shore, sorting it out in piles. Dar spotted their own bags, but kept quiet since there were only six duffels there.

"Anyway," Janet said. "We're going to see what we need to do to continue our trip, and try to make you all as comfortable as possible." She eyed them seriously. "So, I'd like you to just relax and rest. There's a track back into a hollow behind us but I'd really appreciate it if you'd stay here. Just let us get things sorted out."

"Can we help?" Don asked.

"No." Janet's tone was definite. "I appreciate the offer, but just please, stay here." She put both hands out, palms outward. Then she turned and went back to where Doug was coiling up some ropes.

Don lifted his hands and put them on his knees. "How about a game of cards?"

"Might as well." Sally hunkered herself around to face him and pulled over her day bag that she'd strapped around her waist. "I think I've got my deck here."

Kerry unstrapped her own day bag. It held her camera in its case, and had banged her raw through the water. She dug inside and removed a granola bar. "Want half?"

Dar eyed it dubiously.

"C'mon. It's the one with cranberries in it." She opened the bar, broke it in half, and handed a portion over. She bit into hers and watched the crew fasten ropes to parts of the raft in a bid, she figured, to turn it upright.

She heard a faint scraping behind her and glanced back to see Todd move on down the wall, away from the water.

Amy watched him for a minute and then she came over to where the cards were starting to be shuffled and sat down on a flat rock near Sally. "I'm in."

Kerry looked back at Dar, who was licking a bit of granola off her thumb, and suppressed a smile.

"What?" Dar said, seeing the attention.

"Nothing." Kerry indicated a small shelf across from where they were standing that was bathed in sunlight. "Let's do what the lady said and chill."

"Or warm." Dar agreeably joined her and they sat down next to each other, the breeze riffling the drying fabric on their bodies. "Y'know," she said, after a pause.

"You'd rather be doing something to help," Kerry supplied in a mild tone. "Yeah me too.

The crew assembled on the shore and they left off their chat to watch as they all took hold of the ropes connected to the raft and started to pull them taut, in a staggered motion. "Okay, when it comes up, front line get out of the way!" Doug yelled.

Janet was just finished dragging all the recovered gear up

higher on the beach and now she scrambled up to get between the crew and her tour group, watching in both directions with her hands half lifted. "Everyone please stay well back!" She lifted her voice so it would carry.

"I'm glad we don't do this for a living," Kerry commented, as the crew started pulling in earnest, their water shoes sliding on the algae slick rocks near the water. "It's hard work."

"Ours is too, sometimes."

Kerry took a breath to disagree, then memories surfaced of both her and Dar in sweat and grime and a desperate slide across the floor of a grungy Wall Street back office and subsided, with a wry shrug. "Eh. Sometimes." She glanced aside as she sensed Dar moving and saw her body stiffen as she shaded her eyes to look at the raft. "What?"

Dar moved quickly toward the raft. "Hold it!"

Janet intercepted her. "Ms. Roberts, please." She threw her arms out to physically block Dar from advancing.

Dar pointed. "If they let that come over the engine's going to smack on that rock."

"No, it isn't," Janet said. "Please go back and sit down!"

Dar measured again with her eyes. "It is."

"Please, get back." Janet sounded more than a little frustrated. "Just let us do our jobs. Get back!"

Kerry watched, knowing the body language, and knowing Dar like she knew her own heart. She also knew what was going to happen next, because Dar was who she was, and there was no changing that part of her.

"No I won't," Dar said and pushed past. "Doug!" She let out a bellow. "DOUG! Hold it!"

Now Kerry got up and bolted, because she saw Janet go to make a grab for Dar. "Whoa whoa whoa." She got hold of Janet's arm. "Don't do that." She planted her feet and arrested Janet's forward motion, jerking the woman off balance.

Doug heard his name and paused. He half turned, but the team kept pulling so he quickly turned back around, and at that moment the raft reached the halfway point and started down amidst a flurry of yells and warnings. "Not now!" He yelled at her. "Get away! Get back!"

Dar cursed internally. Too late. The raft was too far gone for the crew to stop its motion and she skidded to a halt as she realized it, making both Janet and Kerry collide with her as they hauled up a second too late.

The big craft rolled over and off the rocks. It slammed down onto the ground with a crunching thump of the hard rubber hitting and a scream of metal as the engine crunched down onto a clump of boulders.

"Shit." Janet tore herself loose from Kerry's grip and ran over to where the crew gathered hastily round the raft to inspect the damage. A few of them went chasing off after the gear that had been flung off when it hit.

Kerry joined Dar, and Rich came running over, with Sally and a few others right behind him.

"Holy crap, what happened?" Rich said, shading his eyes. "What did they do? What's wrong?"

"What morons," Todd said. "Snapped the freaking engine in half." He glanced at Dar. "You saw it was going to happen? That what the yelling was?"

Dar sighed. "I did," she said. "Just not in time."

"They're done," Todd said. "Full refund for everyone. What a bunch of idiots." He turned and wandered back over to the wall, flexing his hands.

"What does that mean?" Marcia asked.

The crew huddled around the raft and now five or six of them took hold and lifted the back end up off the shore, while Doug squirmed under it to inspect the outboard engine he used to control the craft.

"Mean's he's got no way to drive that thing," Don said. "Gotta agree with the kid, much as I don't like to. That was a bonehead move. They should have listened to you, Dar."

Kerry sighed. "If I had a dollar for every time I've heard someone say that I could buy this canyon." She took hold of Dar's elbow. "C'mon, no point in all the I told ya sos."

"They didn't really have time," Dar said. "It was already tipping."

Don shook his head. "Shoulda planned that move better. Don't know what they're going to do now. They can't take the raft down the rest of the river like that."

Marcia frowned. "Oh, dear."

Janet had part of the crew around her and she was giving directions. The rest of them were carefully lowering the raft to the ground after Doug emerged from under it. He stood up and looked over at Dar, then lifted his hands and said something to Janet, who nodded glumly.

"We're screwed," Rich said. "What the hell? I thought these guys were pros. That was bush league."

Dar folded her arms but remained silent, her expression somber.

"Yeah," Kerry finally said. "If Dar could see it from this angle, they should have probably checked huh?"

The ring of crew broke apart and started pulling open the gear. Janet visibly squared her shoulders and started toward the clump of watching passengers.

"Here comes the bad news," Sally said. "Poor Janet."

"Nice enough woman, but that wasn't good judgment," Don said. "Don't care for being treated as a mindless mark."

"Let's wait to see what she says," Sally responded. "C'mon."

She fell silent as Janet arrived at their group and paused, waiting for everyone's attention.

"First off, my apologies, Ms. Roberts." Janet said. "You were spot on. We thought we measured, but the water pushed the raft aside enough that we were wrong." She glanced behind her. "Not really sure—"

"I'm an engineer," Dar gently interrupted her. "Let's just move on. No point in talking about it."

Janet took a breath. "Folks, we have a real problem here. As you can see, we've got the raft right way round. My team is going to get things sorted to make you all as comfortable as we can. We lost a lot of gear."

Todd came back over and stood behind Amy. He folded his arms. "You're idiots."

"Thanks, that's so helpful," Janet shot back. "We're going to make camp here, and Doug is going to take the kayak downstream to an outpost and get us some backup. They can lift us down another engine, and we'll be on our way. In the meantime, we've got some hikes planned from here."

"They going to lift all the gear you lost?" Don asked. "Might as well just lift us out of here if not. I'm not sleeping on the ground for the rest of this trip. I'm too old for that."

Janet hesitated. "Well, not all...but we'll get enough to make everyone comfortable. We're going to see what we have left to make for dinner, and get camp set up. Okay?"

The group remained mostly silent, and that went on until it became awkward and uncomfortable. "Sure," Kerry finally said. "We'll make the best of it."

Janet turned and went back to the crew, shaking her head a little in silence.

"Well, we'll see how that works out," Don said. "Let's play some cards in the meantime." He went back to the flat rock with Rich and Sally, where PJ was waiting for them.

Todd removed a small bag from the waterproof sack he'd

been carrying and dusted his hands with the contents of it. He went over to the wall and studied it, while Amy went back to join the card game.

Dar and Kerry settled back on their ledge. "Well, it could be worse," Kerry said, after they'd sat in silence for a few minutes.

"Shh." Dar reached around her shoulders and covered her mouth with her hand.

"MPfof."

"Shh."

KERRY CHEWED ON a stick of jerky, hoping it was the beef it was claimed to be and not anything more esoteric.

They were clustered around a driftwood fire. The crew had put up a tarp that partially blocked the wind between them and the raft, and the small collection of food they'd recovered was portioned out to all of them.

Probably the only in the group who was happy was Dar. She had on her lap three peaches, two pieces of beef jerky, a peanut butter sandwich and a bag of potato sticks.

All they had to do, Janet had told them, was make it through to the morning because by then the re supply would be here and it would be all right again.

Kerry hoped so.

They had another assortment for the morning, but it seemed heavy on granola bars, so Kerry determined she would enjoy her jerky and peaches, and hope for an early helicopter tomorrow.

There was no real shelter. Most of the tents and pallets had been lost. All they had to drink was water that had been boiled over the fire to remove the impurities of the river. They had gone from a relatively luxe experience to rock under the butt bare bones.

At least some of the duffels had been salvaged and theirs were some of them, so after they finished their scraps they were able to unroll the sleeping bags and get as comfortable as they were going to.

"Should we use one and share?" Kerry whispered into Dar's ear. "Don and Marcia lost their stuff." She watched Dar's profile, outlined in the light from the fire, as she pondered the question.

Finally, she nodded and they both got up. Kerry took her bedroll and moved toward the older couple, while Dar unzipped the sleeping bag and spread it out fully to take the place of two of them.

The crew had lost most of their gear and they were huddled near the fire, with their backs to the tarp, passing a large mug around that showed faintly steaming.

Dar sat back down on the sleeping bag, which, spread over a patch of sand wasn't horribly uncomfortable. The college kids had also lost a duffel, but they were sharing what they had along with the contents of a bottle PJ had taken out.

Todd and Amy were near the wall, just at the edge of the light.

Rich and the rest of that gang were also sharing. Rich got out his deck of cards, as the light faded completely out and the sky went inky dark.

Kerry came back and smiled as she sat down. "I'm glad we did that." She settled on the bedroll next to Dar and leaned back against the rock wall. "They'd spread out their jackets on the ground because they didn't want to bitch."

"No real point," Dar said.

"No, but some people would anyway." Kerry laid her hand casually on Dar's thigh, a little hyper aware of how close the rest of the people were, and a little uncomfortable knowing some were watching her.

Watching them.

Dar draped one arm over her shoulders and bit into a peach, offering her a bite, with slightly raised eyebrows. Kerry smiled a little and leaned over, feeling Dar's head rest against hers.

The crew had pretty much lost their spunk and they looked exhausted. Long hours of moving things in and out of the water had worn them out. Two of them were already curled up under some towels fast asleep.

In the distance they heard a howl and then the fire popped a little. Kerry felt a little chill come over her skin as the breeze blew through the narrow canyon.

The passengers all nudged a little closer to the fire and Janet leaned over and said something to one of the male crew, who got up reluctantly and skirted the encampment, heading back into the narrow area beyond. They had piled up a stack of wood, but had whittled it down since dark had fallen and it got cooler. It was obvious they were going to need it.

How cozy their tents had seemed. Kerry pressed against Dar's long body, missing the camp chairs and the mugs of mulled wine, feeling more than a little disappointed at how it had turned out.

Bummer.

"Dogs will be glad to see us," Dar commented. "Want to drive over to Zion and spend a few nights there in our jazzy camper?"

Kerry allowed herself to be distracted. "That sounds fun. Do we still want to stay over in that cabin, or just take off?"

Dar's eyes took on a wry twinkle. "My guess is, better we get out of there. Because I'm sure the end of this trip isn't going to be pretty."

"Mm." Kerry rocked her head from side to side a little. "Do we want to press them for a refund?"

"Nah," Dar predictably said. "I got my money's worth. The rapids were fun, and the pools were cool." She crossed her ankles and wiggled one foot. "But they'll probably offer. They know they got skunked." She moved her chin a little toward where Janet was seated a little apart from the rest of the crew.

She looked worried. Dar wasn't sure if it was about the financial aspects, or about Doug, or something she had no knowledge of. It was an almost painful expression to see, and as though Janet realized it, she scrubbed her face with both hands and then got up and wandered over to where they were lying.

"Hey," Kerry greeted her. "Sorry things went a little south."

Encouraged, Janet sat down on the rock near their joined bedroll and leaned her elbows on her knees. "I should be saying sorry to you," she admitted. "But hey, when the chopper gets here we can get going again. We can make up the time."

Dar eyed her. "You really think they can bring in enough supplies?" She held up a bit of jerky. "I don't mind this, but I don't think you can serve that the rest of the ride."

Janet sighed. "They'll have to make a few runs. It's going to cost us more than we made on this trip, but we'll make it right for you guys. I promise that." She got up and started over to the next clump of passengers.

Dar's eyebrow was still hiked up. "Hmph."

Kerry rested her head on Dar's shoulder. "Maybe we could make this into a foraging trip. You know, we could fish, and find berries and stuff."

Dar's other eyebrow lifted.

"Wouldn't you like to do that?"

"No," Dar responded readily. "I forage in Publix."

Kerry snickered, her body shaking a little with it. "C'mon, I know you know how to fish, Dar. You bring home the hog snapper at the cabin all the time."

"Not the same." But Dar smiled and laughed a little herself, tipping her head back to admire the canopy of stars overhead. With that, and the crackle of the fire, she relaxed and allowed herself to enjoy the moment.

She leaned her head against Kerry's and focused on the moment they were in. It was warm and cool combined, and she spotted a shooting star overhead and lifted her hand to point it out to Kerry.

"Did you make a wish?" Kerry asked.

Dar pondered that. "What in the hell would I wish for that I don't already have?" she asked after a moment. "Chocolate ice cream?"

"Aw." Kerry circled Dar's arm with one hand and gave it a little squeeze.

A soft hooting sound came from a nearby, gnarled tree and it sounded loud as the talking petered out, the river's rushing and burbling covering even the snap of the fire.

Dar closed her eyes and relaxed, the hoodie she was wearing and the warmth of Kerry's body providing as much comfort as she figured she was going to get, until the helicopter showed up.

Chapter Six

BUT THE NEXT morning, there was no helicopter.

They all consumed whatever was left, and drank some herbal tea from the river water, boiled in the one battered pot that had been salvaged.

Their remaining gear was packed up, and everyone was standing around as the sun rose over the canyon wall, bringing no sound of the chopper in the distance.

Janet stood at the riverside on two of the rocks they'd pulled the raft off. She folded her arms, and watched the horizon. The rest of the crew also stood around, occasionally glancing uneasily at the passengers, and the battered raft.

"How long are we gonna stand around here like a bunch of idiots?" Todd finally said in a loud tone.

Josh took his hands from his pockets and cleared his throat. "Should be here any minute."

"Should have been here an hour ago," Todd replied. "What if he ain't coming?"

"Of course, he is. They're probably picking up the engine parts," Josh said. "Place maybe doesn't open until nine. I don't know if they had spare at the shop, so early in the season."

"Should we take a walk down the canyon?" Sally suggested. "If he's right, it could be hours."

"We could do that," Josh said hesitantly. "Let me just let Janet know." He trotted toward the river, as five or six of the crew got ready to join them.

"Better than nothing," Todd said. He had on cargo pants, hiking boots, and a tank top, and he picked up a hat and put it on his cropped hair.

Dar leaned on the rock wall, hands in her pockets, sunglasses on. She regarded the group then glanced at Kerry. "You want to go?"

"Sure." Kerry fastened her little day bag over her shoulder. "Probably give Janet a break from all of us staring at her like a pack of vultures."

In fact, Janet seemed quite relieved, and a good percentage of the crew started off with them, making their way down the narrow slot of the canyon away from the water.

Dar filled a water bottle with some of the boiled river water and put it in her day bag, along with its dwindling store of peanut butter crackers and a pocketknife. She ambled along at Kerry's heels, near the back of the crowd as they were forced to go single file.

It was sunny, and there was a nice breeze. She stretched her legs out and flexed her hands as Josh pointed out markings on the walls. Small lizards scampered out of their way and as they passed a cleft in the rock, Dar spotted a snake inside.

She briefly considered calling attention to it, then decided not to, and passed on, walking in Kerry's footsteps as they moved from the narrow section into a wider one.

The group paused and looked around. The canyon walls were curved and shaped by the flow of the waters, full of striated layers in a range of colors. Kerry had her camera out, and as the sun poured in behind them it turned the space into something beautiful.

Dar saw a small stream ahead. The stone arched over it, as it trickled through past them into a small cave that ultimately would lead to the river. "Wow."

She went over to the arch and put her hand on it next to small yellow flower growing out of a crack. Kerry came up behind her, camera in hand. "Look at that." She pointed at the flower.

"I am." Kerry took a close up of it, framed by Dar's long fingers. "This is beautiful."

Dar watched her, then tipped her sunglasses down and smiled, as Kerry poked her tongue out at her in silent response.

They walked under the arch and past it, and Kerry turned to get a shot in the other direction outlined by the sun. Then they joined the rest of the group in moving on, walking up the narrow waterway farther into the canyon.

The walls grew over them, allowing strips and squares of light to come down splashing over the light green of the stream and the ochre of the walls, causing sparkles of sun to make patterns over their skin.

Amazing and it got all their minds off the wreck. Even the crew started smiling, glad of the rising spirits and eager to show the special parts of the slot canyon off to their guests. They found a little pool in the rocks that was speared by a bit of sunlight and called everyone over for a picture.

Dar got in the back and let her arms drape over Kerry's shoulders as she put her hand in the sunlight, sending a brilliant sparkling across the cave as it caught on her ring.

Amy was on the other side of the pool with Todd. "That's pretty."

"Thank you!" Kerry turned her hand up and cupped the light, as they separated and started around the corner into a darker overhang.

The water was coming out of the overhang and they splashed through it into the cavern, ducking past a low shelf of rock, emerging into a larger, open space.

"Wow," Sally said, after a pause. "That's cool."

It was a high ceiling split in two that went up to the top of the rock wall, and sunlight streamed into the cave giving them a good view. Everyone broke up and started to wander around, examining marks on the wall that looked like pictographs.

"Someone used this for shelter," Don said, indicating a fire pit. "Make a pretty good one."

Marcia sat down and removed a small pad and pencil from her day bag, where it had been rolled up and stashed. She started sketching the interior of the cave and Dar went to the back of the space where the water emerged from a tumble of rocks in a gush.

Josh came over to where she was standing. "Later in the summer that goes away. It's cold."

Dar stuck her hand in, and nodded. "It is." She brought her hand up to her face and sniffed the water. It had a sharp, mineral tang and she resisted the urge to stick her tongue into it. "What was this place used for? Or is it now?"

"Hunter's camp," Josh supplied promptly. "The natives sometimes stop by here, but I've only seen them maybe once or twice in the five years I've been on the river." He tipped his head back to study the open crack emitting the sun. "I heard they did medicine stuff here."

Dar straightened and looked around. "What?"

"You know," Josh said. "Spirit ceremonies. Way I heard it, those guys were sharp. They'd come here winter, and make a big yow yow." He turned and waved his arms, stamping his boots on the ground. "And the spring would start flowing."

Dar's brow lifted.

Josh smiled. "They knew the rain patterns. Cistern fills up about a half mile away, and ends up here." He pointed at the spring. "Made a good show though." He glanced around, but the rest of the group were examining the back wall. He winked at her. "I'm part native. My mam's an elder with the Havasupai."

He had dusty brown hair, and hazel eyes, but strong planes to his face and a thin, angular build. "They wanted me to go study and be an engineer. Wasn't my gig. I'd rather ride the rapids and be outside."

Dar folded her arms and leaned against the rock wall. "Bet this ride's not one of your better ones."

He shrugged a little. "Happens. Though I never had something crack the raft up like that before. I hope Doug's got that chopper headed our way with gear. Wouldn't like to have to hike out. Not enough stock."

"How long would that take?"

Josh also leaned against the wall, his head nearly even with hers. "Week maybe," he said, after a pause. "Hard to say with all you, and the gal with the hurt foot." He shrugged again. "And no provisions. I grew up round here but I ain't no forager."

"Hm."

"Hey there's some paths back here," Amy called out, from the other side of the cave.

Josh pushed off the wall and started in that direction. After a moment Dar followed, catching up with Kerry, who was coming out of another curve in the rock with Sally and Rich.

They followed the group as one of the crew produced a flashlight. Its beam reflected off the sandstone walls, showing lines and patterns and old carvings. Todd and Amy, at the front, showed their first real signs of enthusiasm of the trip.

Dar hooked one finger into Kerry's belt loop and allowed herself to be towed along into the narrowing tunnel. "We probably shouldn't go too far into this," she said. "I don't have any breadcrumbs and I'm not going to waste any of my peanut butter crackers."

Kerry reached back and patted her hip. "Only one way in or out, Dardar."

"Mm." Dar didn't deny the sense of discomfort that caused, and she eyed the uneven ceiling. "Sounds like a single point of failure to me." She sighed. "At least we're at the back of the line."

They heard, echoing through the rock, the faintest rumble of thunder in the distance.

"CAN YOU PUT the light there, Dar?"

Dar extended her arm past Kerry's shoulder and put her flashlight on the wall, where Kerry had discovered a fossil embedded in the rock. "Whole one."

Kerry was carefully focusing. "What is it?"

"Trilobite," Dar answered. "Probably started out in the ocean, a long ass time ago."

It was oval shaped, with segments along it's body and a tiny head. It was embedded in the rock, partially exposed by weathering.

"Really?" Kerry studied it, reaching out to touch it with one fingertip. "So, this was ocean once?"

"About two billion years ago, yeah," Dar said.

They were in an inner chamber, the rest of the group exploring the cave with the entrance they'd come in through at their backs. A steady breeze emerged from it, and on the edges of that Dar could faintly scent rain, which matched the steadily growing rumbling outside.

"Okay, folks, I think a storm's coming in so we should go back and see what the plan is." Josh was at the entrance, beckoning to them. "Maybe we can come back here after we know."

The group straggled over and followed him out down the dark and narrow passageway, emerging into the split roofed cave that already was shedding sheets of rain down from the opening to the ground, increasing the flow of the small spring already running out of it.

It was cold, and they split around the spring to avoid being rained on. When they came to the front of the cave the overhang was almost a waterfall.

"Okay, you folks stay here and I'll run on ahead and see what the deal is." Josh hunched his shoulders and passed through the falls, scampering through the now near knee high little stream in the slot canyon. He disappeared quickly around a bend.

The thunder rumbled overhead and then a flash of lighting lit the far wall. Dar took a step back from the entrance and moved over to the side wall of the cave and found a rock to sit on. She stifled a yawn and crossed her ankles, watching the thin curtain of rain coming down and drenching the inside of the cavern.

With the light coming down it was rather charming, and she was glad to see Kerry getting some pictures of it from different angles.

After a short while, footsteps approached and Josh and Janet came into the cavern. Both were drenched. Both looked worried. Josh watched Janet's face though, and kept silent.

Janet put her hands on her hips, as they all gathered around to listen. "So, folks, as you can probably tell, there's been no sign of anyone coming after us. So, we've got to go with plan B."

"And that is?" Todd inquired.

"We can't hike out," Janet said. "We don't have enough supplies. So, we're going to take the raft down river with paddles and get out at the staging area we sent Doug to."

Marcia cleared her throat. "Isn't that dangerous?"

"Less dangerous than sticking around here starving to death," Todd said.

Dar nodded. "He's right," she said. "We're out of food now. We either go with that, or start scavenging."

"There isn't enough around here to support a group this size," Janet said. "So let's go and pack what we have and get the raft ready. We'll leave as soon as we're done."

The crew looked relieved. They trooped out following Janet, and the passengers trailed after them, out into the rain and along the slot canyon back toward the river.

Two of the college girls helped PJ along, supporting her on either side. "This is so not what I was looking for," One of them said.

"Me either," PJ said. "But I'd rather sit on that raft even in the rain, than try to hop out of the canyon. That's a long, long walk."

Dar and Kerry were the last in line and so they were the last to get back to where the raft was. The rain was coming down harder, but everyone pitched in, carrying gear and the little they'd salvaged onto the craft.

It looked quite woebegone. Most of the storage chests were gone, and some of the seats were bent and twisted, leaving just a metal frame behind. One of the crew put a piece of wood down on the frame and backed off with a shrug, gesturing them toward it.

Todd rolled his eyes and shoved the board back against the back of the frame, examining it.

Dar gave their own seats a tug, the battered metal bent and in one case broken, but intact enough to brace themselves against.

Rich came up and squeezed himself in beside them. "This is gonna be scary. I'm not on the pontoons this time."

No one wanted to sit up front. The pontoon seats were all loose and ripped, and Josh was busy lashing the front of them together with some rope, glancing over his shoulder as the thunder continued to roll on.

"Dar."

"Mm?"

"I've got a bad feeling about this." Kerry had her arms folded over her chest. "We should wait for it to stop raining."

Dar regarded her for a moment, then she turned and headed to where Janet was standing pulling on a rope. "Hey," she said, without preamble.

Janet exhaled. "Yes, Ms. Roberts?" She paused, and turned.

"We really do have a lot to do."

"Is doing this in a thunderstorm a good idea?" Dar asked. "Not sure if you people deal much with those."

Janet took a breath, then she paused. "Do you?"

"Florida is the thunderstorm and lightning capital of the world," Dar said. "Maybe wait until it's over?"

Janet studied her for a minute, then leaned closer. "We' can't," she said, in a low tone. "If it keeps raining, we'll get a flash flood that will come down that canyon and wash us out."

Dar considered that. "Rock, hard place."

Janet nodded. "Thanks for understanding."

"Okay." Dar shrugged slightly. "Keep your head down." She went back to where Kerry was arranging her bags. "No luck."

"I could tell."

They both put on their life jackets and a few minutes later, the crew shoved the raft into the current, jumping aboard as it lunged forward.

Josh and Tony, the tallest of the crew, had hold of long oars. They stood near the back edges of the raft, braced against the frame.

The ride now had a distinct edge of danger, and the surge of the rapids, twisting the already damaged raft gave no pleasure. Dar edged closer to Kerry and put her arm around her back, taking a grip on the chair frames to hold them both in position.

They could barely see the river ahead of them, the rain was coming down that hard and the river was a dark, brooding color with a tinge of red mud on it.

The raft was bucking and rolling and they were heading into some narrows. Dar's heart started to beat faster as she tensed, her body reacting to the danger. She could almost feel the electricity in the air around her and just as that thought crossed her mind a blast of lightning lit up the sky as it struck the wall nearest them.

Someone screamed.

Dar jerked hard in reaction and the hair on her arms stood up straight. She could feel it even despite the rain. She pressed against Kerry as she heard her gasp, and the raft swerved under them as bits of the wall fell into the river.

"Oh crap." Kerry released the hold she had on the seat and put her arms around Dar instead.

The passengers all clustered in the center of the raft, no one sitting, everyone just holding on, looking scared, all keeping their heads down.

Thunder rumbled loudly on the heels of another flash of

lighting, but this was at the crest of the canyon and Janet went to the front of the raft, shielding her eyes, trying to see past the curtain of rain. "Keep right!" She yelled back to the crew. "Keep right, we're nearly in the pass."

"Dar." Kerry pressed her cheek against Dar's chest. "How about a dude ranch next time?"

"There'd be a stampede of three headed cows and a pink goat would end up in bed with us." Dar took a tighter hold as the raft started to pitch and slide sideways in the water.

"Pink?"

"We're girls"

Kerry had to laugh just a little, despite the fear. She felt her mouth dry out as the raft dipped to one side. In reflex she closed her eyes as a surge of water came up over the front of the pontoons and hit them both. It was colder than the rain and she felt a shiver go through her.

"Hang on," Dar said, in an urgent tone. She pressed against Kerry and gripped the metal frame hard.

Kerry did, tightening her grip on Dar as the raft went sideways and then another lightning bolt struck somewhere above them.

"Watch out!" Rich yelled.

The raft spun and Kerry flinched as a rock hit her shoulder. She heard impacts around them and then the raft spun again and they were away from the wall.

"Ow!" Someone said, with a yelp.

"Stay still!" Janet's voice now, out of the deluge. Dar craned her neck to see someone on the deck of the raft with Janet kneeling next to them.

Then they were through the narrows and the raft, rolling and rocking, spun around and went forward, into a wider stretch of the river.

"Keep her steady!" Janet called out. "Everyone stay where you are. Don't unbalance the raft!"

"Who got hurt?" Kerry asked. "Can you see?"

"Can't." Dar faced them back around again and the rain lessened, though the thunder was still rumbling overhead. They could see down the river now, and ahead she saw a wide bend and to one side of it a beach that had a lot of debris piled on.

"Steer in!" Josh called out. "There's the landing. Is that gear?"

The raft started dodging across the river over ruffles and boulders that shook them and made their teeth rattle as the crew worked hard to move the raft sideways toward the far shore. They were moving fast, and three of the crew ran forward and hung onto the frame near the pontoons, swerving wildly as they fought to stay onboard.

They dipped along a set of boulders mostly buried in the water and scraped against the canyon wall, catching against the pontoon and slamming the raft around and backwards into the beach.

Josh leaped off and ran up the beach rope in hand to get it around a rock, hauling with all his strength to keep the raft in place. Two more crew scrambled off, one running to grab one of the crew from the front pontoon that had been thrown into the water and was scrabbling for a grip on something.

They got enough ropes out and the raft was pinned in place, its front smashed against the wall and the rear up against a pile of rubble that had been driven up the beach.

"Fuck!" Todd jumped off, but missed his step and went headfirst into the sand. He rolled over and got to his knees, hands up in a warding off gesture. "That was insane!"

Janet was still kneeling in the middle of the ship. "Josh, after you tie off give me a hand here," she said. "This guy's out cold."

Kerry leaned over and recognized Don's stocky form. "Oh hell." Marcia was sitting on the raft bottom next to him, looking terrified. Kerry scrambled around the frame to get to Marcia's other side, putting a hand on her shoulder. "What happened?"

"I don't know! One minute we were standing still, the next he was falling!"

Kerry knelt. Don's face was pale, and there was blood all over his head soaking his gray hair and staining his heather colored shirt. Unable to do anything to help, she just reached over to clasp Marcia's hand and squeezed it.

Rich came to stand shoulder to shoulder with Dar. "That sucks. Something from up there must have fallen on them."

"Hit us too." Dar kicked a bit of rock off the raft. "But small ones." She glanced behind them. "How far did we come?"

"About ten miles. That was the last big rapid on this stretch," Rich said. "This is the haul out. Sometimes they put boats in here for people who just want a quiet ride." He pointed up the beach. "There's a path cut there, and they keep a cache with a sat phone I think."

"Ah."

"That's where Doug was headed. Rich peered up the beach. "Don't see the kayak though." He frowned. "Unless he hauled it farther up on the beach. But where is he?"

"No other place he could have gotten out?" Dar asked. "Or missed this one?"

Rich shook his head. "Doug's a pro. Like those guys got the raft in here? He could get that kayak in.

The crew carried Don off the raft and they went up the beach, some of the passengers stopping to inspect the wreckage that had washed up.

Janet disappeared ahead of them and they saw an overhang that they all gathered under to get out of the rain, giving the crew space as they put Don down so Josh could look at his head.

Kerry walked with Marcia and they leaned against the wall, the older woman looking exhausted and scared. "We can call for help now."

Don started to moan and Marcia went over to kneel next to him, holding his hand, while the rest looked on uncomfortably, trying to avoid the rain falling everywhere.

Kerry rested her head against Dar's shoulder. "This is kind of getting past us, hon."

"Yeah," Dar said, briefly. Then she pushed off the wall and walked up the small step ridge and back out into the rain, almost inhaling it as she moved past the landing and climbed up the path where Janet had disappeared.

The landing looked well used. There were paths worn in several places, and rusty metal boxes on stilts that came into view as she moved farther from the river. Each one had something painted on the outside, some so worn it was impossible to tell what it said.

The different operations, Dar figured, as she came around a last bend and saw a worn building made from rock and old driftwood that reminded her a little bit of their cabin in the keys. As she walked toward it, the door opened and Janet emerged, stopping when she saw Dar.

Something was wrong. Dar had enough experience with oh shit looks to know one when she saw one. She grimly continued walking until she was up on the uneven porch.

Janet opened her mouth to speak, but Dar lifted a hand in a warning gesture. "Please don't tell me to just go back with the others and sit down," she said, in a very quiet tone. "You're getting to a point where you're risking our lives and I want to know what's going on."

Janet hesitated.

"I probably can't do a god damned thing about it, but I want to know," Dar said. "That little trip we just took wasn't funny."

For a minute, Dar thought Janet was going to blow her off and she started marshaling her arguments, but then the woman's shoulders dropped and she stepped back into the little cabin. "C'mon. I might as well tell someone who isn't going to rip my head off."

Dar followed her inside to find what reminded her more of a garden shed than a cabin. There were bits and pieces of rafting gear and old rags, roughly made wooden boxes with rusty hasps, and the slight, but pervasive smell of old gasoline.

"Phones gone," Janet said. "And Doug never made it here."

Dar stared at her in silence. "Someone took it."

"Someone did. Probably another op, who needed it, maybe the end of last season and didn't bring it back. We all know each other's combos, and the lock was unlocked, not broken." Janet sat down on a dusty table. "So, if you got any ideas, let me have em."

Dar looked around. "No supplies in here?"

"No edible ones. We hadn't stocked it yet. Just some old stuff from last year."

They stared at each other in silence for a few minutes. "Well," Dar said. "I can fish with my bare hands." She paused. "And whatever you got in here, Kerry can probably cook it."

THE MOVED DON into the shack, and set him on top of a pile of canvas tent covers on one of the benches on the edge of the storage area.

"We're going to have to send someone out for help," Janet said, in a clipped tone. "Since the phone was stolen, it reduces our options, and it's probably why Doug isn't here. He could already be near the end of the line, and the pickup spot."

"Or drowned somewhere," Todd said, sardonically. He was leaning against the doorjamb, arms crossed.

"Doug's a very capable kayaker. So, let's think positive. But we're going to send someone up the trail in any case," Janet said. "Josh is going to head out in a few minutes." She looked past him, as the rest of the group wandered up. "So, come on in and let's make the best of it."

Everyone clustered inside, dripping and uncomfortable, and spread out inside the two-room shack finding places to stand and drip. "We should bring all the gear over here. No sense in it sitting over there getting wet," Sally said, motioning to the college students. "C'mon."

Janet opened her mouth to interject, then just stopped and turned to Kerry. "Want to help me scrounge? Your SO said you could cook."

"Sure," Kerry said, and they moved into the second part of the storage cabin, filled with boxes and dust and smelling of old tents.

"I'm going to see if I can grab a fish," Dar said, ducking past the crowd and going out the door back into the rain. She was glad to be out of the musty smelling space, even though the weather didn't show any signs of letting up. She passed Sally and friends on the way back, each woman dragging duffels and gear. "Thanks guys."

"Where are you heading?" Sally said, blinking the rain out of her eyes. "We got everything."

"Trying my hand at fishing," Dar responded, continuing on her way with a wave. "Wish me luck."

Sally watched her go. "But you don't have a fishing pole?"

Dar just waved again.

With a shake of her head, Sally continued.

KERRY AND JANET rummaged around seeing what they could find. Janet surveyed a bag of dried venison. "I'd probably need a hammer to make that edible."

"This help?" Rich came in from the outside wooden shelves with a large, dented, but whole pot in his hands.

Kerry pointed to the one single ring gas burner. "Put her there, Rich." She stacked several packages of dusty dried fruit, six cans of navy beans, a package of barley, a package of rice, and a number ten can of white potatoes on the bench. "This is going to be interesting."

"What is?" Janet came over with a case of shelf stable milk boxes.

Kerry eyed them. "Even more interesting," she said. "Only thing I can think of to do with all this is make a big soup. I can't even think about what it's going to taste like, but it'll be hot and it'll be enough for everyone."

Janet nodded. "Good idea."

Kerry picked up the pot and headed outside with it, as most of the rest of the group sorted through the duffels and started hanging things up inside to dry.

She set the pot outside in the rain and scrubbed it, then rinsed it out and set it down again to fill. The rain was about as clean a source of water as she could imagine and it was coming down hard enough so that it wasn't going to take long.

She could see Dar moving slowly into the river and hoped her beloved would have some luck so the soup would taste of something other than dust and old rags, given she had no spices to work with.

All the condiments had been lost in the wreck. Kerry sighed, and peered into the pot, which was half full already. Then she straightened up and looked around, lifting her arm to shade the rain off her face.

A small overhang was just visible on the far wall and she made her way over to it, ducking under it to get some relief from the weather.

Inside she was surprised to find an irregularly shaped cave. She moved a step or two inside to look around. The walls were rough and scarred, and the space was cramped. She amused herself with peering at the surface looking for more fossils.

The walls had some marks on them, and it looked like they'd been impacted with blunt objects at some point or other. She could see one area that had almost been excavated, and she ran her hand over it, leaning closer in the gloom to see more clearly.

Didn't seem like anything. She shrugged and pulled her hand back, examining the dust covered skin, then she looked back at the wall and saw what seemed to be a little reflection. She tilted her head, then she reached out to rub the surface.

It seemed flat, and planed. She curiously put her thumb into her mouth to get some moisture to clean off the edge with and then stopped. She removed her digit and stared at it. "Holy crap." She gingerly licked her index finger. It tasted of salt. Kerry looked around and spotted a few river rocks and picked one up that was cracked in half. She brought it over to the wall and scraped at the surface, holding her free hand under the area to collect the scrapings.

It took a while, but she eventually had a full handful of the substance and she went back to the overhang, to look at it better in the light. Sure enough it was a crude crystal. With a slight chuckle she closed her hand and went back to the now full pot.

She tipped a little of the water out, then emptied her hand into the remainder and stirred it to clear the debris off her skin. Then she picked up the pot and headed back to the shack, shaking her head and laughing as she went.

DAR EDGED CAREFULLY into the water, keeping to the line of rocks that the river was flowing over near the landing. There was a relatively shallow space there, and a line of boulders that gave her something to lean against and brace against the current.

She wasn't sure this was going to work. She thought the rush of the water was too fast, but she'd opened her mouth about it, so she figured she better at least give it a try.

Janet had seemed very skeptical.

Dar appreciated the skepticism. She saw a narrow break in the flow a few feet over, and she cautiously edged that way, not wanting to do something stupid and end up getting swept downstream.

As she thought that, she realized she hadn't put on a safety jacket and cursed, then she got herself wedged in against the rock and figured she was safe enough for now.

It was cold, and upstream she could see the ruffled gray green water surging down toward her. She took a moment to appreciate again the power of nature.

Humans always thought they were so all powerful. But she'd been on the ocean enough to understand that Mother Nature could bitch slap you into hell and not even realize she'd done it. In this case, she could see the raging power of the river, and the walls on either side of it that it had cut through the millennium.

That river had created this canyon. Mile by mile, eon after eon, just the water, just that river had cut through the rock and made the scene she was looking at. There was an awesomeness to that Dar readily acknowledged.

But.

She tested her footing and leaned over a little, bracing her elbows on her thighs as she focused on the water rushing past the rocks, trying to tune out the roar of the rapids.

Were there even fish? She remembered seeing them where they'd stopped to swim, but in these long stretches of white water?

Then her eyes caught a brief flash and she looked down just in time to see a fish wiggle between her legs, it's tail brushing her calf as it went by.

Ah.

She settled down to concentrate, aware from the corner of her eye motion on the shore. She glanced briefly over to see Todd standing just out of the water, watching her.

"Hey," Todd called out. "What the hell are you doing?"

Oh yay.

"Catching fish," Dar responded.

"No way is that working," Todd scoffed. "Waste of your time."

Dar focused past him, blinking a little as she let her vision adjust to the colors and motion of the water going between her legs, sorting out the ruffles and curls from the rock they were rushing over. She could see some algae on the downstream side of the rocks facing her, and then a minute later she saw a movement coming down.

A flash, and a ripple in the water and in reflex she plunged her hands down between her calves and felt her fingers fasten onto a moving body. With a grunt of satisfaction, she pulled her arms back and straightened up, holding a reasonably good sized fish in her hands.

"Fuck!"

Dar looked aside to see Todd standing up straight himself, shading his eyes. She held up the fish. "Wanna grab this if I throw it at you?"

"Did you just do that?" Todd said, in an astonished tone. "Holy shit."

Dar lifted the fish. "Catch it? You're wasting my time."

He looked around. "Hold on," he said, without his usual sarcastic tone. He went over to the raft and picked up a battered metal tin that had once held beer cans and brought it back over. He put it down and then held his hands up. "Go for it."

Intrigued, Dar readied herself, and then she extended her arms over her head and threw the fish as hard as she could toward him, watching him grimace a little as he caught it, then dropped it immediately into the bin. "Nice catch."

Todd examined the fish in the bin, then he dragged it up a little farther. He returned to the shore and walked into the water up to his knees. "How did you do that? Fucking A."

Dar regarded him. "You just see and grab" She wiggled her fingers. "My father taught me how to do it."

He made his way over to where she was standing. "Do it again?" He demanded. "I want to see that."

Dar went back to her crouch, resisting the urge to elbow him in the jaw. She took a deep breath and released it, then rested her elbows on her knees again.

A flash. Her hands moved before she even thought about it, and the next moment she pulled a larger fish up and out of the water, it's scales reflection the gray light as it fought her grip.

Todd reached out and grabbed her to keep her steady. "Holy

son of God," he said, in a honestly reverent tone. "That's the most useful thing I've seen a woman do in my whole life."

Dar felt a sense of the ridiculous. "Wanna grab this? We've got a crap load of people to feed."

He hooked his fingers into the fish's gills and relieved her of its weight. Then he made his way over to the shore, lifting the fish over his head as he used his other hand to balance against the rocks.

Dar shook her head and went back to her fishing.

"OKAY," KERRY GAVE the pot a stir, and adjusted the gas burner. "Let's let it cook a while and see what we get." She glanced around as there were footsteps at the door and saw Dar follow Todd inside. Todd was carrying a beat up metal bin. "Ah. The protein component."

"Fuckin A." Todd put the bin down. "Never seen anything like that in my life." He indicated the bin.

Janet looked inside. "Wow. Ten? Is that ten fish?"

Dar retreated to her pack and removed a packet of peanut butter crackers and opened them. She popped one in her mouth and munched it, as everyone gathered around her bounty.

"Wow." Rich echoed Janet. "Where did these come from?"

Kerry turned and regarded her huntress, who winked at her with a droll expression. "Nice work, honey." She smiled. "Too bad you couldn't grab any shrimp I could have done some gumbo."

"She fucking caught them with her hands," Todd said. "Fucking amazing."

Janet glanced at Dar, who issued a tiny, modest shrug.

Kerry went over and fished into Dar's pocket for the pocketknife she knew was there. Then she came back over to the table and peered inside the bin herself. The fish inside were all big, and she reviewed them. "We can either add this to the soup, or grill them."

"Too wet to grill."

"Put it in the soup," Rich said. "It'll last longer."

"Sounds good." Kerry pulled one of the fish out and started gutting it, and a moment later Sally joined her and then Rich and Marcia came over.

"How's Don?" Kerry asked.

Marcia looked relieved. "He's better. Has a bump on his head, but Janet fixed that cut up for now. He's mostly hungry."

"Great." Kerry half turned. "Okay everyone? Take the guts out, and cut off the head and tail, and then cut them into cubes like this."

"We should use the heads," Rich said. "My mother always did."

Sally grimaced. "Not the eyeballs. C'mon, I'm making a vegan sacrifice here as it is."

"Those are better roasted," PJ said. "Fish cheeks — mm"

The fish chunks went into the soup pot and Kerry gave it another stir, its contents now starting to thicken up. She judged that even if it wasn't as savory as anyone would like, it would fill everyone up, and they could at least be dry and full.

"Okay." Janet rubbed her arms. "So let's get settled as best we can, and Josh'll hopefully be on the trail head by now." She leaned back against one of the workbenches. "Thanks, everyone. We'll get through this."

"No thanks to you," Todd said. "You're gonna owe us double for this by the time we get out of this mess."

'Let's deal with that once we're back at base," Janet said, sharply. "Then we can talk about what you're owed. In case you don't remember you signed a liability release saying you accept all the risk of the travel."

They had. Dar remembered it. "True," She said before Todd could. "But you also took responsibility for safety and organization."

Todd nodded. "She's right," he said. "And you all know my dad's a lawyer."

Amy came over and stood next to Kerry, checking out the pot of soup. "Thanks for doing that," she said. "I think it would have been good even without the fish."

Kerry smiled. "Thanks. I got lucky. I found some salt crystals in a cave across the way, otherwise it would be pretty darn bland."

"You found salt crystals?" Amy looked at her with more interest. "Can you show me?"

"Sure." Kerry joined her and they walked outside, crossing quickly over the rocky ground and around the slight bend to where she'd found the overhang. It was starting to get dark but there was enough light yet to see the inside of the cave with some clarity.

"Here." Kerry pointed out the area, and swiped her finger over the crystals then put it in her mouth. "Salty."

Amy pulled a flashlight from her pocket and examined the

area, then duplicated Kerry's motion. "It is!" She knocked off a sample, a bit of slanted clear crystal with uneven edges and put it in her pocket. "This is really cool. It means this cave once was under ocean water, and probably the crystals made this split." She indicated the walls.

Kerry was standing with her arms folded. "I was just glad to find something for the soup," she said. "You like caves, huh?"

"Geology is my major," Amy said. "I love it. I want to be an archaeologist after college. Todd just likes climbing. I met him in class." She gave Kerry a sideways look. "He's really a nice guy. He just acts mean a lot." She paused. "He thought you guys were so faux before the trip but now he thinks you're pretty cool."

"Faux?" Kerry's eyes twinkled with amusement.

"You know like some of these people. Just all pretentious stuff, like look at my North Face backpack, and things like that. No one ever really did an outback, like Todd and I did."

Kerry sat down on a rock. "Well we never did white water before," she admitted. "Some of the rest of them did."

"It's true." Amy sat down as well. "But this stuff, this glamping and all that, it's faux," she said. "Todd and I did the real thing. We climbed Half Dome. We did real camping. We went on this, because we wanted to just relax getting from climb to climb. That's what the trip was supposed to be."

"Ah."

"The guys that didn't show? They were climbers," Amy said. "So, this whole thing turned out to be a scam to us. You know what I mean? Then with all those other faux types glamping." She eyed Kerry. "Look, I know Todd's been an asshat, but we saved up for months for this. His dad didn't buy it for him."

"They would have given you your money back, I thought?" Kerry said, cautiously.

"They would, but we're out of time," Amy said. "This was the only break we were going to have before going back to school."

"Ah." Kerry repeated. "I'm sorry about that. I know what it's like not to have time for vacation. This is our first in a while."

Amy nodded. "You guys are cool. We talked about it last night, and that fish thing today was outrageous." She stood up. "I'm sorry it turned out such crap for you guys too. But now it should be okay. That Josh guy's a good hiker." She grinned a little. "And I like fish."

With a wave, she started back out of the cave, leaving Kerry to ponder things for a minute, before she, too, got up and left, shaking her head almost continuously.

A CRACK OF lightning woke Dar up and she was on her feet with hands outspread before she knew where she was.

It was pitch dark and she smelled dust and canvas around her. She felt the chill of a cold wind coming in from her left hand side and then she nearly jumped when a hand touched her knee and she remembered what the hell was going on. "Crap."

"Dar." Kerry's voice sounded, low and burry with sleep. "What's up?"

"Me." Dar sat back down on the pile of old tent material they'd laid down on and leaned back against the shack walls, aware of rustles and motion around them. "Sorry, folks."

"Sokay, blast woke everyone up anyway," Rich said, in a muffled tone. "And I think I'm sleeping on a cam shaft."

Dar blinked a few times, and then looked down, to see Kerry's hand pat her knee. She covered her hand with her own and relaxed, listening to the rain thunder down around them.

It meant nothing good. Not for them, or for the kid trying to hike out to get them help, or to Doug, wherever he was. They didn't really have any supplies, and if they had to walk out they had nothing to travel on except for the remains of the soup.

Which they had no way to keep edible for any period of time. Dar exhaled a little, then turned her head as she heard motion, and saw shadows moving to the door and the shine of a flashlight coming from the back half of the shack where the crew had all taken shelter.

"Make sure the lines are tight," Janet said in a low tone. "Check the water level."

"Got it," A deeper, male voice answered. "I can hear the banging from here."

Dar felt Kerry's fingers contract and a moment later she was sitting up as well, her profile now visible in the faint light entering the shutters. "That doesn't sound so good."

"Mm." Dar grunted in agreement.

The door opened, and the sound of rushing water entered with it, along with a blast of cold air and the smell of the river, and then light flared as the small gas lantern hanging in the center of the shack was ignited, providing a reddish gold illumination.

Everyone blinked into it, sitting up from where they'd bunked out in all corners of the shack, on boxes and bundles, and cramped corners. Janet moved under the lamp and rubbed her hands, looking around at them. "Sorry to wake you all up, folks."

"Is everything okay?" Sally asked. "Except the weather, I mean?"

Janet glanced at the door. "I just sent someone to check. The river's rising again, and we may need some help pulling the raft up higher."

Everyone scrambled to their feet, and Dar reached down to grab her boots and Kerry's, handing her partner's over to her.

"First time they asked for help, huh?" Kerry said, as she swung her legs over the side of the stack of tents and started pulling on her socks.

"Yep." Dar tugged one boot on and started lacing it. "You know what just occurred to me?"

"What?"

"Our dogs are having a better time than we are."

Kerry muffled a snort of laughter.

"Seriously. They're in a spa, swimming in warm water, playing with other dogs and getting massages every day. Here we are getting our asses kicked from every direction. What the hell, Ker?"

"I know, hon." Kerry stood up and reached for the jacket she'd hung up next to them. "We should let them plan the vacation next time." She zipped up the front of the jacket and pulled the hood up, glad of the warmth as Janet had left the door to the shack open. "Worst thing we'd deal with is liver snacks."

"I'd take it right now," Dar grumbled. "I miss my milk dispenser."

Kerry reached over and gave her a one-armed hug. "Hang in there. We'll get through it and have some great stories to tell."

"Peh."

Thunder rumbled overhead, and another flash of lightning lit up the sky outside, sending a flare of silver into the shack as they moved toward the door, joining the crew as a wet figure came running back from the river.

"Hurry!" He yelled. "We're gonna lose it!"

They all piled out into the rain, a crowded clump in the darkness bumping into each other as they hopped off the shallow porch onto the wet ground. "Careful," Rich reeled for balance. "It's gonna be slick."

"Gonna be?" Sally circled him and everyone moved out toward the river, the crew running on ahead with flashlights and yells starting to go up.

"Fucking women stay the hell back," Todd shouted suddenly. "Go back to the shed!"

No one paid him any attention as they spread out along the gravel filled ground. Dar strode ahead and realized after a few more strides that she was moving through rising water and she looked down to see about an inch of it covering her boots. "Uh oh."

Kerry was at her side and reached out to latch on to the back of her jacket. They went slightly to the right of the rest of the crowd and came around a boulder to see the river picking up the raft and yanking it sideways. The crew grabbed onto ropes and looked for an opportunity to hop on.

"Wait for them to tie on, and throw the ropes!" Janet yelled. "Stay back!"

"Sounds like a great idea." Kerry put her back to the boulder and raised one arm to shield herself from the pouring rain, as the rest of the crowd spread out along the shore, the water coming up now to their ankles.

Dar braced her boots shoulder width and pushed her hood back, annoyed at the edges obscuring her vision. She could see past the raft to the river, and it was mostly whitecaps and surge, and the raft itself was bucking up and down and yanking against the ropes that had tied it to the shore.

One of the crew managed to make it on, and he quickly secured one end of a rope slung over his shoulders to a stanchion. A moment later a second of the crew scrambled up to join him, almost falling into the water as the raft pitched.

Dar was glad she wasn't on it. "This is really crazy."

Janet stood in knee-deep water, waiting with her arms outstretched. "Throw it!"

The raft suddenly moved, and careened toward the shore. Janet scrambled back but not fast enough and the edge of the pontoon smacked into her and sent her flying into the water. The movement of the river pulled the raft and her back out again.

Both Dar and Kerry moved as one, and lunged into the water, Dar reaching out to grab Janet's boot as she slid past, hands scrabbling for a hold on the slippery rocks.

Dar got a foot up on a rock and pulled backwards, and almost lost her balance against the wash of the water as Kerry hooked one hand on the pocket of her cargo pants and grabbed Janet's flailing hand and somehow managed to keep a grip on it.

A second later, Todd came past them and got one brawny arm around Janet's waist and lifted her up and clear of the water, and all of them scrambled backwards to the shallow wash, where more arms were waiting to take hold.

"Catch! Hurry!" The crew on the raft yelled, and Rich hopped past them and lifted his hands to grab the end of the rope hurtling through the rain. He caught it and backed up rapidly.

Todd dropped Janet onto her feet and went to Rich's side to grab the rope, both men starting up the slope as more of the crew also took hold. "Get out of the way!" Todd barked.

Dar took a step back and looked back at the raft, seeing the aft pontoon swing inward with the pulling of the rope and the two crew onboard hanging on with tight grips.

Janet had recovered her balance, and had one hand against the boulder bracing against it. "Need another rope! John! Tie off to the midship!"

John hand over handed to the centerline of seats and knelt, quickly removing the rope from around his shoulders and getting the end of it around the metal supports. He had to release his hold to tie the knot and he spread his knees to keep his balance as the raft was being tugged from both sides.

Dar looked down to see the water up to her kneecaps and she turned her head toward where Kerry was standing. "Ker?"

"Yeah?" Kerry had a finger hooked into Dar's belt.

"Maybe you want to go back a little?" She pointed down.

Kerry looked down at the water. It was inching up her thighs and she felt the pull against her balance. "Let's both go," she said, "before they pull that raft right into us."

"Good point." Dar took hold of the belt holding up Kerry's pants and started around the boulder, leaning forward as they came around the edge of it and saw a bunch of the crew heading past them at a run. She resisted the urge to turn around and see what they were doing and kept walking until the water was just splashing against the soles of her boots before she paused.

John had thrown the second line and Dave grabbed it, and was coming around the boulder on the other side where Pete from the crew met him and got his hands on it. On the other side, Rich and Todd were hanging on to the first rope, Todd in the front with it wrapped around his waist and moving backwards with short digging steps.

Janet waved at them. "Bring them around and tie them behind the rock! Nothing's going to pull that out."

The boulder, twice Dar's height, and half buried in the earth seemed a good bet and she and Kerry went over to help with the second rope, and Sally joined them.

"Pull it tight!" Pete said. "Hey, Dar, can you tie them when we get them together?"

"Sure." Dar got hold of the front of the second rope as they came around the rock and the first rope was pulled around to meet up with them.

Todd extended the end of the first rope to her and planted his boots in the gravel.

She got the ends in both hands and quickly knotted them together, memories surfacing from lazy summer afternoons spent on the navy base, learning this skill on cast off loops of hemp worn from long use. She briskly tugged against the knot and made sure it was snug, then backed off. "Done."

The men pulled against the waters grip, and held the lines taut as she got the hitch in place, and then they slowly relaxed, letting the rope take the strain from the plunging raft. A rumble of thunder sounded overhead, and they all looked up, but it was sound only, no lightning lit up the sky.

The rope scraped against the rock and made a rickety sound as the knot tightened, then slacked and dropped, then pulled taut again as the river surged.

Janet moved to the edge of the beach to see the raft. "Okay. That should hold." She came back over as everyone walked away from the shore, retreating up the slope until they were standing on dry ground, a clump of slicker covered figures in the dark. "Thank you," Janet said, in a quiet tone. "I really appreciate everyone helping out."

There was a faintly awkward silence. "Let's go back and dry off," Sally finally suggested. "Last thing we need is for everyone to get sick."

"True that," Rich said. "True that."

"Be nice to have something hot to drink. Except we don't," Todd commented in a sarcastic tone. "Nice not to even keep some chicory in that shack."

They trooped back to the shack and went inside, where PJ and Marcia were waiting. "Everything okay?" Marcia asked, as they started stripping off the wet jackets. "I made Don stay here."

"Good move, grandma." Todd hung up his jacket and stood there, looking down at his wet fatigue pants. "Fuck."

Dar went over to the stack of tents and sat down. She removed her boots and set them on the floor, adding her now soaked socks to them. Kerry came over and sat next to her, extending her feet out and watching the rain drip from the fabric of her pants.

Rich started rummaging through the boxes stacked near the wall. "Let see if we have something we can boil up," he said, as Dave and Sally joined him.

John and Pete came in, looking tired, and Pete came over to the light to examine his hand. "Ow." He grimaced. "Got caught between the raft and one of those rocks getting off."

Janet sighed. "Great."

"You're lucky that's all that happened," Todd said. He sat down and removed his pants, then stood to wring them out as he stood in a t-shirt and his boxers. "Should have just let the damn thing go. We can't go on the river with it."

"We can," Janet said quietly. "But we won't have to, when Josh gets to the ranger station and calls in. I just don't like to give up any of my options."

With uneasy looks, the group all changed into what dry clothing they had, and hung up the wet to dry near the walls, where the ground quickly gained a line of dark wetness.

Dar fished in her day bag and pulled out a packet of crackers, one of the last few she had, and opened it, offering one to Kerry.

"I'm going to heat up some of that soup," Amy decided, standing up and moving to the other side of the shack.

Sally followed her. "We found some old boxes of Lipton tea bags." She held them up. "It'll be a feast."

Janet drew breath to say something, then just shrugged and went over to examine Pete's hand. The rest of the crew wandered around, some taking seats near the walls, a few going back into the area where the cook stove was.

Kerry chewed her cracker thoughtfully, as she listened to the rain outside. She wondered how far Josh had made it. Would he have taken shelter and waited it out? Or pushed forward to the ranger station? What would happen if he also got lost or hurt?

What would they do? She glanced at Dar, who had changed into a dry pair of jeans from their duffel, and was now relaxing, sockless, in the dim light from the lantern.

They were out of food, mostly. They had no real supplies.

"Least we're not outside," Dar commented, passing over another cracker. "Maybe it'll stop raining in the morning."

"Hopefully." Kerry smelled the soup heating up, and wondered if it would be a better idea to save it. "I guess you can catch more fish, huh?"

Dar dusted her fingers off. "I can always catch more fish," she said. "As long as we're near the river." She folded her hands over her stomach. "But you don't have that much gas in that stove."

Kerry considered that. "I've eaten sashimi."

Dar made a face. "I'd rather we get out of here." She lowered her voice. "If there's no sign of Josh, we should walk out. Staying here is going to be trouble."

Kerry hiked up one knee and circled it with both arms. "More trouble."

They heard a rumble of thunder, and then, just after it, the yowl nearby of a cat, sudden and shocking and making them all jump.

Rich went to the door and shoved it closed. "That was a big one." He said. "Did we throw those fish bones out the window?"

"Anyone got a gun?" Todd asked, as they all went silent.

The cat yowled again.

Chapter Seven

KERRY EASED THE door open and poked her head outside, looking around before she emerged into the chill of an early dawn.

The skies had cleared, and the stars were fading from view. She went to the edge of the rough wood porch and looked toward the river.

Janet and Pete were coming back from that direction, and Kerry stepped down onto the gravel surface, taking a breath of the morning air filled with the scent of the water as she heard the door open behind her and the sound of the rest of the group emerging.

She felt a little tired, unable to really get any good sleep after their early waking. They had boiled up more old tea, and she could taste that mustiness on the back of her tongue.

Janet and Pete stopped, as they saw everyone approaching and a moment later they were all in a rough circle as the rest of the crew also came over.

"Okay, folks." Janet visibly steeled herself to continue. "The river's running pretty high. I don't think going farther on the water is really an option."

"What about the kid?" Rich asked. "How long till he gets to the ranger station?"

"That's our second option," Janet said. "Depends on the trail conditions." She washed her hands together. "I think he probably didn't make that much headway last night from the weather. So, I think we should probably start up after him."

Dar nodded, but kept quiet.

"Don how are you feeling?" Janet asked, looking past her.

"Not bad," Don said. "Got a headache, but I'm all right. I just won't be running up that trail." He folded his arms over his chest as most turned to look at him. His head was covered in a bandage and there were bruises along his temple, but he had a healthy flush of color and seemed fine.

Janet looked relieved. "Good. So, let's gather up everything we can find in terms of supplies, and see what we can pack out."

She motioned to the crew and they scattered to start collecting things, while the passengers stood in their irregular circle, regarding each other.

Todd came to stand next to Dar. He folded his arms, and produced a skeptical expression that reflected what Dar was thinking in her head.

They exchanged glances.

"You any good at catching snakes?" Todd asked, in a mild tone.

"No," Kerry supplied at once.

Dar eyed her thoughtfully.

Kerry returned the look. "Please tell me you aren't."

'Well, I have," Dar said. "But not for a very long time, and I didn't really enjoy the experience. But it was either latch on to a cottonmouth or have him bite me and we were out in the bush and no one wanted to have to carry my six foot plus dead ass back to the base."

Kerry made a face, and so did Rich and Don.

"In August. In the Everglades," Dar said. "So how about I get a few more fish and we...I don't know. Smoke or dry them or something?"

"That'll beat eating crickets," Todd said. "I'll give that a try too." He motioned Dar to precede him toward the river and with a faint shrug Dar headed off.

Sally looked up at the sky, then she pulled the one carry bag that her group had salvaged and started sorting through it. "If the weather holds, we should be good," She said to Kerry, who had taken a seat on a rock nearby. "Got to admit I'm not having a real great time now."

"No," Kerry said. "Not much fun." She rested her elbows on her knees, her and Dar's duffle resting next to the rock. She watched as a bird landed on a bit of twisted wood nearby, and pecked at it. "I'll go get that soup pot and get some water in it. We'll need to carry that."

"For sure," Sally said. "Boil it first."

Kerry pushed herself to her feet and went into the shack and picked up the pot. She carried it out and across the gravel back to where she'd found the cave.

There had been a trickle of water and now when she made her way into the cave, it had become more of a gush, carrying the rain runoff from the previous night. She wedged the pot into a corner of the stone and watched it start to fill up.

While that was in work, she turned and picked up one of the rocks littering the floor and went to the wall. She pounded it against the salt crystals, knocking them off into her hand. She kept at it until she had several palms full, which she put into her cargo pants pocket and dusted her hands.

She went back over to the pot and stood watching, then turned as she heard a soft scraping sound behind her. There was no one there, but she spotted motion and her heart rate picked up as she recalled Todd's comments about snakes.

But it was just a squirrel. The small rodent seemed as surprised to see her as she was to see it and scampered quickly out the opening and raced off.

Curious, Kerry went over to the corner the squirrel had emerged from and peeked behind the rock, spotting a pile of debris behind it. She knelt and fished her flashlight out of her pocket and turned it on, peering warily at the ground, then moving her boot a little and moving the sticks around.

There were bits of stone and fluff there, what appeared to be some nutshells. She was about to abandon the pile when the light flashed against something and she paused and then leaned closer. She extended her hand and pushed the fluff aside with the edge of her flashlight then reached down and picked up what the light had exposed.

She stood up and went to the entrance to the small cave and peered closely at the device, a square piece of plastic with two wires extending from it, ending in a pin out cable. "What the hell?" She turned it over, but it had no writing on it. With a shrug she put it in her pocket.

The sound of water overflowing made her turn and she trotted back over to the now overflowing pot and picked it up, holding it away from her body to keep from being doused. With a grunt, she turned and made her way out of the cave into the sunlight.

"WATER'S HIGHER," TODD said as they got to the edge of the river. "Look at that thing."

Dar spared a glance at the raft that looked sadly battered. She could see cracks along the front of the pontoons, and most of the metal structure was bent. "Yeah." She put her hand on one of the struts and then sat down on the pontoon. "Going to change shoes."

She had her day bag on her back and unslung it, then removed the pair of sandals. The sound of the river was loud behind her.

Todd walked over to the other side of the raft and started into the water, moving along the rocks and between the pontoons. He was wearing shorts and an odd kind of shoes that were melded to his instep and had a slight curve to them.

Dar finished putting her sandals on and tied her boots to her day bag, then followed Todd's path into the water, grimacing a little as the chill crept up her calves.

Dar studied the rocks then picked a spot between two algae covered boulders and got a foot on either side of them.

"How do you know where to stand?" Todd asked.

"Find a gap," Dar said, briefly. "We might have to go deeper." She pointed to the right. "It's a lot higher than it was yesterday."

Todd looked upriver. "It is," he said. "No way could we use that raft. It'd come apart under us." He eased sideways and carefully climbed over a submerged rock, getting into the water up to his waist. He almost lost his balance and reeled, waving his arms. "Oh shit!"

Dar grabbed hold of the pontoon strut and swung over. She reached out to grab his wrist and pulled back. For a moment it was touch and go, then he rocked forward and got his footing and braced one hand against the rocks. "Watch it," she said and released him. "Let me get a rope."

"Nah, I got it." He wedged his feet into the crevices and bent forward. "Hey, Amy!" He let out a bellow that nearly made Dar's ears ring. "C'mere!"

Dar reached up and pulled a length of rope that was tied off and circled her waist with it, tying it off before she settled into her spot and let her elbows rest on her thighs. The early light reflected off the water, it's rich green color and pungent scent flowing over her.

Todd stared intently at the water, and then he lunged, grabbing at something. After a moment, he straightened and lifted his hands up, dripping but empty. "Shit." He stared again, then plunged both hands into the water, chasing after something. "Shit," he repeated.

Dar felt the water flowing hard against her leg. "Might be going too fast to do this," she said in a diplomatic tone. Then she felt a bump. Without really thinking her body reacted and she grabbed down by her shin and felt a body squiggling there.

She tightened her grip and pulled her hand up, pulling a medium sized trout out of the water.

Todd came back over to where she was standing. "Fuck. How do you do that?"

Dar threw the fish into one of the broken topped bins on the raft. "It's all in the reflexes." She settled down to wait. "You get in the flow, and you feel the fish hit you. Then you grab them."

Todd studied her legs, his brow creasing. "The fish hit you?"

"See the gap?" Dar pointed to two rocks. "Fish come through and I'm blocking their path." She indicated her leg. "They can't really control where they're going in the flow, so they smack into me." She felt another bump and grabbed quickly, feeling a bigger body that thrashed immediately. "Ah."

Todd got both hands under the water and grabbed and together they pulled a large fish out of the water. "Nice." He looked at it with satisfaction, then peered past Dar to where not just Amy, but most the passengers were standing on the shore watching.

Dar produced a somewhat pained smile, then turned her attention to ridding herself of the large, squiggling and croaking fish. From the corner of her eye she spotted Kerry arrive at the back of the crowd, and she handed off the animal to Todd for him to pose with as Amy focused her camera.

The fish were a little slimy. She stuck her hands into the water to wash them off, and a fish swam into them, making her eyes widen a little as she simply closed her fingers on it. "Hey," she told Todd. "Get rid of that I've got another one."

"What the fuck?" Todd stared down.

"Throw it." She jerked her head toward the raft. "We must be in the path of choice this morning."

Todd laughed, lifting the fish over his head and aiming for the cooler.

THEY ASSEMBLED OUTSIDE the shack, ready to leave. The fish were packed in salt from Kerry's cave find and the cooler rigged so that two of the crew could carry it, along with the rest of the salvaged stores. Water bottles had been filled by the now boiled runoff and they were as ready as they were going to be.

Janet stood in front on the group holding a walking stick. "Okay," she said. "Let's move."

Dar had put her hiking boots back on, and had their duffel rigged for her to carry on her back, while Kerry had both their day bags. It wasn't too uncomfortable, and she bounced a little on the balls of her feet as she waited for the group to get going.

Todd and Amy were the first to start, both using backpack mounted water sacks. They wore the odd shoes that someone had explained to her were for rock climbing.

Kerry had her camera around her neck, and a brimmed and ventilated hat on her head. "Might as well make the best of it, right?" she said as they started walking, just behind Rich and Sally.

"At least you don't have to be bored on the raft," Kerry said.

"True," Dar said. She flexed her hands, and fell into the rhythm of the hike as they headed up and around the corner of the rock wall, following a faint path up a short rise.

It was a nice morning, at least, the rain the previous day leaving clear skies and cool air behind as they continued upward, in the shadow of the canyon walls and the pungent blue sky contrasted with the striated rock and the gravel-strewn ground.

Kerry touched Dar's arm and pointed. "Hey a bighorn sheep. Look at it climb."

Dar watched the animal scale apparently without footing right up the cliff. "How in the hell does it do that?"

"It's got sticky pads on its hooves," Rich supplied knowledgably. "And it keeps moving."

The animal gained a ledge and then trotted out of sight, and they kept moving between the walls. The sound of crickets suddenly loud around them, as grass about knee height grew in dusty tufts around ground that was visibly damp.

They were still climbing up, and Dar leaned forward a little, shifting the duffel to a more comfortable position. She heard a scrape behind her and glanced back to see the crew members repositioning the gear, struggling a little with the big cooler.

Just ahead of them PJ walked, using makeshift crutches that let her keep her weight mostly off her bandaged foot. Her classmates stayed with her, and two of them went back to help the crew, all of them roughly the same age.

Not even a slight protest from the workers, who gladly shifted some of the load.

Dar returned her attention to the trail, pondering if she should go back herself and assist. She looked up to find Kerry watching her over one shoulder, a faint grin on her face.

She reasoned Kerry probably had a good idea of what she was thinking and returned the grin, with a slight shrug of both shoulders.

"Hon." Kerry hooked one finger into the waistband of her pants. "You did your part by providing food for all of us. Honest."

"Pffft."

"And everyone spent an hour scraping salt crystals for it.

We're all in. For a posh luxe ride down the river we're doing plenty of work."

"I know." Dar laid one arm over her shoulders, as the path widened and they could walk side by side. "I had a thought, though. What if we're taking a different path than Josh did?"

"I'm going to pretend you didn't say that." Kerry looked mournful. "C'mon, Dar. Isn't it screwed up enough without inventing more problems?" she asked, in a plaintive tone. "What can we do? Split up?"

Dar sighed. "No, I know." She briefly fell silent. "They just haven't made good choices so far."

And at that, Kerry had to be silent herself, because that was undoubtedly true. She sighed. "Well," she finally said. "They know more about this than we do."

"Yrg."

The canyon was angling to the left, and they were on a steeper path. The gravel was damp and as they spread out a little Dar noticed that there was standing water in some places.

"Folks," Janet said from ahead of them. "Be careful, there's some runoff up here and it can get slippery."

Dar felt the gravel shift under her in fact, and she moved over a little to where there was some scrubby grass growing. Kerry joined her and they kept their eyes on the ground as they walked in and out of splotches of sun coming between the walls.

Their boots slid a little, anyway. Kerry reached out quickly to grab hold of a piece of rock wall to keep from slipping. "Yikes."

Dar frowned. "We should have brought those softball cleats. Not much traction in these."

"Hold up, Dar. We have those collapsible walking sticks in the bag," Kerry said, suddenly. "Let me get them."

"Great idea." Dar paused and unslung the duffel, lowering it to sit on a rock and unfastening it as the crew coming up behind them paused for a rest, and PJ sat down and flexed her hands, with a grimace.

Janet appeared next to them. "What's up? We have to keep moving."

"We're just getting something." Kerry fished around in the duffel until she found the sticks. "Besides, I think those guys needed a breather." She indicated the crew. "How much longer is the uphill?"

Janet looked around. "Three or four hours. But once we get to the top it gets tricky."

Kerry handed Dar one of the sticks and opened one for herself. "Tricky?" She closed the bag and handed it back to Dar. "What does that mean?"

But Janet just walked past them to the crew, and didn't answer.

Dar unfolded the stick and was now testing it, grunting in satisfaction as she looped the leather strap around her wrist. "I got a bad feeling about that." She hoisted the duffel back up and tightened the straps. "But like you said, not much we can do."

The sticks helped, and Kerry made her way upwards with more confidence. They joined the rest of the party up the slope where they all were paused, watching the progress of the load bearing crew, who were picking their way up very cautiously.

Don leaned on his wooden walking stick, and Marcia was seated nearby, a smear of mud along one side of her face.

Janet climbed back up and past them, and the group started off again.

BY THE TIME they got to the top, even Janet didn't demur when they stopped for a break. The crew were all breathing hard. They put down their burdens and went to sit down, shirts drenched with sweat.

Kerry was also glad to stop, her legs tired from the climb even with the help of the stick. She leaned against the rock wall and crossed her ankles. Dar stood nearby taking a sip from her water bottle.

The sky had remained clear, but the downside to that was the sun remained bright. Kerry swung their day bags down from her back and fished inside hers. She pulled out a tube of sun block and opened it.

Dar sidled over and lifted her hair off her neck, bending over to kiss her on the nape before she applied more of the gooey stuff.

A little cool air, a little tickle from Dar's fingertips, and the pleasurable sensation of Dar's lips and Kerry dismissed the discomfort. She glanced up at her partner with an affectionate look as she applied some of the block to her exposed skin.

Dar winked at her.

Kerry winked back, and reached up to put some of the block along Dar's cheekbones. Her base tan was enough to protect her, but there was no sense in taking chances. Dar stood there motionless as the block was applied. "You know what?"

Dar straightened and leaned next to her, setting down the duffel bag she'd been carrying. "What?"

"I love you."

Dar smiled. "I love you too," she responded. "Especially at craptastic times like this." She watched the rest of the party find rocks in the shade to sit on as the sun blazed down overhead. It wasn't overwhelmingly hot. She was used to that.

It was probably around eighty degrees, but dry, and now that they'd stopped hiking up the incline the light breeze made it almost comfortable.

Dar stretched her legs out a little, pushing herself upward onto her toes as she watched Janet talking to the crew in a low tone she couldn't make the words out in.

Rich came over, holding his water bottle. "Now we go down and past that next ridge," he said. "Glad we're up here. If it starts raining again, we're not going to drown."

"Is it likely to?" Kerry glanced up. "Seems pretty clear now."

"Heard them talking." He indicated the crew. "That's why they wanted to hump up here fast as they could." He made a face. "We better find someplace to stop under cover."

Kerry pondered that. "How long is it going to take to get to that ranger station?" She asked. "It sounded like a short trip when they were talking about Josh going."

Rich glanced around casually then lowered his voice. "Three days."

"Three days?" Dar repeated.

"We can't go that fast, because of PJ, and the gear," Rich said. "Josh would have gone faster, maybe a day and a half." He took a sip from his water bottle. "Hope this lasts, or if it rains we can refill. You're supposed to suck down a couple of these a day in this weather."

Dar and Kerry exchanged looks. "Especially with salt preserved fish," Kerry said. "Or was the idea, Josh will get there ahead of us, and we'll meet the rangers on their way back?"

Rich half shrugged. "Yeah, sure. Why not? Makes sense."

Dar and Kerry exchanged another look. "We sure we'll all meet up on the same path?" Dar asked, one dark eyebrow hiked up.

"Well, there's really only one major trail," Rich said. He turned and pointed along the ridge. "Goes along there, and then down that set of switchbacks, and then back up to the slope, then back down there." He shaded his eyes. "The ranger station's on the other side of that mountain."

"Nice," Dar said.

"Should be fine," Rich said. "I'm glad we're off the river. I don't think that raft was going to make it much farther. This way, at least, we're making progress. If we'd dumped off the raft, who knows where we'd end up?" He looked up as Sally called him over, and went to join her.

Dar opened her pack and removed a packet of crackers. She ripped it open and handed half the crackers to Kerry, then relaxed against the stone wall, chewing thoughtfully.

Kerry nibbled one of the crackers. "Know what? Glad you brought these."

"Me too."

THE PATH GOT narrower, and now there was a short, but significant, drop off to their right-hand side. Dar was a pace or so behind Kerry, the soft scuff of her hiking boots audible amongst the silence of the rest of the group.

Kerry looked quickly behind her, past Dar's tall form to see the crew cautiously picking their way along the ridge.

Two of the male crew had rigged a sort of sling between them, with the heaviest of the gear suspended by it. As she watched they paused to trade off their burden with two of the others, the first one swapping the ropes for a handhold on the rough seat they'd fashioned for PJ.

PJ's face showed a discomfort not only for the ride, but for the necessity of it. One of her classmates was walking alongside, the other two were back with the rest of the crew, helping carry boxes.

"Watch it," Dar said, gently, touching her back.

Kerry refocused her attention on the trail and stepped over the rock in the center of the path before she tripped over it. "Thanks."

"Those guys bothering you?"

"My helper gene is bothering me." Kerry admitted. "As in, I want to be able to call in a helicopter or at least a squad of cute llamas to get us all out of this."

"Llamas are cute," Dar said, "but—" Dar straightened as yells came from in front of them. "What's up?"

Kerry stood on her tiptoes. "Hon, if you can't see what's going on what makes you think I can?" She shaded her eyes, but the group ahead had gone past a curve in the trail and were out of sight. "Should we go find out?"

Dar sighed. "Probably. Maybe they ran into a tarantula or something."

Kerry paused. "Can those bite through hiking boots?"

"No." Dar started forward, then paused as the sounds started to come toward them, a mixture of boots and a tattoo of hoof beats. "Hold on."

"I was only joking about the llamas," Kerry said with a nervous grin. "Honest."

They heard scrambling, yells of alarm, and then the sound of the hooves moving fast.

Dar absolutely had no idea what was going on. "Go flat against the rock," she said, pulling herself and Kerry back and sliding the duffel around so she could put her back to the wall.

They heard more sounds of thrashing then a loud, frightened scream. A moment later two large figures came bolting down the path at them at full speed.

"Holy crap!" Kerry flattened herself and grabbed hold of Dar's arm as the mountain sheep, or goats, or whatever they were, thundered past inches away from them. The one in the lead half turned its head as its horns brushed Dar's leg.

Instinctively she kicked out, booting the animal in the ribs and it baa'd loudly, but kept going.

"Watch out!" Kerry yelled after it. "Get to the side! Big sheep! Guys be careful!"

"Mountain goat." Dar started after it. "They may need help if it hits them."

Kerry scrambled after her as the animals reached the struggling crew. In a moment, it was a pileup and two of the crew went flailing over the edge of the path down the slope, as the men carrying PJ stumbled and she was almost launched off the seat onto the now confused sheep.

Without hesitation Dar dove off the path after the crew, landing with a hop as she skidded down the rocky surface and continuing down to where they'd fallen in a cloud of dust and tumbling stones. She kept her balance and just let gravity take her the rest of the way until she was at the bottom of the slope.

"Crap crap crap." Kerry gave the nearest sheep a shove, it's pungent, musky scent something she could almost taste on the back of her tongue. The animal baa'd in outrage but turned and leaped off the path, racing almost sideways across the rocks as its companion followed.

A moment later, they were long gone, and everyone was catching their breaths. PJ was sitting on the ground, her bandaged foot held up in the air, scrapes visible on both elbows.

One of the crew sat down on the cooler they'd almost lost and examined a bleeding cut on his hand. "Hey, are you guys okay?" He called down the slope. "Hey?"

Dar hauled one of the shaken crew to her feet. "You okay?"

The girl was covered in dust, and her knees had lurid scrapes on them. "What the hell was that!" She turned to her companion, a short red headed teenager still seated on the ground. "Pete, you okay?"

The boy grimaced. "My ass is broken. I landed on my tailbone." He cautiously rolled over and pushed himself to his feet, hissing. "Oh shit."

Dar went over and grabbed his arm as he started to waver. "I'll help you get up there." She got one arm around him as he limped forward.

"I'll help too." The girl went to the other side and took his arm. "I just got a few bangs. I landed on my head, lucky me."

Dar frowned. "That's not lucky."

The girl smiled at her. "Just kidding. I landed on my knees and side and rolled. Just road rash." She indicated her legs. "I ride a bike at home, I know how to fall."

Above them, Kerry stood watching, and then Todd appeared at her side. He had a rope circling his shoulders. "Two more people went down up ahead," Kerry yelled down. "One of them was Janet."

"Oh, fuckety do dah," Pete muttered. "Maybe she fell on her mouth."

Dar hastily stifled a laugh. "Toss the rope down," she called up to Todd. "He hurt his lower back."

Todd shook his head, but did as he was asked, throwing the end of the rope down and then backing up a step and bracing his legs as he positioned the rope across his shoulders and around his waist, ready to belay them up the slope.

Kerry slid past him and started up the path. "I'll check it out."

Dar looped the rope around Pete's chest and they started to climb, Todd taking in the slack and pulling as they did to help the effort. Dar took hold of an outcropping and hauled herself up, then she levered her body up onto the path and turned to grab Pete's hands to help him upward. "Easy."

"Ow." Pete grimaced as he got one knee up on the path and then was up onto it. He rolled onto his side. "Son of a bitch that hurts."

The rest of the crew gathered around him and helped him to his feet, and the girl, Tracy, came scrambling up after him, dusting herself off.

Amy came trotting down the path. "They're going to need some med there," she told Todd. "Not sure we can keep going."

"Figures." Dar shouldered past her and moved up the path and the two turned and followed her.

They reached the bend in the path and came around it, to a wider area where the rest of the group was gathered. Two people were seated on the ground, Janet and Sally, and there was blood visible.

Kerry knelt in front of Janet, talking to her. A moment later she turned and met Dar's eyes. "Hon, they're going to need the first aid kit."

"They need it down there too," Dar responded, looking around at the watchers. "But I'm sure someone can go get some bandages." Her eyebrows hiked.

"Right," Rich started and hurried past. Dar heard the snort from Todd, who was just behind her.

Janet had a cut across one knee that looked deep and painful. As Dar came closer she could see how pale the woman was. "That might need stitches," she said. "Anyone here a medic?"

Everyone stood there in an awkward silence. Then Dar folded her arms. "Someone want to go up the trail and find a place to camp? I think our trek's done for today." Her voice changed, a little. Maybe even unconsciously. "Anyone?"

"We'll check," Todd said, after the silence had lengthened and become uncomfortable. "C'mon, babe." He reseated his rope and moved past them, the rest drawing aside to let him by. "See if we can find a crick, too. Need some water for that."

Kerry suppressed a smile. Just like that Dar had stepped into the void of leadership, and even Todd, the asshole, had accepted it. "Let's get you moved into the shade," Kerry said. "Give me a hand, guys." She waved the rest of the group forward. "Over there, against the wall in case some other wildlife decides to come flying at us."

Dave joined her immediately and he and Kerry carefully helped Janet up.

"Let's get the rest of the gear up here," Dar said to the rest of the them. "C'mon." She turned and started down the path and they all followed, with an air of something like relief.

THE SUN WAS starting to go behind the rock walls when Todd and Amy returned. Rich had just finished an awkward attempt at stitching up Janet's knee, and it was hard to say which one of them had suffered more from it. Janet won points, however, for grit as she had her mouth and eyes clamped shut and made no sound of discomfort.

They were all gathered in the wide area of the trail, the supplies piled up around them for a meager kind of protection.

Todd went right over to Dar. "We're screwed," he said without preamble. "There's a cave up ahead, but no one's gonna make it up to the entrance except maybe me and Amy. It's thirty foot up. This is pretty much as good as it'll get." He indicated the wide area.

"You can't use the cave anyway," Tracy said. "That's a medicine cave. It's off limits."

"Okay," Dar said. "Let's make the best shelter we can in case it starts raining again." She eyed Todd. "Cave nearby?" He nodded. "Let me go look at it."

"I said you can't use it," Tracy repeated.

Dar turned and regarded her. "If it's between some rule, and survival, the rule loses," she said, flatly. "Besides if they get pissed at us maybe they'll report us and we can get the hell out of here." She motioned Todd to move forward and he did, with a smirk.

"That's not cool." Tracy frowned, but made no move to interfere, and instead started rummaging in the supplies for a folded tarp.

Kerry looked around. "I'm going to go find whatever wood I can to make a fire," she said. "Anyone up for that?" She was pleased when Rich and Dave joined her, and two of the crew as well. They trooped up the path, to where there was an outcropping of weathered trees and scrub grass visible.

DAR STARED UP at the side of the cliff, where the entrance to the cave was very visible. "Huh."

"No one's getting up there," Todd said, both hands clenched around the rope still circling his neck. "I mean most of those dipshits won't." He regarded the wall thoughtfully. "There's some hand holds."

Dar folded her arms over her chest. "Yeah, I can't see it happening," she said, with a regretful sigh.

Dar looked to the left of the entrance, where a splash of green was visible. "That water?"

Todd looked where she was pointing. "Maybe."

"That might be more useful than the cave." Dar started toward it. "Let's find out." She started up off the pathway, through a slide of rocks toward the bottom of the wall.

"Right behind ya." Todd started up the slope after her, his climbing shoes giving him solid purchase. "Don't have to ask me twice."

Closer to the wall, Dar could now see pictographs, faded and yet with pungent color against the flat part of the wall. "That say keep out?"

Todd just laughed.

KERRY GAVE THE rope tied to the edge of the tarp a tug, and stepped back. The blue fabric was providing a bit of shelter, enough to cover where they were sitting. Janet was laying on a folded piece of canvas, and Pete was curled up on his side next to her, in obvious pain.

Not good. Kerry went over to where they'd dropped their harvest of wood, and both Rich and Dave were putting stones in a circle in preparation to using it.

They heard the scuff of boots and looked up to find Dar and Todd returning, both holding water bottles that dripped faintly on the rocky ground.

"Good news," Dar said. "We found some water." She held up the bottle. "Might want to get everything filled up."

Several of the crew stood up and came over, looking relieved. "We've got purification tabs," Tracy said. "Where is it?"

"Just below that cave," Dar said. "It's coming out of a crack in the wall. You can see the green stuff near it."

Tracy grabbed her water bottle and headed off with the rest of the crew behind her, and a scattering of the passengers. Dar came over to where Kerry was and they stood together in silence for a few moments.

"Really hope it doesn't rain," Kerry said.

"Me too," Dar said. "Now we have three people we have to carry out of here. Don't need any other bad luck."

Kerry regarded the stone circle. "Do you know...oh, yes, that's right you do. I remember you started the fire on the island when we were there the last time."

"I do," Dar said. "But most of these people do too, and I'm better at using a soldering iron." She steered Kerry back over to the shelter, sitting down on a bit of rock outcropping near where she'd spotted their duffel bag.

They were at the end of the tarp, in a small bit of ground that had been cleared of pebbles. They sat down next to each other regarding their surroundings with simultaneous sighs.

Janet heard them. She eased herself over, keeping her leg outstretched. She waved them off as they started to get up to go to her instead.

They settled back down and waited, as she got herself arranged. Her leg was covered with thick bandages but there was a line of dried blood that had seeped through. "This sucks," she said, simply. "Thanks for finding water and getting things sorted out. I hope my severance pay is going to cover taking out these stitches."

She seemed resigned. "I just wanted to tell you both how sorry I am this happened. I know what it's like to wait for a vacation and have something go wrong."

Dar removed one of the remaining packets of crackers from her bag and opened it, handing two of the crackers to Janet and two to Kerry.

Kerry paused to consider. "Yeah, it does kinda suck, not only for us, but for everyone else. Your crew as well."

"It does," Janet said. "I'm worried about Doug, and Josh, and now Pete." She glanced over at the young man, curled in almost a fetal position. "That must really hurt."

"Janet." Dar cleared her throat a little. "This stuff doesn't happen much, does it?"

The woman sighed. "We have rollovers, sure," she said. "It's a wild location, you know? We have stings and knee cuts, and that sort of thing. But all this?" She looked around and shook her head. "No. In my ten years on the river I've never had anything close to this happen."

"Hm." Dar grunted thoughtfully.

"Hm." Kerry echoed her.

Far off they heard a soft rumble of thunder, and Janet sighed again, resting her head against her hand. "Just bad juju. I should have listened to my gut when that other team didn't show. Just started everything off wrong," she said. "But you know, everything was fine until the flood."

"It was," Kerry said. "We were having a great time. You all were doing a great job. And the weather, that wasn't your fault."

"Or the jerk going up into that cave," Dar said, suddenly. "That night."

Janet lifted her head. "What jerk...oh. Todd. Getting the natives pissed off at us..." She regarded them thoughtfully. "You know there is something to all that stuff. Tracy wasn't wrong saying not to mess with the medicine cave."

"Yeah," Dar said, after a moment. "You can call it medicine, or mojo, or karma, but what you put out in the world is generally what you get back from it."

Thunder rumbled again, and as they all looked out from under the tarp, dark clouds were now gathering and obscuring the deep blue sky.

KERRY PULLED HER waterproof jacket more tightly around her, huddling against the stone wall as the rain pelted them, the tarp providing little shelter against its wind driven deluge.

Dar was behind her, and as she shifted, her partner put both arms around her bringing a very welcome warmth against her back abating the shivers that had started. "This sucks."

"This sucks," Dar confirmed. "As in what did we do to deserve this kind of sucks." She glanced past Kerry, where all the rest of the group was looking miserable and wet, and the fire they'd hastily cooked some fish over was now washed out and down the slope.

It was cold. Most of the rest of the group was shivering and Dar could hear teeth chattering, even from where she was. She looked out in to the darkness and tried to think of some reasonable plan of action and found herself coming up empty.

Even climbing up into the cave at this point, was a nonstarter.

Even in dry weather, it was probably a nonstarter. Dar started to consider the very real possibility that they were in true trouble, with little she could do about it.

On the other side of them was Janet. Beside her was Tracy and two more crew members. Then Todd and Amy, Rich and his gang, PJ and the college kids, then the rest of the crew. They had pulled down the front of the tarp as much as possible, but there was no real protection from the weather even with all the coolers piled in front of them.

No one was sleeping. Everyone was miserable, even Todd, who had put on a waterproof poncho and was sheltering Amy under it.

No smartass remarks. Everyone, in fact, looked more than a little scared.

Dar considered that. She hugged Kerry a little more firmly, watching the faint outline of her profile in the weak light from the lantern they'd left going. Her expression was calm, dealing with the discomfort in a stolid kind of way characteristic to her nature.

Kerry wasn't a whiner. Never had been. Dar had recognized that from the start, from the beginning when she'd thrown all kinds of business bullshit at her and had only gotten back either determination or anger.

There'd been a toughness there she hadn't understood until much later, after they'd fallen in love and become partners.

"Know what?" Kerry said, half turning so she was facing Dar. She snuggled up next to her and reached over to wipe some rain off Dar's nose, gazing at her damp profile with gentle affection.

"What?" Dar smiled a little.

"So, freaking glad we timed this to avoid our periods."

Dar started laughing in pure, surprise reflex. "Wasn't expecting that comment."

"Could you freaking imagine?" Kerry sighed. "C'mon, Dar. Gotta take the good where you find it, you know?"

Dar touched her forehead to Kerry's. "I know."

"What's so funny?" Janet asked, softly. "I could use a joke."

Kerry looked over her shoulder. "I was just telling Dar I was so freaking glad we missed that time of the month."

Janet also reflexively laughed, reaching up to cover her mouth. "We use birth control pills." She murmured. "But yeah, what a horror show that would be." She pulled her hat more firmly down on her head and looked out at the weather. "Shit."

Kerry relaxed a bit, the shivers working out of her as Dar's body heat drove them out. She leaned her head against Dar's shoulder, catching a scent of sun block she now wished they still needed to have on. She looked up to watch Dar's face, as she looked out at the storm. A lightning bolt struck somewhere relatively close by and lit the area up in silver.

She saw Dar's eyes pop wide open, pale blue irises ochre in the dim light. "What?"

Dar pointed past her. "What the hell was that?" She asked Janet.

"What?" Janet repeated, in a flustered tone. "I didn't see anything. What did you see?"

Dar's whole body went rigid, as she peered out into the rainy darkness, the muscles around her eyes tensing, and on the side of her face moving her ears forward.

Kerry watched her in fascination. It was pitch black past the lantern and she knew there wasn't anything there for her to see if she looked. "What did you see?" she whispered.

"Some big cat," Dar said immediately. "Big as in, bigger than me." She started to untangle herself from Kerry, hand scrabbling in her pocket for her folding knife. "Like a panther or something."

"What?" Janet yelled, hearing her. "Did you just say you saw a cat?" She started to haul herself to her feet, grimacing in pain. "Mountain lion! Everyone watch out!"

"Fuck!" Tracey and Rich both stood up. "Smell that?" Tracey said. "She's right!"

Now they could all smell it, a musky scent brought in on the rain and in a moment the camp was in chaos. Dar got to her feet and got in front of Kerry with her small knife unfolded in one hand.

"What are you going to do with that, Tarzan?" Kerry muttered. "Where's my shotgun when I need it?"

Todd staggered to his feet, bleary eyed. He and Dave went to the front of the tarp and looked nervously out. "Don't see anything."

"Maybe we scared it off," Dave said.

Todd stooped down and picked up a rock, about the size of his head, and hefted it, throwing it overhanded into the darkness. They heard it hit the ground. On the next flash of lightning, all eyes stared hard at the path and found it empty.

"That was a good idea," Kerry said.

"The rock?"

"Yeah." Kerry moved out from her somewhat ineffective knife wielding partner and used her boots to kick over a few rocks toward where they'd been sitting.

Dar folded up the knife and put it in her pocket then went and joined Rich, Dave, and Todd at the point in the tarp, closest to the fire circle, where they were all standing and staring out into the dark.

"You sure it was a big cat?" Rich asked. "Not just, like a bobcat I mean?"

Dar half shut her eyes. "It was kind of either silver or goldish," she said. "It was hunkered down, but it had a round head not the whiskery kind."

"Huh."

"And it had a tail," Dar concluded. "It was moving back and forth."

"Definitely not a bobcat," Rich said sadly. "But boy, you've got a pair of eyes on ya." He looked at Dar with respect. "Even with the lightning."

Dar was still studying the path, as lightning flashes periodically lit in the distance now. "Photographic memory," she said absently. "Useful sometimes."

Tracey came over to them and pulled her hood up around her face. "I don't smell anything now," she said. "Holy shit that was scary. Good job throwing that rock, sir."

Todd glanced at her. "It's still out there," he said. "What if it comes back?" He picked up another rock and went out into the rain, heading for the spot Dar had seen the cat.

Rich folded his arms. "Guy has balls," he said. "Wouldn't catch me going out after something like that." He looked over at Dave. "But he's got a point, should we do something? Put up some..." He looked around. "Well, there isn't much we can do I guess."

Dar also looked around. "Not much," she said. "We've already piled up the supplies best we can. I guess we can..." She paused. "I guess we can hope the sun comes up sooner rather than later."

"Mm." Rich went back to where Sally was crouching next to Janet, the rest of the group now on their feet and moving around. "Least it's warmer now that I'm up," he remarked back over his shoulder.

"Point." Dar retreated to where Kerry was still studiously piling rocks and looked around in their gear. She picked up the folded hiking sticks and assembled them, propping them against the wall as Kerry straightened up next to her. "Probably more useful than my pocketknife."

Kerry leaned against her. "Hon, the fact that you got out there with that thing and would have done your best with it is truly a definition of your macha. Kind of like you going after that ghost in the buff."

Dar had to laugh, a low chortling noise that was almost obscured by the rain.

"Oh, my God are we going to get ribbed by the staff when we get back," Kerry said, folding her arms and leaning next to Dar against the rock wall. "Almost as bad as our last vacation."

"Yeah." Dar draped one arm over her shoulders. She looked down the wall as the rest of the group repositioned, moving closer to each other. The crew shifted the heavy coolers that had their supplies, making sure they were closed tightly.

She checked her watch. "Three a.m.." She ran her fingers through her damp hair as Kerry put both arms around her and give her a hug. She returned it, and they stood together in silence as Todd came back under the tarp, dripping rain from every surface.

"Nothin," he said. "I checked both ways." He paused. "Found this up the path." He held up a sodden piece of fabric and handed it to Janet. "Guess the cat was chewing at it."

Janet examined the item. "Bring the lantern over, will you Tracey?"

Everyone drifted over and watched as Tracey unhooked the light and brought it over, kneeling next to Janet. "What is it?"

"Backpack," Janet said, briefly. The item was torn and tattered and covered in mud, and she carefully inspected it. "Could have been one of ours," she said, in quiet tone.

"Let me see it." Tracey took the item and leaned close, squinting at it. Then she shrugged and handed it back." It could be, but half the whoohah out here uses these."

"It's true," Janet said. She checked all the compartments, but they were empty. "Nothing there." She put the ragged pack down. "We're about three hours from dawn. We better keep a watch."

"I'll light the other lantern," Dave said and went to the pile of supplies. "Too bad it's raining. Fire'd be better."

The crew went to the line of supplies and picked up whatever they could in the way of sticks and poles. Todd went back to where Amy was seated and took a seat himself, smirking a little when she squeezed his bicep and patted it.

Everyone slid to the center a little, closing ranks.

Dar and Kerry slowly took a seat again, the damp and soggy bedroll at least giving them some padding on the hard rock ground. After a moment, Dar took hold of their hiking sticks and handed one over, then put hers on her lap, putting one hand around it's handle and the other arm around Kerry.

"Everyone get some rest if you can. We need to move tomorrow." Janet said, with as much authority as she could muster.

"If we don't get eaten tonight," Todd said mockingly.

"Got a better plan?" Janet shot back. "Since you've got an answer for everything?"

The rain pattered down in a sudden silence. Kerry turned her head to watch Dar, since she felt the faint shift in the body next to hers.

Dar cleared her throat. "C'mon people. We don't have enough crap flying you need to upchuck into the wind?"

"Yeah," Rich said immediately. "Just shut up."

Silence fell again and Dar waited a moment, then she settled back against the wall with a sigh, as Kerry gave her a little pat on the side. "Peh."

"We're in a tough place, hon." Kerry nestled closer. "Usually when you and I are in tough places we just let our brains do the heavy lifting." She looked out into the rain. "It's really annoying not having all the skill sets, you know?"

"But we do," Dar responded in almost a whisper. "At least as much as the rest of these people do."

Kerry thought about that in silence for a few minutes. "You got those fish," she said.

"You found that salt," Dar said. "You cooked the fish. You herded that sheep."

"Oh, Dar, I shoved the sheep. C'mon." Kerry chuckled.

"You put your knee into its ribcage and made it move. How did you know that?"

Kerry frowned, her eyes narrowing a little as she remembered that moment when she'd reached for that animal in a total confidence whose genesis she really couldn't understand. "I have no darn clue," she admitted. "Maybe I was Little Bo Peep in a former life?"

Dar chuckled faintly.

"Dar?" Kerry lifted her head a little. "You think maybe the reason those sheep were running was because they knew that cat was here?"

"Maybe," Dar said. "I just wish it was morning."

In the distance, they suddenly heard a scattering of rocks come down the path, and everyone surged upright who could, but there was nothing else behind them.

Chapter Eight

"I FEEL LIKE a cold old toad," Kerry said. She rubbed her hands together as she cautiously eased her head out from under the edge of the tarp and studied the sky. It was still overcast.

She peeled out of her rain slicker, but everything she had on was damp and she felt waterlogged and uncomfortable, glad at least she'd gotten an hour or two of sleep out of it.

Nearby, Sally and Tracey started a fire with what wood they'd scrounged and saved. With it they could warm up some water at least for the teabags they'd brought along. Todd, Rich and Dave had taken a walk up the path to check it for storm brought obstacles, and the rest of the gang was working on packing up things so they could move on.

The biggest problem was going to be their now three injured members. PJ had resumed her hastily made crutches, and Janet was gamely limping around on her cut leg, but Pete was unable to stand, much less walk. Even rolling over was painful for him.

Marcia knelt next to him, examining his back. Don and Dar were lashing together the tarp poles to make a litter. At least they hadn't been eaten by a mountain lion during the rest of the very long night.

Kerry went over to the longest of the coolers and pried the lid up, revealing some of their salted fish. She removed one of them and closed the top, placing the fish on it and retrieving the metal plate they'd used as a frying pan.

There was rain in a bucket nearby, and she used it to dunk the fish, cleaning off the salt coating as best she could. She used a piece of wood with a flat edge to manipulate it before lifting it up to let it drain then putting it back on the metal.

She then took out her small folding knife and cut the fish into pieces to make it easier to cook. She heard them striking sparks for the fire nearby, and was glad that she'd had one of her protein bars to start with.

Amy came over to her and put down a big double handful of dried berries. "I had these," she said. "Thought we should share."

"Sure, why not?" Kerry said. "they'll give some flavor to this stuff."

Sally detoured over and plunked down an open can of mushrooms. "And I found this."

"Mushrooms, berries and fish," Kerry said. "I think I'm starting to feel like a bear, which is better than an old cold toad, anyway."

"What?"

"Never mind. Just talking to myself." Kerry finished her cutting and moved the piece of metal over to where they'd lit a fire. She balanced the metal on top and retrieved a bit of metal tent prop and started moving it around.

Sally shoved a metal water pot between two of the stones. "We're earning our camping badges today, huh?"

Kerry eyed her in somewhat puzzled silence.

"C'mon, Kerry. Don't tell me you weren't a Girl Scout." Sally stood up and dusted her hands off.

"I wasn't a Girl Scout," Kerry said. "I don't think Dar was either."

Dar put her pocketknife away as she came closer to investigate what was going on. "Was what?"

"A Girl Scout."

Both of Dar's dark eyebrows shot up. "No," she said, with a brief laugh. "I got my camping skills the hard way."

She went over and felt the bedroll they'd crouched on all night, finding it unpleasantly cold and clammy to the touch. "Yuk." She picked it up and started wringing it out bit by bit with powerful twists of her hands.

Kerry continued her stirring. "Dar grew up on a couple of Navy bases," she explained to Sally. "Probably weren't many troops in the area."

"Ah." Sally nodded. "And you?"

"I grew up between backwoods Michigan and Washington DC." Kerry smiled a little. "I'm sure there were Girl Scouts in the area, but they weren't on my parents radar for me."

"Oh. So, you had family in the government?"

"My father, and now my mother, in fact, were and are Senators," Kerry said. "When my father passed on, my mother took his seat, and now I think she's going to run for reelection."

"Huh." Sally removed the tea bags from the plastic casing they'd put them in. "Was that weird?"

Kerry stirred and considered. "Didn't seem weird at the time, but probably it was. It's like anything else I guess, it's what you get used to."

"True. My folks were serious hippies," Sally said. "That's how I ended up from Colorado. My dad's a health store manager and mom's an astrologer." She chuckled at Kerry's slightly wide-eyed reaction. "All I got from that was the vegetarian deal, and like you said, it's just what you get used to. I never ate anything but vegan until I went to school."

Kerry chuckled in response. "Dar's folks are, respectively, retired Navy special forces and an artist," she said. "A pagan artist who's vegetarian, matter of fact."

"That must be a story."

"It is." Kerry poured the drained mushrooms into the fish and listened to it sizzle. "But they're awesome people. I guess they were so used to being different, that my and Dar's relationship didn't even faze them a bit. They were all in."

"Lucky."

"I know it." Kerry judged if the canned mushrooms were warmed through, then she went back and got the berries to add to the pan. She turned the pieces of fish a few more times, then moved the piece of metal off the stone. "Come and get it."

Dar sidled over and inspected the impromptu fish hash. She eyed Kerry dubiously.

"C'mon." Kerry scooped some up onto one of the cracked plates and moved aside, as the rest of the gang came over to take some. She took a forkful, then offered one to Dar. "it's not bad."

Dar gingerly accepted the taste, and chewed it, then made a low grunting noise and picked up her own fork. "it's not." She swallowed the mouthful. "I like the berries."

"This is good," Amy said. "It's just like what we like to eat out in the wild. No fake stuff." She had her pack already at her feet and her hair tied up in a bun at the top of her head. She was wearing the odd-looking footgear again and she idly kicked a small rock with one of her toes.

Sally took a seat on a cooler and stolidly chewed on her fish. "Those for climbing?" she asked.

"They are. They have really grippy soles." Amy turned one over for inspection. "And they conform to your foot. Only downside is they're better for climbing than hiking."

Marcia came over to them. "Hey," she lowered her voice. "That kid's got a real problem with his back. There's a lump there the size of a baseball."

Sally grimaced. "Ow. Probably cracked something in there."

"Probably," Marcia said. But he's in a lot of pain. I did that to my elbow once." She held up one arm, and pointed to her joint. "They had to operate to relieve the pressure. Was no fun at all." She looked at her husband, who had wandered over. "How are you doing, honey?"

"Doing all right." Don touched the side of his head where a lump had been, and where now he had scabs. "Got a tough skull." He picked up a plate and took some of the fish. "Hope we can make some good time today. Not looking forward to another night like that."

"Nobody is," Sally said. "Hey, Rich! Get some chow!"

IT WAS SLOW getting started. Between the waterlogged material, and sorting out carrying things, it was almost noon before they got moving along the path. The pace was slow because of the injured, and the need to carry supplies. Rich and Dar were in the lead, with Todd and Kerry right behind them. Don and Marcia were just a few steps back.

So far the clouds remained dormant, but the winds blew fitfully against them as they walked past the cave they'd found the night before.

They were quiet, and their steps scraped softly against the sandy ground. Dar shifted the duffel on her back, feeling the dampness still in it. She looked up at the walls. They were pretty, but there was too much worry and discomfort to really enjoy them. Even Kerry had left her camera in its bag, and walked along, eyes on the ground.

Dar reached up to touch a bit of the wall she was going past, and felt a moment of somewhat irrational loss. "Bummer."

"Yeah," Kerry said, in a mournful tone. "I'd rather be back on the river where the worst thing I had to worry about was you being bored."

The path curved between two rock formations and then bent around to the right. The rock-strewn path started to trend a little downward. Dar saw markings up on the left hand wall and pointed her walking stick at them. "Native?"

Rich looked up. "Hard to say," he said. "Some of the stuff is real, and some of the stuff...I think they put some stuff up for the tourists, you know?"

Dar grimaced.

"This is one of the trails they use in the summer a lot." Rich evaded the implicit criticism. "So, they start with a climb down the canyon wall and then they end up on the river, there, where we came out, and they pick up a raft there."

"Huh." Dar gently booted a stone out of the path. "I guess by the time you get down here you're looking forward to riding a while."

"Exactly," Rich said. "Mostly they camp one night up by the shack, have a nice barbecue, then get on a paddle style raft to go the last few days. It's a fun hike. I've done something like it."

Dar imagined doing it, and had to suppress a smile. "To be honest, I'd rather stick to boats and underwater gigs. I won't lie. I'd rather be diving right now."

She imagined being on their boat, coming up from a dive and throwing her fins onto the deck, feeling the warmth of the sun as she sat down and unfastened the gear strapped to her back. She sighed and glanced around, wistfully wanting the smell of salt water around her.

"Guess it's what you're used to," Rich said, with an amiable shrug. "That always seemed so...I don't know. Technical I guess. For this you just need your feet, and maybe a stick." He cleared his throat a little. "Okay, we go down to the left hand side now. See the marker?"

Dar did, in fact see the curved arrow scratched into the rock ahead at a crossroads of the path. "Where does the other side go?"

Dave caught up to them and was now peering past. "Oh...that's where we are?" He nodded. "Yeah, that other branch goes to a dead end in the path, I think, and a nice overlook."

Calls from behind them made them all pause, and look back. "What's up?" Dar called over to Sally, who was just at the curve in the path.

"They're changing bearers," Sally yelled forward. "Ten minute break."

"Hey, then let's go see the overlook," Dave suggested. "Might as well." He gestured to the other path. "It's not far."

"Good idea," Sally said. "Maybe Kerry can get some pictures." She waved forward Amy and Todd, who came striding forward to join them. "We're going to see the overlook down there."

"Why not?" Todd said. "Let them figure it out back there. That kid's crying like a baby." He shouldered past Dave and started toward the right hand side.

The group of them proceeded on down the trail, as Kerry caught up. "Making lemonade?"

"Might as well," Dar said. "They said this path leads to a nice view."

Kerry got her camera out and hung it around her neck. She looked down at the rain-washed ground and paused to pick up a small stone and put it in her pocket. "Hey I'll take a view if I can get it."

The right hand path was rocky, and a little steep, but they made it up to a boulder at the peak of the slope and then Todd stopped abruptly. "Whoa."

Dar was right behind him and looked past his muscular frame. She jerked a little as a puff of wind blew against her face, bringing the smell of death with it. "What... "She eased past Todd and stepped over some fallen rocks as the rest of the group scrambled after her.

There was a bundle of debris near the edge of the drop off. As Dar reached it a cloud of flies dispersed, and she dodged in reflex. She poked at the bundle and it spread a little, exposing a bone.

"Oh shit." Todd knelt near a rock nearby and now he stood up and pointed. Rolled up against the stone was a roundish object cracked in two. "That's a fucking head." Todd backed away from the skull and uncertainly stood nearby.

They all froze in place. Then Kerry went over to where Dar was standing and stared wide- eyed at the scene. Shock was obvious on every face, and for a long moment there was only stunned silence, and the buzzing of flies.

"Okay," Dar finally said. "Someone please go get one of the crew." She very gently moved a bit of torn cloth with the tip of her climbing stick. "Because I think this was one of their shirts." The tip rested on a colorful bit of fabric stained in blood.

"Oh, my God." Sally turned and raced back up the path, as Rich, and Dave and Amy slowly moved down toward them. They gathered together in a clump a few feet away from the remains. Only barely recognizable as a human figure, the flies were busy buzzing around what was left.

A pair of tattered shorts. A half-chewed boot. The skull with scraps of hair still attached. A mostly chewed up leather wallet near the fall off.

"Oh, Dar," Kerry murmured. "So that pack... "

"Probably," Dar said somberly.

Tracey came leaping over the boulder, with Sally and Don at her heels. She skidded to a halt in the gravel, staring at the remains. "Oh fuck, no." She came around and dropped to her bare knees, uncaring. She picked up the piece of cloth, the company patch stained but visible. "Oh fuck."

Todd came over to Dar's side and folded his arms across his chest, his usual attitude suppressed. "Damn," he muttered. "You figure it was that cat?"

"Figure it was something hungry," Dar replied quietly. "Like they reminded us, it's the wild out here."

Todd exhaled. "This just went down hard." He put his arm around Amy, who had walked slowly over, her hand covering her mouth. "We got lucky last night."

"Yeah," Dar said. "We need a better plan. No more making it up as we go along."

"Yeah," Both Todd and Kerry answered in concert. "No more leaving it to someone else either," Kerry added. "We need to get out of here."

THEY SAT IN a close huddle, Janet with her cut leg extended out awkwardly as she held the patch, and the half-shredded wallet in her hands.

Dar stood at the edge of the circle. "So, I think it bears stating, though most everyone here realizes, that we need to shelter in some place that's protected at the end of the day. We don't know what attacked Josh. But if it attacked him, it could attack us."

"Yeah," Janet said. "But I've never heard of that happening before."

"I have," Tracey said. "We just don't hear much about that on the river. I've heard about it from the canyon hikers."

"It's true," Rich said. He was seated on the ground, his arms wrapped around his knees. "The hikes I've taken, we knew. About mountain lions, and coyotes, and all that. The guides usually had guns." He looked at Janet.

"We don't do guns. The management is not a fan." Janet said. "It's a political thing." She turned the patch over in her fingers. "But really, on the river there's no point."

"So, what are we going to do with him?" Tracey asked. "What's left of him?"

There was an awkward silence. "We can't bury him. They'll just dig it back up and eat the rest," Todd said. "Surprised we didn't find any vultures here."

Kerry sat on a rock, leaning her forearms on her knees. "We can cremate what's left." She suggested. "With the pack and everything."

Don nodded. "That's a good idea," he said. "Not just leave him."

"Any wood we use for that, we could use to cook with," Todd said. "Does it pay to waste it?"

There was another minute of awkward silence. Dar was the

one who finally answered. "Yes, it does. It's worth it to me even, if I have to spend the whole night finding more wood, to know I paid respect to someone who died trying to save us."

Todd shrugged. Everyone else looked relieved and nodded in agreement. Kerry reached back to circle her arm around Dar's leg and give it a squeeze.

"So, let's get moving on that," Dar said. "Find some wood, get it done, move on to some place we can shelter safely."

More nods.

Janet slowly struggled to her feet. "Let's go. I think I saw a bristlecone in that last crevice. We can use that."

Everyone was glad to escape the horror that the overlook had become. But waiting for the path to clear Kerry walked over to the edge of the space and looked out over the dusty valley the other path descended into. There wasn't much to be seen, just off gray walls and rocks. At the bottom, in the corner, she saw a small lake whose surface was faintly rippled by the wind.

She imagined Josh standing there, looking out, possibly choosing this spot to rest in She took a breath and released it. Then turned and made her way back past the sad remains of the bright, friendly kid she'd talked with. She joined Dar at the top of the path. "This sucks."

"This sucks," Dar said. "I'm damn sorry for him. Poor kid."

Kerry exhaled. "I hope it was fast. I hope he didn't even realize it happened." She stared back at the fly ridden pile. "I hope he was just looking at something pretty, and then it was over, and his soul went up to God."

Dar put her arms around her and rested her chin on Kerry's head, giving her a silent hug.

"That he wasn't scared and looking into that animal's eyes when it hit him. He was so young."

Dar hugged her again.

Kerry remained silent for a moment, then she looked up. "Do you believe in God, Dar?" She studied the light crystal clarity of Dar's eyes, as Dar considered the question somberly. "You said once, that you believed in something."

"I don't know exactly what I believe in," Dar finally answered. They heard the others returning with the wood. "But I hope he's in a nice place, if there is a place. He was a good kid." She met Kerry's eyes. "And I hope he never knew what happened too."

Kerry studied her in pensive silence.

"Does it matter, if I believe?" Dar asked, after a long moment.

"It only matters that we go to heaven together." Kerry smiled, briefly. "Whatever that takes."

Dar hugged her. "No problem," she reassured Kerry. "Noooo problem."

THE AIR WAS damp, and a little cool, following them down the path as they moved in a silent straggle away from the small rock plateau.

Kerry was convinced she still smelled the acridness of it, and hear the crack and slight pop as the remains were consumed by fire. She felt more than a little sick. She walked along at Dar's heels, her eyes on the path, one hand tucked into the shoulder strap of the bags she was carrying.

No one was talking. Just behind her they were carrying the stretcher that Pete was lying on, his intakes of breath audible when they jarred him. PJ and Janet helped each other along in grim silence.

The sun started to head to the edge of the canyon, sliding out from behind the clouds briefly and then disappearing, sending faint and fitful spears of light down to splash across the rock.

The path was narrow, but as they got a bit farther down into the canyon it spread out and Kerry moved up to walk next to Dar. She turned her head to look up at her partner's somber profile as she came up next to her. "Hey."

"Hey."

Kerry adjusted her shoulder strap a little and remained silent, content to watch their hiking boots move in paired rhythm along the dusty ground. She wondered how much longer they would need to walk before they found a place to stop.

Or would they?

She looked ahead down the path, which wound downward and then bent to the left under an arched overhang between the two canyon walls. It was dusty and shade after shade of ochre and coral, only occasional wispy shrubs and grasses edging the path.

At the bottom the ground changed from dusty to damp. She saw greenery as they reached the bottom of the canyon, and water, slowly seeping into the rocks, but still standing from the rain of the night before.

Dar glanced behind them and then looked forward. "Hold up, folks!" She called ahead. "Let's take a break."

The bearers put down their burdens and sat down, as the

group all gathered along the path. Sally pushed the toe of her boot into a patch of mud and looked back the way they'd come. "Not much cover anywhere near here."

"No," Janet said. "A few slot canyons ahead though. There's one to the right hand side, maybe two hours up."

Dave nodded. "I saw that on the map."

Kerry walked over to where Marcia and Don were sitting on one of the big coolers. "How are you guys doing?" She took a seat on the edge of the box.

"Not bad," Marcia said. "Don and I do a lot of hiking at home, so this isn't too hard on us. I can't really concentrate though, after what happened to that poor boy." She kept her voice low. "I just feel so bad."

"Mm." Don said. "I just don't understand, myself. If they knew about these animals, to let him go alone."

That question also occurred to Kerry. She studied the damp ground. "This is their first trip this year. Maybe they didn't know. Maybe it's new?"

Don pursed his lips thoughtfully. He had a lined and craggy face, with deeply tanned skin. "Could be," he said. "I thought it would be nice, you know? To be on the first trip, but I think I was wrong about that." He dusted his hands off. "You don't know what you don't know."

"Oh, c'mon, honey," Marcia said. "You couldn't have known this whole thing would go like it did. Let's just keep our minds on what we're doing and we'll be fine."

Kerry smiled at her. Then she glanced to her left where Pete was lying on his side. "Hang in there."

He opened one eye and peered at her. "Jesus Christ this hurts. I feel like my whole body's on fire."

Marcia got up and came over. "Do you want some water, hon?" She knelt by his side. "Let's see if we can get you some."

Dar wandered to the front of the group, where Todd and Amy were seated on a rock, staring off into the distance with bored expressions. "You think we'll find some place to hole up?" She asked, in a casual tone.

Todd shrugged. "If not we can throw that derpy kid to the lion. Buy us some time." He thumped his heels against the rock.

Dar eyed him. "Really?"

He shrugged again. "Survival. You want to have it eat you instead?"

"I'd rather we all make it," Dar said dryly. "I don't want to end up as a footnote on a movie of the week."

Todd stared at her, then he laughed. "Hey, maybe we'll get to be cannibals. He can be our long pig."

Dar moved past him and down the path, examining the rock wall and running her thumb over the surface as she slowly looked around at the narrow crevice they were moving through. Open to the sky, but enclosed. She missed the ability to see any distance.

She imagined what it must look like from above, these narrow channels in the canyon like a maze. That would make them rats in one. She wished they were out of it, and out of this, and on their way home.

She looked up as the sun emerged for a moment, and bathed her in light, a comforting touch of warmth on her shoulders and she relaxed into it.

A scuff of boots against the rock made her look to her left. She wasn't really surprised to find Kerry there.

They looked at each other and Dar smiled a little, because she knew they were thinking the same thing, at the same time, for the same reason. The brief wrinkle of Kerry's nose acknowledge that. She reached casually over and brushed Kerry's hair from her eyes and felt her lips nibble gently at the skin on her palm as it passed.

"Miss our waterbed," Kerry said.

"I'd take an air mattress at this point. Or the futon in that RV," Dar said. "Or actually just some privacy," she added, after a little pause.

Dar heard the crew stirring behind them, starting to take up their burdens again. Sally and Rich traded off backpacks, and the rest stood up and got ready to move on. "Time to hike."

They both sighed, and Kerry glanced at the ground, a faint tinge of blood coloring her cheeks that deepened a little when Dar reached over and tickled her nose. "Long day."

"With no sleep." Dar turned and leaned next to Kerry against the wall and they stood in the sunlight together until it faded out behind the clouds and a gust of wind replaced it.

They started off along the path that dipped down and the rasp of their steps went from a dry scrape to a wet sounding thumping. As they came around the bend in the path, they heard a rumble far off. With a glance upward, Dar increased her pace a little, as she stepped over a crack in the path that had a trickle of water draining down into it.

An hour of steady hiking later, it appeared they were going to keep walking the path until dark. Walls were rising on either side of them and presenting no real shelter to speak of. The wind was getting more fitful, and gustier, as the clouds kept gathering overhead.

Dar looked around for any possible protection, with Don at her side, when they heard a yell from behind that brought them all to a halt.

Tracey came trotting forward. "Todd saw something."

Don's brows creased. "That can mean pretty much anything. Good or bad, usually bad."

They went back along the trail until they came to where the rest of the group was clustered, and Todd pointed over their heads to one of the walls. "What is it?" Dar said.

"Waterfall, there," Todd said. "Maybe a cave or something at the base. There's a side canyon there, up this split." He looked past the gap in the path leading off to the left. Just a space between two folds in the canyon, with discolored ground leading out and down where water had recently run.

Dar studied the wall. "Let's go find out," she said. "Let these folks rest." She turned and started up the new path and Todd, Rich and Dave hustled after her, with Kerry at their heels. Don rejoined Marcia back where the tired team was settling down and huddling close as the light began to fade.

Janet sat down on a cooler, with PJ next to her, giving up all pretense of leadership with an expression of almost guilty relief.

THE SLOT CANYON was narrow, and shadowed, the light only penetrating at the tops due to the depth. It was a little hot and stuffy, and the ground was bare of any sign of life.

After three or four twists, though, Dar felt a puff of fresher air and then the path opened a bit into a larger gap where the sound of the water was suddenly vivid. They came out into yet another canyon, teardrop shaped, with a closed end where the waterfall was gushing out and running downward into the ground at the far end.

There was no cave. But as Dar climbed up around the base of the wall where the water was still cascading, she saw some large rocks in a cluster and an overhang of stone that could be shelter. "We can put the supplies here, and then that only leaves that area open."

Todd looked at the meager, but present overhang of rock and nodded. "Sucks," he said. "But we're not going to find better." He turned around. "I'll go get the rest of them."

Rich and Dave started toward the base of the cliff. "Think I see some brush there," Rich called over his shoulder. "Get a fire going."

Kerry joined Dar near the wall. "At least we're up on a slope here," she said. "If it rains it'll drain downward and we won't be sitting in water all night." She unslung the bags on her back and set them down, stretching her body out and twisting from side to side.

"True." Dar examined the tumble of rocks. Then she looked up at the wall. "Guess this all came from up there." She inspected the overhang and gave one of the stones an experimental shove, but it seemed solidly anchored in the debris and not inclined to move.

Rich called out and they turned to see him and Dave coming back dragging what looked like an entire dead bristlecone pine tree behind them. "Look what we found." He produced a brief smile. "There's three of them at least, back in the corner there."

Which meant they would have fuel to keep a fire going. "Good job," Dar said. "Let's put a fire ring together," she said to Kerry. "Over there?" She pointed to a rough half circle on one side of the tumble of debris and they went over to it, booting the rocks center out to the edge.

The ground was sandy rather than rocky, and Dar paused for a moment, and then she unstrapped the duffel she was carrying and set it to one side, near the back wall, before she rejoined Kerry in sorting out the fire pit.

They gathered some head sized stones and put them into position, as the sound of the rest of the group arriving echoed behind them. Rich was just outside the shelter, breaking up the tree, and he called greetings to them, the words sounding over the cracking sound as he worked.

Don ducked past the overhang. "Well, it's no fancy cabin," he said. "But it's a hell of a lot better than nothing." He backed out of the way and motioned behind him. "C'mon in, kids. It is what it is."

The stretcher bearers carefully maneuvered inside and set Pete down.

"Better than last night," Tracey said, as she shook her hands out, looking exhausted. "And at least, we've got something around us."

Pete eased himself up to one elbow and looked around. "Yeah," he said. "Warmer too. I was so cold." He licked his lips. "I hope there's some tea left. I sure could use it." He leaned forward a little. "Or even hot water really."

"We can manage something," Kerry said. She looked at the cooler of fish. "I think I'm going to be ready for a cheeseburger when we get back to the RV, Dardar. Or maybe a pop tart."

"Moooo, me tooooo," Dar predictably responded. She picked up one of the plastic buckets. "I'll get some water." She walked down the slight slope to the side canyon the waterfall was falling into.

She could feel the mist as she got closer, and she licked her lips, tasting dust and minerals on the liquid as she stuck the bucket under it and let it collect, the spray randomly dampening her arms.

Just down slope, she spotted the crew managing to set up their camping loo, the poles that held up the tattered and almost ragged tarp around it bent and crooked. One of the crew looked up at Dar and shrugged and she gave him a thumbs-up for at least trying.

The previous night, they'd all just walked out into the rain and did what they had to do. Dar had felt a distinct envy for the men, who'd had a definite advantage. Even Pete, who couldn't walk, was able to do the needful since the driving rain just washed everything away.

They would be able, she hoped, to get more rest tonight. Her eyes felt sandy and sore, and though the hike hadn't been very strenuous, the lack of sleep was wearing on her. She was looking forward to being able to sit in relative comfort, preferably dry, tonight.

The bucket was full, and she started back down the slope to where they were making camp. Dar heard cries of pain. "What happened?" She asked Rich as she reached where he was standing.

"Pete," Rich said, briefly. "I think someone hit his back or something."

"You stupid piece of shit!" Tracey's voice echoed suddenly, in a raw angry tone. "I'm going to kick your ass!"

Dar sighed. "Oh boy. Just what we needed." She started for the shelter, and Rich came right after her, holding a large branch in one hand.

THE SCENE WAS unfortunately dramatic as Dar came around the side of the rock wall and skidded to a halt, the bucket of water splashing a little around her boots.

Pete was on the ground, writhing in pain and crying out. Tracey was standing over him, arms outstretched, face red with anger.

Todd stood with his hands lifted, palms outward, a smirk on his face.

Dar moved sideways to where Kerry stood, hands on hips. "What happened?"

"That asshole kicked Pete in the back," Kerry pronounced crisply. "Before you ask, for absolutely no good reason."

"He's just a fucking baby," Todd said. "I got tired of his whining."

Dar shifted her head just a little, tilting it as she stared at him. "So, you figured kicking him would make that stop? You're stupider than I gave you credit for." She put the bucket down and started walking toward him. "C'mere and let me kick you in the nuts. See if that helps your attitude."

Kerry hesitated, caught between wanting to comfort Pete and wanting to back Dar up, who actually didn't really need much backup.

"You can't touch me," Todd scoffed.

Dar's eyes twinkled, not with amusement. "Want to bet on that?" She came to a halt about a body length from him, and shifted her center of balance up over the balls of her feet, her knees unlocking and taking on a slight bend. "Last time someone thought that I ruptured their middle ear canal from this distance."

Todd stared at her intently.

"Hurting people who can't defend themselves is the act of a coward," Dar said in a quiet voice. "No one respects that."

"Ah, screw you all." Todd backed off and stomped out of the shelter, shaking his head. Amy hurried to keep up with him, turning to look at Dar as she passed, but remaining silent.

Dar relaxed as Kerry came past her and gave her a pat on the back. "I feel ya, hon. But honestly, do we need more hurt people? I've seen what that kick can do."

"Mmph." Dar grumbled. She followed Kerry over to where Tracey was now kneeling next to the rough litter and they both joined the young woman as she gently eased the sweatshirt Pete was wearing up and exposed his back. "Oh crap."

There was a lump on his spine about the size of a baseball, and bruising now extended on either side halfway across the small of his back. "That piece of shit," Tracey uttered. "I'm going to go smack him." She started to get up, but Kerry gently grabbed her arm. "Let me go."

"He's not worth it. Stay with your friend," Kerry said.

Tracey stared at her. "You were going to let her mix it." She pointed at Dar. "I can kick him just as fast, probably faster"

Kerry regarded her seriously. "Are you a black belt in martial arts?"

"No," Tracey admitted.

"Dar is. So, chill and let's see if we can help poor Pete." Kerry put her hand on his hip. "Wow, that's so swollen."

Dar was now kneeling next to her. "Probably why it hurts so much. Pressure," she said

Don came over to look over her shoulder. "Wow. I was a medic, back in the day. We might need to drain that." He very gently touched the skin above the bulge, getting a howl from Pete. "Easy, son. Try to relax, heh?" He got closer and removed his glasses from his vest pocket and put them on. "Don't suppose we have any first aid stuff left have we?"

"I'll check." Tracey got up and went over to the now stacked supplies, opening a plastic box and rooting inside it as the rest of the group slowly dispersed to set up the camp as best they could.

Kerry gave Pete a gentle scratch between his shoulders. "So sorry you have to suffer like this, Pete. It's not fair."

Pete was now half rolled on his stomach, his head resting on one arm. He looked back at her and smiled a little, tears visible in the lashes of his eyes. "I've never gotten hurt like this," he said. "I mean, you know, sprained my ankle, stuff like that, but nothing like this."

"I dislocated my shoulder once, and have had cracked ribs." Kerry scooted over a little to give Don space. "Of the two, the shoulder was worse." She offered him one of the water sacks that had a sip spout. "

Willing to be distracted, Pete focused on her. "How did it happen?"

"A building was collapsing on top of me," Kerry said. "I was trying to visit my sister, who was giving birth at the time, while avoiding seeing my parents, and something blew up."

Pete blinked at her. "For real?"

Kerry nodded. "For real. The ceiling came down on us and Dar had to put it back in place. My shoulder I mean. We were trying to get out ahead of a huge fire and not moving wasn't an option."

Don turned his head and looked at her, both eyebrows lifting.

"But it really hurt," Kerry said. "Still moves a little weird."

"What about the ribs?" Pete asked, peeking back at her.

Kerry's face scrunched up a little. "You know, I'm not

actually sure I can tell you about that. It might be classified." She glanced at Dar. "Is it?"

"Mm." Dar wrinkled her nose. "You can tell them you slipped and fell into the corner of a raised floor," she said. "I wouldn't mention where the raised floor was."

"Or about the rats."

"Now I'm dying to know," Pete said. "But thanks for distracting me."

Tracey came back with a plastic kit, and put it down next to Don. "Whatever we have is in there," she said. "Did you say you were in an explosion?" She asked Kerry. "Did I hear that?"

Dar got up and went over to the fire pit, helping Rich arrange the broken pieces of pine for the campfire. Dave came up and pitched in, both men watching her from the corner of their eyes. It was funny, a little. "That lump looks bad," she finally said.

"Yeah, poor kid," Dave said.

"You were really going to kick him?" Rich finally gave voice to the question they both obviously wanted to ask her. "I mean, he's a big guy."

Dar considered that, as she continued to break the smaller branches. "Well," she finally said. "Kerry's right. We don't need any more injuries. We might need him at some point."

She looked up to find both staring at her with wide, round eyes It made her chuckle audibly. "I would have if he got me mad enough and hadn't backed down," she admitted. "I have an asshole triggered temper." She picked up a large, thick main branch and braced her hands on it then brought her knee up sharply and snapped it in two. "Gets me in trouble sometimes, but gets other people in more trouble more often."

She put the two pieces down on the back side of the fire and dusted her hands off, somewhat amused at their expressions. "Not all nerds live in their mom's basements spending all their time playing video games."

Rich gave her a thumbs-up. "Rock on." He returned to getting the fire started, kneeling and shoving a handful of dried pine needles into the center of the kindling, then striking a match to set them on fire. "Tonight will be a better night."

"Let's hope so," Dave said. "But wow I'm getting sick of fish."

DAR SAT AGAINST the back wall of the little shelter, relatively content with her grilled fish and portion of canned peaches dug up from the box of leftover supplies they had hurriedly grabbed. Kerry was curled up on the ground next to Dar, with her head in Dar's lap.

Across from them the fire was sedately burning, the occasional spark popping up into the air. They had moved Pete to the other side of the fire. Don was seated next to him. Don had Dar's pocketknife in his hand, and was holding the blade in the fire, applying heat in the attempt to sterilize it.

Everyone was silent. Todd and Amy were in the far corner, watching with noncommittal expressions. Tracey was holding Pete's hand.

Dar felt her eyes wanting to close, and she shifted her head a little bit against the folded shirt placed against the rock to provide some small amount of comfort.

Kerry was already dozing. Dar could feel her steady, even breathing under the arm she had draped over her, their fingers tangled together loosely. She really wanted to join her, but she was also curious about what Don was going to do to help Pete.

No one could agree if it was a good idea or not. Pete was in the desperate place where he was almost past caring, just wanting something, somehow to relieve the constant pain he was in, made worse by Todd's asshatery. Don was the closest thing they had to someone who knew what they were doing.

"Okay," Don said, having heated the blade up to his satisfaction, and now was watching it cool down. "I'm just going to make the smallest cut possible, to let all that pressure out."

Pete nodded briefly. "Okay."

Don swiveled around on the small rock he was seated on and then carefully got down onto the ground next to the litter. Marcia was sitting nearby, holding the packet of small antiseptic wipes they had found in the first aid kit, and a roll of gauze.

It was an almost surreal scene. The light of the one lantern, and the fire, painting everything and everyone in gold and tarnished silver. The rest of the group watching in silence.

Dar felt a shiver go down her spine and she blinked a few times, tightening her grip on Kerry's fingers. She watched as Don leaned over Pete's back, and Tracey winced in reflex seeing the point of the knife press against his skin.

Don pressed forward, and Pete gasped as the blade pierced his skin. The sound was loud and Dar jerked a little, but then she heard a slight popping sound and her own body tensed as Don's hand twisted a little to widen the hole he'd made.

"Oh shit." Tracey got out from between gritted teeth.

Dar looked away, not wanting to see the blood, feeling a distinct sense of nausea.

"Okay, son, its finished," Don said. "Marcia, give me that gauze."

"I've got it." She leaned across and pressed a large wad of the fabric against Pete's back. "Oh my."

Tracey peered over. "Wow." She watched as Don pulled the gauze back to reveal a mixture of blood and pus that was ochre tinted and profuse. "That's gross." She returned her attention to Pete's face. "There's all kinds of stuff coming out."

Pete let out a long held shuddering breath. "Ohh." His head fell against his arm and his fist relaxed, fingers spreading out along the pallet. "Boy oh boy."

Don applied the gauze again, and shifted, and pressed very gently. "How does that feel?"

"Better," Pete said. "Oh my God better." His voice was weak with relief. "Thank you."

Marcia patted Don's arm. "Good job, honey."

"Okay." Don replaced the gauze with some of the antiseptic wipes, and carefully cleaned the area. "Here's the problem. This kinda thing, it keeps filling up if you don't put a drain in it and we don't have any drains unless someone has some surgical tubing in their gear." He looked around at the group. "No, huh?"

Not something they would have packed. Dar thought, regretfully, as she shook her head no. "Nothing in that kit?"

"It's just for scrapes," Janet said. "We lost the big one. We had all kinds of stuff in there, but this is just the basics."

Amy got up and went over to their backpacks and knelt.

"What are you doing?" Todd asked.

"I have some tubing as part of my water system," Amy said. She stood up and walked over to where Don was. "I don't know if this is what you need but..." She handed him something.

"Hey! You need that!" Todd stood up and scrambled over, but not before Don had taken the item and examined it. "Give me that, old man!"

Amy got in his way. "Todd, leave it alone," she said. "It's mine to give if I want to." She frowned at him. "Stop being a jerk."

Dar's eyes opened a bit wider, and she slid one booted foot up to get ready to rise. She relaxed, though, as Dave, Rich, Tracey, Sally, and Janet all got up and got behind Amy.

"Okay fine." Todd rolled his eyes and went back to his spot, thumping down and extending his legs out across the sandy floor.

"When you dehydrate don't come asking me for one of mine."

"No problem," Dar said. "The rest of us will share with her." She felt a squeeze on her hand and looked down to find Kerry looking up at her through half open eyes.

Don examined the bit of rubber. "That'll do I think, young lady. Let me clean it up, and see what we can make of it. Thank you."

Amy smiled briefly and went over to the other side of the fire and sat down to feed it some twigs, while the rest of them dispersed and went back to what they'd been doing.

Kerry wriggled a little bit closer and closed her eyes again. "The Grand Canyon trip to hell, where some men are men, and some women are also men."

Dar chuckled softly.

"And other men are weasels," Kerry concluded. "I think you're encouraging them to find their backbones, Dardar."

Dar snorted slightly in brief laughter. "Always like to be a bad example."

Kerry patted her leg in affection.

Dar relaxed at last, the gaps in the rocks blocked by boxes, and the fire giving as much of a sense of safety as she reasoned they were going to get. She let her eyes close and felt an almost immediate sense of dislocation as the sounds took on a slight echo.

It didn't even seem like it was going to rain.

THE NEXT THING Dar knew it was morning, and there was a faint pink light catching the edges of their shelter. She was half on her back with her head pillowed on one of their day bags, Kerry pressing up next to her still asleep.

She blinked a few times, surprised she'd slept through the night. She looked around the little campsite and saw the rest had done so as well.

It was quiet, and across from her she could see the faint glow from the banked fire that had burned down, and the air held a damp chill. She heard wind whistling through the stone walls, and far off, the waterfall hitting the ground across the valley.

Kerry stirred and rolled over, hiking herself up on her elbows as she regarded their surroundings. "Morning."

"Morning," Dar said. "That wasn't completely awful."

"Wasn't completely awful." Kerry sat up and twisted her body back and forth. "Want to take a walk?" She lifted one of their day bags and looked at Dar in question. "Be the first at the watering hole?"

Dar nodded and gave her a thumbs-up.

They both stood up, trying hard to be quiet, and walked around the rest of the sleeping camp to step over the cooler, and emerge into the canyon. The sun wasn't yet visible, but the sky was painted in golds and corals, and the effect on the stark landscape made them both stop and just look.

"Wow." Kerry took in a breath of the cool air.

They continued walking, crossing the center and turning up toward the water, the pressure of its passing having carved out a little channel overnight.

There were birds overhead, and Dar glanced up at them as they drew close to the pool near the wall. She felt the spray, carried with the wind, dampen her face. "What a difference a morning makes," she said, holding out one hand to catch the water.

Kerry smiled, and put the day bag down, going over and putting her own hands under the flow, testing its temperature. "That's not actually too bad." She stripped out of her jacket and put it on the rock then studied the water. "Its less than yesterday."

"No rain last night." Dar also removed her jacket. "I think I feel like a shower," she said.

Kerry quickly looked around. "Um." She glanced back to find Dar removing her shoes. "You know, hon..." She started to say, then stopped, deciding on a slight shrug instead. "You know what? Me too."

Dar grinned and pulled her shirt off, then her pants, then she removed a tube of the biodegradable soap they'd brought and stepped under the water. It was cool, and made her inhale sharply, but she squeezed a bit of the soap out and scrubbed her skin with a sense of pleasure.

Though she'd spent most of the previous day damp it felt good to get clean, and a moment later it felt even better as Kerry joined her and took the tube from her hand. She smiled as their bodies pressed against each other and she reached around to scrub Kerry's back as her partner did the same for her.

It was too cold to completely enjoy, but the contrast of the chill of the water and the warmth of the skin touching provided a moment of intense sensation, and she took the opportunity to kiss Kerry, as the water pounded down on them.

It was like a massage, a little, and Dar surrendered herself to the experience. Kerry's hand dropped lightly to her thigh and the chill was driven back by sensual heat.

A little dangerous, and a little wild, and they both started laughing as they parted and didn't want to. "Someone's going to catch us," Kerry said.

"Maybe."

"Wanna risk it?"

"Maybe."

"KNOW WHAT I figure, Dardar?"

"You figure soon some scandalous picture of us is going to be posted on the Internet?"

Kerry chuckled. "Well, it could have been worse."

Dar ran her fingers through her hair to start it drying. "Could have been worse. We'll be out of here and in our camper van soon enough."

"Mm." Kerry appreciated the new light as they walked back across the canyon. It painted the rock, and with the mostly clear skies the scenery was, at least for the moment, a little charming again.

A steady breeze blew against them, and the air was drier than it had been. Kerry wondered if maybe their luck was changing.

The rest of the party was emerging from the shelter as they approached. They headed over to the waterfall, one of them carrying the pot dangling from one hand. "Pretty bad when I wish we had oatmeal," Kerry said

Dar smiled. "I'd take a sticky bun at this point."

"You don't like sticky buns."

"My point."

"Early birds," Rich said, spotting them. "How's the water?"

"Cold." Kerry said, with a somewhat cheeky grin. "Bring your own heat with you." They met up in the middle of the flat path. "But it's a nice morning."

"Lot nicer than yesterday," Dave said. "We should make good time today. Pete's standing up!'

"Yeah?" Dar said. "That's good to hear."

"Yeah. Don did a great job," Rich said. "I'm glad he's feeling better."

Kerry and Dar eased past and headed for the shelter, pausing as they reached the entrance and heard someone coming in the opposite direction.

Kerry took a step back and got out of the way, glancing down at the ground as she spotted a shadow on it. 'What the..." She crouched to get a better look.

"Easy." Tracey said, as she helped Pete limp gingerly along. "Don't go too fast."

"I won't, no fear," Pete said. "Just glad to be vertical." He gave Dar a brief, wan grin. "Hey, thanks for standing up for me last night. I really appreciated that, after that bozo kicked me." He glanced behind them at the shelter. "Customer or no, boy I could have whacked him."

"No problem," Dar said. She edged out of the way to let him pass, and watched him as he did, then turned to look at Kerry who was standing at her side with a somewhat urgent expression. "What's up?"

Kerry pointed down between her boots.

Dar leaned over and then she knelt, putting her fingertips down on the ground. "Hm." There was an animals' footprint, larger by half than the one she'd seen from the bobcat. In the dew damp sand, it was clear and distinct, right up to the indentations from flexed claws.

"Holy crap," Kerry said, in a low tone. "Dar, it was right here." She looked around and then back at her partner. "Wasn't it?"

Dar stood up and dusted off her hands. She glanced over her shoulder at the group, some wandering across the sand while waiting their turn at the toilet. "I think those are fresh so It was." She scuffed the print out with the toe of her boot. "But it's gone, and no one got eaten. No sense in freaking everyone out."

Kerry took a breath to protest, then paused and thought about it. "Yeah," she finally said. "I'm really glad we found shelter. That being out here, for who knows how long, creeps me out."

"Me too." Dar put her hand on Kerry's back and guided her inside. "Let's get packed up. Hope we get as lucky tonight."

"Hope we find a taco stand."

Chapter Nine

THEY WERE THROUGH the canyon and heading up the mountain trail hours past noon before the weather started to turn. Clouds gathered, bringing a cold mist down, obscuring the top part of the canyon wall.

Kerry paused and put one boot up on a nearby rock, retying her laces as Rich and Dave went on ahead to see what they could find. Dar leaned against the wall next to her, listening to the thunder rumbling in the distance. "Not good."

"Not good," Kerry said. "But we made some progress today." She shaded her eyes and looked back the way they'd come. "Did they say around this mountain and down and then we'll be at a ranger station?"

"They did," Dar said.

Just down the path, Tracey and Pete stood, Pete with both hands on a gnarled stick Don had salvaged from the remains of the pine tree they'd burned for fuel. He was still in pain, and he was sweating through it, but he'd managed to move along with them as best he could.

Relief for the crew, who now just had the dwindling supplies to worry about carrying. But on the other hand, they were now climbing up hill and everyone was tired.

Water containers were passed around, filled that morning at the falls. Dar took a moment to uncap her water bottle and take a swallow, grimacing a little from the faint taste of iodine they'd used to kill anything in it.

They'd passed on lunch, and she was hungry. She thought she had one package of crackers left in her backpack but she resisted getting it out, feeling a bit self-conscious about chewing on them while everyone was watching.

Then something occurred to her, and she swung the pack around and fished the somewhat battered crackers out, opening it up and handing one over to Kerry. "Here."

Kerry eyed her. "How in the hell did you know I was just thinking about that?"

"Been a long time since breakfast." Dar crunched contentedly on her own cracker. "I don't want you keeling over before we can stop."

Kerry stuck her tongue out, covered in crumbly peanut

butter. She paused to swallow, and wash down the mouthful with water. "I'm not looking forward to more of the fish tonight," she said ruefully. "It's getting pretty funky."

"Salty," Dar said. "Kind of dried and chewy."

"I can soak it I guess. Maybe make a soup again, but we don't have anything else to put in it."

Dar pondered that. "Too bad we didn't catch one of those sheep."

They were both silent for a few moments, standing there in the mist. "Mm." Kerry sighed. "Now I really want lamb chops. Damn you, Dar."

Dar offered another cracker in mute apology.

Janet came up behind them. "We better get moving. We don't want to get caught on this path in the rain. Runoff comes down it, see?" She pointed at the ground with the stick she was using. "I don't even know if there's some place to take shelter but we better find something out of the water route."

Dar tightened down the pack on her back and started up the path, leaning forward a little and using her hiking pole as she climbed, listening for Kerry's steps behind her, and the chance of Rich and Dave returning from ahead.

The mist was giving her skin a clammy feel, and she licked her lips as she put her hand on the rock wall to keep her steps steady.

She knew behind them was the crew, and behind the crew, bringing up the rear was Todd and Amy. Everyone had ignored Todd the entire day but he apparently didn't care, and Amy stayed at his side as the group moved gamely up the path.

Dar heard rocks tumbling down ahead of her. She paused and braced herself as the fog came down and blocked the long view. "Rich?" She called out.

"Yeah we're here!" Rich answered. "Not much to see!"

Great. Dar continued up and came around a slight bend of rock to a more even part of the path and saw Rich and Dave ahead of her. They stood looking through an overhead arch that covered the path. It was too thin to provide any real shelter and they moved past it.

The walls were again on either side, and the rock-strewn path provided uneasy footing. "Careful!" Dar said. "Lot of pebbles."

Kerry slid a foot just as Dar said that, and quickly caught her balance with a hand on the wall. "Whoa." She got her pole ahead of her and got closer to Dar. They caught up to Dave and Rich a moment later. The two men were speaking in low tones, and they turned to greet them.

"There's a few more arches," Dave said. "I've seen this hike on the Internet. It's supposed to be like a two day'er from the ranger station. If we can get through this part, it goes down again and maybe by sundown tomorrow we can get some help.

"That sounds fantastic," Kerry said. "If the weather doesn't kill us again."

Rich made a face. "Yeah." They started forward and walked along under the rock overhangs, all mostly thin and without any promise of shelter. The walls were also straight up, with no shelves they could even duck under, and of course the thunder was getting closer.

Dar started to look at the walls, trying to find any shelter as she felt the first isolated drops of rain, along with a rising of the wind that was gusting through the canyon.

The path started up again and they all leaned forward, now relatively far ahead of the main group, though they could hear the voices back behind them.

There was no wood around, Kerry noticed. No trees or even shrubs, and she realized the rain was going to probably make building a fire unlikely.

Now she was sorry they hadn't stopped for lunch. "This is going to be a mess."

"Yes," Rich said. "But maybe...hey, yeah." He pointed ahead of them as they came around a bend. "There! Look!"

It was another arch, but this one was wide, and on either side had a deep undercut that they reached just as the rain started coming down harder. Rich dropped his bags down and started back up along the path, waving at Janet as she struggled up the rise. "Hey! We found a spot!"

Todd made his way up to the front and now pushed past Janet. "At least its big enough to be away from you and the rest of the pussies." He went over to the far side of the path and motioned Amy with him.

"Assholes R Us," Janet muttered under her breath. They all worked to get the supplies under cover before the rain really started. The fog came all the way down and they stumbled around in the mist. Two of the crew and Sally climbed up farther, braving the weather to see if they could find some wood.

Dar knelt next to their duffel. She looked up when she heard a yell of alarm, to see something relatively small scurrying toward her at a high rate of speed.

"What the hell!" Janet got up and almost fell as it went

between her legs and jumped over one of the boxes, careening toward the other side of the arch. "Hey! Hey!"

The animal raced toward them and in utter reflex, Dar reached out and grabbed at it, feeling soft fur and muscle under her fingertips. It turned and fought her grip, and she saw large teeth go for her hand and she froze for a moment, not sure whether to hold on or not.

"Dar!" Kerry bounded over to her. "It's going to bite you!"

Dar got it around the neck and held it up as the rest of the group came over. "It's a rabbit," she said. The rabbit panted in fear, eyes round wide in a terrified expression. Kerry arrived, lifting her walking stick in defense of Dar. "Take it easy, slugger."

"Oh." Kerry relaxed her stance, then reached over and touched a fingertip to the rabbit's ear, which twitched violently. "Aww. I wasn't sure what it was. Poor little bunny."

Dar looked at the rabbit, then at her beloved. "Weren't you the one who was just wanting lamb chops?" She asked, in a quizzical tone.

"Psht. Dar." Kerry touched the rabbit again, this time with more confidence. "We can't eat this thing. We don't even have any wood to cook the dried fish."

"Rabbit's good," Dave said. "But more important, if it came from around here, there must be grasses and stuff for it to eat. We can burn that."

Dar sniffed reflectively and peered at the rabbit, who had calmed a little, and was now eyeing her back with a twitch of its nose. Its long ears drooped and she felt one brush her hand with a feeling of damp velvet. She gave it a little scratch on the bottom of its jaw with her thumb.

Then, without warning, she lowered her hands and released it, giving it a toss down the path. She watched it recover itself and race off just as a protest lifted from her companions. "G'wan, bunny."

"Why'd you do that?" Rich said. "We're all hungry! We'd have figured it out!"

"Go catch it yourself then." Dar stood and dusted her hands off.

Rich took her at her word and trotted off through the rain, in the direction the rabbit had scuttled, pausing to pick up several stones on his way. After a minute, Dave followed him.

"Why did you do that?" Kerry asked. They started to lay down a much-folded tarp, and blocked out an area right on the edge of the overhang.

"Why did I do that," Dar repeated, as she moved down the path in the mist, collecting rocks and bringing them back over to put them down to make a small wall. "Because I knew you'd freak out if I broke its neck." She knelt to arrange the stones. "And I really didn't want to kill it."

"Aww." Kerry leaned over and gave her a kiss on the shoulder. "You're such a sweetie."

"And because butchering it and letting that blood smell get out is probably not a good idea," Dar added, under her breath. "Know what I mean?"

Kerry laid down the edge of the tarp for Dar to put her rocks on. "Hadn't thought of that. Kind of like not going diving that time of the month?"

Dar paused and looked at her. "Kinda," she said. "Or with open cuts as if jumping in salt water wasn't enough to keep you from doing that."

"Mm." Kerry looked past the arch, where rain was now dampening the ground. "Good point."

Dar came around and under the overhang. The arch started along the ground about ten feet, and though low, it was definite shelter. She sat on the ground to save her head from smacking into it, and rubbed her fingertips together, still feeling the struggle of the rabbit's body in her grip.

Why, really, had she released it? It wasn't as if she hadn't eaten rabbit in the field, back in the day. That and frogs, and once, a big lizard. It hadn't been tasty, but she wasn't a cook and neither were the guys she'd camped with.

After that they'd brought MRE's stolen from base with them.

She licked her lips and grinned, remembering the canned chicken with hot sauce on crackers, and PBJ in packets, and wished she had some right now.

"What's so funny?" Kerry regarded their little corner and grunted in approval.

"Nothing." Dar stretched her legs out and glanced to her right, where they were getting Pete settled next to her, with Don and Marcia on the other side. "How's the back?"

"Hurts," Pete said. "But still better than it was." He was on his side, brushing pebbles away and moving small stones from under the ragged sleeping bag Tracey had put down under him. "Hey." He looked up at Dar. "Glad you let the bunny go."

Dar smiled.

"Me too." Tracey was sitting cross-legged on the other side of him. "I'd rather be hungry. Honest. Those guys are just wankers."

Kerry sat quietly, waiting to see what the results of the wood hunting was going to be. "They aren't really," she said. "They're mostly nice guys. I just think the whole situation here is making people kind of crazy."

"Kind of?" Pete gave her a wry look. "Those guys are getting hangry. Seen customers get that way, you know? We have times we stop, and times we need to keep going, and they get all aggro because they're hangry. You're smart to have brought those crackers."

"Hangry." Kerry repeated the word.

"That's why Janet is always running around passing trays," Tracey said. "Speaking of, let me see if we've got anything left in the supplies. I thought I saw maybe some rice crackers." She got up and went to the pile of boxes, notably smaller than it had been.

A minute later Sally and the two crewmen returned with large armfuls of what looked a lot like sagebrush.

"We managed to find this. Did you guys see that rabbit? We surprised her out of her burrow."

"We saw it," Kerry said. "Dar grabbed it but she let it go."

"Great, because it has babies back there." Sally set down her burden. "I'm going to go back and get more brush, there's a whole patch up about five minutes from here." She looked around. "Anyone want to help?"

The two crew members put their bundles down and pushed their raincoat hoods back, as PJ stood up and limped forward. Both she and Sally disappeared back into the mist, along with Tracey, who looked back over her shoulder at Dar and winked.

Dar and Kerry looked at each other. Without comment, Kerry lifted one of Dar's hands up and brought it to her lips, kissing her knuckles. Then she pulled their duffel over and started rooting around in it.

Dar folded her arms as she listened to the rain increase, and the thunder rumble now more closely overhead. "One more day," she said, watching the center of the path start to gather a little water in it. "One more day."

DAR WIPED MIST off her face for the nth time, watching the lightning bursting outside the shelter of the arch, outlining the driving rain and the flow of water down the center of the path.

Kerry sat next to her, arms wrapped around her knees, and her chin resting on her forearms. She was in her waterproof jacket and its surface was shiny with moisture.

The grass had allowed for a fire, but a fast burning one, and so they'd cooked as they could, and put what they hadn't eaten back in one box for the morning, hoping that would be the end of that. They emptied out the cooler the fish had been in and washed it, and now were storing things in it they were hopeful of keeping dry.

Including enough grass to burn to heat water to drink in the morning, as they were out of any kind of tea or other leaves.

Across the arch, Todd and Amy had set up their own, isolated camp. If Dar squinted a little she could see their outline tucked into the corner of the arch on that side, much as she and Kerry were on the side they were on. "Be glad to finish this," she said.

Kerry merely straightened and leaned toward her, resting her cheek against Dar's shoulder. "Glad we're at least up here, not down at the bottom of the path."

"Mm." Dar pulled the sleeping bag around their shoulders, and glanced at her watch.

Only two a.m.. She rested her head against the wall and diverted her attention, trying to ignore the discomfort long enough to get some rest.

Dar picked up the cup she'd filled with rainwater and sipped from it, her mouth a little pinched and dried on the inside from the saltiness of the fish they'd had. She offered the cup to Kerry, who accepted it and then set it down between them.

"Too wet for cards, huh?" Kerry remarked wryly.

"Wish I had a Rubik's cube," Dar said.

Kerry regarded her. "I've seen you solve that underwater, Dar. What challenge would this be?"

"Dark."

"Mm."

The lightning flashed again, and suddenly Rich let out a yell and pointed below them. "What was that?"

Dar's hand fitted itself around a rock and leaned forward to look out, waiting for the next flash. It came, and she took in the whole area, seeing nothing but rock. "What?"

Rich was half standing, hand on the curve of the arch over his head, blinking. "I swear I saw something."

Everyone got up on their knees and stared.

There was only the sound of the rain, and the swish of the water passing through the center of the path, and the thunder rumbling overhead. But even repeated flashes showed nothing downhill from them. Dar got to her feet and looked intently at the path.

Had she heard something? Her ears twitched, as she was half convinced she'd detected the scrape of something against stone, a scratching sound. Then she saw a few rocks tumble off the top of the arch and fall to the ground right in front of her.

She went still, and in reflex, looked up at the underside of the arch as her heart started to pound. She felt all the chill of the rain vanish as blood flushed through her muscles.

"What?" Rich said, staring at her.

"I think I heard something up there." Dar pointed at the arch. "On top."

"Fuck." Dave pulled his hood up and ran to the upper side of the arch, and into the rain, shading his eyes from it and whirling to look up. "Nothing from this side!"

Thunder rumbled, and then they all heard it, a rasp and rattle of something big on the ledge overhead. Everyone was awake and got up in alarm.

Dar dropped the rock in her hand and took her pocketknife out of her pocket and opened it, feeling the blade lock as she tightened her fingers around the hilt. She felt Kerry take a firm hold of her belt. She looked around, to see her partner braced. "What?"

"What what?" Kerry hissed back. "Just what do you think you're doing?"

Dar half turned and almost laughed, when she heard more sounds overhead and quickly turned back to see something fall through the air to the ground. Lightning lit up again and she saw a large animal getting its balance back and turn toward her.

"Oh crap." Dar exhaled realizing how large the cat was. She spread her boots out at shoulder width as her body recognized the threat. She let out a booming yell in the animals' direction, waving her arms in a motion that did nothing to deter the cat.

Someone screamed behind her and she heard Kerry yell a warning. A stone came flying past her to miss the cat and go bouncing down the slope into the darkness.

It rushed at her, and for a second she froze, then instinct took over and she lashed out with a kick aimed at its head and felt it connect, sending the cat skidding to one side as its claws scrabbled in the wet gravel at the unexpected attack.

Then it lunged forward again and she leaped at it, reaching for the teeth coming at her knees in a perfect moment of unreal insanity. Its eyes met hers in a flash of silver light and two feral souls met with no time to do anything but act according to their natures.

She wasn't cognizant of the knife in her hand, but the blade tip hit something hard, and with her momentum penetrated. Her other hand grabbed at the cat's neck and shoved its head away from her, teeth missing her wrist as it twisted to meet her, claws extended.

She landed on top of it with all her weight and shoved it to the ground. She heard it yowl in pain and surprise and her knees came down on top of the cat's hind legs. Her forearm pinned its neck to the ground, her thinking mind suddenly wondering what the hell she was supposed to do next.

Then without warning, Tracey landed next to her with a thump and a splash, a long blade grasped in both hands. She stabbed the animal repeatedly with a screaming of her own, nearly slicing Dar's hand as she struggled to get the hell out of the way.

Dar had to get off the cat's body, or risk being impaled. She jerked back hastily. "Hey! Look out! Stop!" She yelled in alarm. "Hey!"

The cat twisted and scrambled free as Dar's weight came off it. The cat ran off limping. It shook its head and disappeared into the rain.

"Fuck!" Tracey panted. "I wanted to get it for Josh." She stared at the knife in her hands. "Little bastard!" She watched the dark stain of blood rinse past with the driving rain and put one hand down into it.

"You damn near stabbed me!" Dar said, in an exasperated tone.

A rush of people was now at their back, and Dar felt hands lifting her to her feet as she stood there shivering in reaction, with Kerry's arms wrapping around her.

"That was insane," Rich said. "That was freaking insane."

"Nuts," Janet said. "Are you guys okay?"

Dar was silent for a moment, feeling the beat of the rain on her skin and the afterimages of the cat and its vivid eyes, and its yowl fading. "Yeah," she finally said, motioning them all back under the arch. "I'm fine. Just wet and freaked out."

They all clustered back under the arch, and then Todd pushed through them. "What in the hell just happened?" He asked, getting to Dar's side. "What was that?"

"That was the mountain lion," Kerry responded. "Or a mountain lion."

"Yeah," Rich said. "So, Dar kicked it in the head and then she and Tracey jumped on it and started stabbing it. Pretty rad." He eyed the two women with bemused respect. "It went up onto the arch. Was stalking us."

Todd's eyebrows hiked up, as Amy peered from around his broad shoulder. "Oh shit." He looked out. "It got away?"

"It's got holes in it," Don said. "Better it than us." He pointed down the path. "Went that way."

Todd grabbed one of the walking sticks and ran in that direction. "I'll make sure."

"Todd wa—" Amy flinched as a flash of lightning cracked overhead and they all ducked backwards, and when the afterimages faded.

Don grabbed her arm and held her back. "No sense in both you out there," he said, in a practical tone. "That thing's gonna die soon. He'll be back."

Dar felt her heart settle, and she pretended everyone wasn't furtively staring at her. She turned and regarded Kerry, who, after a brief pause grimly smiled. "That sucked." She edged back under the arch and out of the rain, now soaked to the skin and shivering.

Kerry took the knife out of her hand and unlocked the blade to fold it closed. Then she put her arms around Dar and exhaled. "Jesus." She could feel the vibrations running through Dar's tall frame and she closed her eyes, giving her a gentle scratch on the back.

Courage was such a funny thing. You couldn't buy it, couldn't even develop it inside yourself. It was just something you had. Or not. She felt Dar's body slowly relax, and she guided them both back to the spot they'd picked and sat down, listening to the rain coming down all around them. Listening to all the people talking around them. Hearing again the angry howl of the cat.

Hearing again Dar's answering yell, bold and fierce and without fear echoing in her memory. Kerry looked aside, watching Dar's profile in the faint light. She reflected on the realization that most people, especially most people who had lives like theirs, never got to test where they fell on the flight or fight scale.

Strange. She watched the rain fall. Strange, and often on the edge of heartbreak.

Dar sighed. "I shouldn't do shit like that." She shook her head a little. "Idiotic."

Kerry tasted the truth of that. "You can't help doing shit like that, Dar," she replied, understanding the truth of that, as well. "We joke about you being a crusader, but you know..."

"I know," Dar answered. "But is that fair? I seem to remember promising you to think about us first."

There was something so woebegonly charming about that it made Kerry smile. "You did." She took Dar's hand in hers. "But that was only for the stuff you could think about."

Dar grunted a little. "Yeah, I guess this is different. No time."

Odd moment of epiphany. Kerry clasped her fingers with Dar's. "Let me tell you something about you and me, Paladar Katherine."

"Uh oh." Dar eyed her.

"If there's a fucking mountain lion coming at us, we jump on it," Kerry said. "We don't let it eat us."

Dar regarded her in silence for a moment. Then grinned, just a little.

"Besides." Kerry consciously lightened the tone. "Can you imagine me telling the gang at the office about this? You'll end up having ridden a Tyrannosaurus Rex while singing God Bless America."

Dar chuckled silently, clasping her hands over Kerry's, with a light shrug of acceptance. Then she leaned back against the rock and extended her boots out a little, as the rain started coming down harder.

MORNING WAS DISMAL. Literally, because it was still raining, and figuratively since there was only leathery dried fish cooked the night before. Everyone was tired and had little sleep.

They had an uphill climb to face on top of it, and the only positive note was they'd gone through all the supplies so there was little left for the crew to carry. Everyone had a pack on their back, and that was it.

"Let's get this over with," Dar finally said, taking the lead out into the rain.

"Fuck yeah," Todd said. "Too bad I didn't find that cat. I wanted a souvenir." He dug his walking stick into the gravel and walked steadily upward. "So, what are you really?" He asked Dar as they trudged along.

"What I am really what?" Dar replied shortly.

"You a circus performer? Some reality thing for Animal Planet?" Todd asked. "You aren't no computer geek."

"I'm a computer geek."

"Nah."

Dar just shook her head.

The center of the path was a continuous stream of water, so

they walked on the edges, the party split into two groups one on either side.

Dar and Kerry were on the left hand side, with Todd, Amy and most of the crew. The rest of the passengers were on the other side, with Rich and Dave in the lead. Everyone walked carefully, and slowly enough that the three injured were able to keep up.

They reached the plateau that they'd gotten the dried grasses from, finding it soggy and barren. "Should we pick up some of this stuff for later?" Rich asked, pointing at the remaining grasses, beaten down and ragged.

"No, we'll be at the ranger station before mid-day even at this pace," Janet said. "No sense carrying wet grass."

Kerry dug her stick in as they reached a slightly steeper part of the path, leading up to a turn that bore to her left, and would then pitch downward to the station.

She hoped.

The canyon walls curved on either side of them, providing no shelter and just a funnel for the rain pouring down, the sky overhead solid, uncompromising dark gray.

But, she thought, they'd left the lion behind them, and they only had a short distance to go, then it would be over.

She could almost taste the hot cup of bad coffee she knew would be there, at the end of the trail.

Chapter Ten

DON LEANED AGAINST the rock wall with his arm lifted to block the rain. "Can't believe this weather." He was breathing hard, and next to him Marcia looked patient but miserable.

But of course everyone was, in this march up a steep, sometimes slippery path into the rain.

They were taking a brief rest, both to catch their breaths and to allow the deluge to lessen a little. Dar was braced against a large boulder, providing a rain break for Kerry, as well as Tracey and Pete, huddled behind her. The water down the path was now a solid rush. It came up over their boots as they stood in a tiny facsimile of the river they'd left far behind.

"We'd be hip deep if we were back where we'd stopped last night," Janet said. She was seated on a bit of rock out thrust, her cut leg stretched out, her face white with exhaustion. "But hey, at least no one's dehydrated."

Tracey chuckled shortly. "True."

"That's the usual problem out here," Rich said. "Man I'm looking forward to a hot shower and dry clothes."

Todd shook his head. "What a bunch of pussies," he said. "You think this is bad? We did a hike in the Yucatan where we didn't have nothing for a week."

Kerry tipped her head back and allowed the rain to fill her mouth, swallowing it and licking her lips. It tasted of nothing and everything, sky and cloud and fog and as pure as water was going to be.

Ahead of them, maybe a ten minute walk, was another large arch. Just past that they could see the path cresting. Water was running off the arch, making a curtain across the path. She could already feel the pounding on her head and imagined what that would be like.

"Only morons pay money to be miserable," Dar said. "I'd rather spend the week on my boat."

"With fresh caught lobster and a nicely chilled white wine," Kerry said.

"Please shut up," Tracey said. "Most of us can't afford lobster."

Kerry eyed her. "Sorry. We can, but we never buy it. We catch it in the ocean." She paused. "Besides, we earned what we have. I'm not ashamed of it."

"No, sorry. I didn't mean..." Tracey held up a hand. "Didn't mean to diss you. Just jelly."

Janet stood. "We should get moving."

They all picked up their bags and shouldered them, starting up the path toward the arch in a straggled line as thunder rumbled over head again.

Dar leaned forward and focused on the top of the path, looking forward to achieving it and the downhill stretch beyond it. "I think—"

"Always and constantly," Kerry said. "Regular as lizards on our porch."

Dar chuckled. "I think I appreciate Miami's flatness for the first time. Now I know why I steered clear of the stair climber in the gym."

Caught thinking that very same thing, Kerry just chuckled in response.

They'd gotten perhaps twenty feet up the path when a huge crack sounded overhead that made them all duck. Lightning hit the top of the arch they were climbing toward and lit the area with such pungent white light they all turned to the side and closed their eyes.

"Shit," Janet yelped. "Oh shit!"

Thunder boomed. Then as Dar blinked the after image out of her eyes, Tracey let out a bloodcurdling scream. Suddenly Rich pushed her to the side toward the wall. "What the hell..."

"Avalanche!" Dave yelled. He grabbed Kerry and they all pressed against the wall amidst a rapidly escalating sound of crashing stone.

"Get out of the way!" Pete bawled. The crew started running down the path, back the way they came, unable to find shelter against the walls as thick pieces of rock thumped and tumbled down after them, gaining momentum.

Dar felt the sting of debris against her skin and she pressed her body against the rock and closed her eyes, feeling a thick rumble so deep it vibrated the bones inside her. She heard things smashing against the wall and opened one eye to see Kerry looking back at her, scared.

Instinctively, she put her hand over Kerry's as she felt a rock hit her shoulder. Dave yelped in pain and she turned slightly, to put the pack on her back between her and the moving debris.

Rich looked down the path and hesitated, but then pressed himself more tightly against the wall on the other side of Kerry.

"Stay here! Don't move!"

Dar grimaced, as another piece of rock slammed into her. "What the hell."

"Arch collapsed," Dave said, his eyes closed. "Jesus Christ this trip is haunted."

They had gotten lucky, tucked behind a slight bend in the wall. After a minute or two the noise abated, and then there was only rain, and the faint sound of stones bounding and skipping down the path behind them.

Dar pushed back and looked over at the arch, stunned into speechlessness when she saw the upper trek they were heading for. "Oh crap."

"Jesus!" Both Rich and Dave spoke at once.

"Oh my goodness," Marsha gasped.

The top of the path was completely blocked with stone rubble and huge chunks of the arch that had collapsed completely, closing in the slot canyon.

Everyone was briefly silent, stunned and wide-eyed.

Todd came up to stand next to Dar, and they stood shoulder to shoulder regarding this new impediment to the end of their journey. "We're fucked," He said, after a few moments. "Seriously."

Dar tried to consider a rebuttal, but failed. "Yeah," she said, putting her hands on her hips. "This is terminal suckitude."

No supplies, no food, no way around the rubble. Dar turned and looked down the path, where the crew was now climbing back up to rejoin them, having evaded the falling rocks.

She looked at Kerry, who looked back at her, the same knowledge in her pale green eyes.

No way to let people back home know what was going on.

Kerry came up next to her and put her arm around Dar's waist. "This just got very complicated."

Dar responded. "Yeah."

"Fucked," Todd concluded succinctly.

"Cursed," Rich added. "Seriously."

"Shit." Tracey said.

For once, it seemed that the entire group, leaders, passengers and crew were in total agreement.

THE ONLY BRIGHT spot to be found was the rain stopped. They gathered at the base of the avalanche, where the path had started to even out and provided a flat space for them to stand.

The clouds lifted and they were splashed with random sunlight as they stood in a rough circle of mounting consternation.

"So now what are we supposed to do?" Marcia asked. "Do we go back?"

Janet shook her head. "It's flooded back there, and I don't know if the raft is even still there after that storm."

"What choice do we have? Sit here and starve?" Rich said. "Seriously?"

Dar was half ignoring the discussion, her eyes studying the mountain of debris blocking their way. "Can we climb this?"

Todd tilted his head back and looked up. "Too loose," he said. "End up bringing down crap on everyone and falling on our asses." He hopped up onto a bit of the rock and immediately jumped clear as it detached itself and came out from under him, tumbling a few feet down the path.

Kerry had gone to one side of the wall and experimentally pushed one of the rocks with her boot, sending it rolling downward. "Can we move it?"

Dave picked up a rock and threw it. "We can't move a lot of that, too heavy." He pointed at one slab of debris. "Take a backhoe."

Dar sat on a rock and braced her elbows on her knees. "Anyone got any other ideas? If not, we pick the best of the worst of them." She eyed them all. "The worst of the worst being just sitting here doing nothing."

Kerry walked over to a relatively flat piece of rock and regarded it. "So what do we have to work with?" she said. "Let's see what we're all carrying."

Grudgingly the group surrounded the rock and started putting things on it, emptying packs and pockets randomly onto the damp surface, except Pete, who was sprawled over another large rock, with Don checking the injury on his back.

His shirt was stained with blood and pus, and his face showed pain and exhaustion, having stumbled and fallen running from the avalanche. PJ sat next to him holding his hand in sympathy, her bandaged foot likewise tattered and stained.

Janet upended her pack, dumping a tattered and much folded map, a camp fork and spoon, a set of keys, and a compass.

Dave pulled out his hygiene kit, a book, the pack of cards, stained brown, and a small set of binoculars. "All great stuff to carry on the raft, and fegging useless here."

They had their canteens, and packs filled with water from the morning. "Save it," Amy said. "If it doesn't rain again we're going to run short." She put down another compass, and a large handful of carabiners and other climbing gear, along with a tightly wound coil of rope.

Dar's pocketknife joined the collection, and Kerry half shrugged as she put what was in her pack down, a pair of sunglasses, a safety pin, a towel, and a piece of black plastic she found in the bottom of it.

"Hey." Janet limped forward and picked up the plastic. "Where did this come from?" She stared at Kerry intently. "Where did you get this?"

Kerry frowned and her eyes unfocused, as she tried to recall. "Not sure I remember," she said.

"You picked it up near the shack," Dar said mildly. "You had it in your pocket after that." She regarded Janet. "What is it? Piece of something?" She rested her wrist on Kerry's shoulder and peered at the item.

"It's the battery from the sat phone," Janet said. "Now if we only had that. Holy shit, I wonder if the phone was out there too."

Everyone stared at the module, resting silently in Janet's hand. Then Todd snorted. "Wouldn't do a fucks worth of anything this far down in the canyon. They'd never hear it. He turned and went over to the far wall, examining it thoughtfully.

'That's true." Janet put the battery back down. "Anyway, Amy's right about the water. Looks like the weathers drying out." She looked up at the sky that showed patches of clear blue past the clouds. "Of course, since we need water."

"We should set up some shelter anyway," one of the crew said. "If we're not going to start back, I mean." The man pointed down slope. "Should we?"

Dar folded her arms and stood in perplexed silence for a moment. "How long will it take for the flood to drain out?" She asked Janet.

Janet looked thoughtful. "Depends. If we don't get more rain, maybe a couple days. But let me look at the map and see if we have any alt routes, even if they're not great." She spread the map out and studied it.

"Might as well." Rich indicated the tarps. "We'll help. C'mon, Dave." He and Dave went over to the unpacked shelter supplies, most of the tarps tattered and torn, and the poles all bent and in two cases, cracked in the center. "Not much to work with, but maybe we can...do we have any tents left?"

"We can set up what we have," Janet said. "Flat enough here."

"Get the bag over there." Sally went toward the pile of gear they'd dragged up, and retrieved from the headlong rush down the path from earlier. "There, with the stakes. I think we can get them."

Kerry handed Dar her pocketknife. "How in the world did you remember when I grabbed that?" She asked. "Holy pooters, Dar."

Dar smiled. "I always pay attention to you."

Kerry looked at her in mild exasperation. "You pay attention to what I put in my pockets?"

Dar winked at her. "I do."

"And actually I remember where it was now, in the cave I got the pot of water from before we left the shack," Kerry recalled. "Wish we were back there now."

"Me too." Dar slid the knife back in her pocket. "Let's go help." She indicated the pile of canvas bags. "We're going to be here for a little while at least I guess."

IT WAS ONE of those few times in her recent life that Dar acknowledged she was really hungry. She and Kerry lived in a world where the longest wait for food was the drive to and from work, and it was only in dim memory of her younger years that lack of food had been a problem.

And that only voluntary when she'd been out on hikes in the sawgrass and learned the hard way to take snacks with her instead of relying on the other kids, or on scrounging.

Dar studied the little encampment, sad and ragged in the brisk wind swirling through the now closed canyon, and shook her head.

She could see to the bottom of the path, and the moving figures that were the rest of the party scouring the area for anything useful.

They had set up the four remaining tents, and two tarps that were fluttering harshly in the breeze, along with a rope clothesline that held a variety of sleeping bags and clothes drying.

There was nothing organic visible. The rain and the floods had stripped out any vegetation. The crew climbed back down the path to find anything that might have gotten caught and left, with a hope of some wood to burn for heat.

Kerry was nearby, talking to Janet. She had her waterproof jacket tied around her waist and her arms folded. Her blond hair was in ruffled disarray and Dar watched her profile shift as the muscles in her jaw tensed and squared.

Resolute. Dar smiled to herself as she stood up and flexed her hands. She walked to the side of the avalanche and examined the debris and wondered if putting the shelters that close was really a good idea. It provided a wind break, but what if another storm hit?

Todd wandered over and kicked one of the stones at ground level. "This sucks," he said to her. "I thought it sucked before, but this is another level of suck."

Dar nodded. "I'm trying to decide if there's any option that doesn't have — we're screwed — written on it in ten inch high letters."

He reached out and put his hand on a bit of the rock. "Best idea was climbing out over this." He said. "But it's unstable. You can feel it." He pushed gently. "Maybe me and Amy could get partway up, but not this bunch."

Dar glanced at him. "You could?"

He shrugged. "Maybe."

Dar turned to face him. "Why don't you go get help? Climb over this and go to the ranger station? Can't you do that?"

He stared at her, eyes narrowing a little. "You don't know a fucking thing about it."

"No, I don't. I live in South Florida, where the highest elevation that isn't a garbage dump is six feet," Dar said. "But you do."

For a long moment Todd just stood there. "Too vertical," he finally said. "This stuff's too soft, too few places to hang onto. Probably end up taking a header. You saw this thing come down." He picked up a piece of rock and slammed it against a second.

It cracked and powdered in his big hand. "See?"

Dar observed it. "So," she looked at the rock walls, "wrong kind of rock."

Todd nodded. "That's why this thing came down so easy," he said. "Stuff crumbles."

"What the hell were you going to do with this op then?" Dar asked. "You wanted to use them to get you to some place to climb?"

He tossed the rock aside and dusted his hands off. "Not here," he said. "Not the slot canyons. There's walls you can climb. Just not this."

Was it true? Dar studied his face. He had a flat profile, and what appeared to be a nose broken more than once, and very sparse facial hair, even after the guys had stopped shaving. She concluded silently it probably was true, if for no other reason than she figured he would enjoy lording it all over them otherwise.

Damn. "Too bad," she said. "Waiting it out for the flood and walking back is going to be a serious suck."

"Yeah." he said. "Especially with this bunch of lame-o's." He turned and headed back across the loose surface to where Amy had joined the small group around the table rock.

That left Dar by herself next to the debris wall and she went and sat on a rock. A beetle trundled past on the ground, making a detour around the toe of her boot. She watched it thoughtfully, wondering if her choice of letting the rabbit go earlier was as stupid as it felt right now.

What were they going to do?

BY DUSK THEY still had no answers. The weather was still clear, and it appeared they would have a dry night, but the whistling winds were chilly and everyone was hungry.

They had enough to burn to heat some water, and they'd done that. They added three peppermint candies found in Rich's pockets to add some taste to it.

Dar was seated on their now dry sleeping bag tucked between two rocks, with one of the tarps wrapped around the back of the rocks to form a tent like shelter. It was preferable to arguing over one of the four tents. The tarp smelled of the river. It had come from the bottom of the sack they'd salvaged from the raft.

There was room between the rocks for two people. With the tarp overhead, Dar figured it was about as good as it was going to get.

Kerry came over and sat down next to her, the small day bag from the raft between her hands. "Dar."

"Yes."

"I have something terrible to tell you."

Dar's eyes popped wide and she turned to look at Kerry in alarm."What?"

Kerry carefully looked both ways then leaned closer to her. "There's one granola bar left in this bag."

Dar blinked. "That's terrible?"

"I don't want to share it with anyone."

"That's terrible?" Dar repeated, in a quizzical tone.

Kerry tucked the bag behind them and leaned back against the rubble, her booted feet sticking out from their little shelter. "In Sunday school they taught us to share with everyone. Nothing there covered something like this though."

"No." Dar snuggled in next to her and folded her hands in her lap. They both watched the group of people arguing around the table. "They still at it?"

"I think the whole situation is getting to everyone," Kerry said. "Everyone's scared too."

"Are you?"

Kerry pondered the question in silence for a minute. "I'm not, really." She sounded surprised. "I'm worried, you know? About our family and the people at the office. I know they really depend on you and me. And I'm worried about the dogs."

"Mm."

"But as long as we're together, it's hard to really be afraid." Kerry smiled a little. "I feel like it's always been that way," she added. "I remember how out of sorts I was, in Washington, until you got there. Then I was still freaked out, but I just felt like it was okay because you were there."

"Yeah," Dar said. "I was scared because you were there where all the stuff was going down. Alastair knew. It was hard for me to concentrate on anything."

"Really?"

"Really." Dar gazed fondly at her. "C'mon, Ker. I left Miami without even my driver's license, laptop, or anything. You figure my head was screwed on straight?"

"Mm."

"So I'm not scared now. Just pissed off," Dar said. "I'm pissed off that nature is kicking our ass, and that these people were not prepared, and that we made so many bad choices. We could have been at the end of the river by now, flying back and chilling in our RV." She lifted her hands. "We're here. We're screwed. We have no plan on how to get out of here besides trying to hike back the way we came, with no supplies."

"Yeah." Kerry sighed.

"People have accused me of being a control freak." Dar took a breath.

"You?" Kerry's brows lifted in mock surprise. "Really?"

"But this is why," Dar said. "I want to be in charge of

everything so I only have myself to blame."

Kerry patted Dar's thigh under its covering of cotton. She could see the group around the table rock breaking up now, and felt a sense of relief that they were not going to have to go over there and intervene. The crew all went over to one tent.

"Cozy," Dar commented.

Eight squeezed into a tent made for four. Kerry was glad they were in their own little shelter, as the rest of the group split up into male and female clusters, and took two of the remaining tents. With a smirk, Todd and Amy took the third.

Kerry shook her head. "Dudley Douchebag."

Dar hiked up one knee and circled it with her arm. "I think we should hike back tomorrow. Regardless of what these other people do."

"By ourselves?"

Dar nodded. "Only one way back. I'll rig what's left of that raft and we can go down the river."

Kerry thought about that. "So just leave these guys behind?" She asked. "What if they want to go to, some of them?"

Dar was saved the need to answer by a yell, and then a scream. They started up out of their little nest as Todd and Amy exploded out of their tent in a scramble of arms, legs, and debris. "Motherfucker!" Todd bawled at the top of his voice.

The rest of the gang came pouring out of their two tents, but the crew flap stayed shut. Dar got to her feet and stood in front of their shelter, hands in her pockets, unsure of what was going on.

Kerry stepped around her and went over to where Amy was slapping at her arms and legs. "What's up?"

"Ants!" Amy said. "Ow! Shit!"

Todd was brushing himself off, so Kerry went over and started helping Amy out, since she was visibly covered by the insects.

The rest of the gang, after watching a moment, went back inside. "Better check in here for them," Don said in a philosophic tone. "Though with any luck the only ass with ants is that one."

Todd paused and stared at him, but Don just pushed aside the tent flap for Rich and Dave and ignored the look.

Todd jerked back as Dar walked behind him, but she merely started to brush off the visible ants on his shirt. "Thanks," he said, grudgingly.

"Hard to believe a nest of ants lived through all that water." Dar paused to peer inside. "Oh, crap." She stepped back. "Its infested."

"Assholes had it in storage." Todd shook his arms viciously. "Fuckers."

"Bet they knew," Amy said.

Kerry glanced at the shut tent of the crew, and mentally acknowledged the truth of the idea. "I think I got them all," she told Amy. "Sorry about that."

"Jerks." Amy carefully stamped out all the live insects who scurried in all directions.

After a moment, Kerry helped her, not wanting to lead them to their shelter. They were large, and dark colored, and had vicious jaws to bite with.

Todd pulled the tent down and dragged it after him, heading a little ways down the path. Then he stopped, paused, turned around, and came back. He stopped next to the closed crew tent before he started shaking the infested one out.

"That probably won't do much," Amy said. "Unless he cuts a hole in that canvas."

Kerry went back to their shelter, carefully inspecting the ground, and her boots, before she crawled back inside.

Dar looked around the empty canyon, listening to the wind whistling down it and the soft clink of the rocks tumbling out of place in the landslide behind them.

It felt barren and unsafe. She was unhappy being where they were, and she didn't see the conditions improving in the short or long term.

She was hungry and thirsty. She wanted some milk. Most of all, she wanted to be somewhere else. With a sigh, she rocked up and down on her heels and watched the pink of sunset painting the top of the canyon, the rest of it cast already in twilight blue.

Amy came over and stood next to her. "Todd and I are going to hike out tomorrow morning. You and your SO want to come with us?" she asked. "Between us we have the best chance of getting out."

Dar regarded her somberly. "Leave the rest of them here?"

Amy nodded. "If everyone goes, we're going to take six forever's to get out, if we even do. You know that. You've got brains."

It was true. She did know it. And after all, hadn't she just been talking to Kerry about doing the same thing? It was also true that Amy and Todd, assholes that they were, had skills. "Yeah maybe," Dar said. "Let me talk to Ker about it. We gotta get out of here."

Amy looked relieved. "If we get back to that raft, we can do it."

"And I can catch us more fish." Dar's lips twitched a bit.

"Though right now I'd rather catch a cheeseburger."

Amy smiled. "Me too. And a big plate of French fries." She turned and went over to where Todd was still shaking the tent out. She grabbed hold of one side, leaned close, and whispered to him.

Dar went back to their little shelter and sat down. "You hear?"

"Uh huh." Kerry leaned against the rock with her hands folded over her stomach. "That's a crappy thing to do, hon."

"You rather stay here?"

"No," Kerry admitted. "It's a crappy thing, but staying here is crappier. We can send help back."

"We can," Dar said. "But who knows? We could be flying off into space by the morning with all the insanity that's been going on around here. Or be attacked by a sheep."

"Not if it knows what's good for it," Kerry replied. "Stop making me think of lamb chops" She took out the last protein bar and split it in half, handing Dar a portion. "Actually, at this point, I'd take some of those crackers."

Thus prompted, Dar pulled her bag over and started rooting in it, as though by wishing she'd find some inside. She upended the bag and dumped the content out, a pair of sunglasses, an empty water bottle, her book, a t-shirt, and, last of all, a packet of crackers.

With a satisfied grunt, she handed it over to Kerry. "There ya go."

Kerry stared at it. "I thought you didn't have any more?"

Dar shrugged. "Maybe it was wrapped in the shirt, or maybe it's just because you wanted it." She smiled at Kerry, and winked.

"Should we save it?" Kerry asked. "Just have our bar, and save this for the morning?" She studied the package. "At least it's something." She handed it back. "Especially if we're going to start hiking."

"Okay." Dar put the packet back in her bag. "Better than roasting and eating those ants. Or eating them raw." She closed the bag and put it away, then turned to see Kerry staring at her. "What?"

"Have you actually done that?" Kerry winced, seeing Dar nod.

"Dar, no!"

"They taste kinda lemony," Dar said, after a pause. "It's better than starving." She crossed her ankles. "Lot more stuff to eat in Florida than here, though." She nibbled on the edge of her protein bar. "Best thing we had was—"

Kerry covered her eyes. "Please don't say palmetto bugs."

"Rabbit," Dar admitted. "But squirrel isn't bad either if you put enough hot sauce on it." She studied Kerry's horrified stare. "Give it a rest, Yankee. You were just asking for lamb chops."

Kerry drew breath, then made a hmphing noise. "Bunnies are cuter than sheep," she muttered, then fell silent for a moment. Then she turned and regarded Dar.

"Yes, its crappy to leave everyone," Dar responded promptly. "I just don't know if there are any good choices at this point."

"You can read my mind."

'Yes."

Kerry studied her profile, as Dar tilted her head a little to return her gaze. "Or I'm that predictable," she finally said with a slight grin.

Dar's eyes warmed and gentled. "You wear your convictions on the outside."

One of Kerry's blond brows quirked. "Says the shining old soul."

Dar stuck her tongue out.

THE CLOUDS WERE back the next morning, and they all gathered together around the table rock, regarding the sky overhead and each other. The wind was shifting and fitful, blowing their hair in varying directions as they felt the renewed moisture in it.

It meant nothing good.

There was nothing but hot water to drink, and they did, burning the last of the grass and standing in silence until it just got too uncomfortable to bear.

Dar finally bent to the pressure. "Okay. We can't stay here. We can't climb over this thing, we can't go anywhere but back the way we came. That's it."

"It's true," Janet said. "But if it starts raining again it's going to flood out. "She looked around. "At least this is high ground."

"High ground to starve to death in?" Todd asked. "You're an idiot."

"No, there's still Doug," Janet said. "If he got down the river, there will be people looking for us. We just have to hang in here. We've got people hurt, and it could be dangerous if we get caught in another flood."

"But what if he didn't?" Dar asked, in a mild tone. "How

long do you wait?"

"Well..." Janet hesitated, but looking around at the crew showed nothing but noncommittal faces.

"You can't hike out, because you're too weak?" Amy said. "We have to move out." She indicated herself, then Todd. "We're going to go." She looked at Dar, and Kerry. "You coming?"

Kerry nodded. "We have to move," she said. "There is literally nothing here for us." She looked around their surroundings. "At least on the other side of the valley, there was brush and a chance of finding something to eat."

Don nodded as well. "That's true. We can't stay here."

"Yeah," Rich said, reluctantly. "Wish you'd kept that damn rabbit," he muttered, giving Dar a slit eyed look.

Dar was actually wishing the same thing, but remained silent regarding that and changed the subject back. "So we should pack up and move out before it starts raining," she said. "Sooner we start, sooner we can get somewhere useful."

Reluctantly, Janet nodded in agreement. "Let's see how far we can get." She motioned to the crew to start breaking down the tents. They all separated and moved around in grumpy silence to gather their things up.

Dar unhooked the tarp they'd used and folded it up, tucking the bungee cords away as Kerry rolled up the sleeping bag, much the worse for wear. But at least they'd gotten some rest. From the bleary eyes of the other passengers, it seemed most hadn't.

And they'd had their crackers. Kerry tried to feel guilty about not sharing them, but failed miserably. "Know something?"

Dar eyed her. "You're never going to tease me about snacks in my pockets again?"

Kerry just smiled. "Anything to keep me from eating ants."

Nearby, Rich and Dave rolled up the tent the rest of the men had shared. On the other side of them Sally and PJ were doing the same with theirs. Pete was limping gingerly around, and Janet was shaking out the cooler they'd stored the dried grass in.

Rich stood up with the rolled up rain shade in his hands. "Hey, something's in here."

"More ants?" Todd asked sarcastically. "Or maybe some scorpions?"

"No." He unrolled the canvas, and as he did something fell out, rectangular and black. It clattered onto the stones at his feet. "What the hell?" He stared at it. "What is that?"

"I was sleeping on it I think," Dave said, rubbing his back. "I thought it was a rock."

Janet pounced on it. "It's the sat phone!" She felt in her pocket for the battery as the rest of them gathered around in excitement.

Todd said what they all were probably thinking. "Are you fucking kidding me? You had this the whole time?"

Kerry clapped her hand to her forehead mutely, as Dar turned and stared off into the distance for a brief moment. Then she turned back around and put her hands on her hips, her body language expressing a singular level of silent frustration.

"OMFG," Sally said, after a shocked pause.

"How could you have missed that?" Marcia added.

"No one knew. Trust me." Janet fit the battery to the phone and closed the module in, then turned on the device, waiting for the screen to come on. "Not much batt left but we don't need much." She stared at the readout impatiently. "C'mon."

After about twenty seconds of charged silence, she turned in a circle. "We're blocked. Can't see the sat because of the walls."

"Turn it off," Dar ordered. "Let's move down the trail until we get back to that open area and try again." She looked at Todd. "Or we find a wall hard enough for you to climb."

After a pause, he nodded. "Rock on." He went back to shoving his and Amy's gear away. "Let's move."

Janet turned off the phone and started to put it in her pocket, but Rich came over and took it out of her hand. "I'll take that. Don't want you to lose it again." He put it in his cargo pocket and buttoned it. "Sorry. Gotta agree that was bush league."

Janet shrugged, and turned away. The rest of the group continued packing and getting ready to move.

THEY WERE TWO hours down the trail when it started raining. Dar got her hood up and tightened around her head as she felt the impact of the drops. Behind her, the party was clustered into a group, but Todd and Amy were ahead of them, stumping stolidly along using their hiking sticks in short, digging motions.

Kerry unfolded their sticks and handed Dar hers, pausing to pull her own hood up and trying not to think about bacon and eggs.

She didn't even usually like bacon and eggs. But right now, she was imagining them both in their kitchen, with second cups of coffee and plates of breakfast. She felt herself getting angry, at the situation and the people around. And more than anything she wanted it all to end.

End, end, end. She slid a little in the gravel and flexed her hand around her stick, as the rain increased. Perversely it was driving against them rather than coming from behind.

Of course.

Behind her she heard Rich and Sally sniping at Janet. Tracey had her arm around Pete, supporting him as he limped along with his hand curled around a branch. From where she was Kerry could see he was sweating.

Don quickened his pace, and caught up to her. "That back of his is getting worse," he said. "Hope we find that open spot soon."

"Me too," Kerry said, briefly. "I'm trying to remember how far it was from this bottom part back to that camp we made the other night."

"Downhill, after this bit here," Don said. "Should be faster." He wiped the rain out of his face. "That arch wasn't much of a shelter, though. We should go past it."

"True." Kerry shaded her eyes with one hand, blinking the rain from them. "Maybe we'll find a better spot." She slid a little again as the gravel got wet and a moment later felt Dar's grip on her arm. 'Thanks, hon."

They walked quickly across the bottom of the valley and then up the slope, between the striated walls that had lost their picturesque beauty and become stubborn impediments to their escape.

"Ugh." Don exhaled in frustration.

Ugh. Kerry echoed silently in agreement. Her cargo pants were already wet and she felt the water coming through her hiking boots. She decided to do as Dar had done and switch to her sandals at their first break.

She wished that she'd already done that, though the boots provided better protection against the rocks, and any snakes. She glanced around, acknowledging any snakes in the area were comfortably tucked somewhere, laughing at them, smart enough to avoid both the rain and klutzy tourists.

Ugh.

Dar took a sip of water, then tucked the bottle back in her pack and took a grip on Kerry's belt, as they leaned forward to start the climb up into the headwind blowing against them. Despite the lack of snacks, she felt relatively energized and was more than willing to lend that out as long as it lasted.

It was completely different, this hiking, than their usual

physical activity, and in a perverse kind of way a little bit of her enjoyed it.

It was a challenge, and she didn't often get physical ones as their day-to-day lives usually required her to provide a mental response instead. It was a somewhat new experience for her to rely on her body in this kind of way, and despite the rain and discomfort, she was extracting some satisfaction from it.

A little like way back in the day, when the need to not only keep up with, but exceed the guys. Dar smiled a little in self-deprecation as she considered what those old friends would have said seeing her face off against a mountain lion.

A mountain lion. Dar was human enough to admit slight disappointment that Kerry hadn't gotten a picture of that, though she strongly suspected it would have ended up framed in their office if she had.

Probably right over Dar's desk, in fact. Where it could be put to appropriate purpose during contract negotiations. Dar laughed silently at herself.

Kerry felt it, through the contact with her arm. "What's so funny?"

"Tell ya later."

A yell, behind them. Dar turned and put her back to the rain. "Damn." She released Kerry and they both started back to where a cluster of people were now stopped around someone on the ground. "Now what?"

They arrived to find Rich kneeling next to Dave, who'd slipped and ended up landing on his hand. "Dude, that's nasty," Rich told his friend. "It bent all the way back, I saw it."

Of course it was. Dar dropped to one knee and held her hand out to him. "Let me see it."

Without hesitating, Dave complied. She gently cradled his injured hand in hers. She could see the bruising starting already, a deep, blue-black stain spreading across just above the wrist. "He's right, that's nasty."

Kerry knelt next to her. "What can we do?"

Janet sat down on a nearby rock. "Not much." She produced the battered aid kit. "Nothing in here for that."

The rain came down harder. Dar studied Dave's hand for a minute. "Anyone got some sticks? A shirt we can cut up?" A certain engineering mindset took over as Dar made a picture in her head of what she thought might work for this injury. Then she eased her knee forward and rested his arm on it.

Rich came plopping down, a little out of breath. "I passed

this back there." He displayed two branches, spindly and bare, about a finger width in size.

Dar took out her knife and put it down on her knee as the rest of the gang gathered around them, some standing with their backs to the rain blocking it somewhat. She broke the branches midway along their length and then picked up her blade and used it to trim off the edges.

"Okay, let's see if we can at least make it so it doesn't move."

Rich nodded. "That's the ticket."

Janet looked past them. "Hey, someone run after those other two and tell them to hold up," she said, motioning to the crew standing around.

"Screw them," Tracey said, bluntly. "They'll figure it out."

"Or they won't," Don said. "But I agree with the lady. Let 'em go." He edged over a little to watch what Dar was doing. "They wanted to go off on their own anyhow."

"And I've got the phone," Rich said. He ripped a shirt into strips of cloth that were twisting and wet in the rain as he handed them to Kerry to hold for Dar.

"But he can climb the wall," Janet said.

"I can climb it," Rich said. "I've done half dome too." Everyone looked at him. "I just keep my mouth shut a lot more than he does."

"Got a plan B then. Good," Don nodded.

Dar lay the sticks along Dave's hand, holding them in place as Kerry carefully wrapped a strip of cloth around them putting the binding just exactly where she would have in some odd synchronicity between them.

A momentary flash of almost memory flickered through the back of her mind, of kneeling in just this way, using the roughest of tools. In that memory too, there was rain, and the close presence and steady unremarkable assistance at her side.

Then it was gone and she was cautiously tying the cloth in a knot. "How's that?"

Dave looked forlornly at his hand. "I can't move it."

"That's the point," Don said. "C'mon, give me a hand getting him up on his feet." He waited for Rich to scramble up and they got Dave under the arms and lifted. "Good job there, lady." He gave Dar a brief grin, as Tracey hiked Dave's pack back up on his back.

"Dar has pretty much unlimited skills," Kerry said, as they turned and started their march back up the path. "She's a human Swiss Army knife."

Dar gave her a droll look.

Kerry shrugged, and patted her on the back. "Well you are."

THE ARCH, WHEN they got back to it, seemed somehow less of a shelter than it had the previous day, with the rain now coming down in earnest.

There was still some daylight left, and they stood under the arch regarding the way forward. There was no sign of either Todd or Amy, and no one said anything about that either.

Kerry folded her arms and leaned one shoulder against the rock wall. "After what happened to that other arch? Not sure I want to stay under this one anyway. If we'd been camped there last night, I'm pretty sure we'd all be toast."

"I've never seen that happen before," Janet said. "It was a freak chance."

"Everything in this trip's been a freak chance," Rich shot back. "I'm with Kerry. I don't want to take it."

They were tired, grumpy, and hungry, and at least some of them scared.

"We should keep going," Dar said, after a pause. "Let's see how far we can get." She opened her water bottle and stepped out into the rain, watching it fill from a torrent coming off the arch. "At least we have this."

"At least." Dave tried to hold his bottle one handed, giving Tracey a look of gratitude as she came over to help. "I'd rather walk. If I sit down, this is going to hurt so much it'll drive me crazy. Walking at least I can think of something else."

Kerry removed her pack and fished out a small case, opening it. "Want some Advil?" She offered him the tablets, which he eagerly accepted. "I've only got about a dozen, but you're welcome to some."

"Thanks, Kerry." Dave gulped them back with a swallow of his water. "They burned through what was in that little aid kit." He clipped the water bottle back to his belt and took hold of his stick again, waiting for the rest of them to start moving.

Everyone got up and stood briefly, watching the rain come down before reluctantly starting back out into it. It was downhill now. They could see water pooling at the bottom of the trail, as sheets of the rain washed down the rock path.

Kerry glanced behind them, then sighed and continued on.

DAR SLID THE last few feet into water up to her shins and immediately felt the pull of the current as it rushed along sideways. "Careful!" She yelled back. She felt Kerry thump against her, the impact almost taking both of them down.

"Oof. Sorry." Kerry got her balance and they paused as the rest of the group caught up.

"Oh crap." PJ said as she held on to her stick, balancing on her good foot and lifting her cut one up out of the water. "This is cray cray."

Dar peered around the bend. "Let me see how bad it is." She waded carefully into the current, using her stick to balance as she felt the shove of the water against her calves. It was cold, but a little warmer than the rain driving against her and she blinked a few times to clear it from her eyes.

This was going nowhere good. Dar made her way down what was becoming a fast running stream, hearing the rumble of thunder over head with a sense of surreal irritation. About halfway down the steep decline there was a curve in the wall. Past that the path sloped down and to the side again, but left an area clear, with a little elevation.

There was no shelter, but at least they'd be able to stand. Dar turned and waved them forward, pointing behind the rock. There was even enough clear space between the walls that there was a chance the phone might work. She braced one arm against the wall and stepped back out into the current as she watched the rest approach.

They could put the tents up. That would have to be enough shelter. It was getting dark and she was shivering in her jacket, pretty damn sure all of them were going to end up sick as hell.

Maybe if the rain stopped, they could move on to the lower valley, where the cave was. That was even more open. She figured that open space she and Kerry had walked across to get to the waterfall might have room to land a copter,.

But first they would stop and rest on the ledge. She kept an eagle eye on Kerry's progress, hoping no one else would slip and fall. They were reaching their limits, all of them.

She reached out her hand to Kerry and they clasped, and she pulled her behind the bend in the wall and up onto the ledge.

Kerry put her back against the wall, now out of the wind and the driving rain. "Dar this is nuts!"

"I know," Dar said. "Going to continue that way." She grimaced as two of the oncoming bodies slipped and tumbled, but they got up and kept moving toward the shelf. "I thought maybe we could rest a little then try to get to the valley down there."

Kerry took a few steps to the side and looked down the path, where the rain rushing was gaining real volume. "I dunno, hon." She glanced down at her soaked boots and sighed. "But there sure isn't much up here."

The rest of the group clustered onto the high spot and spread out, shielding their heads from the rain as best they could.

Dar put her arm across Kerry's shoulders as the crew put the long cooler down, the repository of pretty much everything dry. The injured sat down on it. Everyone was tired.

Dar studied the path downward.

"Best of evil choices?" Kerry put her arms around Dar and savored the warmth of the contact, and the relief from the driving rain. She closed her eyes and felt, for a minute, like she could just fall asleep standing up there in this momentary spot of almost comfort.

Sally came to lean on the wall next to them. "We can't really stay here."

Rich sighed and folded his arms. "Well, we can. But I sure don't want to. Maybe we can at least get some stuff farther on to make some tea. Or salad. Or anything."

Pete knelt on the ground, his elbows and chest resting on the cooler. "I feel like such crap."

Dave sat next to him, his bandaged hand resting on his knee. "Me too." PJ was at his side, her foot propped up. Janet, the last of the injured, was leaning against the wall, keeping the weight off her cut leg.

Marcia sat on the edge of the cooler, her face pale. Everyone was shivering, half obscured in the heavy rain.

Dar considered them. "Let's put up the tarps best we can and get some relief," She finally said. "I think that slope's pretty dangerous with the rain right now."

Rich glanced past her. "We could make it."

Dar turned and met his eyes. "Not all of us, maybe. And if someone else gets hurt, we're running out of people to help carry them."

Grudgingly, he nodded. "Yeah."

Tracey watched him. Then she turned and went over to where Pete was kneeling. She crouched down next to him and helped him up as they opened up the cooler and removed the top layer of tarps.

The sound of the rain on the fabric was loud and sharp. Dar

turned and studied the wall, then she released Kerry and went over to the edge of the tarp and took one of the bungies attached to it. It had a ball in the middle of it and she tucked the ball into a crack in the rock above her head.

That immediately got everyone moving, and in the small triangle of rock they quickly found spots for the other balls, raising a shelter over them that everyone gathered under.

"That's better," PJ said, wringing her jacket out. "At least, a little better."

It was better. Kerry kept her jacket on and zipped up, waiting for the shivers in her body to subside. After hours of the rain pounding on her head, it was a relief to just stand there without it. She glanced up at the gray sky, then ran a hand through her hair and tried to brush some of the water out of it.

Dar came up behind her and put her hands on Kerry's shoulders, gently massaging them and granting her a moment of solace out of proportion to the action.

They all fell silent, staring out at the rain.

Chapter Eleven

THE RAIN FINALLY slowed down. Dar wrung out her clothing as best as she could, but put the damp garments back. She figured the wet was going to continue, and getting two sets of clothes wet made no sense.

Standing in the rain made no sense, sitting in the rain made no sense, waiting to get so cold they started chattering made no sense. Dar exhaled.

The wind was dropping, at least. She went to the edge of the shelter and looked out over the path, judging the rush of the water still heading downhill.

Kerry came over to stand next to her. "Whatcha thinking?"

"Thinking I don't want to stay up here," Dar answered. "Want to go looking around for a better place with me?"

Kerry smiled. "Is that a serious question?"

"Not really, no."

Kerry folded her arms and rocked up and down on her hiking boots a little. She had her hood down, exposing her short pale hair in damp disarray. "It'll be pretty slow going if everyone joins us."

"Everyone's not joining us," Dar said calmly. "No saying we'll find anything better before it gets dark. We come back if not."

Behind them the rest of the group was sitting down on the remaining tarps, just trying to stay as dry as they could. No one was talking. Rich had made no effort to get out his cards. Pete was still draped over the cooler, resting on his belly with his arms folded under his head.

Don wandered over. "You gals want to sit down over there? We got some space." He gestured vaguely behind him. "Not real comfortable, but it's something."

Dar shook her head. "No." She stuck her hand out and judged the rain. "I think we're going to go see if we can find a better place to shelter."

"It's too cold to just sit out here," Kerry said. "My lips are turning blue."

Dar inspected them. She leaned over unexpectedly and covered Kerry's lips with her own for quite some seconds, then pulled back.

Kerry's cheeks were now pink, and she gave Dar an abashed look. Dar leaned forward and kissed her again, cupping her hand around the back of Kerry's neck, and willing the body heat to transfer. Then she paused and examined her face again. "Better?"

"Yes." Kerry cleared her throat. "Better stop though. I'm getting lightheaded from blushing."

Dar chuckled briefly, then released Kerry and put her hands in her pockets.

Kerry cleared her throat again. "So I agree with Dar. We should see if we can find a place with more shelter, where we can find something to light up so it's not so cold."

Don nodded. "Good idea. Let me and one of those fellers come along too." He turned and went back over to the group, pulling Rich aside and speaking to him.

Dar's eyes narrowed. "Did I ask for company?" She muttered.

Kerry patted her side. "It'll be good to have company. Especially if we have to make a hand bridge over water or something like that." She turned. "Let me get my pack and our sticks."

Dar zipped her jacket up and put the hood up around her head, snugging it tight under her jaw and fastening the throat flap of the waterproof garment.

Don and Rich came over, with their packs on their back.

"Good idea," Rich said. "I'm really sick and tired of being here." He tightened the sleeves on his jacket around his wrists. "I'm starving."

"We all are," Don said. "So let's see if we can find a better spot. You got that radio phone?"

"Got it." Rich said. "We told the rest of them where we're going." He put up his hood. "Told em if we found some place we'd come back and get everyone."

"And if it got dark we'd shelter ourselves under someplace," Don said. "They can catch up in the morning. Easier to find shelter for four."

Easier to find for two. Kerry could almost hear Dar's thoughts audibly as Dar adjusted the straps on the pack she was carrying, brow puckered. She gave her a pat on the hip and took a deep breath, pausing to sip a mouthful of rain water from her bottle, hoping it would quell her complaining stomach.

"True that," Rich said. "Let's go."

Dar led the way out into the gray light, starting down the path. The rushing water covered her boots, but presented no real impediment to her progress. She probed the ground with the stick Kerry handed her, and they made their way down the slope and out of sight of the camp with relative speed.

"Glad to be out of that bunch," Don said, after about twenty minutes walking. "Rather be doing something constructive."

"Yeah." Rich maneuvered around a half-submerged boulder. "It was getting cold just standing there. Kerry's right. We're going to end up with hypothermia."

"Better walking." Kerry felt herself warming up, despite the fact her pants were once again drenched with rain. "If we can get back to that shelter from the other night, there were those sagebrush bushes, and those trees near the waterfall."

They could see the bottom of the trail. "Could be," Don said. "Looks like it's not too bad there." He looked around. "You figure those other two came this way? We should have caught them by now, yeah?"

Dar started slightly. "Crap. Forgot all about them," she admitted. "No telling which way they went. Not like this ground holds footprints."

There were several bends in the path ahead of them and they went down the slope sideways, unable to really see their footing with all the water. The rain, as though in cooperation with them slowed to an annoying mist, droplets fine but still stinging.

"Florida rain's sure not like this," Kerry said, after a brief silence. "Drops big enough to knock you over."

"Tropical," Don said.

"Part of it, yes," Dar said. "Bottom three counties are tropical. Above that's sub-tropical." She evaded a rush of water over a big rock and moved closer to the right wall of the canyon. "But all of it's hot."

"What was 9-11 like for you ladies?" Don asked. "Must have been strange with all those pilots being trained down there."

Dar and Kerry exchanged glances. "I was out of the country the day it happened," Dar said. "Kerry was in Michigan. We didn't get back until most of that was over."

"I was at work," Rich said. "We had a big promotion starting that day so we were all in early getting ready for it. I'd just sat down with a bagel when one of the admins came running in and told us to all come into the breakroom and watch CNN."

"I was cleaning the garage," Don said. "Marcia came in and told me a plane had hit the World Trade Center. I thought it was a Piper Cub or something. Some sightseeing thing, you know?" He shook his head. "I said, yeah, so what?"

Kerry amiably joined in. "I was eating breakfast with my family. Or, actually, brunch I think. Dar called me from the UK."

Dar nodded. "I was on the line with my admin, ordering a marketing kit. I heard from one of our staff through the phone something was happening and we turned it on where we were."

"Everyone remembers where they were right then," Don said. "It was that kind of moment."

Rich nodded. "They sent us home. We didn't come back in for a week. You guys?" He looked at Dar and Kerry.

"Not exactly." They both answered in unison, then looked at each other again. Kerry tilted her head in Dar's direction.

Dar reached the next curve and peered around it. "Company we worked for did some work to help the recovery," she said, briefly. "We were tied up with that a few weeks."

They continued around the corner and across the next narrow area, where the flowing water was puddling at the bottom of the path. It was halfway up Dar's lower legs, and she pushed through it to the next angle that started upward.

Don examined some debris on the wall. "Must have been pretty high here. Don't think we should bring those hurt people through unless it drops."

"Hey, wait," Rich said, suddenly. "I remember seeing you on the news!" He caught hold of Dar's arm. "I knew I'd seen you somewhere before! I saw you interviewed about something you were doing in New York!"

They paused and Dar looked at him. "Yeah." She turned and kept going. "C'mon, we're getting soaked here." She climbed around the corner and they started up again, quickly getting past the pooling and back onto higher ground.

"We worked with the city on restoring some services," Kerry said, after they'd hiked upward for about five minutes. "I remember that interview. We were at our offices in Rockefeller Center and they were asking us about some of the things we were doing."

"Stock exchange?" Don asked, giving her a shrewd look.

"Something of that, yes," Kerry said. "Some other things, services for the city, things like that."

"Uh huh," Don said. "Pal of mine works for Verizon." He sidled up the slope sideways. "He was there. I remember him telling me some crazy stories."

"Mm." Kerry grinned briefly. "It was a strange time."

The rock ground now was quite slippery, and Dar focused on leaning forward and keeping her boots from slipping on the wet gravel, still feeling the rain hitting the hood over her head. She started looking forward as they climbed up along the track, then saw motion ahead of them. "Whoa."

"Hey, it's a sheep," Rich said, with some excitement. "Let's catch it!" He started to plunge up the path, slipping and sliding as he dashed after the animal.

Don groaned. "He's going to kill himself. Hey! Watch it! Be careful!"

Just as Don said it, Rich slipped and then he tumbled back down toward them. Kerry dodged over to get in the way but found herself hauled back out of the way as Dar pulled them both to one side. "Let him go," she said. "If he hits you you'll both go down."

Don had also jumped clear, and Rich was unable to stop himself until he was at the bottom of the slope, rolling into the pool of water.

Dar sighed. Then she started down with the rest of them hastily following.

"YEAH, IT WAS stupid," Rich said. He was sitting on a rock, his pants leg rolled up exposing a bloody kneecap. "You don't have to tell me. I'm just so damn hungry all I saw was a chance to get something to eat."

Dar finished wrapping a strip of shirt fabric around the bruised cut. "Unless it was a girl and we were going to milk it, wouldn't have done much for us." She stood up. "There, try that." She looked around. "Does it pay to keep going on?"

"Oh, don't let me be the one to squish this." Rich got up hastily and stamped around in a circle, his boots splashing in the edge of the pooled rainwater. "Okay, let's go." He picked up his stick, grimacing as he eased his elbow out straight. "Sorry guys."

The wind picked up again as they started uphill, this time on a path free of mammals. Rich was limping, and he tucked his left arm close to his body, using his stick with his right hand.

Dar took the lead again and they climbed steadily up, keeping speech to a minimum as the clouds drifted grumpily overhead, spattering down rain that smacked against the rubberized surface of their jackets and sounded like large caterpillars dropping out of the sky.

They got to the top of the rise and up into the small pass, where the walls narrowed and cut the wind, and the tall walls arched over and gave them some protection and relief. Walking on flat ground was a relief as well, and Dar flexed her legs that were burning a little from the climb.

The canyon angled to the left, and they crossed under two thick arches as they straddled a thin stream of water running down the middle of the path. They had just started through the narrow passage that would lead to the larger valley when they heard hoof beats again.

Dar, in the lead, stopped and lifted her hand up. "What's that?"

"That sheep?" Rich eased up behind her and peered past her shoulder.

Dar got both hands around her hiking pole just in time as a large animal skittered through the end of the passage and headed right for them with its horns down in an aggressive charge.

"Holy shit."

"Get against the wall." Dar braced herself and lifted the pole as the animal came right at her. "Kerry get behind me."

"Gotcha." Kerry put her arms around Dar and braced her legs.

Don and Rich flattened themselves against the wall as the bighorn lunged at them. At the last minute Dar slammed the pole end into the animal's face and let out a loud yell. It veered to one side and then turned, trying to butt her.

Kerry released her hold and grabbed the horns, yanking the sheep to one side and letting out a yell of her own. The sheep stuck its tongue out and baa'd in frustration. It jerked it's head back and forth as Dar took the opportunity to kick it in the ribs.

"Where's your knife!" Rich yelled. "Let's kill it!"

Kerry released her hold and the sheep reeled backwards, smacking itself against the opposite wall before it dashed off in the opposite direction, heading through the narrows back the way they'd come.

Rich went after it, and Don as well, running as fast as they could after the creature.

Kerry drew a breath. "Should we have killed that thing, Dar?"

Dar watched their companions throw rocks after the sheep, as it plunged downhill as fast as it could go. "Do you know how to butcher a sheep?"

Kerry blinked. "No."

"Me either," Dar said. "Most I can handle is a rabbit or a squirrel. What the hell are we going to do with a quarter ton animal?" She asked. "We left the pots and pans and everything behind, Ker. Everything's wet."

Don and Rich came jogging back. "Damn it," Rich said. "We had it! We coulda killed it! That thing'd feed us for a week!"

"You can be in front next time and grab it," Dar said. "If we find another one closer to the shelter I'll jump on it with ya." She went quickly to the passage the animal had come down. She passed through it and down into the plateau where they'd burned Josh's body, the remnants of the fire, and his bones, already washed long away.

IT MADE DAR feel better, being out in the open, despite the rain that kept coming down and the wind that was making her eyes water. Off to one side she could hear the waterfall, and all of them breathed audible sighs of relief.

"That overhang's still there," Rich said. "Let me run back and get the rest of them. I think they can make it, right?" He looked overhead. "Maybe just after dark?"

Dar shaded her eyes and looked across at their former shelter. "Yeah," she said. "You guys want to go back and get them? Kerry and I will start hunting around for some wood we can dry off."

"Sounds good," Don said. "You ladies going to be okay by yourselves?"

"Yes," Kerry said. "I think I see some dead bushes over there we can use for kindling. And who knows? Maybe Dar'll find a...um." Her voice trailed off. "Something."

Dar chuckled. "I'll try."

"We'll look too," Rich said. "If I find that sheep I can get the rest of those guys to help carry it." He flourished his walking stick and started back up the path. After a moment Don followed him.

"Be careful!" Don yelled back over his shoulder.

Dar watched them climb back up the slope. Then she turned and regarded Kerry. "At last."

"We're alone," Kerry completed the thought.

Dar extended her hand and they clasped fingers, then turned and started along the narrow track that wound through the valley floor. The rain pattered softly against their rain jackets and made the puddles on the path dance.

"You know what's weird?" Kerry said, after they'd walked in silence for about five minutes.

"Those two jerks disappeared."

Kerry sighed. "You really can read my mind," she said. "Yeah, that's it. It's only one path back, Dar. We have the phone."

"He has the phone." Dar pointed over her own shoulder. "I was thinking about those guys. We should have caught them up."

"You think they climbed out?"

Dar looked at the canyon walls, towering over them. "Maybe. You'd think we could see them, though. He said the walls back there were too soft to climb. Maybe these aren't." She shaded her eyes again and started searching the dark gray surface. "This looks like different rock."

It was getting dark. Twilight was already putting the valley in shadow, but the light tan of the pocket canyons they had come out of was definitely different than the cliffs the waterfall was pouring out of. There was no sign of anyone scaling them, though.

Dar put her attention back on the trail. They were moving down into the flat part of the valley and there were dripping scrub brush on either side of the path. They passed three or four sodden logs that were split and cracked.

No animals though. Dar kept walking, aware of how hungry she was. The weather had driven everything under shelter, and as she tipped her head back, there weren't even any birds to be seen drifting overhead.

Not that she had anything to catch one with anyway. Dar sighed.

Kerry squeezed her hand gently. "We'll get through this, hon. It just seems like a walk through hell right now."

Dar listened to the rain for a moment. "We've been through worse." She felt her shoulders relax as they increased their distance from the rest of the party, at least for the moment. It was nice not to hear voices around them, or the sound of things being moved.

There was just the wind swirling around them, the soft sounds of their boots against the rough path, the waterfall in the distance.

"You know what I wish we had?" Kerry spoke up, after a pause.

"Dinner."

"A horse."

"For dinner?" Dar's voice lifted in mild outrage.

"To ride on." Kerry chuckled a little. "Wouldn't it be nice? We've been walking all day. I'm tired. I want a nice palomino horse to ride."

"Those other guys would want to eat him," Dar said. "We'd end up defending the damn thing with my pocketknife and your makeshift frypan."

Kerry wiped the rain out of her eyes, her shoulders shaking with laughter. "Oh God I can imagine that too. I mean, would any of us know what to do if we did catch a sheep, Dar? Seriously?"

"Seriously I'd hope it was a lady sheep," Dar responded, as she skirted a deep puddle. "I do know how to milk goats and it can't be that different."

"You do?"

"Yup."

"Can you milk a cow?"

"Yup."

Kerry eyed her. "Dar, you grew up on a Navy base, not a farm. What's up with that?"

"Moo," Dar warbled. "Okay, so we were on the base that was south of the Redlands," Dar said. "Remember I said I had a buddy who had some horses I learned to ride on?"

Kerry frowned, then her expression cleared. "Oh, yeah, sure. When we went on that ride on our first vacation, and my horse got bee stung. I nearly got bucked off to the next state. I should have gotten the warning about vacations with you right then."

Dar chuckled. "With me? That was my first vacation in a decade."

"Mm."

"Anyway, my buddy had a couple dozen of everything there. Horses, cows, goats, and chickens. You name it," Dar said. "So I learned to milk the cows and goats." She smiled in memory. "He was the original farm to table guy, decades before it was trendy."

"Did he make his own cheese and stuff?" Kerry kicked a rock ahead of them. "Like, it was a real farm?"

"He did," Dar said. "He was gay. And talking to him, made me realize I might be too."

Kerry blinked. "How old were you?"

"Twelve, thirteen maybe." Dar shaded her eyes and watched a bird circling overhead. "He was maybe thirty? His parents had owned the farm and they passed on. He had come home after living in San Francisco for five years."

"Culture shock?"

"Kinda. The Redlands were a little thin on liberalism. Still are." Dar studied the sky. "Those look like vultures." She turned her head and regarded Kerry. "That could be gross but sort of okay, or really horrific."

Kerry eyed the birds. "Well, let's go find out." She increased her pace, and they moved doggedly up the path and through the weather ravaged bushes, hopping over streams of runoff.

Some were too wide to jump, and Dar paused as they reached what was in truth a small creek, the water clear and in motion. She took a step into it and sank up to her knees, throwing out her hands for balance. "Whoa."

Kerry cautiously followed her, grimacing at the chill of the water as it soaked her pants immediately. They waded across as fast as they could and climbed up the other side, then continued on the path as they closed in on the overhanging shelf they'd sheltered under previously.

The shelf was there, intact, and Dar spared the spot a few moments attention before she tipped her head back up again and focused on the vultures.

Condors, actually. "Let me go see what that's all about." Dar eased out from behind the rocks that had formed their protection from the mountain lion. "This is going to be about as good as it gets I guess." She took out her flashlight and unstrapped the pack on her back.

Kerry hesitated. "I'll come with you." She put her pack next to Dar's and followed her as she emerged back out into the rain.

It was growing dark. The weather was getting worse. "Keep an eye out for some stuff we can make a fire with," Dar muttered. They went up the path around the side of the valley back in the direction that would lead them eventually back to the supply hut.

The condors were circling lower, and Dar saw one coming in for a landing. She got up to the pass just in time to watch the last of the light fade over the scene of a kill. The birds were already plucking at a carcass.

Too small to be a person. Dar felt relieved. She exhaled as Kerry put a hand on her back and they moved cautiously forward, hearing the rasp and squawk of the birds as they landed.

She smelled the blood, and as they got closer, saw the outline of the animal and it's matted, already shredded coat. "I think..." Dar picked up a rock and threw it at the body, hitting one of the condors.

Kerry resisted the urge to close her eyes as they got closer.

Dar waved her arms, as the condors hopped awkwardly out of her way and cawed in disgruntlement. "It's a deer." She went over and knelt next to the carcass, already stiff in death and missing it's eyeballs. "Yeah." She touched it, seeing the front of its throat torn and stained with blood. "A mule deer. Something killed it."

"One of those lions?" Kerry hazarded a guess as she reached Dar's side and had a better view. Its neck was twisted and its mouth was gaped open, tongue protruding and half missing. "Something chewed it."

"No idea." Dar regarded it. "I guess we should take some of the meat. "She studied the dead animal that, aside from the eyes and tongue, was mostly intact.

Kerry grimaced. "It's sorta like road kill, isn't it?"

"Sorta." Dar reached back and patted her leg. "It's better than crickets, right?"

Kerry sighed.

"Or beetles." Dar pointed at one, scurrying away.

"Okay, okay."

'Want to gather stuff for a fire?" Dar looked up over her shoulder. "This gets kinda messy."

Kerry looked at her affectionately. "Thanks, honey. She leaned over and kissed Dar on the top of her head. "Thank you for being the cave woman in the family."

Dar chuckled silently. "Ooga ooga."

"The super macha cave woman." Kerry ruffled her hair. "Let me see what I can do about the cooking part." She turned and started back to the overhang, turning on her flashlight and letting it play across the ground as she walked.

Dar put her own flashlight in her teeth and removed her pocketknife, opening it and setting it down so she could rearrange the dead deer to cut it open.

It was by far the largest thing she'd ever tried to cut up and she pulled it around in a few different ways, a little glad it was raining to keep the flies back and rinse the blood away. She tried to remember how she'd done this to the small brown rabbits and squirrels they'd caught in the swamp back in the day.

She wasn't entirely sure of what she was doing with this. Nearby the condors hopped and cawed, anxious to get to the food now just out of their reach. Dar realized with the dark, and the rain, it was also possible other creatures would be out there equally as hungry as she was.

Far off, she thought she heard a yell. She paused and listened, but it wasn't repeated. "Ker?" She called out over her shoulder.

"Yeah?" Kerry's voice floated back. "Something wrong?"

"Nope. Never mind." Dar went back to her work.

KERRY DRAGGED A small fallen tree behind her as she made her way up into the shelter of the overhang. She pulled it clear of the rain and paused to wipe the rain from her face. "Phew."

Inside the little cave like space it was dark, and she turned on her flashlight and played it over her recent labor, now tucked against the back wall. Arms full of dead grass, waterlogged bushes, numerous dead tree-branches and twigs.

All soaking wet. She began breaking up the tree she'd dragged in behind her, putting the limbs up against the wall out of the rain.

Then she went to the edge of the shelter and peered out, seeing a bit of light dancing nearby that was Dar still at work. As she considered going out to help, the light disappeared, then reappeared as Dar turned and started back up to where she was standing.

No sign of the others, yet. Kerry waited as Dar ducked to enter, a bundle of blood smelling, dusky animal smelling stuff in her hands. "Ew."

"Yeah, ew," Dar said. "I left the rest there. I think a coyote was somewhere nearby growling."

Kerry shone her flashlight off past Dar into the darkness, and thought she spotted some motion. "Oh. That's not good."

Dar put the bundle down on the rock they'd previously used as a table, then went over and stuck her hands out into the rain, scrubbing at her skin and letting the water run down to clean the blade of her pocketknife. "Yeah, and this stuff is not going to burn much." She sighed.

"All I could find," Kerry replied, somewhat defensively.

"I know, hon." Dar went back and sat down on another rock. She picked up one of the pieces of wood and cut into the bark, working to peel it off. "Grab a handful of rocks, huh? In case we need them."

Kerry went over to the fire pit they'd made the last time they were there, and started collecting hand sized rocks. "Not a good mental image."

Dar split the bark and peeled it away from the inner core of the limb, exposing a somewhat dry surface underneath. She used the blade to split the inner branch into several pieces, then set them aside and started working on another piece.

Kerry carefully put the dry pieces up near the wall, and set the rocks next to them. Then she started stripping small twigs and pine needles off and putting them together with the dead grasses she'd found. "Dar?"

"Huh?" Dar wiggled the blade of her knife under the bark and levered it off. "Gonna ask me how I knew to do this?" She pointed at the branch.

"No. You come from the thunderstorm and lightning capital of the world, hon. I'm sure you know all about what to do with wet things," Kerry said, then paused and chuckled.

Dar chuckled as well. "I'll take that as a compliment."

"Punk." Kerry went back to drying her twigs.

It was an odd moment. There was something ancient and strange, and yet familiar about the place she found herself in right then, kneeling in chill discomfort, listening to the scrape of metal against wood, thinking about how good the fire would feel.

She stood up and went over to pick up more grass, stopping to peer out across the darkness of the valley. There was no sign of the rest of the group and she frowned. "What do you think is taking them so long?"

Dar glanced past her. "Maybe they decided to stay up there?" She said. "They don't know it's any better here."

Kerry grunted. Then she roamed around the cave and picked up a flat stone, bringing it back to the fire circle. She started arranging the stripped limbs Dar was peeling in a square, wedging in the smaller pieces on all sides. "Well, fine. More for us."

"They have all the supplies," Dar said. "The tarps and all that."

Kerry dried the grasses off on her shirt and stuffed them between the wood. "I have all I need right here." she said, after a moment of quiet. She looked up to find Dar looking back at her, a smile on her face. "And we have fire and deer meat. Who needs tarps?"

"Good point." Dar handed her another peeled limb. "Let's get this lit. I'm freezing."

Kerry looked up at her. "We have any matches?"

They both regarded each other. "Crap," Dar finally said.

Kerry sat down and then splayed herself backward. "Son of a bitch."

Dar got up and went to her pack, opening it and digging inside. "Maybe I have something I can use...aha!" She pulled her hand out in triumph. "Thought I remembered picking this up!"

Kerry lifted her head up. "What is it?"

"Bit of flint." Dar came back over and removed her knife from her pocket, taking a moment to wipe it off on her shirt and the piece of stone as well. She settled herself on a rock near the fire and turned the rock in her hands, then she scraped the knife blade against it.

Nothing but sound.

She scraped it again. Still nothing. "Too wet." Dar dried both off again, as Kerry sat up and wriggled around to see what she was doing. Then she turned the rock over and tried again, this time rewarded with a single spark. With a grunt, she settled closer and started smacking the rock with the knife, as they heard a rumble of thunder overhead.

On the two or three dozenth time, a shower of sparks fell into the dead grass, and a minute after that, they had a somewhat smoky little tiny blaze going, which Kerry quickly started sticking some of the twigs into. "Aha!"

"Aha," Dar said. "Took long enough." She resisted the urge to wipe her brow, scooting a little closer to the pile of smoldering brush.

Kerry could already feel the warmth against the skin of her fingers, and the light from it outlined Dar's angular profile as she continued to throw sparks into the center of the pit. She exhaled in relief, already imagining how much warmer they were going to be in just a little while.

The larger branches smoldered and popped, releasing the moisture inside them and Kerry reached over for more of the dead grass to keep things going, while Dar carefully surrounded the fire with stones. The warmth was spreading out to fill the space and providing them with light enough so that Dar turned off her flashlight to save the battery.

"Boy that feels good." Kerry held her hands out. "When that rock heats up I can throw your road kill on it and we can almost be civilized."

Thunder rumbled overhead. "And maybe we won't freeze." Dar scooted a little closer. "We can drag more branches in here to cut the wind."

They studied each other across the fire. "I hope those guys did stay in that shelter," Kerry said, after a moment. "We can go find them in the morning."

"And bring them some road kill," Dar said. She got up and retrieved the bundle of deer meat, and sat down cross legged on the sandy floor and started cutting it into gory, pungent strips.

THE DEER WAS small, but had provided plenty of food for

them both. Kerry had even found a little bit of salt in one of her pockets, and after the rock heated next to the fire she used it as a pan and grilled the strips Dar had cut on it.

That had worked better than she'd expected. Dar sharpened some discarded twigs into makeshift skewers and what had ended up was something that she could convince herself resembled Thai satay, except without the delicious peanut sauce and all that curry.

It wasn't a great taste. She never really cared for venison, but the animal had been a young one, and for sure it was better than nothing. It was hot, it filled her stomach and her body was grateful for the application of protein.

It was that, and rainwater, they had plenty of, and after they dragged all the brush they could find into the shelter, they built up the fire enough to dry their clothing and boots while the rest of the venison was cooked off for the morning.

Or for their companions, if they decided to hike up in the dark.

There was nothing to sit on, but they had put the brush between the rocks that had fallen in front of the overhang and made sort of a shelter from the wind and rain that was tolerable. Or really tolerable because there wasn't any choice.

Was that what survival was like? You just got reduced down to looking at what positive you could find because of the negative that all implied? Kerry turned over another stick full of meat and regarded it thoughtfully.

Dar was sitting next to her, using the stone she'd used to make the sparks to sharpen the blade of her pocketknife, idly drawing it across the surface making a soft scraping sound. "I feel better," she said, after a pause. "Glad we got to that deer before whatever killed it did."

"Me too," Kerry said. She picked up one of the cluster of leaves and waved off the smoke from the fire, pushing it toward the gaps in the rock and away from them. "So, what's the plan?"

Dar cocked her head. "What's the plan?" She asked back.

"C'mon, Dar. You're a lot more experienced in this stuff than I am. My entire experience of camping was in a cabin with room service, and you know it."

Dar scratched the bridge of her nose, then settled her elbows on her knees and regarded the fire. Her pocketknife was still clasped in one hand, the sharpening for the moment forgotten. "Two choices," she finally said. "We either go back along the trail to find the rest of them, or we continue on to the shack."

"Right."

"I'd rather keep going to the shack," Dar said. "I'm tired of all the other people." She reached out and took one of the skewers, biting off a piece and chewing it. "I don't want to deal with them. I just want to deal with you."

Kerry was a little abashed by how much her internal dialog agreed with what Dar had just said. "Shouldn't we help the other people?" She suggested anyway.

"We should," Dar said readily. "But I don't want to." She munched on the grilled venison. "Nothing on earth really requires us to do that, Ker. We're not legally mandated to be selfless martyrs."

Kerry flipped a few of the strips. "No, I know," she said, in a quiet voice.

"Like I said, last couple times I did that I got a kick in the head for it," Dar said "Couple of times I stepped in on this trip? Also got my head kicked. How much of that do I want to take? I'm kinda done."

It was all honest and true and Kerry knew it. She considered in silence for a few moments then she just shrugged. "Okay. I'd rather just be with you too." She rested her head against Dar's shoulder and listened to the fire pop and crackle a little. "Besides, they're the ones with the sat phone. They've got a better chance of getting a ride out than we do."

"True," Dar said. "Could be they'll come after us and find us. I just don't want to have to give up the progress we made today."

"Right."

They both looked at each other, then, after a moment they both started laughing. "We're so full of shit," Kerry said. "How about we stick around here in the morning and see if they show up, then go on."

Dar was still laughing. "Rampaging boofheads." She sighed. Then paused, as they both straightened a little, as sound drifted in from outside the shelter. "What was that?"

Kerry frowned. "An owl?"

They went quiet and listened. The wind outside whistled against the rock, and the rain pattered, but there was a sound again past that which sounded strange and a little unearthly. A bit like howl, or moan and wordless.

Dar got up and went to the edge of the shelter, poking her head out from the branches that were blocking the rain. "I thought I heard something like that when I was cutting up that deer. It stopped though."

"When you called me back?" Kerry stood and came over to her. As they stood in silence, it sounded again. "Is that an animal?"

Dar shook her head. "I don't know." She went back to the fire. "Could be." She half turned as it sounded again. "Can't think of what kind, but there are a lot of animals out here I'm not familiar with."

"Could it be a coyote?" Kerry asked, folding her arms over her chest. "It sounds a little dog like." Then she turned and eyed Dar. "This isn't some bad Lassie nightmare where our dogs followed us is it?"

"No." Dar chuckled a little. "I don't think Labradors howl like that."

Kerry listened again to the sound as it drifted in on the wind, then she shrugged and rejoined Dar, both of them settling down close to the fire again. After a few minutes, the sound stopped.

Kerry rearranged her drying cargo pants. "These are going to smell like bad barbecue. But at least we have a chance to dry everything. I think those guys behind us are going to end up just wet. There wasn't enough shelter there to block the rain."

"True." Dar took a breath to continue, then stopped when the sound returned, and this time, another sound accompanied it. "That's not an animal."

Kerry put down the skewer she'd just lifted. "That's someone yelling for help."

They both stared at the fire, then stared at each other. Then Dar exhaled and picked up her drying pants and put them on, while Kerry picked up her boots and put them down next to her as she removed the dry shirt she was wearing and replaced it with her damp one.

"We could pretend we don't hear that," Kerry said, continuing to dress.

"We could flap our arms and fly to the moon, too," Dar said. "C'mon, Ker. I can talk bullshit about not wanting to help people, but I can't ignore someone screaming."

"Yeah, I do know." Kerry sighed. "But damn to the little baby Jesus I just got dry."

Dar eyed her, while tying her laces. "You learn that in high school?"

"No, some stupid sitcom. C'mon."

THE FLASHLIGHT WAS waterproof and Dar was glad. She

let it shine ahead of her and Kerry to light the path as she kept her other arm upraised to shield her eyes form the rain.

It pounded down around them everywhere, large drops impacting them as they searched the narrow valley past where they'd found the deer. It was rocky and steep, and they tried to be careful as they went along to save a fall.

"Hello!" Kerry yelled out, her hands cupped around her mouth. "Hello!"

For a minute there was just the sound of the rain and the wind. Then, relatively nearby they heard a yell in response, and heard motion to their right. Dar lifted her flashlight and stopped walking, shining it out into the brush.

"Hey!" Out of the darkness a form appeared, running up to them.

"Amy! What happened!" Kerry asked, as the girl came to a halt. She was wet through, and her hands were covered in cuts, the fingertips bleeding.

"Just come help. We're so screwed," Amy gasped. "I've been calling for hours, c'mon." She started back the way she came and Kerry and Dar exchanged glances before they started after her.

"Bet I know where this is going," Dar muttered.

"Yeah." Kerry almost tripped over a stone, but ended up hopping over it as Dar grabbed after her. "Me too."

They chased after the dim figure in the rain, dodging past boulders and brush flattened by the water. They turned a corner and approached the canyon wall as thunder rumbled unexpectedly over their heads.

"Great." Dar shoved her hood back as they reached Amy's side and she pointed up.

In the dark they could see pretty much nothing. Dar played her flashlight up the wall until it found something not rock and stopped. "What in the hell?" A rope dangled down the wall and flapped uselessly against the stone.

"He was trying to climb up." Amy got up onto a rock. "Todd! Todd! I found some help!"

The figure pinned up on the wall moved slightly. "Fuck!" Came floating down weakly. "Someone just fucking shoot me!"

Dar turned the flashlight off and put it in her pocket and turned to face Amy. "What happened?"

"Do we have to talk about it?" Amy said. "Just help him."

Dar folded her arms. "What exactly are you expecting us to do? He's up on a wall in a storm. Neither of us can climb up there. You apparently tried."

Amy stared at her. "I tried. He took all the ropes and I couldn't. He made the swing up there." She pointed to an outcropping. "One of the ropes broke and something happened to his arm. He can't get down."

"Ugh," Kerry muttered.

"And he can't go up," Amy finished. "We have to help him!"

Kerry reached out in instinct and put her hand on Dar's arm, sensing the shifting of the tall body next to her. "Look, I know you're really upset, but Dar's right. We can't climb up there, we need to go get help. We need to go get the others. They have some ropes, and we can figure it out."

"Are they with you? Where are they?" Amy shifted gears. "They have ropes, sure I remember now. Let's get them." She started back down the path.

"Hold on." Kerry chased after her and grabbed her arm. "They're not with us. I mean..." She held up her other hand in a calming gesture. "They stayed up in the pass, we guess. We went on ahead to set up a shelter."

Amy stared at her. "What?"

"So if we go look for them it's going to take a while," Kerry said. "So let's just hold on a minute and figure it out"

"You left them?" Amy said.

"Like you did?" Kerry's brows lifted.

"That's different. We know what we're doing."

Kerry looked at her, then up at the wall, then back at her.

Dar turned her back on them and looked up at the wall as a lightning flash outlined the body pressed against the stone "How long has he been up there?" She asked.

Amy came over to her. "He started up about two hours before sunset. He wanted to see if he could see anyone up at the top, and get a ride back."

Dar pondered the scene in thoughtful silence for a minute, going over to take hold of the dangling rope. "What's this for?"

"Safety," Amy said. "It's so if he slips...but it was too wet. I couldn't stop him."

"Dar, let's go back up the trail and find the rest of them," Kerry said. "We can't do anything here."

Dar removed her rain jacket and set it on the ground, then gripped the rope. "This tied off?" She asked Amy. "As in, to something that's not gonna just come down on top of us?"

Amy hesitated, then nodded.

Kerry lowered her voice. "What are you doing?" She walked around to the other side of Dar and put a hand on her arm.

"I can't climb that rock wall," Dar said. "But I can climb this rope." She gave Kerry a wry look. "At least, I think I can. I might end up on my ass here in a minute."

Kerry regarded her in utter seriousness. "Does that make sense?" She whispered. 'Shouldn't we just go get help"

Dar's eyes were visible in the light form the flashlight, sharp and clear. "He's been up there for hours. Might be good to see what it is we're going to need to get help for."

They stared at each other, rain pouring down on them and pattering against the rain jacket Kerry was wearing.

"Be careful," Kerry finally said. "I don't want to see you get hurt too."

"Okay." Dar tugged on the rope experimentally. "I'm going to see what I can see." She took a step and shoved herself up into the air, grabbing the rope and hanging there a minute before she got her boots onto a bit of rock and started climbing upward.

"Holy shit," Amy blurted.

IT WAS HARD. Dar felt the strain immediately and spent a minute wondering if this was not a good, or even a reasonable idea. It would make more sense to get the hell back down on the ground wouldn't it? She glanced beneath her, barely able to see Kerry's steadfast form below her.

She had her boots braced against the rock and she pulled herself up hand over hand, moving up the rock wall. There were some footholds, and she got herself wedged against one piece of rock as she looked for another higher up to get to.

The rain faded, a little and she focused on putting one hand over the other, feeling her body flex as a small piece of stone from above bounced against her shoulder and went tumbling down past her as she got up about a standard building floor above the ground.

She squinted upward into the rain, and lightning helpfully flashed showing Todd's dangling body perhaps another two floor lengths above her. Then it went dark, and she wondered, again, if this wasn't a very bad idea.

He was tied, she wasn't. Dar understood if she lost her grip once she went past this point, falling would be painful at best, lethal at worst.

She paused, braced against the rock, hands gripped around the rope. "I shouldn't be doing this," she said, aloud, and knew it for truth. "I can't do this."

But another voice answered, in her head. "You can." It was deeper than her own voice sounded to her, and eternally confident. "G'wan. You won't fall."

Weird moment. Dar frowned. Then she shook her head and took a breath. When she released it she felt an odd sense of calm, and started upward again, the wet rope, despite its sodden damp, gripping against her skin.

There was a ledge. She climbed up onto it and then found another foothold and made that one as well. The rain was pushed to the back of her mind and she focused on the task as the strain moderated and her body responded with more confidence.

She thought about being back in the day, climbing up the rope wall with the guys. Always looking to prove herself their equal. Dar felt her face tense into a grim smile. Their equal?

No. She found a spot with no footholds and she pushed herself up a little, wrapping her legs around the rope and moving up like she had back in those days. Not their equal. A picture flashed into her memory of being at the top of the rope tower and turning, releasing one hand off and holding herself up with just the other, boots tensed against the thick strand below her.

She swarmed upward, feeling a sense of odd euphoria, a warmth that pulsed through her body and gave her energy, as a faint laughter echoed in the back of her mind.

Lightning flashed, and for a moment she jerked in reaction, eyes fluttering shut against the after flash as she heard Todd cry out in anguish. That was echoed with an alarmed yell from Kerry waiting on the ground below.

Instinctively Dar hung on as she felt rocks pelt her. She hoped like hell one of them wasn't going to end up being what the rope was fastened to.

Then a huge thump made her jerk to her left, as a boulder crashed past her, knocking down others on its way down. "Watch out!" She yelled down past her.

Then the rumbling died down.

Dar waited. "Ker?"

"Fine!" Kerry yelled back. "Hurry the God damned hell up, will you!"

She got the message, hearing the ferocious anxiety. "Got it!" She stopped the daydreaming and inched herself upward until she reached the body dangling against the wall, swinging in the ropes. This close now the damage visible.

Todd's arm was hanging in an awkward position in a far too extended way from his body. She got up another foot and braced her boots against a tiny bit of outcropping, taking the strain off. "Hey!"

He opened his eyes and looked at her. It wasn't difficult to imagine the bloodshot ochre of them. "Fuuuuck." His voice was hoarse and almost unrecognizable. "Just kill me, will ya?"

Dar took a tighter grip on the rope. "Your shoulder's dislocated."

"No shit." He feebly tried to get his feet on some kind of ledge. "Can't even think it hurts so fucking bad."

Dar released one hand cautiously and took out her flashlight, turning it on to examine him. His lips were blue and there was a gray tinge to the rest of his skin. There was a rope wrapped around him, fastened to two carabiners wedged in the rock, a third and fourth supporting the rope she was climbing.

The ropes had cut into his skin and Dar had it into her to feel sorry for him. "We need to go get help," she said. "We can't move you."

He just stared at her. "Hurts too bad," he finally said. "Couldn't move anyhow." He paused, and breathed for a minute, his mouth open and sucking in the air. "Help me."

The thunder rumbled overhead and it felt a little like it rumbled through her as well, the words sounding a gentle, far off chord in her ears she had no understanding of the source of. "We will," she said. "Just hold on."

The thunder rumbled again, but more softly.

Chapter Twelve

"WHAT'S SHE DOING?" Amy asked.

Kerry half shook her head. "Probably talking to him. Figuring out what to do." She shaded her eyes from the rain and squinted, barely able to discern what Dar was doing in the faint reflection from the flashlight. "Wish she'd hurry up."

Amy folded her arms over her body as she too stared upward. "This is so screwed."

Kerry couldn't find it in her to disagree. "Hope that rope's tied down freaking tight." She felt a sense of impatient anxiety and wished with all her heart they were somewhere else. Anywhere else. Even New York under the subway, else.

Dar moved position and edged over to where Todd was slumped, her boots wedged on a small outcropping just around the level of his chest. She shifted her grip over to the ropes holding him up and then, with a glance to her right she took the rope she'd been climbing and tied it around her waist.

"What is she doing?" Amy asked again.

"No idea." Kerry watched as Dar lowered herself into a crouch, hand wrapped around the ropes as she leaned out a little. "Really no time for us to be asking." She folded her arms over her chest, feeling utterly helpless at the moment.

"Okay." Dar found a purchase for her left boot that was deep enough to feel stable. "So, I'm going to pick up your arm and get my knee under it. "

"Fuck."

"Yeah it's going to hurt," she said. "But if I can get some leverage, and you can take it, we maybe can pop your shoulder back in place."

"Fuck." Todd repeated.

"Want me to just leave you?" Dar said. "Your choice."

His head was pressed against the rock and she could barely see his eyes in the darkness. But she knew he was looking at her. After a pause he nodded. "Don't...I don't care. It hurts so much, how much more could it?"

Dar felt a moment of compassion. "Okay, hold on." She drew a breath and then exhaled, shifting forward and grabbing the fabric of his jacket over his elbow, pulling it up toward her.

His body arched and he let out a hoarse scream, then biting

his lip and muffling it.

Dar shifted her weight over and got her knee under the upper part of his arm, resisting the urge to throw up as she felt the unnatural motion. "Move toward me."

"Can't," he grunted out.

"C'mon." Dar put some pressure on his elbow. His arm was so muscular it resisted manipulation and the angle was wrong for it.

He let out a muted scream and his boots scrabbled against the stone, pushing him against the motion she was causing trying to relieve the pain. Dar swung closer and grabbed him right under his upper shoulder and then she swung backwards and pulled.

He went limp, his head thumping against the rock with a sodden crack as she felt the joint come back into place. She released her hold and moved her knee, letting his arm fall back down against his side, this time at least in a more normal position. "Hey."

No answer.

"Ah crap." Dar sighed. She straightened back up and stood there a moment, waiting to see if he came to again, but there was no response to her nudges. She examined the pressure of the ropes and could see scrapes and bruises in the light from her flash.

What to do? Anything to do? Dar decided not. She backed away from him and untied the rope from around her body, then grabbed it and shifted her weight to it, pushing away a little from where he was hanging.

She felt her body start to shiver a little as she made her way hand over hand down the side of the rock, bumping against the wet stone as she decided to just use the rope and felt her boots get purchase on it, wanting nothing more than to be once again on solid ground.

Kerry used her flash to light the way down as she saw Dar's form outlined against the faint light from the clouds overhead. She felt a sense of relief as Dar passed the halfway point and she moved forward to get next to the wall as the sound of the rope scraping against leather came to them. "Jesus."

She drew in a breath and then released it, and then inhaled sharply as she heard a sudden cracking sound. "Dar!"

At the same time, Dar let out a startled wordless yell, and there was the sense of sudden motion over her head as rocks came tumbling down.

Kerry lifted her hands in reflex to shield herself from them.

She ducked and felt something come past her very fast.

Then she heard boots hitting the ground and Dar was sprawled next to her, as a coil of rope came down on both of them with a slithery thump. "What the!" She grabbed Dar's arm as she got to her feet and heard Dar's grunt of surprise.

Amy came running over. "What happened?"

"Rope came loose," Dar said. She looked back up at the wall. "Came out of the rock I guess."

Amy grabbed the rope and sorted it with experienced hands, coming to the end and looking at it. "Wow." She held up the piton still tied on it. "Look at that." She looked up as well. "Is Todd okay? Did you talk to him?"

Dar grimaced as she looked at her hands in the light, scraped and raw. "He now has something in common with you, Ker. I put his shoulder back into its socket."

"Oh fuck," Amy said.

"And?" Kerry looked around. "Did that help?"

"When he comes to, probably. He passed out." Dar flexed her fingers. "Let's go find everyone." She started away from the wall and toward the path, with both of them hurrying after her. "We need to move."

"You okay?" Kerry asked her, as she caught up. "How far did you fall?"

Dar remained silent as they walked for a long moment. "Not that far I guess," she finally said, as they came down from the rise and got back onto the path. "I was pushing off against the wall and it just came loose." She flexed her hands. "I just..." She frowned.

"Just?" Kerry put her hand through Dar's elbow and squeezed her arm.

"Felt like I was tumbling for a minute, but then it was okay," Dar said, with a shrug. "I guess it was wasn't as far as I thought it was."

Kerry eyed her. "Glad you came down on your feet. No matter how high it was."

"Mm."

They made their way back to the shelter and ducked inside, where the fire was still crackling in a low, comforting way and Amy knelt next to it and held her hands out. "Oh my God that feels so amazing. You have food here?"

"Venison kabobs." Kerry handed her one. "Something killed a deer before."

Dar knelt next to their bags, studying them. "Does it pay to take this, or just go with what we have?" She asked. "Does it pay to change into dry pants? I don't think so."

"Probably not." Kerry knelt next to her. "I'm going to put on another shirt under this jacket though. At least I can keep a little warmer"

"Good idea." Dar put her jacket down and pulled off her shirt, setting it aside as she paused to regard what she had in the pack she'd been carrying.

Kerry suppressed a smile, as the light from the fire splayed crimson against Dar's sun darkened skin, the underlying strength of her body very evident as she moved.

Dar sorted through the cloth and pulled a dry long-sleeve shirt from her bag. "What a waste of time." She sighed. "A set of radios would have been a good idea." She put the shirt on and tugged the sleeves down.

"No power." Amy was chewing the venison, crouched next to the fire. "They'd have to keep them charged. The whole point of the eco stuff is to not need that."

Dar considered that as she donned a second shirt, feeling much better despite the stress from the climb and her scraped hands. "Screw it," she said. "When we get back to Miami I'll design some system of power and make a million bucks selling it to campers."

"I like that idea." Kerry got her jacket on and fastened. "Solar?"

Dar tucked her pack and Kerry's in a niche at the back of the wall. "On this trip that would be pointless." She zipped her jacket up. "Make it kinetic. Use all the hiking and crap to charge it. Let's go." She pulled her hood up. "He's pretty cold up there."

Amy scrambled to her feet and followed them out into the rain, and they started back up the trail.

FOR ONCE, ON the trip, they got lucky. They were no more than halfway across the valley toward the waterfall when they saw flashlights ahead and then heard Dave's voice call out.

"Hell yeah." Kerry breathed a sigh of relief. "Dave! Rich!"

"Hey!" Rich came trotting toward them. "Hey! We found you!"

Tracey was right behind him and they met on the path. "Is that rock shelter still there? We're freezing."

Janet limped up, then trailing them the rest. "Glad we caught up." She gave Rich an ambiguous look. "Oh...and you caught up to the other two?"

'Sort of." Kerry said "Yes, the shelter's still there. We just left it to come find you."

"You found us," Rich said. "We've got the tarps, so we can get out of the weather." He rubbed his upper arms, as they all gathered around. "Hi there." He nodded at Amy. "Let's hurry up."

"There's a problem," Dar said, bringing everyone to a halt abruptly. "Her SO tried to climb the wall and got stuck."

For a long moment there was just a bunch of people silently staring at each other. Then Tracey snorted. "Screw him," she said. "Hope he croaks up there, the asshole."

She pushed past Dar and headed toward the shelter, with Pete limping after her.

Don and Marcia sidled silently after them, with a glance at Amy.

"Sorry." Rich shrugged, not even slightly uncomfortable as he also pushed past Amy. "Got what's coming to him."

Amy stood there and watched them pass. Dar and Kerry stayed with her, until all of them had gone ahead and they had few choices but to follow. "Huh." Dar shook her head.

Kerry sighed.

"Screw them." Amy turned and walked quickly away, angling to the side of the line the others were taking, on an angle that would bring her past the shelter back toward the wall Todd was hanging from.

Kerry put her hands on her hips. "We go with them or with her?"

Dar rocked up and down a few times, her arms folded over her chest. "That's like asking me if I want lettuce or tofu."

Kerry half shrugged. "I don't think we can do anything for her or for him until it's light out," she admitted. "Maybe we can talk these guys into helping."

"Maybe we can," Dar said. "At least we can try."

"So let's go with them," Kerry said, and they walked down the path that would take them to shelter. "That's where our stuff is anyway."

Dar followed her in silence, going over and over their options and ending up right where Kerry had, no matter how she tried to make them work out differently. So she left off trying and turned on her flashlight, playing it over the ground in front of where Kerry was walking.

Her shoulders ached from the climbing. Her hands hurt even

more from the rope. She still felt the jarring shock of falling in those milliseconds of, holy crap, before she hit the ground.

Now that she had a few minutes to think, she did think about falling.

She remembered that moment of panic when she felt the rope give way and she'd gone head over heels downward. Then somehow in midair she'd found herself twisting round like a gymnast to get her legs under her and her knees unlocked before impact.

In the dark. In the rain. Like a cat. It had gone from being terrifying to ordinary in a breath, and she really had no idea why.

No idea. Ahead of her she heard the group talking, and the pace picking up as they approached the shelter. Voices rising in relief as they found the shelter in the glow of their flashlights. But for some damn reason her mind was focused on that kid she'd left up on the wall.

She had zero obligation. She'd done all she could. Had risked her life in the bargain. It could have been a completely different story, and then what? What if she landed and been crippled? Broken her back or her legs?

Or her neck?

"Dar?"

Zero obligation to him. "Yeah?" But what obligation did she have to her own conscience?

What obligation did she have to Kerry? Was any risk worth the heartbreak getting herself hurt would cause Kerry? Or if she'd died? Dar's face tensed into a grimace. For that jackass?

Ugh.

Kerry paused, just at the edge of the rocks. Dar came up behind her and put her hand on her shoulder, and nudged her gently. "Let's go inside," she said. "At least to get our gear."

They went around a boulder and into the calm of the overhang, where the rest of the group was already spreading out with looks of relief. They were all wet, many were limping, and the expressions of exhaustion were not in the least feigned.

"You got a fire here?" Rich was kneeling down, his hand extended. "Holy shit that feels amazing!"

"Yeah, Dar got it started with her knife and a rock." Kerry came over and pulled her pack over to her, opening it and pulling out the plastic bag she'd put the remaining venison in. "Here."

Voices lifted in surprised delight. "Holy crap!" Rich sat down, putting a shaking hand up to his head. "I'm about to fall down I'm so hungry."

"It's not much, but..." Kerry handed the bag to Marcia, who had come over to sit next to her. "Something killed a deer a little ways away."

Marcia divided the contents and everyone just sat down where they were, wet or not, dressed or not, and started chewing on the tough, greasy meat without restraint, even the vegans.

Kerry got up and went over to sit next to Dar, who was leaning back against the rock wall, eyes slightly unfocused. "You know what?" She asked, after a few moments of just watching the rest of them.

"I'm about to know something." Dar smiled briefly, reaching over and putting her hand on Kerry's knee, the edge of her thumb rubbing gently against the wet fabric "And knowing you it'll be worth the knowing."

Kerry paused and regarded her in silence. "I love you."

Dar's pale eyes twinkled a little, now visible as the fire had been stoked. "I do know that," she said, clearing her throat a little. "That what you wanted to say?"

Kerry cocked her head to one side slightly. "No. What I was going to say was that we know what the true value of loving each other is."

And as she said it, and as they stared into each other's eyes, she felt a deep resonance she'd only felt a few times before. A sense of a history between them she knew logically did not exist. She knew she'd only met Dar a few years back.

They hadn't known each other before. Their backgrounds were completely diverse.

But when Dar lifted her hand up and she fit her own into it, and their fingers clasped, it was like they were sharing a private joke of the subconscious that echoed down a far longer stretch of time than that. It was a strange synergy that was there for a moment, and then gone as the situation they were in reasserted itself.

"So what did that moron do?" Rich asked, looking up at them. "Sorry to be an asshole but there was no way I was going to go haul him out of a ditch."

Kerry half turned to face him. "Well, he was trying to climb the wall to see where they were, and if they could signal someone. He slipped and pulled his arm out of its socket, and he's hanging probably three stories off the ground."

She had everyone's attention abruptly, focused and tense.

Janet stopped chewing. "Shit. How long has he been up there?"

"Couple hours," Kerry said. "So Dar climbed up to try and help him." She rested her hands on her knees. "There was a rope hanging down so she went up it and got his shoulder re-set. That's crazy painful, by the way. Anyway, on the way down the rope came loose, but low enough so that Dar could land on her feet."

"Whoa," Rich said, sounding impressed.

"But we knew there wasn't much else we could do but come find you all for help. I felt bad leaving him there. Dar said he'd passed out from it. But what else could we do?" She made her tone gently inquiring. "People are still people, you know?"

The apprehensive discomfort from the group was almost a tangible thing. Kerry worked to keep any judgement from her expression and her words. "So, Dar and I are going to go back there with them, even if they've been really jerky." She paused. "I know how I would feel if it were me, with someone I cared for stuck up there."

Dar waited until she was sure Kerry was finished with her sweetly Midwestern kicks in the groin. "He's probably going to die. It's too cold," she said, briefly. "We'll take some of those tarps."

Kerry got up and shouldered her pack, handing Dar's over. Then she pulled her hood up and went to the edge of the shelter, not turning her head for an instant as she moved back out into the rain with an inner sense of rightness impossible to ignore.

Useful or not, smart or dumb, maybe pointless. Did it matter? "We should have grabbed that damned sat phone," she remarked, as their boots crunched against the gravel.

Dar smiled into the darkness. "I did. They were all too busy grabbing meat to notice"

"Ahh, my hero."

"Soggy froggy hero."

IT WAS A little difficult to find their way back. Dar finished a backtrack that ended nowhere and found Kerry where she'd left her, in a crossroads standing with her arms crossed and back to the wind. "Nope." She closed her flashlight to save the battery. "Dead end."

"Figures. If we weren't looking for them we'd have crashed into them three times already." Kerry pointed a second direction. "Let's try that one."

There was no more screaming, and it was too dark and rainy

to remember which way they'd gone before. Dar flicked her light on again and they moved off along another gully, the sound of the rain thrumming down on the ground around them, a low, rumbling white noise.

Impossibly loud, in all that wilderness. Off to one side Dar heard water coming down the rock wall and she moved gingerly toward it, reasoning if they kept along the cliff they'd eventually find the man hanging from it.

The weather was uncomfortable, but as she made her way around a half-buried boulder with Kerry's hand on her back, she was glad they'd left the rest of them behind.

"You think they'll come behind us?" Kerry asked, after they'd splashed through a water filled gully.

"Do you care?"

"Well." Kerry cleared her throat a little. "If we want help we probably should care, hon."

"Mm." Dar grunted. "They'll come." She decided. "Some of them will, anyway."

"Don and Marcia." Kerry predicted. "And probably Rich and Dave."

"Probably."

"Maybe Sally."

Dar nodded and then she made a noise of satisfaction. "That's the trail." She indicated a spot. "I remember that log."

Kerry studied the log as they went past it, trying to decide if there was something special about it that Dar had remembered. "We could use it to start a fire after we get the tarps up," she said. "Then maybe...oh crap look out!"

Dar had seen the shadow in the dark coming at them and grabbed Kerry, pushing through a sodden bush and pressing them both against the wall as something large and musky scented came barreling past them and smashed head first against the rocks.

"What th—" Dar hopped out of the way as whatever it was fell, hooves scrabbling on the rocks as it rolled over. "Another sheep? All of them nuts?"

"I'd rather it be nuts." Kerry peered at the animal. "Could they have rabies or something, Dar? They're acting weird. Aren't they?"

Dar moved another step away, nudging Kerry ahead of her. "How in the hell would I know?" She asked plaintively.

"You're the one who knows how to milk a cow aren't you?"

"It's not a cow." Dar edged away from the animal. "But damn

it, now I want a glass of milk."

Kerry snorted, and covered her mouth with one hand. "Oh, Dar." She chuckled. "I'd settle for being in traffic in a Miami thunderstorm."

"Mmph." Dar pulled her pack off and held it between them and the sheep defensively. "Go away!" She yelled at it loudly.

The animal got to its feet and rambled off, limping slightly, it's tongue hanging from its mouth, but without a backward glance.

"Let's get out of here." Dar shook her head and they started moving faster. "With any luck that thing will go the other way and those guys will find it and finally have something to kill."

"If it has rabies, and they eat it, we could have lots worse problems," Kerry said as they started going up slope a little. "But that would be kind of par for the course for this trip. This is the point in the movie where they eat the rabid sheep and become zombies, right?"

"I don't think it has rabies." Dar shoved past a wiry bush and slid sideways between the rocks and the wall, spotting the shadowy form against the stone as lightning turned the sky to silver. "There he is." She pointed.

With a sigh of relief, Kerry caught up to her and they climbed up the rise to where they could now hear someone, presumably Amy, rustling around.

"Amy!" Kerry called out. "You there?"

"Who is that?" A male voice came back, immediately. "Get the fuck out of here!"

Dar and Kerry exchanged glances. "That's not Amy," Dar said. "We better..."

"Go see what's going on." Kerry finished the sentence. "C'mon."

They sped up and made it into a small clearing where they could see two figures struggling. A moment later Amy let out a scream, as though her mouth were suddenly released.

Dar got close enough to see what was going on and her body reacted without any thought. "Stop it!" She let out a bellow and leaped forward, getting her arms around the torso of the taller of the two figures. "Hey!"

She yanked herself to one side, pulling the figure with her around in a circle, using momentum to send her adversary flying into the rocks as she released him. She heard him curse, and felt Kerry dash past her to go to where Amy had just bounced off the cliff wall and stumbled to her knees.

"What was that for?" The male voice snarled as the man she'd wrestled with got to his feet and faced her. "You'll pay for that!"

Dar got herself between Kerry and the guy, and got her pocketknife out, opening the blade in a one handed flick. She spread her other arm out to the side and got her balance set, feeling nothing but anticipation. "C'mon," she growled at him.

Lightning flashed, and for a moment they were both outlined in silver. Then the man hastily hitched his shorts up and took a step forward, revealing a lean, muscled bare torso and dark, braided hair. "Who the hell are you?"

"Who the hell are you?" Dar shot right back.

He took another step forward, and now even in the dim light she could make out his features, finding them planed and angular and younger than she'd expected. "Ira Stormcloud," he said in an ordinary tone. "Hey, you're a woman?"

"Last time I checked," Dar said.

"Huh. Never had a woman pick me up and throw me before," he said. "That was crazy. Who are you people?"

Dar straightened and folded her knife away. "We're tourists." She indicated herself and the others. "We were on a river rafting trip that went south."

"Oh." He put his hands on his hips. "Crazy tourists, huh? I wasn't gonna hurt her." He pointed to Amy. "Just trying to keep her mouth shut so she wouldn't draw a big old cat over here." He looked around then folded his arms over his bare chest. "This ain't Disney World you know?"

Dar was momentarily silent. "Yeah, I know. We already ran into one of those cats, a few days back."

"You did?" Ira sidled a little closer. "Big one? We have some man eaters around here. The ops know better than to be out here without guns and stuff." He looked up at the rain and licked some drops off his lips. "I was just taking shelter under that flat rock there and heard all the commotion." He peeked past her. "Sorry I scared you."

Amy glared at him. "Asshole."

Ira snorted a little. "Serves me right trying to do a good deed."

"I feel your pain," Dar said dryly, and then pointed up at the cliff wall. "But give her some slack. Her SO tried to climb out and he's stuck up there."

"Wait, what?" Ira tipped his head up and looked. "Holy shit. You all are crazy." He moved over to the edge of the wall and Dar went with him. "He did that in this weather?"

"Long story," Dar said. "Any idea how to get him down?"

Ira pointed his thumb at his own bare chest. "Me? You gotta be kidding me, lady. That's nuts. My people survived out here long as we have by not doing dumb shit like that."

Kerry exhaled. Yes. It felt crazy. The whole thing felt like she was running on the edge of insanity in fact.

It was like being in a bad dream, and briefly she wondered if that wasn't exactly where they were, because this was just nuts. Really, just nuts. She stepped to one side as Amy finished getting herself dusted off and stood up next to her. "What an ultimate clusterfuck."

"No shit," Amy said. "That goon just jumped on me when I was trying to clear out that little hollow back there. I thought he was a mountain lion." She sounded more than a bit rattled. "I freaked out."

"He apparently thinks he saved you from one." Kerry folded her arms. "I would have freaked out myself. Glad we decided to follow you though."

Amy exhaled, and remained silent for a moment. "Yeah, me too. Are those tarps?" She indicated the pack. "We can use them? Get something over our heads?"

Kerry unstrapped the bundle and they started to sort them out, as the thunder rumbled again overhead. "Really tired of the rain." She found a crack in the rock to wedge in one of the bungies and stretched the tarp along the wall over her head as she listened to Dar and Ira talk behind her.

"That's crazy," Ira said. "You did what? You climbed up a rope?"

"He had a line dropped down but when I was coming down it came loose." Dar picked up the coil of rope and held up the piton that had come loose from the stone. "I was just lucky I was almost to the ground."

"Yikes." Ira examined it. "Not my gig, climbing," he admitted. "I'm a river runner, mostly. Like those guys you were with, but we're a native op." He looked up at the wall. "What the hell was he trying to climb up there for?"

"Long story," Dar muttered. "You got any way to communicate out of here? We'd really like to get out of this damn holiday from hell."

Ira shook his head. "You can walk out though. It's just over the next ridge there, path to the ranger station." He pointed. "But these guides know that." He looked at Dar's shaking head.

"What? Sure it is. I came in that way."

"There was an avalanche," Dar told him. "An arch, one of those stone things came down and blocked the way. We were almost there. So we had to come back. They're out of supplies, and some of them are hurt."

Ira stared at her. "Are you shitting me?" He said. "I came up that path not a day ago, checking some traps," he said. "With just a couple of sandwiches in my pack," he added with a wry look. "Really blocked?"

"Really. Probably twenty feet of debris."

"Holy shit." He reached up and clutched both sides of his head. "Dude, that's a big deal. They're going to have to send a rock mover up to clear that. It's the only way down out of this part of the canyon."

Kerry sighed. "Figures."

Dar shrugged. "Lightning hit the top of the arch and it just went kabam."

"You saw it?"

"Saw it happen."

"I knew the weather was a bitch but didn't expect that," Ira said. "Never heard of that happening before, not recently anyway."

Dar shook her head. "One of the other guys with us is a climber. Maybe tomorrow he can get up there. I've got a sat phone, but there's no signal down here." She indicated the tarps. "Since you're stuck here now too I guess."

He sighed. "Let me go get my gear. I got a few rabbits and a snake if you white people can stand it." He grinned briefly. "Maybe I can help you get your buddy up there down too if you share your sat phone and get us a ride out of here."

He turned and jogged off, the rain bouncing off his skin as he disappeared into the darkness.

Dar shook her head and went over to help put up the tarps. "Keeps getting crazier." She stretched the tarp over a stack of rocks and wedged the bungie into place. "Every single minute."

IRA WAS SEATED against the rock wall next to Dar, with Kerry on the other side of her. "Y'know," he said. "If you were right about how cold that guy was, he might be croaked by now." He unrolled the sleeves on a thick flannel shirt down to his wrists and fastened them.

"I know," Dar answered in a low mutter. "But there's nothing we can do."

Kerry shared the last of the venison and they all had travel cups full of rainwater. There was, she knew, no hope of a fire. It was too dark to search for anything burnable, and they had nothing to dry it with. So they sat against the wall, with the tarps over them at an angle, tolerably dry.

Tolerably warm, with all of them next to each other.

Ira, it turned out, was just a kid. "So I just got out of high school, you know? It was a drag," he said, his hands resting on his knees. "I couldn't wait for it to be over."

Kerry eyed him. "So what now?"

"What now what?" He said. "Now I get to just hunt and fish and stuff. My dad owns the trading post. I'll do work for him." He licked his lips. "That was pretty damn good deer. You people bring that in?"

"We found a carcass," Dar said. "Kerry had some salt left from some cave back toward the river."

Ira looked at them. "Not bad for white city folk." He smiled at them, proving to be just a little charming after all. Even Amy grudgingly smiled back. "You all are city folk, right?" He looked at Kerry.

"I'm about as white a city folk as you could get," Kerry said, with a brief grin. "But I can cook."

They both looked at Dar.

"I can't cook," Dar said. "I'm from Miami."

"Oooh. Miami." Ira cracked his knuckles. "You got the Everglades down there," he said. "You go out hunting?"

"No." Dar laced her fingers together. "I'm not into shooting animals."

Ira eyed her. "You are from the city. There's some good eating out there and it's free." He added. "My mom only needs to shop maybe once or twice a year. Me and my brothers bring in game the rest of the time, and we eat great."

Kerry leaned forward. "Dar does hunt, just not on land," she said. "We have a cabin down in the Keys."

"Huh." Ira wriggled his nose.

"And a pair of Labrador Retrievers." Dar's lips twitched. "Who would freak out if they were faced with a duck."

"Or a crab."

Two hours later, the rain was slowing down. They could hear it in a fitful patter against the surface of the tarp. The wind was coming down too. The surface of the fabric no longer flapping with it.

Dar felt cold and stiff, though, and she drew up her knees

and rested her forearms on them. Kerry leaned against her, cheek coming to rest against her upper arm as they listened to the thunder fade off into the distance. After twenty or thirty minutes, the rain stopped.

The wind stopped.

They heard the faint sounds of foliage moving, and far off, a few pebbles plinking against the ground. Then it got very quiet.

They sat there in the silence. Then it was broken by two sounds. One, a low moan from above them that brought Amy upright and moving out from under the tarp, and second, the sound of boots crunching against the gravel of the path, coming their way.

"Looks like we're going to do something other than just sit here," Kerry said.

"Good." Dar got up and emerged into the darkness of a canyon night, where the sky overhead was clearing and stars were beginning to show intermittently. Kerry followed her just as the moon came out, and the scene was lit with eerie silver.

She looked up, to see a faint motion against the rocks, then she looked out over the canyon to see moving figures coming toward them in a large group.

Two unexpected things. Ira came out behind her and peered past her shoulder, his head roughly even with hers. "Rest of your gang?"

"Rest of my gang," Dar confirmed. "And maybe our luck's getting better." She pointed up at the sky.

"Shh." Kerry poked her. "Don't even say that."

"Umph."

"SO WE FIGURED there was more shelter this way anyhow," Rich said, as he stood next to Dar near the wall. "And your SO was right. It's the right thing to do" He looked up. "What did that moron think he was trying to accomplish?"

"Good question." Dar felt the light breeze, dry now, fluttering the shirt she had on and riffling her hair. "Climb out?"

"To where? There's nothing up there," Rich said.

Dar shook her head. "If he took the phone I'd get it."

"Crazy. Need the rock to dry out before I start up there, for sure." Rich said. "I guess we get him down once it's light."

Janet limped over. "Okay. We got a fire going, and we're going to use that bark we peeled off to make some tea. Good idea there, by the way," she told Dar. "Peeling the bark, I mean."

Dar nodded briefly. "Lot of wet camping areas in Florida."

"Thunderstorm and lightning capital of the world," Janet said. "I remember."

"And Ira's going to share his catch," Sally said. "I guess I really picked the wrong trip to be a vegetarian." She tipped her head back. "Anything we can do for doofus up there?"

They all studied the dim outline against the now star filled sky. "Amy." Dar turned and looked over at the girl. "He has water with him?"

She nodded. "Of course. You'd have to be an idiot not to."

Janet cleared her throat. "What was he going to do up there anyway?"

Amy had been stripping twigs, and now she stopped and regarded Janet. "He's got a mirror in the pack. He was going to try and signal a sightseeing plane or helicopter," she said. "There's at least a half dozen who come over, right?"

"That's true," Janet said. "But not this weather. I haven't heard any of them in the past few days."

Kerry came over. "But the weathers cleared now," she said. "Maybe that could be a plan B for tomorrow?"

"What's plan A?" Sally asked.

"Me to climb up to the top there, I guess, and see if I can get a signal on the phone," Rich said. "But yeah, signaling's not a bad idea if they're flying tomorrow."

Amy gave him a skeptical look. "You think you can make it up there? I doubt it." She added. "Not to be a jerk, but he got messed up trying to get across that gap there and he's bigger than you are." She pointed up to a shadowy cleft. "See that? He jumped and got a finger hold, then one of the pitons came loose and he twisted around."

Rich shrugged. "Let's wait till the morning. No sense arguing about it until we can see what the deal is. Maybe there's another route."

"If there was another route he'd have found it," Amy stated flatly.

"If you know so much, how come you didn't climb up there to help him?" Rich shot back. "If Dar could climb that rope, I'm sure you coulda."

Kerry took a breath to do a subject change, but subsided when Amy just shrugged, then turned her hands upmost and displayed them, showing palms bruised and scraped, and broken nails.

"I tried," she said. "I only made it part way up and couldn't go any farther." Amy glanced at Dar. "You're pretty gonzo for a computer geek."

Kerry scratched the bridge of her nose, then glanced up at Dar's face, which had a blandly amused expression. "Well, we're going to have to figure it all out so we might as well get everything else settled." She put her hand on the rock face, which was damp and cold under her touch.

Dar hooked her arm through Kerry's and guided her back over to where the rest of the group was milling around, PJ and Cheryl talking animatedly with Ira.

"They surprised me," Kerry muttered in an undertone. "I didn't expect all of them to come."

Dar regarded the group. "Peer pressure. Once you kick started their consciences, to stay back would have been jackass."

"Do I get a cookie for that?"

"Sure. If I had cookies I'd give you all of them. But know what I want?" Dar sat down on a rock and patted the spot next to her, which was cold and damp but Kerry sat on it anyway. "I want one of those Star Trek transporters."

"Mmm."

"I want to just call up someone and have them beam us from here to our house."

Kerry considered that. "I'd settle for our RV." She braced her hands on the rock and extended her legs out, wiggling her hiking boots back and forth a little. "Cause if they had to beam our dogs home, they'd end up with poop in their transporters, let me tell ya that."

Dar chuckled silently.

The soft crunch of boots against gravel made them look up to find Don and Marcia dusting their hands off as they came over to join them. "Hi."

"Hello there, ladies." Don sat down on the ground, and leaned his back against the wall. Marcia was about to join him but Kerry stood up and offered her seat up instead and the older woman took it with a grateful smile.

"I'm going to see how the fire's going." Kerry patted Dar on the shoulder and walked past her.

Dar leaned back against the wall and stifled a yawn, then she turned her head on hearing the rattle and scrape of rocks falling, hastily getting to her feet as several bounced down the wall and hit them. "What the hell?"

"Whole damn trip's been one big—what the hell." Don sighed, as he hoisted himself up and they both went around the angle of the wall to see Rich partway up it, paused in contemplation. "Oh my lord, what is that boy doing?"

Amy had a flashlight played on the rock ahead of him. "To the side there, yeah." She directed. "That's the shelf he went onto."

Rich glanced down. "Just want to make sure he's okay," he called down. "Not going all the way up." He carefully inched his way farther, fitting his fingers into the cracks between the rocks and moving very slowly in a more horizontal than vertical path.

He had the rope that Dar had climbed looped around his body, and he paused with his knees pressed against the rock to take the piton on the end of it and wedge it into a cleft, using a piece of rock taken from his cargo pants pocket to hammer it into place.

Kerry came over and joined Dar, head tilted. "Oh for cripes sake."

Rich got a hitch up, then his boots slid on the wet rock wall and he swung sideways with a little yelp.

That caused another scattering of pebbles to tumble down, and as one, the group watching took a step back. "This is nuts," Don said, in an undertone. "Be careful!" He added, in a louder tone. "Don't need you laid up too!"

Rich waved at him, then he snugged the rope a bit tighter around his body and inspected the rocks, looking for another handhold. "Don't worry! Just wanted to show my skills."

Kerry looked over at Amy, who avoided her eyes and stared up at the cliff instead. "That little bitch," she said, in an undertone. "She conned him into that."

Dar patted her back. "He let her."

THE WEATHER STAYED calm after that. Rich only made it halfway up, enough to exchange a few words with Todd, most of which were curses. Now he, Dave, Sally, and her sister were under one opened up sleeping bag, against the rock wall.

Dar was seated on her and Kerry's' tattered sleeping bag, with Kerry cuddled against her, the two of them warming each other in as much meager comfort as was going to be had.

It was dark outside, and quiet. Dar pulled Kerry tight against her, feeling Kerry's steady breathing as she slept.

At least one of them was getting some rest. Dar was just uncomfortable enough, and not exhausted enough to be able to sleep. So she'd spent an hour or so running a programming problem through her head.

She heard the sound of something flying outside and listened hard, but the sounds drifted off into the distance and silence once again fell.

Far off, something howled.

She thought she heard a plane in the distance.

Finally it was sunrise. Dar walked out from under their shelter and looked up at the sky, thankfully free of clouds.

The air was dry and cool, and she pulled on the one dry shirt she had left. She rubbed the skin of her arms to dispel the imaginary dampness she was convinced she still felt.

She heard steps behind her and turned to find Ira ambling over, reviewing the sky with a satisfied nod. "That's better," he said. "Now we can maybe get somewhere." He turned and looked up at the wall, where Todd's body was visible, now wedged in a different position in a corner of the rock.

Rich and Dave emerged, and a moment later, Don was with them, and then Sally as well. They gathered under where Todd was hanging and Dar and Ira joined them.

"We gotta get him down," Rich said. "So I figure I climb up, we get the ropes rearranged and then we belay him."

"Let get going," Dave said. "Sooner the better."

"Nothing else to do anyway," Rich said. "I don't want any more of that bark tea. Made me piss all night." He felt the surface of the rock, grunting in approval. "Drying out."

Amy appeared. She pulled her hair back and put it in a tail as Rich lifted himself up onto one of the boulders embedded in the wall about waist level.

The sun peeked over the rim of the canyon and lit up the wall. Rich got a rope fastened around him, flexed his hands and started moving up, duplicating his path from the previous night.

Kerry emerged from the shelter with an armful of cloth. She moved out across the ground to where there were several sunlit rocks to drape the wet fabric over. The sun crept across the canyon floor and she held her hands out to it in relief as it warmed her face.

Janet limped out to join her, but stood in silence for a moment. "We should have called into main base yesterday," she said finally. "Someone'll be looking for us."

Kerry folded her arms and regarded the trip leader. "No matter if we find a way to signal or not."

"Right," Janet said. "With the sun up, it won't take them long to find us." She licked her lips. "That's why I convinced the rest of them to come down out of the slot canyon. We can at least have them winch us out of here."

Kerry felt a sense of relief. "So we're just really listening for the sound of the chopper while they get Todd down."

Janet nodded confidently. Then she looked around. "Please don't repeat that to the rest of them, though. The way this trip's gone it'll start raining again."

"And Godzilla will appear over the horizon. Got it," Kerry said. "I won't say a word."

Janet wandered off and Kerry remained where she was, leaning one shoulder against the rock wall as she just enjoyed the sun finally warming her. Though they'd had a fire the night before the persistent damp, and the long days of chill, had left her cold at her core. Now she closed her eyes and savored the sensation.

She almost imagined she heard the sound of a helicopter. But after a moment's focus, it was just a cicada rattling away nearby in the desert grass. She opened her eyes and hunted around the area, searching the ground for anything else that might be of use.

It was strange, and yet familiar. Kerry knew there was in no way anything here she'd had her privileged WASP behind involved in doing before, but there was still something about the self-sufficiency that made her smile.

She heard a faint thump and looked over to find a rabbit there, frozen in mid motion, staring at her.

Kerry looked around quickly, then put her finger to her lips. "Shh."

The rabbit flicked it's ears, then hopped off rapidly, heading for a hole nearby that it disappeared down. Kerry tiptoed back around the rock and resumed her scrounging, stifling a rueful laugh. "Hope I don't regret that," she mused to herself.

Then she spotted a twisted bristlecone pine and went over to it. She found several pinecones, along with a handful of the needles the tree had sparsely along its branches, the scent of them rising to her nose and making her think briefly of Christmas.

Or a car air freshener. She chuckled and collected a few more pine cones.

RICH WAS VISIBLY sweating. "Okay, I'm going to try that way," He yelled down. He got a hesitant grip into a crack in the rocks and crouched a little, then pushed upward with both feet. He shoved himself sideways along the rock to another slight protrusion.

His feet slipped and he scrabbled for a foothold for a moment until he found one, testing it carefully and then slowly shifting his hands. "Shit."

Todd's foot was about six feet over his head. If he looked down he would see the whole group of them, gathered in utter uselessness at the foot of the cliff. If he fell, he'd probably kill half of them and now he was fiercely regretting volunteering to climb.

He hadn't lied. He knew how to do it. The fact he was where he was up on the wall testified to that, but it had been a long time, and he hadn't really conditioned himself for this when he'd expected just to be riding on his butt on a boat down a river.

He looked down again and spotted Dar Robert's tall figure coming to the wall, one hand falling to rest on the rocks. From this perspective he could see the breadth of her shoulders and the length of her arms and wished it was her up here and him watching.

Why hadn't he stepped back and let her do it?

With a sigh, he got another handhold and paused, then shifted. There was another crack but it was far enough over his head that he'd have to jump for it and he had slim confidence he'd get a firm grip. If he did, then he could pull his feet up and get almost to where he could do something useful, but if he missed he might end up hanging from the piton.

He looked up, to find Todd looking down at him, haggard and serious of face, with none of the mocking attitude he'd become used to. "Hang on." He steeled himself, and then jumped for it, getting his hands into the crack and grimacing as his weight came onto his fingers.

With a lot of effort he hauled his feet up, and with a sense of relief, felt his toes catch onto the crack he'd had his hands on. He straightened up and his head was even with Todd's knees.

"Nice," Todd rasped. "That last one."

"Thanks." Rich let the shaking work its way out of his limbs. "How are you doing?"

"Sux," Todd said. "Got my arm strapped up. Can't do nothing with it" He indicated the limb tucked close into his body with his shirt fastened over it. "Fuck it hurts."

"Bet it does." Rich debated punching his shoulder, to get a bit back of Pete's torture, but he sighed instead "Okay, how much rope ya got up here," he asked instead.

"Long length in my pack." Todd shifted a little, lifting himself up with a grip on the line over his head and turning to expose his back to Rich. "Maybe it'll reach."

"Let's find out." Rich released one hand and undid the fastening.

Chapter Thirteen

DAR GAVE THE second rope an experimental tug and then leaned back and pulled hard on it. Rich had just set the piton, and she jumped into the air and let her weight come down on the line, tensed to react if it released.

It didn't.

She turned and looked at the group. "Anyone want to have a turn?"

"Long past my days of that," Don said, with a tone of regret. "Sorry."

"Afraid of heights," Sally said. "And I can't climb a rope anyway."

"Me either," Tracey said, with a more authentic tone of regret. "I've done some rappelling, but not the other way around."

"Not with this hand," Dave said, holding it up.

The rest of the group was busy foraging, so Dar gave a little shrug and turned, pausing to rub her hands on her pants and then take a grip on the rope. She paused, then she crouched and jumped and was dangling, feeling her spine stretch out as she coiled up her legs around the rope and took some of the weight off her arms.

She started up, the feeling of hemp crisp and hard under her grip. She shifted her hands upward and climbed, her body scraping against the stone wall. As the last time, it didn't take her long to get up to the level Rich and Todd were at. She locked her boots around the rope and paused as she came even with them.

"Get on that ledge there," Rich said. "Need some help setting the belay."

Dar spotted the ledge and swung over to it, getting a firm foothold. Then she wrapped the rope around her and tied it off. "Now what?"

"Okay, so we got this." Rich sidled up next to her and showed her a long spike with a wheel on it. "We can get this in here, like this. "He pointed at a deep cleft. "Then get that rope on it, and if those guys down there keep hold, he can get down."

Dar inspected the rope. "Going to take all of them," she told Todd. "You're a big boy."

His face, scraped and raw from the wind, crinkled just a little bit into a grimace that might have been a smile. "You're a fucking monkey," he said. "Where'd you learn to climb like that?"

Dar ignored him. "Let's get this going," she told Rich. "I don't want to temp the weather fate."

"Too right," Rich said. He positioned the belaying rig in place and shoved it into the cleft, using his rock to pound it down as far as it would go. That left the wheel exposed. He untied one of the ropes Todd had been using and threaded it through the pulley, letting it dangle down to the ground. "Okay."

Todd reached out and clipped the end of the rope to his climbing harness and shifted over.

"Grab hold of that!" Rich yelled downward, then he looked at Dar. "Help me get him turned around facing the rock." He glanced down again. "Hold it tight, you all! He's heavy!"

Dar shortened up her rope until it was holding her to the wall, and then she released both hands and pushed Todd away from the wall and toward Rich. His weight came onto the dangling rope and he slipped down a little, and a yell came from the ground.

"Don't be pussies! Grab the damn rope!" Rich bellowed. "Jesus, these people!"

"Augh." Todd slammed against the rock and tried to steady himself as he skidded down the wall thumping his injured shoulder against it.

"Hold on!" Rich yelled. "Pull!"

Dar had hold of Todd's belt and she leaned back until the pulley went taut and the rope was taking his weight. She released her hold cautiously, then she ran the rope she was on through his harness then back over her shoulders and braced herself. "G'wan."

Rich gave a tug on his rope and eased himself down. "Little at a time," he said. "Grab hold here."

Todd used his good hand to take hold, and they started downward. Dar stayed braced on her ledge, slowly letting out the rope as the two men retreated down the cliff wall. The sun splashed over them all and the sedate blue sky stretched overhead as though the past few days of weather had never happened.

Dar started to be just a little bit optimistic that the worst was over, then she immediately squashed the thought and pictured a hailstorm instead.

Just in case.

"A LITTLE MORE!" Rich had one hand in a hold, and one hand around the rope circling Todd's body. "Pull left!" He was braced against an outcropping, his hand clenched around his own rope. "Left!"

Don and Dave were anchoring, and they shifted hastily.

Rich pushed to his right and got a grip on Todd's belt. "Got to get you around this point."

"Shut up, I know that. Get the fuck out of my way and let go of me!" Todd got his boots wedged and crossed his good hand over his body and curled his fingers into a cleft, pushing outward and pulling sideways at the same time as he hauled himself around a corner of the rock.

Rich let him go and backed away. "Whatever you say, dude."

Todd's momentum spun him around and a moment later he slammed his shoulder into the wall and lost his footing, making Dave yell in alarm and both Tracey and Janet jump to the line to help keep him from sliding downward. "Fuck!" He let out an agonized moan.

"Stop being a jackass!" Dar yelled from above.

"Ow ow ow," Todd yelped, as his body twisted.

"Jesus Christ." Rich exhaled in frustration. "Swear to God you've got the brains of a sewer rat." He grabbed hold of Todd's belt again and pulled back, easing him away from the wall. "Lower!" He called down to the rope handlers. "C'mon."

They got around the boulder and then they were sliding down the last part of the wall to the ground. Rich grimaced as he tried to keep his balance and hold onto Todd at the same time, and he abruptly lost his footing at the last moment, with only his climbing rope clenched in one hand holding him up.

Kerry scrambled up onto the ground littered boulders and reached up to grab his legs. "Hang on!"

"No choice!" Rich slid down a foot. "Ow!"

Kerry got his boots to a foothold and then grabbed Todd's leg at the knee as Amy climbed up next to her. She could smell the acrid scent of sweat and old dampness. "All yours." She got out of Amy's way and went to help Rich to the ground, as both men inched down to safety.

Dar felt the weight come off her safety rope and she gladly released it, tossing it away from her as it slithered down. "Watch out!" She warned.

Everyone jumped out of the way, then surged back to gather around the two climbers. After a moment, Amy led Todd away without looking back and the two disappeared under the tarps while the group watched them go.

"You're welcome." Rich looked up at Dar and exaggeratedly shrugged his shoulders. Then he motioned her down, gesturing at the rope she'd wrapped around her and holding his hands out.

Kerry appeared next to him and made a come hither gesture, then put a hand on the rock and patted it. "C'mon, hon." She called up. "If you're waiting there for gratitude, don't."

"What a jerk." Rich shook his head. "I realize it's embarrassing but holy cow."

"Dippity douchebag." Tracey made a face. "Ugh." She turned and headed back toward the shelter herself and Sally joined her, leaving Rich and Kerry alone by the wall.

Kerry wiggled her fingers again. "C'mon!"

Dar considered them both, looking around to see what her movement options were. She removed the rope she'd climbed up and threaded it through the pulley, then dropped the end down to the waiting hands, waiting for it to get caught and held.

So. Dar prepared to start climbing down after it, giving it an experimental tug with her hand closed around both the rope around her and the one dangling, satisfied with the lack of motion, finding herself roughly where Todd had been caught.

Could still smell him, a little. Dar wrinkled her nose and moved a little aside, taking a breath and expelling it, as her body relaxed.

She looked up, seeing the handhold Todd had been trying for, when he'd hurt himself. Thoughtfully, she put the end of the rope from the pulley around her and clipped it into place then she shifted over and up a step, raising her body so she could see more clearly.

There was a significant gap that he'd tried to jump over, and gotten a handhold that had left him hanging, his heavy body twisting around and popping his shoulder out of place. She could see it in her head, happening. He hadn't been able to reach the second handhold.

Could she? He'd tried it in the middle of a storm, stupid beyond belief but now it was sunny, and the rock was mostly dry. She touched it experimentally. Yes it was.

Setting aside her reservations, Dar crouched, then leaped for the hold, shoving off with both feet and reaching out as far as her arms would go, getting one hold and then thinking she wasn't going to get the other one for a long moment until she thumped against the rock and her fingers caught.

For a breath she was dangling just from her fingertips then

she contracted the muscles in her forearms and then her lower body and brought her legs up trying to find a foothold.

One boot caught, and then she felt the weight come off her arms as she was straightening up and her other foot settled into place.

Phew. Dar eyed her position, not entirely sure what she'd just done was a good idea. Why was she doing this again? Just to prove she could? Her heart pounded and her knees shook. She took a minute to collect herself.

"What's she doing?" Rich asked. He put the end of the rope Dar was now attached to around his back and set himself as an anchor.

Kerry watched Dar's head tilt. "She's trying to figure something out." She saw Dar move over and flex her hands. "Oh, Dar don't do that."

"What?" Rich looked around.

The rope suddenly moved against the rock as Dar leaped upward and both of them made a grab for the safety rig. Rich hastily pulled it taut around his back and prepared to brace. "Hey!" He yelled out in alarm. "Watch it!"

But Dar's hands caught on a crack in the rock and she swung over and brought her legs up onto a second outcrop above where Todd had been hanging.

"What the hell?" Rich moved over a little. "What's she doing?" He repeated. "She should just come down!"

Kerry sighed. "She's probably got a plan." She put her hands on the rope. "Shit I should have told her what Janet told me."

"Told her what?"

Kerry bypassed the question. "I think she's going to see if she can use the phone," she said. "Call for help," she clarified. "Now that she's halfway up there."

"Oh right!" Rich relaxed a little. "Sure that makes sense."

Kerry sighed. "Yeah, t does."

DAR INSPECTED THE wall, making a picture in her head of what she wanted to do next. She hadn't intended to try and climb upward, but now that she was this far, it occurred to her that she might as well see if she could get up high enough to get the phone in her cargo pocket to work.

That would at least give her a reason to do what she was doing, right?

It seemed safe enough. The rope and pulley had held Todd's

bulk. She glanced down and studied Kerry's body language. Kerry didn't seem freaked out so Dar resumed studying the wall.

It became like a puzzle. She'd always liked puzzles. She'd studied Rich as he climbed and decided it was a matter of problem solving, really, She started the climb and the feel of stone against her palms, and the smell of it, triggered a sense of wry nostalgia that came from she didn't know where. Maybe early childhood? Maybe climbing around the old ships mothballed in the bases she'd grown up in?

Dar shrugged it off.

She saw another small ledge and climbed up to it. She was approximately halfway past where Todd had been. Then the rope became taut and ran out of slack.

She was on a small ledge that had tufts of grass growing in its cracks, and on one side of it a tiny gnarled tree with its roots gamely clutching the rocks. She looked at the angle of the rim and then turned and put her back to the wall.

It was a nice view. She could see the wall where the waterfall was just at the edge of her vision. The sun slanted across the wall and she wished she had Kerry's camera to get a photo of it. Instead, she fished into her pocket and drew the sat phone out and triggered the power button.

The battery warning came on first. She waited patiently as the phone cycled and tried to bring up a signal. She was surprised when it indicated it had.

"Huh," Dar said out loud. She used her other hand to open the dialing pad, pausing when she realized she had no idea who to call. She looked at the phone to see if there was any contact information on it, but the one piece of paper taped to the back was worn to nothing.

She tried 9-1-1.

The phone just sat there, waiting for further digits. Dar glanced at the battery LED, which was red and blinking, then she shrugged and dialed a number from memory and hit send.

The phone thought about it, then dialed and she put it to her ear and listened. After two rings it was answered. "Mark, this is Dar. Sat phone about to die. Track it," she said, getting back a half enunciated oath before the line cut off and the phone died.

Dar regarded the phone with some disgust and put it back in her pocket. Then she turned around and started making her way back down.

KERRY WAS WAITING at the foot of the cliff. "Hey."

"Hey," Dar responded. She untied the rope. "Got signal for about twenty seconds up there."

"Yeah?" Rich said. "Any luck calling?"

Dar shrugged. "I made a call, but I don't think I was connected long enough for it to be useful before it died." She returned Kerry's hug. "But I might want to try wall climbing when we get home," she said. "That was cool."

Rich chuckled. "It grows on ya. And you've got the arms for it, for sure." He studied Dar thoughtfully. "The longer the better."

"Helps with swimming too," Dar said. "But anyway, that's that for the phone."

"It's fine, hon. Janet said since we were due to call in yesterday they'll be looking for us. So even without the phone, they're on the way."

Rich looked at her in surprise. "She told you that?. Why didn't she tell the rest of us?" He demanded. "What the hell?"

Kerry held out a calming hand. "After everything she probably didn't want to raise any expectations. Just like I'm sure Dar's not going to say anything about being able to make even so brief a phone call." She eyed Dar. "Right?"

Dar nodded solemnly. "Since it immediately disconnected."

"Yeah I guess," Rich grudgingly said. "Least that's done." He coiled up the ropes and put them over his shoulder. "Thanks for the help. Maybe we can climb for fun someday." He smiled and then turned and started off toward the shelter, where the rest of the group were half in and half out, conversing.

Kerry patted Dar on the side. "Sorry I didn't tell you before," she said. "Everything happening too fast I guess."

"No problem." Dar leaned against the wall, in no rush to rejoin the others. "I called Mark, but I don't really think the signal was on long enough."

Rich reappeared and waved at them, motioning them over to the shelter. With echoed sighs, they walked down the short slope to where they'd arranged the tarps. As they did most of the rest of the group emerged and stood around in a clump waiting for them.

"I think we should get to the cabin," Janet said as they arrived. "People are starting to get sick. We need solid shelter." She fell silent, waiting.

"Good idea," Dar said, after a very awkward pause. "Everyone okay to walk?"

"Rather that than hang out here," Tracey said, gruffly. "We'll all manage." She had her pack on her back, and now she hitched her thumb through the strap. "We can't stay here."

The group nodded in agreement.

"Let's get moving," Don said. "Don't want to spend any more nights outside." He put his arm around Marcia, who was hugging herself inside her jacket, her face pale. "Someone get those kids."

Dar and Kerry ducked under the tarps and paused as Todd and Amy looked up at them. Todd looked pale and drawn. He was clutching the elbow of his injured arm. "What?" he said. "G'wan and get with them. We're staying here."

Dar headed for their gear, while Kerry went over to the two and crouched down, resting her forearm on her knee. "You don't want to come with us?"

"He was hanging onto a wall for half a day," Amy said. "It's fine. You can leave us here. We'll follow you to the cabin tomorrow. We both want a night's sleep."

Dar stood up with her pack on her back, Kerry's hanging from its straps from one hand. "I get it," she said. "But If I were you I'd come with us." Her voice was calm, but forceful.

Both of them stared at her in silence. Dar stared right back. "Get your stuff and come. We're all safer in a group. "And we might need these tarps, so staying without shelter here is just stupid."

"We'll be fine," Amy said.

"No you won't," Dar stated. "You're just going to be one more thing we all have to worry about, like you were when you went off the last time. I don't want to be hiking back here to save your ass."

"No one asked you to help us." Amy's head lifted and her body posture stiffened as Dar moved closer and put her hands on her hips.

"Wrong. You asked me to help you." Dar smiled grimly at her. "And I did. Now get your gear and c'mon both of you."

For a minute it was a finely balanced thing. Kerry ran through a few arguments in her head, and prepared to join the verbal melee, but held off, sensing Dar's powerful presence was probably more effective.

"Move," Dar said, her voice going down in pitch. "Not going to ask again."

Todd shrugged his one good shoulder. "Yeah." He stood up. "With the luck we've had a fucking dump truck will come down the side of that wall and kill us. C'mon Amy."

Amy looked like she wanted to protest, then she looked like

she didn't. She got up and went to their gear, as the sound of the tarps being torn down was suddenly loud around them.

Kerry stood up and went over to Dar to take her pack and swing it up onto her back. "Nice work, Maestro," she said under her breath, smiling when Dar rolled her eyes. "Glad we decided to have dogs not kids?"

Dar let out a sarcastic bark of laughter and nudged Kerry toward the trail.

IT WAS ALMOST sundown before they reached the last slope that would lead them into the valley the cabin was in. The light streaked across the canyon in a pretty kind of way, but no one was really in the mood to appreciate it.

Except possibly Kerry, who fished out her camera for the first time in days. She was last in line on the trail, just behind Dar as they started down the trail. The light was a deep and burnished gold and she paused to focus, then trotted to keep up.

Ahead she could see the bend in the path that would open up to where the shelter was. She was looking forward to seeing it, and being able to sit down under a roof after their day's arduous hike. "Tell you what," she said, as she caught up to Dar. "Glad we spent the time we did in the gym."

"True," Dar said. "Didn't really think it would be required for a vacation, but then again." She frowned.

"Then again our last one did too," Kerry said with a brief grin. "Was that one worse than this?"

Dar pondered that, as they turned the bend and saw the cabin squatting in the crimson light ahead of them. "Hard to say," she said. "Less ocean, more assholes this time."

"Mmm." Kerry's eyebrows twitched and she lifted her camera as a bit of sunlight outlined Dar's profile. "Might be a draw by the end."

"Might be."

"There's the place!" Rich called out. "C'mon peeps. We're almost there."

"Shut the fuck up," Todd snarled.

"You shut the fuck up, you jackass," Tracey yelled back at him. "We'd have been here hours ago if it wasn't for you."

Dar sighed, and pinched the bridge of her nose. "Not doing anyone any good," she said, in a loud voice. "We're still stuck with each other, people."

The group fell grumpily silent, but the pace sped up as

everyone was now going downhill, and their goal was in sight.

Four of them, Marcia, PJ, Pete, and Janet were all sick, sneezing, shivering and promising to spread the germs to the rest of them. On top of that, they were all still in pain from their various injuries.

Don's head, at least, had healed. But Todd's shoulder was swollen and tight, and Dave was still favoring his hand. No one was happy. Everyone was a level of miserable.

But at least there was the shelter, and the sunset, and the prospect of the river ahead of them.

THE CABIN THAT once had seemed so ratty now looked like heaven. Kerry looked around the inside of the structure and exhaled a little. She put her pack down and stripped off her jacket. "Whew."

"Whew," Sally echoed. "I didn't really see a moment I'd be so glad to see this place again." She sat down on one of the driftwood benches, looking tired and ragged around the edges. "Glad just to have a night of peace."

"Shh." Kerry sat down on the bench next to her. "Don't tempt fate." Now that they were there, and sitting down she could acknowledge how tired she was. "But yeah, glad we're here."

"We probably should have stayed here," Sally said. "She folded her hands on her stomach and leaned back against the wall of the shelter. "That poor kid would still be alive, and we'd have passed on most of the gimps."

That was probably true, Kerry acknowledged, but since they hadn't there wasn't much point in discussing it. "Yeah, if we'd only known then what we know now." She eyed the space against the wall to claim for the night.

After a moment she tossed her pack over on top of the empty floor space, then draped her jacket over it.

"We're going to go check out the raft," Rich announced. "See what's left of it." He led a small group out the door, the rest of them staying behind as Tracey dragged the small cooktop out and picked up the pot to add to it.

Pete limped in with a box. "Found the teabags. And some bouillon. I can't wait to drink something hot, my throat's killing me."

"Aren't we all?" Sally smiled briefly. "Hell I can already taste that tea." She looked around. "Where'd Dar go?" she asked Kerry.

Kerry extended her booted feet along the floor and leaned back against the wall. "She probably went to grab a fish or two."

Todd and Amy went to the wall under the screen covered window, and Todd eased himself down onto a stack of tents. "Fuck." He let out a groan. "Any whiskey in here?"

Pete looked at him. "For once, dude, I'm all in with you. I could use a shot of anything." He leaned against the table and grimaced. "Or a handful of Demerol."

"Let's see what we've got left." Kerry got up and went into the storage area. Most of the supplies had been rummaged through, but she saw two boxes on the makeshift shelves that were covered in dust and untouched. "Hm."

She went over to the shelves and pulled one of the boxes out and propping it on her thigh so she could open the top and look inside.

After a moment, she grunted in some surprise. "Water pistols. Don't think we need those. She put the box down and pulled the other one over, flipping open the top. "Ah."

The box held neatly packed cans of Spam. Kerry turned and carried it with her into the other room, where Don was busy heating up a pot of tea. "Look what I found."

Don peered into the box, then started to laugh a little. "Oh my God."

"Hey, we got a fry pan?" Kerry put the box down and picked up the cooking implement. "I can stir-fry it." She inspected one of the cans. "How did we miss this the last time?

"Thought we wouldn't need it, probably," Don said. "Sides, we had all that fish."

"Found a can of peanut butter." Pete had it clutched to his chest as he hobbled in. "Party time!" He gave the room a wan grin and set the big can down on the makeshift table next to the cooktop. "If we can find something to open it."

Don started dipping out tea into the pile of chipped and dented cups, and those in the room drifted over to get some.

"Better than nothing," Pete said, sipping his. "Definitely better than we've had the last few days." He slowly knelt on the ground and rested his elbows and chest on one of the benches. "Hard to believe we started this thing out worried about running out of chardonnay."

Janet shook her head. "Boy would I love that to be my problem right now."

"Given what we paid? Us too." Don's voice had a bit of an edge. "We were so looking forward to this trip."

Janet merely nodded. "Yes, I know. It doesn't mean anything, but I'm really sorry." She sat down and clasped her hands. "Really sorry."

There was a little silence and Kerry glanced over at Todd, expecting a snarky comment. But the climb and the pain had knocked the jackass out of him and he just kept his eyes closed, wind burned skin rough and painful looking.

"Shit happens," Kerry said, in a mild tone. "Let's get out of here first."

Marcia sneezed explosively, and clutched her head.

DAR PICKED HER way along the canyon floor toward the river, conscious of Ira ambling along at her heels. The sun was gently folding into the cliff walls opposite and Dar blinked into its reddish gold ambiance.

She heard the rush of water and it was hard for her to decide if she welcomed it or not. Water was usually a welcome companion, but after the rain and the floods of the previous few days she wasn't sure she wanted more of it in her immediate future.

But at least there would be fish. Dar glanced ahead, seeing the ruffled white of the flowing water. To one side, the raft was still there, still tied up to the boulders on shore, still with its frame bent and dented, but afloat and apparently more or less in one piece.

So there was that. She didn't think anyone in the group was going to be up for a ride on it, though. There seemed to her to be a better chance for most of them to be thrown off and sent ass over teakettle downstream than to get any place useful or safe.

No engine, no way to steer, most of them sick or injured. Dar shook her head. Best wait for rescue.

Ira caught up to her. "So, hey. One of those girls was telling me about you and the cat."

Cat. Dar frowned, then her expression cleared. "Oh, the mountain lion," she said. "What about it?"

"What about it?" Ira echoed. "They said you had a fight with it. As in, mano a mano." He paused. "Well, womano a cato."

They reached the river and skirted the battered raft. Rich and his gang climbed over it, shouting in some incoherence as they scaled its frame.

Dar left them to it and worked her way over to the shoals she'd fished before. She rolled her sleeves up and started into the river. "We were in a canyon, sheltering under an overhang and it came after us." She paused thoughtfully. "Happened pretty fast."

The river seemed a bit lower than it had been, and it was much easier for her to get into position, or at least she thought it was. The flow seemed less as well, and she was able to get settled as Ira followed her into the water.

"So what happened?"

Dar rested her elbows on her thighs and watched the water. "I stabbed it." She paused, catching a flicker of motion. "It ran off."

Ira digested this. "You stabbed it? With that pocketknife I saw you had?"

Dar nodded.

"So are you like the girl Steve Irwin or something?"

"No." Dar made a grab into the water and caught a fishtail. She gritted her teeth as she scrabbled quickly and got a hold of a set of gills. She pulled her hands out and a medium size trout came with them. "I didn't have many options at the time."

Ira pointed at the fish. "Nice. My uncle can do that. I got bit by a carp once and I don't like doing it." He held up one hand and displayed a scar on his finger. "Got infected and hurt like hell. I stick to trapping."

Dar threw the fish onto the shore, then went back to searching. "I live in Miami. I stick to the supermarket," she remarked dryly. "But my dad grew up in the country. He taught me to do this."

"I thought you were a computer geek." Ira waded out and picked up a discarded tub and turned it over. He tossed the fish into it. "Someone said you were."

"I am." Dar made a grab at another fish "I have a degree in electrical engineering and a second in computer programming."

Ira looked over at her. "Wow. That sounds expensive."

Dar straightened up and regarded him. "I went on scholarship," she said. "But it was a good investment in the long term. The long term being my current paycheck." She indicated the tub. "Move that over to the shore so I can pitch into it."

"Sure." He lugged the tub over and set it down. He paused to look at something as the stripes of red gold started to fade. "Ah ho. What d'we got here."

She glanced over to see Ira inspecting the ground, moving sideways and around to let the fading sun hit the sand in front of his boots. "What?"

He knelt, and touched the sand, and Dar sloshed out of the

water and put the fish into the tub. "What?" She repeated.

He looked up. "Helicopter was here," he said. "Probably this morning." He pointed at the sharp edge of a depression in the sand. "Still clear," he added, as Dar came over and crouched next to him. "I flunked mostly everything, but they still teach us the old skills, you know?"

"Also worth the getting." Dar studied the marks that meant exactly nothing to her. "How do you know it was a helicopter?" She asked. "And when it was here?"

"Heavy." He indicated the depression. "Nothing you all would carry would make a mark that deep. Not even that raft. "He jerked his head toward the craft. "And you can see the wash from the rotors." He pointed at the sand, which in fact had a pattern in it spraying outward.

"We wouldn't have seen it yesterday with all that rain," Ira said. "And I can kinda still smell the gas on the air." He opened his mouth and lifted his head. "Just a little."

"Huh." Dar stood up. "So, what does that mean? You think they were here looking for us?"

Ira shrugged and got up. "Some copter was here, looking for something. Could have been these guy's outfit, could have been some other outfit, could have been smugglers." He grinned briefly. "Tracking skills only go so far."

"True." Dar folded her arms. "But with the luck we've had on this trip chances are it was them and now they're looking everywhere but here for us."

"Could be," Ira said. "Let's get more fish. At least we can eat."

"True." Dar's eyes twinkled a little. "And it's something we can do something about."

"True." He followed Dar back to the water. "So like with the lion. That's pretty rad. If you were one of us, you'd get something for that."

"What, a spanking?" Dar grinned briefly, as she went back into the water.

"No, I mean, that's something you'd get known for, you know? Maybe they'd name it your spirit animal." Ira sloshed after her. "You're not a Christian or whatever are you? I don't want to freak you out or anything." He added after a brief pause, "People can get weird about that."

"No." Dar settled back into position. "I don't screw around with religion much." She noted the fading sun, and the water taking on a black hue obscuring most of her vision. "And if I had a spirit animal it would probably have rabies."

Ira laughed. "That's funny, but don't say that in front of any of our elders. They won't think so." He braced his legs against two boulders with a fast running stream of water between them. "People who come onto the reservation like to make fun of our traditions. Pisses us off."

"People do, when the traditions aren't theirs," Dar commented. "Human nature I guess."

"I guess." Ira studied the water.

"I didn't mean any disrespect." Dar sensed motion at her knee and grabbed at it. "I'm just logic driven. I don't buy into the spiritual."

Ira regarded her with a quizzical expression. "You're tickling fish out of the mother of rivers after facing down the hunter spirit of the canyon and you don't buy into the spirits? Really?"

"Really. Excuse me." Dar tossed the fish over her shoulder and into the tub, then washed her hands in the water. "Too dark to keep this up." She pointed to the shore. "That'll have to be enough."

"That's too bad." He followed her to the shore. They climbed out together and walked toward the tub. Dar could hear feeble thumping sounds as the fish inside struggled weakly. "Part of why I love being out here in the canyon is feeling that life spirit."

He spread his hands out. "You can taste it in the wind, in the water...I feel like I'm part of the earth when I'm out here with no one else around." He took one handle of the tub as Dar took the other. "My grandfather says it's the one gift they can't take away from us."

Dar considered that in silence as they walked. "I've always liked nature," She said thoughtfully. "I just never felt like I wanted to know it any better." She heard coughing from the shelter. "I spend most of my time under the water anyway, scuba diving."

"THAT REALLY WASN'T that bad," Sally commented, swallowing her last bite of fish. "I don't think it would ever have occurred to me to use peanut butter as a sauce."

"You don't live with me." Dar was seated on the floor, leaning back against the wall with her forearms resting on her knees. "I really like peanut butter."

"She really does," Kerry confirmed. "I use it any time I can." She paused. "Except on pizza."

A couple of wan chuckles echoed across the shelter, as most of the group started settling down to get some rest.

Dar waited until everyone's attention was distracted with trying for some level of comfort. "Want to go look at the stars?" she asked Kerry, who sipped a second cup of tea. Without a comment, Kerry put the cup down. They strolled to the door and outside into the darkness of the canyon night.

It was cool and there was a significant wind blowing up from the river. It fluttered their clothing against their bodies. They found a rock about midway to the river to sit on together.

Kerry licked her lips reflectively. "I really don't like spam," she said. "I'm glad you got those fish." She leaned against Dar and rested her head on Kerry's shoulder. "Jesus Christ, I hope this is almost over."

Dar braced her arms behind her and peered up at the sky, which was clear and crisp and full of stars. She could see the Milky Way and it was a moment of quiet content.

Only a moment. "Got some bad news."

Kerry whined like Chino did at a closed door.

"Ira found tracks he thinks are from a helicopter." Dar sighed. "From today."

Kerry whined again, then she turned her face into Dar's shirt and thumped her head against her chest. "You mean they missed us."

"Probably." Dar said mournfully.

"Crap, Dar." Kerry groaned. "Is there nothing about this trip that we catch a break about?"

Dar put her arm around Kerry. "Rich thinks we can float the raft and just go down the river. I know everyone's trying to talk him out of that idea, but we may not have much of a choice. Unless we want to wait to see if they come back."

"That's why you didn't say anything about that." Kerry sighed. "I thought you were being suspiciously quiet."

"I was bored," Dar said. "And, actually, I like spam. My mother used to make spam and spiral noodles with ketchup when I was a kid."

Kerry picked her head up and looked at her. "Did she put ketchup on the spam, or the noodles?"

"Yes."

Kerry was silent for a moment. "Please don't tell me you want me to start making that at home."

"I don't." Dar lifted Kerry's hand and kissed her knuckles. "I love you too much for that."

Kerry smiled. "So we should try the raft? It looked pretty ratty to me." She glanced to the right, where the raft was tied. "I don't think I want to chance that, Dar."

"Let's wait for tomorrow," Dar said. "Who knows? Maybe they'll circle back, or maybe it was someone else." She curled her fingers around Kerry's and regarded the stars overhead. "I don't think it's a good idea either."

They watched as a shooting star suddenly streaked across the sky and disappear. "I wish we were home," Dar said aloud. "I also wish I didn't have to think about having spam for breakfast, or sleep on the floor, or not have coffee."

"That's a lot for one star."

"You don't ask, you don't get."

DAR STOOD ON the shelter's porch, arms folded over her chest as she regarded the clouds now blocking the view of the sky. She listened to the rumble of thunder.

Well, fuck. She sounded the word in her head as she smelled the rain on the wind. Fuckity fuck fuck fuck. She felt like irrationally stamping her feet but held off, letting out a long, frustrated breath instead as she resisted acting like a cranky twelve-year-old.

At least the long, uncomfortable night was over.

Kerry came out of the cabin, closed the door behind her and stood next to her, taking up the same stance. They stood in silence for a long moment, listening to the sounds from behind them, loud voices and a long bout of hoarse coughing.

Dar sighed.

"We should go soon if we're going to," Kerry said. "Miss as much of the rain as we can."

Dar sighed again.

"I know you don't want to."

"I'm afraid that raft is going to kill us," Dar said bluntly. "It's not a matter of what I want." She pushed the long sleeves of her t-shirt up over her elbows and resettled her hands, tucking them against her ribs. "It's a matter of risk."

"Maybe we shouldn't have mentioned the helicopter tracks," Kerry said, in a mournful tone. "Well, we can let them all go then if they want to. You and I can..." She paused. "We can do something else."

Dar eyed her. "Like what?"

After a moment Kerry shrugged, then put her hands in her

cargo pants pockets.

Dar kicked the floorboard with her boot. "Sorry I'm being an asshole." She glanced sideways at Kerry's profile.

"You're not, really." Kerry sighed. "We're just in a cornucopia of suck."

Dar chuckled briefly. "We are. I so badly want to be out of here but I also so badly don't want to have that damn thing capsize on us in the middle of a rapids."

Kerry pondered that. "Could have anyway. Before—on the trip."

"Before the trip it had a damn engine, and someone who knew what to do with it."

"Hm. True."

"And half the people weren't sick or hurt," Dar added. "This is just such a mess."

"Also true," Kerry said. "Like I said, a cornucopia of suck." She removed her hands from her pockets and stood behind Dar. She began to massage Dar's shoulders. "Oh, Dardar. Next time let's just stay on your island and toast marshmallows."

Dar could almost taste the sweet, burnt crispiness of them on her tongue. "Mm."

"Maybe a few lobsters in a boil," Kerry continued, keeping up her motion. "I'd even take some peach pizza right about now."

Dar half turned as the cabin door opened, and Ira came out. He shut it and moved away. "Hey," she greeted him. "Getting pretty rough in there?"

Ira joined them and leaned against the overhang support, which creaked softly under the pressure. "People get aggro when they're sick. I know my family always does."

Dar nodded. "Yeah. I'm just not sure how many choices there are. So all the yelling's pointless."

Ira nodded. "River, or sit tight, or hike another way."

"Is there another route out?" Kerry focused on Ira with some interest. "That you know for sure?"

"Not really." He shrugged. "My dad or my granddad might know. I mean, at some point there has to be an outlet, you know? The canyon doesn't go on forever. Way back that away is the reservation." He pointed to the right. "But there's a lot of dead-end slot canyons round here."

"We saw some of them on the way down," Kerry said.

"So, I dunno," Ira concluded. "Yeah there's ways. I just don't know any of them for sure."

Dar unfolded her arms. "Okay let's go look at that damn raft again. Maybe it got better overnight." She started off the porch with the others following. "Better than hanging out inside."

They walked down the slope and around the bend to the shallow canyon they'd landed the raft in. It was there, lashed to the rocks and shifting with the surge of the river, banging dully against the stone with a sound like hollow melons being thumped.

Dar walked along the shoreline, looking at the pontoons. There were dents and dings in all of them and the middle one had crumpled inward as though some giant had punched it in the nose. The upper level behind that, where she and Kerry sat, was sagging to one side, the seats bent and the aluminum framing tangled.

After a moment's pause, she climbed onto the pontoon nearest the shore and made her way carefully across the deck – now missing several planks.

"Careful, hon," Kerry was right behind her. "You can break a leg up here."

"You too."

Dar sidled between the front row and the second row, where all the rattan seats were gone leaving just a bare metal housing. She regarded it thoughtfully. Under the steel structure were metal flaps, and she lifted one up to see stacks of life jackets underneath.

The smell of mildew made her wrinkle her nose. She closed the flap and latched it, then sat down and braced her boots against the row in front of her and kicked against it.

It was more solid than she'd expected. The metal was welded down to the decking structure and though it wasn't comfortable she didn't get a sense it was going anywhere. "Huh." She stood up and yanked at the rail.

Kerry went past her to the back row, where the two comfortable chairs had miraculously survived, and the captain's station behind it, sans the engine of course. The supply lockers had been taken off leaving open spaces on the deck, but the supports were close enough together she felt relatively secure walking.

She turned and looked out over the river, wanting suddenly and pungently to be gone from the canyon. Despite the ragged condition of the raft, it felt like it was capable of floating and she wanted more than anything to be riding on that current out.

Screw the risk. Walking out would be a risk. Staying where they were would be a risk.

Life was a risk.

Dar jumped up and down on the frame, holding onto the rail by the second set of seats, and she looked up and their eyes met. Dar stopped her shenanigans and wandered over, as Ira inspected the pontoons on the side.

"Let's just do it," Dar and Kerry said, at the same time.

"The rest of them want to and what the hell, we can swim," Dar concluded. "Let's get our gear."

"Done deal." Kerry said.

Ira looked up as they approached. "Hey, I was looking at this and..."

Dar waved him off. "Yeah, we think so too. Let's get moving," she said. "We wasted enough time." She hopped off the pontoon to the ground and turned, offering Kerry a hand.

Kerry's eyes twinkled a little. She accepted the help and leapt to the rocks then headed off toward the shelter at a brisk walk.

"Sure." Ira followed them. "Only live once, right?" He lifted his hands in a shrug as he followed them, head shaking slowly back and forth. "Shoulda gone with Mom to the mall, damn it."

"SO, FOR YOU guys let me see if I can rig up these tarps." Rich rambled around the back row, where Todd and Marcia were sitting in the comfortable chairs. "Keep the rain off ya." He started opening one of the somewhat worn and tattered plastic sheets and Dave went to help him.

Marcia got sick, fast. She was coughing almost continuously, and huddled in both her jacket and Don's, with the sleeping bag they'd used tucked around her. She clutched a steaming cup, the last bit of the tea.

Though the clouds were building overhead, and the wind came up a little, so far the rain had held off as they humped all the gear down the slope to the shore and maneuvered it onboard, finding places to stow it amidst the wreckage.

Pete and Janet were huddled near the back of the craft with Ira standing by next to them and most of the rest were in the second row trying to find a way to tie things down.

Dar was in the first row, studying the wreck of it, and Kerry was helping PJ wrap her foot up with the last of the gauze she'd found in the aid kit.

"After all that stuff, I dunno," PJ said, stifling a sneeze. "Oh crap."

"Yeah." Kerry ripped off a piece of tape and applied it. "It's all a mess, but Dar figures it's better if we give this a try than stay back there and I'm with her on it." She straightened up. "I mean, we almost had a whole mountain come down on top of us, been washed away by crazy rain..."

"What a drag," PJ said in a mournful tone.

"Yeah." Kerry finished her taping and put the roll back in the battered kit. "At least that looks like it's healing okay." She gave the girl a pat on her ankle. "One good thing."

PJ looked at her appendage. "I should have known when this happened it was going to go downhill." She glanced around and then back at Kerry. "Hey, can I ask you a question?" she said. "Since we're still getting ready here?"

"Sure."

"Is tech really a good career?"

It was the last thing on earth Kerry expected to be asked, and it made her laugh a little in surprise. "You mean in general?" she countered. "Or for women? It's tough in some areas for us. You go to most of the really technical conventions and it's a sausage fest," she admitted. "That gets old sometimes."

"Is it easier for you being gay?" PJ asked, after a moment's thoughtful silence. "I mean, with the guys?"

Kerry had to consider that. She sat back and folded her arms, watching Dar out of the corner of her eye as Dar banged a strut into place and used a bit of the climbing rope to secure it. "Well," she finally said, "I never really thought of it like that."

"Or do they hit on you anyway?" PJ asked, with a knowing grin.

"When I was single, yeah." Kerry smiled a little. "It happened. But when I'm with Dar, now, no." She shook her head. "Dar has such a reputation in the industry most of the time when guys come up to me and talk it's because they want me to ask her something for them."

PJ laughed. "Really?"

"Really." Kerry set the kit down and stifled a yawn. There was too much coughing and sneezing for good solid sleep and she felt lagged from it. "It's kind of funny, actually, because Dar never minds sharing what she knows, but everyone's afraid to ask her because they don't want to look dumb. So they test the question on me first."

"Dudes."

"Yeah, some women, too, though," Kerry said, "Dar can be intimidating. And she's got no reluctance to expose you for being an idiot if you are and most anyone who's been in the industry for any length of time knows it." She watched Dar take a step back and regard the two makeshift seats she'd made for them. "But in answer to your question, yes."

"Yes?"

"Yes, it's worthwhile to make a living at," Kerry said, briskly. "It changes enough so you don't get bored. I like it." She felt the motion as the crew lifted the last of the supplies, scant though they were, into the raft and then stood by on shore to lose the ropes. "Whoops. I guess we're going."

"I guess," PJ stood up carefully and limped to where Sally and her sister were tying down gear. She sat down on one end of the metal bench and tucked her foot up under her thigh, settling herself. Her companions came over and joined her. Sally moved up to the front row next to Dar.

"Okay." Janet got up onto one of the steel cabinets in the back of the raft. "We're going to get moving. We have a couple of paddles back here, and a steering pole, and we'll do the best we can with Ira's help."

Ira was standing by with his hands in his pockets, his plaid flannel shirt half unbuttoned, hair braided back and fastened into a knot at his neck. His expression was noncommittal.

"Everyone please put on your safety jackets. Please tie everything down." Janet continued, "Please try to be safe." She got down and motioned to the crew to cast off the lines and board, the raft already half loose and jerking against the final ropes.

Kerry moved to where Dar was standing, holding a float jacket in her hands and as she came closer Dar opened it up and she put her arms through it. "Here we go," she said.

"Here we go." Dar braced herself as the ropes came loose and the frame of the raft shuddered, creaking and groaning as the water current grabbed them and pulled them out into the river, now seeming strange and dangerous after being off it for so long.

It felt a little out of control, and Kerry wedged her boot against the bare metal frame in front of them as she felt the raft dip and turn abruptly, with no engine to counter the motion. She jerked to the side with some violence. Dar grabbed hold of her and she relaxed, just a little.

They swept around a wide bend and then they were in a relatively straight length of river, churning and rustling around them but with no big rapids. Thunder rumbled overhead and the wind pushed at their back. She poked Dar in the ribs. "Put your jacket on."

For a minute, she thought Dar was going to ignore the request. Dar had that look about her. But then she released her hold on Kerry and removed the jacket from the back of the aluminum support and slipped it on. Kerry helped her buckle it, then she turned again to the front, as they rushed past the towering walls.

This part, at least, seemed okay. "Hope it stays like this," she said to Sally, who stood, braced next to her. "Maybe we can make good time."

"Faster than walking that's for sure," Sally said. "But it won't. There are rapids just past that next curve. I've been through them."

"Bad?"

Sally shrugged. "Class 4's. Not really that bad. We've been through the worst already."

"Oh." Kerry felt heartened. "Great."

"Yeah, we should have done this to begin with." Sally shook her head, and her sister did likewise. "Hindsight's twenty-twenty."

"This was the worst option couple days back," Kerry reminded them. "It just became the best option when it was the last one, really."

"Better than staying in that shack," PJ piped up from behind them. "At least we're getting somewhere."

Don had a long paddle, and he was on the port side of the raft, Rich and Dave were on the starboard. Ira had the steering pole, and as Kerry looked behind her, he pushed off some rocks with casual expertise that relieved her slightly.

"Yep, we are," Kerry said. "About time."

Dar nodded. "About time."

Chapter Fourteen

THE RAIN STARTED as they rolled through a narrow, fast stretch that rocked the raft with some violence. Dar sat on her makeshift seat with her boots braced against the bare aluminum framing. Kerry stood between her knees with Dar's arms wrapped around her middle.

Kerry blinked into the rain, which was cool and tasted of the clouds now socked in overhead. With the jacket, and Dar's hold she felt warm and secure, despite the uncertain motion of the raft under her boots as they rolled along the — for now — straight path forward.

At least they were making good time. The flow of the river caused small whitecaps but the section they were in had no rapids and she could see a bend in the distance.

Behind her she heard Marcia and Todd coughing. Pete knelt in a sheltered corner, his elbows braced on a bench and his hands curled around the front of it.

Sally and her sister had gotten a tarp up over the second row of seats, and now Sally was cautiously pulling the end of the tarp over where Dar and Kerry were. "Want to grab this and tie it?"

Kerry turned around and took the edge of the tarp and tied the bungee cord to the framing next to Dar's boot. It gave them a bit of shelter and Dar wriggled backwards a little to take advantage of it pulling Kerry with her. "Thanks."

The blue tarp fabric rattled in the wind. "Best we can do for now." Sally said, as she took a seat next to Dar and secured the fourth end of the tarp on the other side of her. "Rich you need a swap out?"

"Okay for now." Rich was sitting at the side of the raft, holding his paddle. He'd taken a piece of the climbing rope and passed it around his body, and snapped a carabiner to one of the supports with a top piece missing. He dangled his legs over the side, his boots ruffling through the water.

Don handed his paddle over to Dave and went to Marcia's side. "How about some tea?" He took a battered thermos and uncapped it, tipping it to pour some of the tea from the camp into the cap. "Before it gets cold?"

Amy was seated on the deck of the raft next to the big seat where her fiancé was slumped, wrapped in a hoodie and jacket and cargo shorts that showed the raw scrapes and cuts he'd gotten from the climb. He coughed and held his shoulder to try and keep it from moving.

Kerry eyed him. "Should I give him the Advil I have left?" She asked Dar in a low tone.

"No," Dar said calmly, tightening her hold. "With our current luck we'll both get our period and need them for cramps."

Kerry chuckled wryly.

"Not kidding."

"No. I know." She leaned back against Dar's body, ignoring the rain that dampened her knees. "I just remember what that felt like." She let her hands rest on Dar's thighs, feeling the solid muscle under the denim, with a sense of security, as she was held in place.

"Besides someone else like Pete might need them more," Dar said, after a brief silence.

Kerry glanced behind them. "That's true. Poor guy." She faced forward again. "And I just remembered that jackass kicking him in the back so forget I said anything to begin with."

Dar smiled grimly.

PJ leaned forward from behind them. "I heard them talking," she said. "In the back, I mean." She lowered her voice. "They're worried about the rapids just past that turn there."

"I'm worried about any rapids in this thing so that's not a surprise." Dar said. "Is it a big one?"

Sally joined them. "You talking about the whitewater coming up?" She asked. "Rich was saying something about it being pretty treacherous."

"It is," PJ said. "There's a big rock in the middle of the stream, and if you go on the wrong side they were saying we could easily capsize."

"Nice."

"Well they can paddle," Sally said. "And the guy back there seems to know what he's doing with the steering pole."

"True," Dar said. "We can help too." She indicated a stack of worn wooden paddles that were lashed under the row of seats behind them. "Maybe up on those pontoons, where Rich and they were sitting."

"Mm." Kerry watched the water wash up over them.

"No that's true," PJ nodded. "Even I can help. That doesn't need a foot." She got off her seat and sat on the deck of the raft instead and started to work at the lashing that held the paddles.

"We should get ready."

"At least get those closer to us," Sally said and joined her.

"Hmph." Kerry studied the bend ahead, which now seemed a lot closer to them. "If they do this all the time, how bad can it be really? The other operations use paddling boats."

"Did you have to say that?" Dar sighed.

Kerry half turned and gave her an affectionate look. Then she reached up to wipe a raindrop off Dar's nose and tweak it. "Sorry, hon." She turned around all the way and rested her hands on Dar's shoulders, spending a moment just gazing into her eyes. "It is what it is."

"It is what it is." Dar smiled in return. "Just remember, if we get tossed off this thing hold your breath."

Kerry's head tilted a little to one side. "You mean under the water?"

"Yes."

"Should I have to remember that?" Kerry asked, in a somewhat puzzled tone "Isn't it a natural thing?"

Dar cleared her throat and glanced past Kerry's shoulder to gauge the distance to the bend. "For normal people sure. Even babies will hold their breath when they go underwater."

"How would you know that?"

Dar paused, then chuckled. "Probably read it in a book. Anyway, when you dive what's the first thing you do when you step in?"

Kerry's eyes went a little unfocused, as she thought about that. She put herself on the back of their boat, hand on the ladder brace, taking that step off into the water in a plunge and... "Suck in a breath off my reg," she said. "Matter of fact I did that when we snorkeled the last time and didn't realize I was so deep I got a mouthful of seawater and nearly choked."

Dar nodded. "Helps not to have the reg in your mouth, but think about it if you get tossed in," she said, in a practical tone.

"Got it." Kerry leaned forward and gave her a kiss on the lips, tasting rain water and a hint of the morning's tea. "Thank you, my love." She touched her forehead to Dar's. "For always keeping an eye out for me."

"Always." Dar confirmed. "Turn around."

Kerry did, and saw the bend coming at them. She squirmed around and braced her legs, glancing over as Sally handed her one of the paddles. "Not sure I'm going to do anything useful with it, but sure." She tucked the paddle down between her hip and Dar's leg.

"What's the plan?" Dar was calling back to Janet. "We need to do anything?"

They could hear the roar of whitewater now in the distance. Janet squirmed up between the two rows, looking more than harried. "Okay, so." She looked past them. "We're going to steer hard near the inside wall there, and just ride the right-hand side through the rapids. It'll be fine," she said. "Just hold on tight."

The raft started into the bend and both Rich and Dave paddled like mad men, with seemingly little effect. Ira was at the back left corner pushing with his pole, and as they came around the corner they could see what the issue was.

It was a short stretch of river between them and the next bend ahead, which was visibly lower than they were. The water was racing and bubbling, and in the center of the passage was a craggy island of rock. On the right side, a relatively smooth path, but on the left, it went into a whirlpool that was all white and green.

"Eh," Kerry uttered.

"Ho boy." Dar straightened up and released her. She took hold of the paddle that almost fell in the motion of the raft.

"Need some help!" Rich hollered. "We gotta get to the wall!"

Dar got out from behind the framing and scrambled down onto the back of the middle pontoon, immediately soaked as a wash of river water came over the front of the raft. She ignored it and plunged the paddle into the water, pulling to her right as hard as she could.

Moments later, Kerry was on the pontoon next to her, the paddle she'd grabbed from Sally in her hands, and right after that Don was on the third, and they were all pitching in.

The raft plunged right down the middle, and hesitated, between two flows, slid sideways as voices raised in alarm. Dar lifted herself and splayed forward, digging into the river as deeply as she could as the water came over her.

Ira jumped to the side of the raft and hooked a leg around one of the supports, reached out with his pole. He heaved at the last second possible and let out a yell. With a hitch the raft swirled in a circle and took the right path.

They skimmed the center rock and went to the smooth side gliding past the maelstrom and along the canyon wall before pitching downward toward the next bend.

"Yay!" Rich lifted his paddle in triumph. "We did it!"

Dar shook the wet hair out of her eyes and pushed her hood back. She looked around at the river and then at the rest of the raft, waiting for her heartbeat to settle.

"Holy crap," Kerry said. "People pay to do this?"

Don let out a wry laugh. "Thinking of a spa next time?"

"Thinking of staying in my living room next time."

"Bedroom." Dar corrected her.

"Dar." Kerry covered her eyes with one hand, the other gripped around the paddle.

There was a sense of euphoria around the raft though, as they swept through the narrows and around the next bend, this time to the left and into a long, wide, straight stretch that had only minimal white ruffles and a much gentler motion.

"Phew! Good job folks!" Janet called out. "We're golden for now."

Dar rolled onto her back and pulled herself back up onto the frame and ducked under the tarp as Kerry crawled up after her. "Break out the peanut butter," she said. "Might as well party while we can."

"Whoo." Kerry ruffled the rain out of her hair. "Wasn't as bad as I thought it would be."

"Me either."

Dar stashed the paddle and took her seat and pushed the hood on her jacket back as the raft's motion moved from a rough rambled to a smoother glide.

Ahead of them was green blue water, and the rain had modulated from a heavy sheet to a light mist. Tracey passed around the can of peanut butter, and for the moment things seemed all right.

"DAR."

Dar started a little, coming out of a light doze to find Kerry at her elbow, and the light around them starting to fade. "Huh."

"Looks like a conference is coming." Kerry offered her a cup of water. "We probably want to be in it."

Dar felt a bit disoriented, but she stood and took the cup, drinking as she glanced around the raft. Two more tarps were strung up and everyone was under cover, even Ira back in the corner.

Most of the group was hunkered down with cups in hand, but Janet had come up between the first and second row of seats and motioned Rich and Dave over.

"Okay." Janet said, bracing her hands on two of the frame supports. "I don't think we can find a spot to pull off before it gets dark," she said. "But on the bright side, we've got calm water all the way to probably after sunrise tomorrow. We can keep making decent time."

They were all silent for a moment. "Not the most comfortable thing, being on here," Don spoke up. "Got sick people. We need some heat."

Todd punctuated that by coughing violently.

"Even if we did find a spot, no guarantee we'd find anything to make a fire with." Rich said. "Or shelter, or anything At least on here we know what we have."

"True," Tracey wiped her sleeve across her face. "We can put up a few more tarps. Block all the wind."

"I'd rather keep moving," Dar said, after a short silence. "Rich's right. Could be worse onshore."

Janet nodded. "Yes, I agree also. I know it's uncomfortable but at least we're making progress out of here. Once we get through the rapids tomorrow morning, we'll be close to a pull out where I know there's campgrounds."

"And people," Ira said. "Supply shack."

"Well, that sounds good," Don said. "Sure would be good to see some civilization."

"Let's just make it as good as we can on the raft," Sally got up and started to pull over one of the coolers they'd filled with supplies. "It sounds great to me to keep going. I don't want to stop now."

"Sounds good to me." Kerry adjusted one of the bungees to bring the front of the tarp a little lower to block the rain. "We'll just make the best of it."

They did. Rich and Dave worked on getting more shelter in place, and as they did, it cut down the wind as well as the rain, and with all of them clustered together it got warmer.

They all changed into the driest clothes they had. Dar was standing behind her seat, shaking out the rain from her jacket as the last of the light started to fade around them.

Kerry joined her and held out a bit of paper towel, on which two lumps of peanut butter were deposited. She settled on a piece of the brace next to her and waited as she hung her jacket up. "Here you go, hon."

Dar took the paper and took a bite of the peanut butter, chewing it stolidly as she watched Tracey offered a cup of water to Pete. "Mmm." She licked her lips. "I remember going through a can of this stuff a week when I was a kid."

Kerry grimaced a little. "Really?"

"Really." Dar took another bite. "Didn't stunt my growth any."

"Probably was the gallon of milk offsetting it." Kerry put a piece of the smoked fish from the previous day in her mouth and chewed it slowly. "Wish I had some milk right now."

Dar licked a bit of peanut butter off her thumb. "We're almost out of this, Ker." She glanced behind her, toward the front of the raft. "I'm glad we didn't stop."

"Me too." Kerry rested her elbows on her knees. "My God I can't wait to get out of this damn canyon." She stifled a yawn. "I want a big cup of coffee, and a doughnut."

Dar reached over and ruffled her hair. Then she sat down on the frame next to Kerry and pressed against her, offering the last of her peanut butter.

Kerry eyed it. "Doesn't really go with the fish, honey." She nudged it back toward Dar. "All yours."

Dar shrugged and popped the last ball into her mouth, savoring the sweet and salty taste as she watched Rich and Sally drag the cooler over and shove it into place on the other side of them. They took seats on it as Dave and Tracey sat down with their backs to them.

"So here we are," Rich said. "Floating down the Colorado River, in the dark, in the rain."

"Here we are," Dar said.

"We should try to get some rest." Janet was behind the second row, in a corner next to Pete who was still kneeling in place, now resting his head on his crossed arms. "So we're ready to face the rapids in the morning."

Ira was seated in the back, legs sprawled out in front of him. "Should be a nice ride. Water's really clean right here."

Amy was seated on the arm of the chair Todd was laying in, her arm draped over his shoulders. Don was on a box next to Marcia.

Janet cleared her throat. "I saved this." She removed a box from her kit and handed it to Tracey. "Pass it around. There's not much there, but it is what it is."

Tracey opened the box and peered inside. "Oh." She removed a piece of something from it and passed it on. "Thanks, Janet," she said. "Smells great."

Kerry took the box and looked inside, her nose already detecting the scent of honey and sesame. She removed two pieces of the candy and passed the box on to Sally. Then she offered one to Dar and put hers into her mouth, savoring the sweet and nutty taste.

It was nice. It cleared the taste of the smoked fish out of her mouth, and it was a bit of comfort all out of proportion to what it was. Kerry chewed it slowly, wanting to make it last.

"Mm." Dar had bit hers in half and was munching on it. "What is that?"

"Just something my mom makes." Janet said. "Our family's from Iran, though I don't talk about that much these days." She had her hands folded and her elbows braced on her knees. "None of us talk about it much. Too many people think we should have been packed up and shipped off."

There was an uncomfortable silence.

"But anyway, glad you like it," Janet said. "I'm kind of out of I'm sorry's so it's the best I could do."

"Well," Rich spoke up finally. "Thanks." He looked around. "Right?"

"Thanks," Kerry said. "We all really needed a pick up, and that was a good one." She smiled at Janet. "Especially since it wasn't expected."

Janet smiled back. Then she cleared her throat. "I'll keep a watch on. Everyone get some rest." She went to the back of the raft, sitting down next to Ira. "Let's hope for a nice, bright morning."

KERRY HAD HER eyes closed, the burbling of the water enticing her into sleep as she sat on the small metal ledge, leaning against Dar's body. It wasn't really comfortable, but with the tarps it was acceptably warm and she could feel Dar's steady breathing as she slept.

She could taste peanut butter, on the back of her tongue.

She could hear the wind outside, whistling a little, and it flapped the edges of the tarp, but she allowed herself to imagine getting off the raft in the warmth of a new day and then, probably, taking a helicopter back to the lodge.

It would be nice. In her mind, she drew a picture of them escaping to their RV, unhooking the connections and starting it up, driving up the long road far enough to get the place behind them out of site, and then finding a spot to just chill out together.

Maybe go back to the little barbecue joint they'd passed on the last turn toward the canyon. Go in and just share a rack of ribs together in messy contentment.

She could taste the tang of the sauce, and the musky chill of a cold beer and the knowledge she would spend the night in warm comfort wrapped in Dar's arms in the RV's cute little bunk made her smile a little.

It was almost over.

She heard a low voice and opened her eyes to see Janet back in the back talking to Ira. She reached out to take the steering pole. Ira settled on the bench in the back, curled up and put his head down on his arm with a relieved sigh she could almost hear.

Janet hitched herself up on the far back metal brace, the wind tossing her short hair as she wrapped her arm around the pole and looked over the tarps, down the river.

Kerry could see her face, in the faint silver light, lined and tired and visibly worried.

She'd come around to feeling sorry for Janet, again. Kerry put her cheek on Dar's shoulder and closed her eyes. In fact, she'd come around to feeling sorry for all of them, for the people who were sick, and those that had gotten hurt and were miserable — all of them.

Even Todd. Even Amy, who was curled up with her head on Todd's uninjured shoulder.

She and Dar had just really been inconvenienced. Gone a little hungry, been a little bored, a little more frustrated, with their vacation gone south. But they were both in one piece, had not truly suffered as some of the others had, and would walk away from the experience with not much more than some more wild vacation stories.

At least these she could tell all of to anyone. Not like last time.

Eh. Kerry felt sleep stealing over her and she let the sound of the wind and the river fade out as she felt Dar's fingers close over hers in a warm sure clasp. She heard the softest rumble of thunder far behind them.

At least they had some time to rest.

DAR SENSED IT before she felt it, her body tensed, and her eyes blinked open seconds before Janet let out a yell that broke the relative silence of the night before the sound of white water followed it, and the creak and hiss of the raft bending against the force of the current. "What the hell?"

"What's going on?" Sally blurted, coming upright.

"Get up!" Janet bellowed. "We're going into the rapids!"

"Oh shit!" Rich pulled himself upright. "Crap. Crap. Crap!!!!"

Dar stood and pulled a startled Kerry with her as Rich rolled off the bench and crashed against her knees as he grabbed for the aluminum framing. "Watch it!"

"Sorry!" Rich got up and out of the way, scrambling for the paddle under the frame.

She stepped over him and ducked under the edge of the tarp in time to see the white churn ahead and the flash of lightning. "What the hell?" She turned around. "I thought you said we'd have till morning!"

Ira scrambled to the back and grabbed the pole. "Must have let the dam loose again." He yelled back. "We went faster than we shoulda!" He craned his neck to look over the tarp. "Ho boy! Hang on!"

Marcia struggled to sit up and Don was at her side, grabbed her arm, and stared ahead at the river as Tracey climbed up past them. She got behind where Dar and Kerry stood and pushed herself up to look past them.

The front of the raft was already pitching down and they swung sideways as Rich and Dave stumbled and hand over handed to the sides, yelling incoherently in alarm.

There was thunder, rain, lightning and the roar of pouring water. The raft lurched sideways toward a huge hole in the river full of frothing white and the dark black of rocks, swirling around an island in the center with two up thrusts of stone in the middle. They were headed straight for it.

"Oh damn!" Rich hung on to a part of the frame. "This thing will come apart!"

"We're not going to make it past that!" Janet screamed, real fear in her voice. "We can't! We're going under! Everyone get your vests hitched!"

People started to panic. PJ struggled into a vest, her hands shaking. Dave was standing on one side, jaw slack, staring at the water.

"Oh wow." Kerry inhaled. "Jesus, Dar. What the hell are we going to do?"

For a moment, Dar felt like everything went still, and she could hear her own heartbeat as her mind took in all the factors and the potential outcomes. She moved across the raft, put her hands on the frame behind the front row of seats and vaulted over it.

"Dar!" Kerry yelled. "What are you doing?"

"Stay here!" Dar yelled back, as she bent and scooped up one of the coiled lines they'd tied the raft to the shore with and ran across the pontoons to dive into the white water ahead of them.

The impact nearly made her inhale a breath of water and she battled her own instincts. She clamped her jaw shut and forced some air out of her nose as the chill shocked her.

She felt the water close over her head and she fought to the surface. The river's force swept her through the huge trough in front of the island. The water went from froth to chill black and the cold soaked her through.

Yells from behind her.

Dar ignored them as she made a picture in her head of the path she wanted. She rolled over in the water and kicked off against an underground rock just in time to force her way between one boulder and a second, the rush of the current shoving her forward.

She wanted to get between them, then get up onto the island. She squirmed through the opening she'd spotted and stopped.

Underwater and suddenly stuck there.

The jacket wedged her in place. Dar unsnapped it and wriggled out from the straps. She opened her eyes to swirling dark green water. She turned sideways and squiggled between the rocks the rope clutched in one hand.

The current helped her along and she got through, almost piling into the rocks head first "Uf," she grunted. Her head broke the surface and she saw the island edge ahead of her.

She grabbed hold of a boulder and pulled herself up. Her boots slipped on the slick surface. She propelled herself onto the island and hauled the rope with her as she got from her knees to her feet. She bolted for the tall stones in the center.

She got around the nearest one and passed the rope around the rock and came around the side of it just as the raft surged past it. The rope pulled hard taut.

Dar felt it start to slide and she got the other end around the stone again and dropped to her knees. She got the rope into a knot just as the weight of the raft came fully on it. The rope twanged like an overstressed guitar string.

It creaked and stretched and Dar paused, hands off it, hoping it would hold. She thought that it shivered under the strain and she decided getting out of its way was a good idea just in case.

A spattering of water from it dusted Dar's face as she got up and jumped over it, put her hands on the rock and climbed half up it to see the raft.

It swung around and slammed into the island. She saw two bodies tumble off it and into the water and realized one of them was Kerry.

How did she know in the darkness and the storm? By the grab at her heart and the sense of shock at hitting the water. She knew the feeling belonged to Kerry.

Without thought, she vaulted up to the top of the rock and dove back into the river, into the rolling wash. She popped to the surface to keep Kerry's bobbing head in view. She started into a crawl as fast as she could manage after Kerry.

Behind her, she heard the slam of the raft against the rocks and incoherent yells. She was glad in a way to leave it behind her. She ducked a wave and let a side wash of the current go over her as she went from a smooth stretch into a tangle of rocks and boulders in the center of the river. It tossed her in every direction.

She thumped against rocks and through crevices feeling like a shoe in a washing machine as she was pulled under the surface again and again. She realized she had no safety jacket on and then she was in midair, shooting out from the other side of a raceway and into a whirlpool.

No way to know which way was up, just a lot of water, and incredible force, but she held her breath and stayed calm. The pressure and the darkness around her produced no panic.

She rolled over again in the water and flexed her body in an undulating motion, heading for the surface. She broke through it just as the whirlpool grabbed her and threw her out the side and into the rush of a mini waterfall.

That sent her tumbling and as she stretched her arms out to steady her motion she spotted Kerry's head about a hundred feet in front of her. "Kerry!" she made use of the current, dodged the rocks and then slid over the last of them as she caught up to her. Kerry was being kept afloat by her bright orange jacket.

"Dar!" Kerry grabbed on as Dar almost crashed into her and then they were swirling around in the current in each other's arms. "Son of a bitch!" They were face-to-face. "This is nuts!"

"You okay?" Dar went onto her back, using a scissors kick with her legs to steer them. She looked behind them, barely able to see past the whitewater to the dark outline of the raft stuck to the side of the rock island. "Who came off with you?"

"No idea." Kerry said. "One minute I was yelling my head off, the next I was in the river." She took a tighter hold on Dar. "I remembered what you said though. Held my breath."

Dar got a good grip on the jacket straps and managed a grin. "Me too."

Kerry turned around and looked over her shoulder. "You

tied them to the rocks? Holy shit Dar!" She stared into the darkness. "That was crazy! You scared the crap out of me." She looked back at Dar. "How did you do that?"

Dar shook her head. "Just got that rope around some rocks and got out of the way." she said. "Then I went after you."

Kerry studied her in silence for a moment. "I was a second from going after you before I got thrown off. We're nuts, you know that?"

Dar smiled briefly.

"But in a good way." Kerry reached out and stroked Dar's cheek. "I think you saved them, hon. If some of those folks got tossed in the water they'd been in real trouble."

"Well, seemed like a good idea at the time." Dar watched the raft recede in the distance. "Kinda sucks for us though. Unless we find a place to get out."

Kerry regarded the current taking them at a brisk pace down the river. "Yeah. But at least I'm with you."

It was dark, and the water was very cold, and on her back going down this strange river in a storm, Dar accepted that as an inevitable truth. "Back at you," she said, watching Kerry's face, it's outline starkly plain with her pale hair wet and slicked back.

They went down a raceway and turned in a tight circle, then dropped down an incline and then, for a moment, it was quieter.

Dar looked to either side of them, but the walls went straight up and the river filled the space between them for as far as she could see, giving them no real way out other than staying in the water.

She looked at Kerry, and saw the acknowledgment of their predicament clear in those pale eyes looking back at her. She watched Kerry fish something out of her pocket, then used the carabiner to clip the straps on her jacket to Dar's belt fastening them both firmly together.

"Where you go, I go," Kerry said, after a moment of silence. "Wherever that ends up being."

Dar smiled, as they twisted in the middle of the river and went sideways. "Any regrets?"

"Not one," Kerry said.

Dar pulled her closer and put her arms around her. "Me either." Dar watched the clouds overhead and blinked into the rain, as lightning flashed over the horizon and outlined the canyon walls in stark silver and black.

She could hear the roar of the rapids behind them and the sound of the river in front of them and... Her brow furrowed.

"You hear something?"

"Hear what?"

"Buzzing." Dar squinted into the darkness, but all she could see was the outline of the surface of the river. She blinked at the pouring rain that smelled wet and stone like and contrasted with the strong green scent of the river.

She felt Kerry put her arms around her and the sound of the rapids faded behind them, but a roaring sound was increasing from ahead of them, and in a flash of lightning they saw another set of rapids approaching, churning the water into froth.

"Ah," Kerry said, after a pause.

"Yeah." Dar responded. "Well, just stay with me, Ker. I'll try to get us through it."

Kerry paused, and bit her lip, turning her head to look at the walls for a moment. "If anyone in the world can, it's you," She finally said. "Is that the last one?"

Dar shook her head, as she watched the maelstrom approach. "Should have paid more attention to the plan. Too much the tourist."

"Well, we were supposed to be tourists." Kerry took a few deep breaths as Dar fought the pressure to make them turn in a circle. Dar took a firmer hold on her and then they were in the churn.

They went over some rocks and Kerry got a quick breath of air before they were under the flow and her ears surprisingly popped as they dropped into a gully and then shot out the other side emerging into the air again before being turned around violently.

It became scary then as they were out of control and tumbling over and over until Dar got her feet on a piece of rock and kicked outward, taking them both out of the turmoil and into a clear area of fast running water. Kerry expelled the air in her chest and sucked in a fresh supply as they tumbled down a series of stepped rocks. Dar kicked outward again and they plunged feet first into the pool at the bottom of the rapids.

They were lifted upward and a moment later popped to the surface. "Whoa!"

Dar shook the hair out of her eyes and they both held on as they whirled in a circle. "Wasn't as bad as I thought it would be."

Kerry spat out a mouthful of river water. "Kinda fun, actually. In a scary, screwed up sort of way. Like a post-apocalyptic water park."

Dar laughed in pure reflex. "Maybe we'll get lucky and that's it before the pull out."

"Maybe our RV will grow wings and pick us up from it."

"Mm," Dar kicked and turned them so they were faced forward as thunder rumbled overhead. They were moving past some rocks and then...

And then there was motion, sudden, unexpected and very close. A second later Dar felt disoriented as she smelled rubber and hands abruptly grabbed her and hauled both of them out of the river, over the side of a rounded surface and into the bottom of a boat. The engine vibrations rattled right through her.

What in the hell? Dar raised her arm to shield herself from the downpour as a figure knelt over her and she was looking up at someone she didn't know, dressed in dark, waterproof clothing with bright yellow stripes. "Uh."

"Stay down," a firm, authoritative voice said. "We got you. You two all right?"

"Yeah." Both Dar and Kerry answered at the same time.

Hooked together, it was hard to maneuver but Dar managed to get herself hitched up on her elbow as the figure turned a flashlight on and played it over her face. "Who are you?"

"We're friendly," the man assured her. "Just relax." He turned the flashlight off and straightened up. "Go to the right, Jack. See if we can pick up anyone else." He turned back around, swiveling on the gunwale. "You with one of the river groups?"

"Yes," Dar said. "We ran into some trouble."

"More of you back there?"

"Yes, there's more," Kerry spoke up. "At least one other person went over the side with me, and there's a bunch on a raft, two rapids back."

The man regarded her. "Thank you, ma'am. Save my ass the trouble. Jack you hear that?"

"Heard that." A very low rumble came from behind them. "Give 'em a jacket, Ronnie. Like some drowned rats up there."

Dar managed to get herself unhooked from Kerry and sat up as she was handed a safety jacket. The shape and smell of the craft suddenly became familiar. "This is a zodiac," she told Kerry, who was trying to get herself sorted out. "It's military."

"I figured." Kerry leaned back against the rounded pontoon, resting her forearms against her upraised knees. "Any bets on which kind?"

"Hm."

IT WAS STILL short of dawn when they got to the pull out. The boat they were in landed first greeted by several anonymous men in dark rain gear who pulled the craft up onto a short sand beach and allowed them to climb out. Kerry noticed more boats behind them.

Behind them was a large, dark green tent, and halon lights. The tent flap opened and the welcome scent of coffee wafted out of it.

It was organized and there was a sense of purpose and order about it, and in response to gruff orders men with stretchers hustled out and headed past them to the shore.

Someone else who knew what they were doing was in charge here.

It was a relief. Dar and Kerry entered the tent and moved to the side out of the way, pausing to look around. There were boxes of gear and one part was cordoned off with mesh partition where bags with red crosses were hung.

A woman in green came over to them. "You need any first aid?" She asked, briskly. "They said the first boat didn't but it's always worth the asking."

"No, we're okay," Kerry answered. "Just wet and cold."

The woman nodded. "Good to hear. You can get some joe over there, and there's blankets," she said, then hustled off before they could ask anything else.

Kerry lifted a hand in a brief wave. "Thanks." She went over to the table with thick stacks of green fabric and regarded them. "It's funny they won't say who they are," she said, as she took off her jacket and folded it, picking up a blanket to wrap around her.

"They will eventually." Dar did the same. "Let's find a seat. I really don't care who they are. Even if they're bozo's dad's private troops I'm glad they found us."

"True."

They spotted some canvas chairs to one side and went to them, claimed two and sat down to take off their sodden boots and socks. Dar stood up again and took off her pants, wrapped the blanket around her waist before she sat down.

"Good idea." Kerry felt the shivers receded as she followed suit. There were portable heaters in the corners of the tent and stacked along the edges were utilitarian folding cots.

Two men offered up some cups of coffee, and as Kerry sipped hers, without sugar or cream and strong as all get out, she appreciated it none the less. it was hot and she savored the sensation of it going down into her stomach only realizing after it had that it had some alcohol in it. "Oh."

Another woman came by, and offered them dry t-shirts. "It's not fancy. But it's dry."

Kerry took both and waited for the woman to continue on to where Rich and Dave were now sitting. "I don't care who they are. I like them. They have common sense."

Dar took her wet, long sleeve shirt off. "I think they're Army," She said, setting the garment aside and pulling the dry t-shirt on. "Ah." She ran her hands through her hair to sort it and leaned back in the chair.

Two more men were going from person to person with a notepad, asking questions. Todd and Marcia were on stretchers, in the cordoned off area and Pete was there as well, leaned over a chair with someone looking at his back while Tracey looked on, a blanket wrapped around her body.

Don was seated near the partition, talking to a man with a medical kit at his waist. Don looked utterly relieved, and briefly he pointed to where Dar and Kerry were seated, saying something emphatically.

PJ limped in, with her dorm mates all talking to the two men supporting her.

"Looks like everyone made it," Dar commented, as Ira and Sally came in, with Theresa behind them. "Good. Makes all that half assed crap worth it."

Kerry nodded a little bit. "In the ends justifying the means department. It turned out okay." She took Dar's hand in hers. "As our shenanigans often do. We must have a guardian angel, Dar."

For a brief moment Dar found an image in her head, of a towering figure with dark wings and a deep, throaty chuckle. "Sure," she said, with a smile at the thought. "There must be a patron saint of nerds. Which one is it?"

"Not my denomination, honey." Kerry squeezed her hand. "But I know there must be one because you and I have squiggled out of more horrific situations than anyone else I've ever heard of." She exhaled and regarded the interior of the tent.

Another man had Janet in the corner and it looked like she was being grilled, the man's body language tense and aggressive. "Now what's that about?"

She was crying. Kerry nudged Dar and motioned toward her. "Like she needs to be smacked around."

Dar put her coffee down and got up, heading across the sandy floor toward where the group leader was being questioned.

Kerry took a sip and put her own cup down, then followed.

"And then you know?" She said under her breath. "Sometimes we just bring this stuff right down on us. We're nuts."

"Look, I told you. A lot of stuff happened. Nothing was on purpose." Janet was saying as Dar arrived at her side. "Oh, sorry, um..."

"Can I help you?" The man asked Dar, shortly.

"Can I help you?" Dar asked him back. "Why are you messing with her?"

The man regarded Dar. "Why is it your business why I'm asking her questions? You people were doing stupid things on the river and we had to risk a lot to go rescue you. I can ask anyone anything I want."

"Captain, really, we owe this lady a big round of thanks. She's the one who tied us up onto that island," Janet said. "We would have been toast in the rapids."

"Really?"

Dar shrugged.

"You should still stay out of this business," he said. "Has nothing to do with what you did or didn't do."

Which actually was true. Dar had to admit in her head. "I'm a jackass and I make things my business." She agreed readily. "It's a reflex I can't help. Glad you showed up, but nothing that happened calls for you to be a jerk to her or any of us."

The man folded his arms. "Lady, you have no idea who I am."

Dar smiled. "You have no idea who I am. Bet we'd both be a little surprised."

Janet put her hand on Dar's arm. "It's okay." She said. "Thank you, but let him get it over with so I can go and sit down and maybe get a bandage on my leg."

The man eyed her. "Are you hurt? Why didn't you say so?" He motioned another man over. "Get this one over to the docs. We can talk later." He watched one of the medics hurry over and help Janet to a stretcher.

Then he turned to Dar. "Now as for you."

Kerry arrived at that moment and took up a position next to Dar, arms folded. "Now as for us," she said.

"Stay out of this, for real," he said, seriously, his attitude moderating perceptibly. "Those people are in a lot of trouble, and you can't help them so just go back over there and sit down and let us just do what we do."

"Why are they in trouble?" Kerry asked. "It was just a river rafting trip."

"Lady, go sit," he said. "Please. We got work to do and it's been a long night." He looked around and both his voice and attitude changed even more. "Besides I do know who you are. Do those guys know?" He indicated Janet.

"Just a name on a credit card."

"That's what I figured." The man said. "Please do me a favor and just go relax. You really, really don't want to know what the deal is here." He paused. "Honestly."

Dar and Kerry exchanged looks. "Okay," Dar said. "Guess we'll find out later."

"I'm sure you will." His nose crinkled in a somewhat appealingly wry grin. "Just please don't hack my paycheck, okay?"

They walked back to their seats and sat down. "This is a little weird," Kerry said.

"This is a little weird. But I think that's tuna noodle casserole so for right this minute I don't care."

"Tuna what?"

Dar leaned back and exhaled, the long night finally catching up with her too. "Tuna fish, mayo, spaghetti and peas."

Kerry closed her eyes. "Urgh."

"No, it's good."

"You said that about peach pizza." Kerry sighed. "Jesus Christ at least it's not Spam."

Chapter Fifteen

THE SOLDIERS SET up cots as Dar and Kerry finished up their meal. It was like heaven to lay down on one. Dar stretched out her long body and was happy to close her eyes, feeling the warmth of Kerry's hand clasping hers in the next cot over.

She was full and dry and in some comfort. Now they just had to wait for a break in the weather.

The roof was being pounded by rain, and there was a lingering scent of noodles and coffee in the air as thunder rolled outside and the occasional crack of lightning was visible, but the tent was waterproof and secure and the generators kept right on rolling.

"That really wasn't as bad as I expected," Kerry said, in the muted darkness of the shelter. "That noodle stuff. It didn't really go with the Gatorade though."

"Needs milk," Dar said, stifling a yawn.

Kerry chuckled a little. "Doesn't everything?"

"Mm. But pretty much anything's good if you're hungry enough."

More thunder rumbled, and they could hear the rush of the river past the rain, but it was hard to even remember being stuck out in all that now.

Dar briefly thought about the cave shelters, and the wood fires, and beyond that to the comfortable glam camping they'd done at the beginning of the trip and it all seemed faded and unimportant.

Now there was this—the smell of canvas, the comfort of dry cotton and looking forward to getting into their RV and seeing their dogs.

Looking forward to going home. The heat and sunshine of Miami. The strong smell of salt on the air. The thousand shades of green that were so different than this place they'd come to that it was almost like a different planet.

The canyon was beautiful, but alien. Dar was glad she's seen it, glad they'd had the experience no matter how crazy it had been. Whatever it was, she certainly hadn't ended up bored.

"Hey." Ira was sprawled in the cot next to Dar and his head was turned as he looked at her. "That thing you did was crazy."

"What thing?"

"Jumping off the boat into the rapids. That was seriously insane."

Dar nodded. "Looking back at it, yeah."

"Were you scared?"

Dar regarded him thoughtfully. "Wasn't time to be scared. I didn't want that raft overturning. Wouldn't have been a good thing for anyone." She shifted a little. "Only choice really was that island I just was hoping the rope would hold."

He watched her with serious intent, his dark eyes equally thoughtful. "You have a good spirit in you," he finally said. "You should come meet my granddad."

Did she? Dar thought about all they'd been through.

"I don't think your spirit animal has rabies, either," Ira continued. "I'm glad we got to work the water together."

"Yeah," Dar answered. "This is a beautiful place."

"It's a fierce place." Ira crossed his ankles. "The earth here is very sharp, and very angry because it wants to stop the river and it never can. The river just keeps changing it."

"Humans can change the river," Kerry said. "And they have, with the dams and all that."

"They can, but you know, that won't last forever," Ira said. "It's been here way before us, and it'll be here way after we're gone. It's permanent. We're not."

Dar nodded. "That's true." She listened to the rain for a minute. "But you can feel the time here. You can see it."

"Yep, you can."

IT SEEMED LIKE she'd only been asleep seconds when the sound of helicopters rattled the air in place of the storm. A soldier shook them awake. Kerry sat up, blinked her eyes, feeling almost as exhausted as she'd been before sleep. "Whoa."

"Sorry, time to go." The man who shook her shoulder moved on. "Get ready."

Dar stood up and stretched, glancing across the tent to where the medics were preparing to take Todd and Marcia out, along with Pete and PJ. "Be stupendously glad to see that damn RV."

There was coffee in a big oatmeal colored thermos on one remaining table and they headed for it, along with Rich and Dave, who were rubbing their eyes and looking a bit somber.

"Something's going down," Dave said, as he dispensed coffee into paper cups. "They took Janet out first and Tracey's really freaked. Not sure what's going on."

She remembered their earlier conversation. Kerry just kept silent and sipped her coffee, hoping it would clear some of the fog.

"I'm sure we'll find out eventually," Dar said. "Right now I just want to get the hell out of here."

"Heard that." Rich said emphatically. "Want to get out, and get to civilization and have a hot shower." He said. "Hope they got that ready back at the ranch."

The soldiers were packing things up, and as they took their coffee out into the canyon they found a cloudy, but not rain filled, sky and two helicopters bearing Army markings.

Kerry had her dry bag, all she'd had on her when she'd fallen off the raft. In it she had her camera and Dar's book, if nothing much else. Dar had nothing at all, just the clothes she'd jumped in the river with now dry, and somewhat stiff feeling.

"Ended in a bummer," Rich said. "But we were lucky there finally." He took a sip of his coffee. "Next time I go with one of those paddle ops."

Sally looked at him. "Next time I go to Cancun."

"Next time we stay home," Kerry added wryly.

They watched the stretchers being loaded, and Amy and Don climbed into the first helicopter along with PJ and Pete. They were all silent, and as the door closed the soldiers motioned the rest of them toward the second chopper, and they ducked under the wash and climbed onboard.

Hard seats and webbing, not at all like the helicopter that had dropped them to the canyon floor. Dar slid to the last seat and grabbed hold as Kerry tucked herself in next to her and the rest found space as they closed the door. A moment later they were lifting and rising up past the canyon walls.

Then they were in free air, and the chopper went from vertical to horizontal flight and they were moving across the rim of the canyon heading back toward the ranch.

After a moment of silence, Kerry put her head next to Dar's. "Can't wait to call home."

Dar snorted faintly, the motion jerking her shoulders a little. "Bet they can't wait either."

THE HELICOPTER SETTLED to the ground and they gazed out the window as the rotors spun down and several of the staff from the river operation ran forward to meet them.

There were police cars gathered near the gate, and men with

guns standing by.

"Mm," Kerry grunted softly.

"Thaaat doesn't look good," Rich said, from the webbed seat next to her.

"They probably heard about Josh." Sally said, briefly.

Josh. Dar inched forward as the door slid open and she hopped out, keeping her head down as she moved away from the helicopter. She'd almost forgotten about Josh, the kid's death now seemingly part of a foggy past where so many other things had happened.

"Okay folks, come on this way. We've got a table set up in the lodge for you." It was Tamara, the girl who had first greeted them at the check in desk, now in a ragged hoodie and jeans with a somewhat overwhelmed expression.

Dar looked speculatively at her, then she paused. "I'm going to get our phones out of the RV." She stated, turning and heading toward the parking lot.

Kerry stayed with the group, who waited for Tamara to move off. "Relax," she said, after seeing the girl's expression. "She's not leaving."

"Okay." Tamara nodded. "They want to talk to all of you."

"I figured." Kerry motioned her forward. "So let's get it over with."

Looking slightly reassured, Tamara led them through the gates over to the lodge. They went onto the porch and into the lodge, around the side of the desk to the restaurant and bar area where they'd first met.

Seemed like a year ago. Kerry settled at one end of the biggest table, while the rest of them picked chairs around it. The staff hurried over with platters of sandwiches and pitchers.

Against the wall was another table, with piles of paper on it and three police officers, who grabbed pads and pencils.

Kerry took a sandwich and inspected it, then took a bite of the simpleness of turkey and swiss cheese, and chased it with a sip of plain hot coffee. She turned her head slightly as Tamara came in, washing her hands together

"Okay, thanks everyone. So these officers just want to talk to you for a few minutes, then you can get on your way if you want to, or absolutely you can stay overnight here until you sort out your travel." She hesitated. "Absolutely free, of course."

"Yeah, I bet," Rich said, with a wry, brief smile. "Along with our refunds for the trip, right?"

Tamara hesitated then nodded. "Yes, of course. We're getting the paperwork all together." She hurried out and they all exchanged looks, as the police came over to them. "Richard?"

Rich held up his hand.

"Could you come with us please? We're just going to interview you, in that room there." The officer pointed and Rich got up to follow him. "We appreciate you folks cooperating."

Kerry watched them disappear into the small office off the bar and close the door. "As if there was choice involved?" She commented in a conversational tone.

"Yeah, right?" Dave leaned on his elbows and grabbed another sandwich. "Just hope it doesn't take too long." He glanced at Kerry. "You all going to stay over or take off?"

Kerry smiled. "If I had to bet, I'd bet on taking off."

DAR UNLOCKED THE RV and stepped inside, greeted with the smell of leather and new carpet. She glanced around, but the interior seemed untouched and as they'd left it. She went to the cabinet near the driver's seat and unlocked that, too.

Inside were both of their Handsprings and she took them out and turned hers on, waiting for the device to boot up and activate.

It was quiet in the RV, and she sat down in the driver's seat feeling a sense of relief and comfort to be back here in their own space. Even if it was temporary, she'd gotten used to the sedate interior and she looked around at the two dog beds in one corner, and the scattering of toys on the floor.

After a moment she got up again and went to the refrigerator, which the campsite connection had kept running. She opened it and removed a milk chug, setting down the phone to open it with a smile of anticipation.

The phone's message light fluttered. She gulped down the cold milk in long swallows and picked up the phone, thumbed the speed dial, called up her office's number and dialed it.

It rang once, then picked up. "Roberts Automation, how can I help you?"

"Hey Christy. It's Dar." Dar said. "Is my..." She paused as the receptionist let out a scream and then started yelling, muffling the receiver. "Ah." She pulled the device away from her head and studied it. "I hope that means they missed me."

Probably they did. She was generally well regarded by their staff though most usually went to Kerry first for anything but the nerdiest matters.

She had just time to finish the last swallow of milk when the receiver was grabbed and a male, breathless voice emerged. "Dar! Dar! That you? Holy crap! Are you okay? What the hell happened!?"

"It's me. Back in civilization." She paused. "Hi, Mark."

"Holy crap." Mark repeated. "They found you? Dude your dad went bananashit and started calling all these people I do not know who in the hell he was talking to," he said. "After I got that blip from you I mean." He clarified. "So I called him about it, y'know?"

Ah. "Yup, I get it. Good call." Dar smiled to herself. "They found us. Some army unit with a craptastic attitude, but who cares." She opened the refrigerator and removed another chug. "Thanks for calling them in. What a clusterfuck."

"Dude," Mark said. "Like no shit. I had military people crawling all over my ass for that one squilch of GPS info." He exhaled in relief. "So glad you're okay. You are okay right?"

"Just fine." Dar put the chug between her knees and unscrewed the top with her free hand. "We'll be heading out of here in a little while to go get the dogs. All good."

"Oh, phew." Mark exhaled again. "Wow after what we heard I'm glad you made it out okay." He paused. "What in the hell really happened?"

Dar sipped her milk. "What didn't?" She sighed. "Tell you all about it when we get home. Typical vacation for us."

"Oh boy."

Dar smiled. "Tell everyone we say hi, and everything's fine. I'll call my parents."

"Will do boss," Mark said. "Glad it all worked out. Bye. Talk to you later."

"Talk to you later," Dar said and hung up the phone. Then she dialed another number and waited, this one going to voice mail. "Hi, Dad, it's Dar. Just wanted to let you know they found us, and we're fine. Call me back when you get a chance."

She stood up and slid both devices into her pocket then exited the RV, heading across the still muddy ground toward the lodge as the helicopter landed again and the remaining crew emerged from it.

Ira was with them and he started to head off, then paused as he spotted Dar and waited for her to catch up. They walked toward the lodge. "So, hey."

"Hey," Dar said. "They going to let those guys loose or what?" She indicated the crew. "Lot of cops here."

Ira nodded. "Not sure what the deal is. They told me to take off and mind my own y'know? But I wanted to say hey." He offered a hand. "Glad I met ya."

Dar paused and they both stopped walking and she returned the clasp. "If you ever decide to come to Florida, look me up. You showed me your place, I'll return the favor."

Ira smiled. "You got it." He released her and turned on his heel, heading back down the road leaving her to walk on alone.

The crew had already disappeared. The police cars were parked haphazardly. Past the lodge she could see the corral where two of the horses were idly grazing and one of the staff was standing near one, hugging its neck in a woebegone kind of way.

It made Dar a little sad. They'd had fun, right up until they hadn't. She continued along the path and onto the porch, pushing the door open and going inside.

KERRY CAUGHT SIGHT of the milk chug and had to chuckle. She watched Dar come over and take a seat next to her, reaching over to hand Kerry her phone. "Thank you, honey."

"I called the office," Dar said. "And my folks."

"Sure." Kerry was checking the texts on hers. "Oh, Dar. We got that contract from Monroe County." She almost felt a sense of relief at this return to a familiar world. "Great."

"Great, because we will finally be able to get decent internet at our cabin." Dar remarked, reaching out to take the last of the sandwiches. "I figured at some point I'd have to do that myself."

Kerry chuckled. Then she looked up. "What did the office say?"

"Lots of expletives," Dar said. "Mark told my dad, who made a bunch of calls and apparently resulted in this." She circled her hand over her head. "So my stupid climbing heroics were not, after all, in vain."

"Nice."

It didn't even seem strange, for that to be true. Kerry continued inspecting her texts. They had been so involved with so many different bizarre experiences in the past that if Martians had landed in their backyard and knocked on the door asking for Dar to debug one of their engine scripts she would not have even blinked.

Well. Maybe blinked.

"Okay folks, please come with us."

Dar and Kerry both looked up to find the police there, pads in hand, waiting. They got up and followed the officers into the small room, taking seats opposite a paper filled table, as one officer sat down behind it and the other closed the door.

"Okay." The officer behind the desk pulled over a folder. "You are Dar and Kerry Roberts."

"Yup." Kerry responded. "That's us."

"We're here to discuss the finding of Josh Albert's body," the officer said, glancing up at them. "So tell me about that."

Obligingly, Dar did. "So I came up over the little rise in the path and I saw a bundle of debris, with a lot of flies around it."

The officer nodded.

"It really wasn't," Dar hesitated. "It was hard to tell what it was until we moved it around and saw the bones."

The officer nodded again. "That's what the rest of them said. What made you think it was that missing kid?"

"We found his backpack earlier," Kerry spoke up. "And the scraps of cloth in it...he was wearing khaki shorts with their company logo."

"That's really circumstantial," the officer said, in a mild tone.

"We're not police officers,." Dar said. "But we knew he was on the path, we knew it was his backpack and we knew there were mountain lions around so it wasn't out of the question." She paused. "Wait, and they found his wallet."

"They did?" The man checked his notes. "I don't see anything about that here."

"They did." Kerry confirmed. "It was halfway chewed, but you could see his driver's license."

"Huh." The man across the desk leaned forward. "What made you burn the body?"

Both Dar and Kerry were silent for a few minutes. "Just respect, I guess." Kerry said. "I don't really know."

"Who suggested that?"

"I did," Kerry said. "I guess just the thought of animals eating at him bothered me."

The officer scribbled down some notes. "And the rest of the group agreed?'

"Some did," Dar said. "I did, Don, the crew. Todd wanted to save the wood for cooking." She cleared her throat a little. "I decided it was the right thing to do and we did it."

The officer looked up at her. "You did."

"I did."

"Did it occur to you that you were destroying evidence?"

Dar shook her head. "No."

"No?" The officer queried. "Really, Ms. Roberts? You find a body in a canyon and you never considered it might have been foul play? Never thought some other member of the group, or some vagabond out there might have done him in?"

"Really, no," Dar responded, with another shake of her head. "The bones were chewed."

"Could have been after he was killed, you know," the officer said. "Doesn't mean he was killed by what was chewing on them."

"Do you really think that happened?" Kerry asked. "Josh headed off before the rest of us to try and hike out. No one followed him." She fell silent. Was she sure? It had been dark and raining. "I don't think," she finally admitted. "There was a lot going on."

"We don't know," he said with a faint shrug. "And now we can't know, because you all burned the evidence."

"But there wouldn't have been any left even if we hadn't," Kerry said. "By the time you found us, between the rain and everything it would have been gone."

The officer eyed her.

"She's right," Dar said, with a faint smile. "Wasn't a lot left even then."

Kerry took a breath, paused, and just released it instead of speaking.

There was a knock at the door, and the officer leaning against it opened it up. A tall man in green entered, glancing around, "There you two are," he said. "Jackson, I need these people." He stared at the officer behind the desk, who then just shrugged and pushed the folder aside. "Are you done?"

"I guess I am," Jackson said. "Everyone has the same basic story. Not much else I can do." He stood up. "All yours."

Dar and Kerry got up and filed out, as the man in green held the door open. He followed them closing the door on the two officers.

"Sorry about that," he said as they went across the porch area and into the restaurant, where a number of the Army staff were seated, having coffee. "They don't like us stomping in here. Gives them a hive." He offered them a seat at one table, which had a coffee pot and cups on it. "I won't keep you long."

"Do they really think someone killed Josh?" Kerry asked.

"Who?" The officer sat down and poured himself some coffee. "Oh, that kid? Who knows?" He took a sip. "We don't think so. I heard the story. Sometimes a pickle is just a pickle, you know what I mean?"

"Yeah." Dar said, taking some coffee and pouring a cup for Kerry. "Walks like a duck, quacks like a duck, probably not a raccoon."

The Army man chuckled. "Okay, so now," he said, resting his elbows on the table. "You people who have friends in high places who bum rushed my butt from the beaches of San Diego to this hole in the ground, tell me. This all just a series of unlikely coincidences or what?"

Kerry and Dar looked at each other.

"That's what I care about, and my bosses. Seems like an awful lot of trouble to happen in one place to one group without there being some evil intent somewhere." He cocked his head, covered in a ragged gray cap. "You're smart, smart people according to what I'm told. What do you think?"

Dar merely stared benignly at him. Kerry folded her hands on the table and produced a wry smile. "Have you ever heard about a vacation curse?" she asked.

"What?"

"Like a WTF vortex?"

"I THINK THE Army thinks we're weird, Dar," Kerry said, as they walked out of the lodge and down the steps. Outside, three of the four cop cars were gone and a vehicle from the local reservation was pulled up next to it, covered in mud.

"Yeah, probably," Dar said. "Or monumentally unlucky."

Kerry cleared her throat a little. "I was going to tell those cops, you know, that I think I have some pictures of Josh's body in my camera."

Dar stopped and turned to look at her. "What?"

"I took pictures," Kerry said in a mild tone. "But I was afraid they would just confiscate my camera or the card, and you know, Dar, I've got a lot of other pictures in there I don't want to lose."

Dar blinked.

"So I'll send them to the police department, after I copy it," Kerry continued, putting her arm through Dar's. "C'mon. Let's skedaddle."

"Isn't withholding evidence illegal?"

"Isn't burning evidence illegal?"

Dar frowned.

Kerry smiled. "You'd have made a lousy politician,

sweetheart." She tugged her forward. "They never asked me about pictures, so I never had the opportunity to say I didn't have any. I could have forgotten I took them. A lot of stuff happened between then and now."

"All true," Dar said. "Besides, it wouldn't tell them a damn thing anyway."

"Nope, but it might convince them it wouldn't."

The sun had come out, and it was painting the area in warmth. They walked through across the grounds, a light wind blowing the scent of sagebrush and pinon over them. The rest of the group they'd been in was standing around a picnic table, listening to a tall man in khakis holding a clipboard.

Todd and Marcia and Pete were long gone to the hospital, Amy and Don with them. "Sorry we won't get to say goodbye to Don and his wife." Dar said. "They were nice."

"They were. I liked them. And Pete."

"Mm."

They paused near the table, and a man motioned them over. "We need to get a record of your lost gear so we can reimburse you." He added, "I'm David Scintah. I own the operation."

He was tall, and spare, with gray hair cut close to his scalp and a clean shaven face. He had clear gray eyes and was dressed in a company polo shirt and jeans.

The others were busy filling out forms, but they looked up and waved as Dar and Kerry joined them. "Do we want to be reimbursed for a bunch of clothes?" Dar mused. "Really?"

"Meh." Kerry waved off the form. "We're okay," she said. "Nothing there of much value."

"Hey, don't make us all look bad!" Rich protested "C'mon!"

"Sorry," Kerry said. "We knew we were going to go on a river so we packed our oldest and rattiest stuff. And we didn't have the fancy camping stuff you all had." She paused and eyed Rich. "Right?"

He grinned. "Right." He went back to filling out the paperwork.

David put the rejected form back on his clipboard with a snap, without any sign of regret. "We've already put a credit back on your cards for the trip, and the night you stayed before we left," he said. "I'm really sorry. I don't know what else to say."

"What I say is it's a lucky thing Dudley Douchebag isn't here or this would never end." Rich scribbled another line on his form.

Dave said, "I don't wish bad stuff on anyone, but he got what he deserved."

The owner perched on the edge of the table. "Is that Todd Evangeline you mean? The fellow with the dislocated shoulder?"

"That's him." Rich stood up and handed over his form. "I'm sure you'll be hearing from his father, the famous lawyer."

"Hm." The man seemed thoughtful. "How did he get hurt?"

"Trying to climb up the wall out of the canyon," Rich said. "After abandoning the rest of us."

Dar put her hands in her pockets. "What really went wrong?" she asked. "Were your people just that unprepared, or we just that unlucky?"

The man put the clipboard down and folded his arms over his chest. "That team was very experienced," David said. "Real river veterans. I talked to them, and I think I can defend most of their decisions. Though not all of them. Everyone makes mistakes, sometimes."

"True," Dar said.

"And the weather is the weather," David said. "Not sure they told you all, but we found Doug. He had hauled out and was making his way down an old riverbed and ended up in a washout. One of the guys from the reservation found him."

"That's great," Kerry said, sincerely. "I was hoping he was okay. It was a really brave thing he did, trying to get help for us."

"I'm just really glad that Army group was doing their training exercise and spotted you all. Now that was a bit of luck," David said, with a faint smile. "What with them having all that gear, and the helicopters and all and in the right place to see you coming out of the rapids."

"No kidding, was I glad to see 'em," Sally said. "Never say a bad thing about the military ever again."

David nodded gently and smiled. "Yes." He looked over at Dar and Kerry. "I hear you ladies did some brave things too."

Dar shrugged.

Kerry shrugged.

"We did our part," Kerry finally said. "Anyway we're taking off so we wanted to say goodbye you all." She could feel the tug of the RV, and privacy and somewhere down the road, a cheeseburger. "I think you all gave me your e-mail addresses for copies of pictures?"

"You got mine for sure," Rich said. "And I have Don's in case you don't."

"Here's mine." Sally handed over a folded slip of paper. "I'll share with the college kids. They're at the hospital with PJ."

They stood up and hugged awkwardly. "Won't say it was

fun, but it was an adventure," Rich said, wrinkling his nose. "Give me plenty of stories for next time."

"Yeah, enjoy your drive back home," Sally added, stepping back. "Nice to have met you."

"Okay, see you all." Kerry lifted her hand in a wave. "Bye."

"Bye!" Sally and Rich said together, and the others waved back. "If the rest of them come back from the hospital we'll say goodbye for you."

They walked away from the table, along the rock lined path that led to the road and the RV parking, somewhat aware that they were being watched by the group, by the owner, probably by the staff lingering on the grounds.

Dar put her arm around Kerry's shoulders, and pulled her closer, giving her a kiss on the head. "Glad the Army didn't out us."

"Me too. Didn't really want to have to explain all that," Kerry said. "Let's get out of here before someone changes their mind."

"Booyah."

DAR DISCONNECTED THE connections on the RV, slid the hoses inside the hatch on the side and closed it up.

There were two other campers near them, and as she came around to the front again a new RV pulled into the lot and trundled past them, headed for an open spot nearby. Dar looked at her cell phone and grunted. "Is tomorrow really Sunday?"

She opened the door and entered, closing it behind her. She settled into the driver's seat to start up the engine. "Ker?"

"Yes?" Kerry arrived at her side, sans shirt. "Want to take a shower before we move this thing?"

"No." Dar started up the engine. "I want to get away from this place before our vacation curse hits the next set of people who want to have an innocent ride down the Colorado River." She glanced aside. "But go ahead if you want to."

"I will." Kerry winked at her, then retreated back into the body of the camper, to resume removing her clothing as Dar started to back out of the lot.

It felt amazing to be back in their little temporary world, without anyone else around. Kerry opened the door to the small bathroom and slid inside, turned on the shower and ducked under the lukewarm water with an appreciation even for the slightly chlorinated scent of it.

She picked up the natural sponge scrubbie and added some

soap to it, enjoying the scrape of it against her skin. Even though they had spent most of the week wet, the shower felt warm and good and she spent a moment shampooing her hair, sure she could still feel sand from the canyon in it.

Ah. She stepped out of the shower and pulled a towel around her body, tucked the end in under one arm as she picked up a brush from the tiny sink and glanced in the mirror.

The RV rocked gently as she met her own eyes in the reflection facing her. "That could have gone a lot worse than it did. Our guardian angels must have been fist fighting with our WTF vortex and they won."

Because really, that was true. Through all the chaos and danger, she and Dar, unusually, had come through without a scratch.

Literally. Where others had gotten cut, hit poison oak, suffered back injuries, arm injuries, terrible colds...despite Dar climbing walls and her wrangling mountain sheep, here they were, having suffered no more than hunger and in Dar's case, milk deprivation.

Pretty amazing, actually.

She shook the brush at the mirror then she slid out of the bathroom and into the back section of the RV which had a slide out and contained the queen size bed and small closet. She changed into clean clothes and gave the bed a wistful look, before she went out into the main area and over to the galley. "Feel like coffee, hon?"

"Feel like a steak and a baked potato?" Dar asked. "Want to find a restaurant for us to stop at?"

Kerry came over and sat down in the seat next to her in the cockpit, relaxing into the comfort of the soft leather as she regarded the road ahead of them. A mostly empty trek.

Mostly empty, because there were two cars coming toward them at a good clip, and as they passed them they felt the RV rock a little from the air displacement. One was a sleek looking Mercedes and she considered the possibility that it was Todd's father zooming to his rescue.

She was glad they were headed in the opposite direction. "Let me see what the Handspring can find." She started tapping on the device as Dar shifted a little in the driver's seat, leaning forward as another pair of cars came up over the horizon and sped past them.

They were both momentarily silent, then they looked at each other. "Anything at the end of that road but the ranch?" Dar asked. "Anything past that?"

Kerry shrugged a little. "I don't think so."

"Hm."

Kerry went back to her search. "Hon," she said, after another moment's silence. "Are you thinking about turning around?"

Dar cleared her throat and tapped her thumbs against the steering wheel. "I was." She admitted. "But honestly, Ker? What the hell are we going to do? Whatever it is – not a problem we can solve."

"True."

"Besides, the Army is there, and they have my phone number. Find me some spuds."

"How about Big E Steakhouse and Saloon?" Kerry suggested, with a grin. "I think they've got us both covered and we can bring a doggie bag for the doggies since it's about ten minutes from their spa."

"Now that's a damn plan."

KERRY KICKED BACK and crossed one knee over the other as she regarded the sparsely seated patio around her, and the pretty scenery in the distance. It was dry and sunny, but a nice breeze fluttered past and she gave the waitress a benign smile as she set a frosty mug down in front of her. "Thank you."

"Anytime. You ready to order?" the woman asked. "Or should we wait for your friend to come back."

"We can get started. Since your patio is pet friendly she went to go get our pets," Kerry said. "So let's go with two of the ribeyes, with baked potato and mushrooms, medium rare. And we'll need a porterhouse cooked rare and cut up in pieces."

The woman was scribbling. "For the pets?"

"For the dogs," Kerry said. "Thanks."

"No problem." The woman took the menus and disappeared, and Kerry settled back in her seat with her mug of local amber.

Her phone rang, and she lifted it. "Hello."

"Oh, Kerrisita! Are you and Jefa okay?"

"We're fine, Maria," Kerry reassured her. "Dar just went to pick up the dogs, and I'm about to start on a beer. We're on our way back out of the canyon area."

"Thank goodness!" Maria said. "We were all so worried! Especially since we saw that place you were going to on the television this morning!"

Kerry took a sip of her beer. "Yeah, I guess the rescue got

some press. Anyway how are things there? Everything okay?" She paused, then frowned. "Wait, you saw it on television in Miami?"

"Si, on the CNN," Maria said. "Things are very good here, yes. Two of the new contracts have signed the legal, and Mark has put in some more bandwidth. So you will be coming home now?"

"Yep, we will. We'll probably stop at some swanky camping place tonight and then get a full day drive in tomorrow. I know Dar's looking forward to getting back." She spotted the RV approaching the front parking lot. "And here come the dogs. Let me call you back, okay Maria?"

"Si, no problem Kerry. I am glad you are not with the dangerous people anymore," Maria said. "I will talk with you later, bye-bye."

The call ended, and Kerry leaned back and took another sip of her beer. "CNN? Wow it must have been a really slow news day, huh?" She mused, then frowned. "Wait, the dangerous people?"

DAR SCRIBBLED HER name on the release form and handed them back to the smiling attendant behind the desk. "Were they good kids for you?"

"Oh, Ms. Roberts, they're wonderful," the girl said, with sincere enthusiasm. "Everyone loved them and I think they had a great time."

The inner door opened, letting a cacophony of pet sounds emerge. A man, dressed in dark purple scrubs, came out with two dogs on leashes.

"Hey guys." Dar smiled as the dogs spotted her and let out howls of happiness, making the attendant lunge forward as they bolted toward her. She knelt quickly and then was freight trained by Chino, as half-grown Mocha galumped in her wake. "Hey girl."

Both dogs started a tail wagging, foot dancing lickfest of her as the two spa workers stood there with indulgent smiles. They had new, woven, desert themed collars on and smelled like sage, and Dar was glad to hug them both.

"Hope you had as much fun as they did," the man said. "You went rafting, right?"

"Right." Dar took possession of the leashes. "Now we're heading home. Ready kids?"

"Grouf." Chino sat down next to her and barked, her tail

sweeping the floor.

"Hey, you weren't by any chance in that whole thing on the news, were you?" The girl asked as she walked around Dar to open the door for her. "That sounded crazy!"

Dar put her sunglasses back on and got herself sorted out with her two pets. "Haven't seen the news, so I have no idea," she said. "Gotta go. Thanks for taking care of them."

"No problem. Anytime!" The two waved as Dar got down the steps and headed for the RV. "Come back soon!"

"Nope, sorry." Dar glanced down at the bouncing dogs. "Glad to see you guys, you know that? We missed you."

"Yap!" Mocha hopped along and stood up, his paws now almost reaching to her hips. She gave him a pat on the head and opened the RV door, waiting for the dogs to rush up the steps and followed them. "Let's go find your other mom, and some steak. How about that?"

"Growf!" Chino hopped up onto the couch and sat down.

Dar started up the RV and backed out, pausing when her cell phone rang. She glanced at it, then hit the button to answer. "Hey, Dad," she said. "Thanks for sending in help I..." She paused. "What?"

"Growf." Chino repeated, tongue hanging out.

"What?"

KERRY SMILED AT the sight of the two Labradors, full-sized Chino and half-sized Mocha bounding toward her with ears flapping and tails wagging so hard they were just a blur. "C'mere kids!" She held out her hands to them and wiggled her fingers in welcome.

Dar jogged behind them, leashes over her shoulder. She hauled up as Mocha hurtled through the air and landed in Kerry's lap. "Mocha!"

Kerry just had time to squawk as she ended up with an armful of brown puppy, rocking her back in her seat as Mocha eagerly licked her face. "Hey, little man!" She spluttered. "Aw, I missed you too!"

Dar dropped into the seat across from her and patted Chino's back, as the cream colored lab waited her turn for attention with far more decorum. "Hey."

"Hey." Kerry reached past Mocha and gave Chino a scratch behind her ears. "Hey, Cheebles! Did you miss us?" She glanced at Dar. "That rescue they did ended up on the news, I hear. I talked to Maria."

"It did." Dar regarded her. "Mostly because CNN's reporting the op was full of suspected terrorists."

Kerry went still. "What?"

"Remember Janet said her family was Iranian?"

Kerry blinked. "What?" She repeated. "How does that mean they're terrorists?"

"Mom and Dad just landed at a nearby airstrip." Dar soldiered on. "They got Alastair to fly them here. We're going to hear all about it in about fifteen minutes."

"What?"

Dar gave her a commiserating look. "Just go with it, hon. We're lucky we kept going."

The waitress returned. "Oh, you're back. What cute dogs!"

Dar leaned her elbow on the table. "I'm back and bringing more friends. We're going to need a bunch of steaks and a bunch of vegetables and a gallon of beer."

"Great!" The waitress didn't miss a beat. "Are the friends people or more dogs? I need to know for the dishes."

"People," Dar said.

"No problem." She whisked off and headed for the kitchen.

Kerry managed to wrangle Mocha down to the ground. "Terrorists?"

Dar sighed.

"Dar those guys weren't terrorists," Kerry said. "Janet? C'mon."

Dar shrugged. "We don't know everything. But apparently my dad has some intel so I guess we'll find out soon as they get here." She looked up as the waitress returned, with another young man behind her, carrying a tray with a mug of beer on it, which he put down in front of her. "Thanks."

"No problem. Can I pet your dogs?"

"Sure." Dar picked up her mug and drank from it, her eyes fastened on Kerry's across the table as the two servers made much of their pets.

After a moment, Kerry just started laughing, covering her eyes with one hand.

DAR SECTIONED HER steak into neatly cut squares and forked up one of them, putting it into her mouth and chewing it. She watched Kerry leaving her own plate aside for a minute, as she took the two plastic dishes the restaurant had given them and portioned the dogs' lunches out first.

Mocha and Chino stood next to her, eyes glued on the plates, tails wagging in unison. "They know." Dar commented, after swallowing.

"Of course they know." Kerry put the plates down and got out of the way. Then she went back to her plate and dove in herself, really glad to be eating something of her own choice for the first time in a week. "I can't believe they dragged Alastair out here."

Dar chuckled. "I think retirement is boring him," she said. "He sent me a bunch of cat videos before we left and an animated gif of a pony."

Kerry paused in mid cut and stared at her. Dar merely looked back at her as she chewed her steak.

After a moment, Kerry shook her head. "This is good." She indicated the steak.

"Anything would be good after what we went through the last few days," Dar said. "But yeah, it is." She glanced up at the television on the wall, which was now showing a basketball game. "Wish they'd get here already. I want to know what the hell's going on."

"Want me to call Maria and ask what's on CNN?" Kerry offered.

"No. I don't want to freak her out."

"Mm."

A taxi pulled up, and disgorged three people who advanced toward the patio. Chino, seated on a chair next to Kerry sat up on seeing them and barked.

"Ah." Kerry lifted a hand and waved. "There they are."

Dar turned and then stood, as the three marched up the steps and came over to the table. "Hi, Mom." Dar greeted the first of the new arrivals, a short silver blond woman in a colorful patchwork jacket.

"Hey, kid," Ceci Roberts said, as she stepped aside to let her tall husband sidle beside her. "Hey Kerry."

"Hallo there, Dardar," Andrew said. "Kumquat." He winked at Kerry.

"Hey, Alastair." Kerry stood as well, holding firmly onto the dog's leashes as she extended a hand out to their former boss. "Nice to see you."

"Have a seat." Dar gestured. "They're bringing out chow." She sat back down as Andrew picked up Mocha and set him on his lap. "So. What's going on?"

"What isn't?" Ceci eyed her. "I gotta say, you kids are trouble magnets."

"You all do get into the damndest things," Andrew said. "Ah swear."

Alastair McLean sat back and smiled. "This time, I'm just along for the ride." He said to Kerry, who was sitting next to him. "Can't wait to hear what's going on. But it was nice to be able to take the plane out longer than just to Galveston."

The wait staff returned, with a cart. "Welcome," the girl said. "So we have steaks, and vegetables and beer. You have anyone else coming?" She looked at all of them. "More people? Or dogs?"

"Maybe a pony?" Her male counterpart suggested. "We have carrots."

"That's all for now," Dar said, as they put the platters down. "Thanks."

The servers left. There was a brief lack of conversation as the three newcomers took plates and sorted out their edibles, then Ceci cleared her throat. "Okay."

"Growf." Chino barked at her.

"Shh." Kerry tweaked the tail of their pet.

"We were in the office, just doing a few things when Mark comes running in, looking for Andy," Ceci said. "Wanted to know how to geolocate someone using a sat phone."

"Lord." Andrew cut his steak up into squares just like Dar's.

"So, of course your father asked him what he was looking for." Ceci said. "And turned him upside down and shook him until he coughed it up when he didn't want to tell us."

Dar could easily imagine the scene. "Glad we have health insurance. I'm sure he just didn't want you to freak out."

"Ah swear," Andrew said. "So then I done called some feller I knew back in the service, and he plugged in them numbers and told us where you were."

Kerry took a sip of her beer. "That sounds pretty simple actually."

"Oh, it was," Ceci said. "What wasn't simple was by the time we got that, and we were figuring out what to do with it, a spook arrived."

Dar blinked. "A spook?"

"Somebody from the Miami office of the NSA," Ceci said. "Who was super interested in the coordinates Mark gave Andy because they were apparently running an operation in the area. Unfortunately, he wasn't willing to share any of his information so your father boxed him on the ear and sent him on his way."

"Jackass."

Dar rested her chin on her fist. "So then what?"

"So then we called Gerry," Ceci said. "Because what is the point of having a family friend who's a general if you don't call him when you need the army?" She shrugged seeing the wince on her daughter's face. "There wasn't anyone else really to call, Dar. You were lost in a national park, and the bimbos you were with weren't answering their phone."

"I see," Dar sighed. "Yeah I guess they were probably running around trying to help."

"They were stonewalling ev'rbody," Andrew said. "Wouldn't tell no one nothing."

"They probably didn't know anything," Kerry said, in a mild tone. "Except that we missed the check in call. It's not like we were sending text messages out there."

"Anyhow somebody out there tipped off them spooks that them folks that ran that place were from the Middle East," Andrew said. "And they were investigating."

"A lot of people are from other places, Dad," Dar said. "It's not against the law."

"No," Ceci said. "It's not. But the man who owns that rafting operation was housing three of the guys who hijacked those planes on 9/11."

Everyone sat in silence for a long minute.

"Jesus Christ," Alastair finally said. "Is that really true?"

"That's what they done told us." Andrew looked at Dar. "Gerry called us and done told us they were taking care of all that business and to just keep still and wait."

Dar was blinking, her eyes wide. "Son of a bitch," she said after a long pause. "That totally was never in the picture." She added. "No one said anything about that to us."

"Not at all." Kerry was shaking her head. "Never would have even crossed my mind."

"Wow," Alastair commented. "What are the odds, huh? What made you pick them?" He asked. "You get a recommendation from someone or what?"

Dar sat back and thought about it. How had they come to her notice? She shook her head a few times. "It was just random," she said. "I went through the travel agency on the island. They had brochures for a bunch of things and I picked that one. Because it had a picture of a horse on it."

Kerry looked over at her, eyebrows hiking slightly.

Dar shrugged apologetically. "Really nothing more than that.

Just that they were a full- service outfitter and it looked like fun."

"They seemed legit," Kerry said. "Some of the people we were with had heard of them, had picked them because they'd been around a while and had a good rep." She paused thoughtfully. "Most of the crew were kids. Kids from the area, matter of fact."

Ceci seemed pleased at the response to her news. "And how it came to light, apparently, is some of the people who worked for them got stopped crossing the border from Canada. They were on some list."

Dar's jaw dropped a little, and she and Kerry exchanged looks. "Didn't they say that jackass's raft team was from Toronto?"

"They did," Kerry said. "There was this couple who were supposed to take a trip down alone so they could climb cliffs and things that weren't on the usual program." She explained. "But the team that was supposed to take them couldn't make it so they ended up on our raft."

"Uh huh," Andrew grunted.

"Some rich kid and his fiancé," Dar said. "Father's a big shot lawyer or something."

"Yeah," Kerry nodded. "He ended up dislocating his shoulder. Dar had to rescue him." She added, almost as an afterthought. "But that was after the raft flipped, and the flash flood and the collapsed arch."

"And the mountain lion." Dar looked up at the abrupt silence, to find three sets of eyes staring at her. "There was a lot going on."

The waitress returned. "Anything else right now for you folks?"

Alastair folded his arms. "I think we're going to need another round of beer."

"Coming right up."

Chapter Sixteen

"SO ANYWAY, THE first couple of days were fine," Kerry related. "It was nice, we got some good pictures."

"It was getting boring," Dar added. "But there were fun parts too, we got to see waterfalls, and do some slides and we saw a bobcat."

"And mountain goats, and there was an owl that landed on Dar's arm, and all that." Kerry went on. "But then they started to get worried about the weather."

"Uh huh." Andrew grunted. "Wonder if that was all they was worried about."

"It started raining when we got to shelter that night, and it was pretty bad." Kerry said. "But it was weather, you know?" She sat back in her chair. "But the next day, it got crazy."

"The raft flipped and we got thrown off," Dar said. "They got everyone out, but the boat got damaged and one of the crew took a kayak to try and get help and supplies."

"That's when they lost the phone," Kerry said. "And a lot of what they brought with them."

There was a little silence, as the waitress brought around a platter of assorted cookies and two large dog bones. "On the house." She smiled and put it down. "Let me know when you want more drinks," she added, and left.

"So you went from a posh river tour to an episode of *Gilligans Island*," Ceci said, taking a cookie and nibbling on it. "Is that what I'm hearing?"

"It was getting that way," Kerry said. "But then it got a lot worse."

"Dar, at any time did you think any of this was deliberate?" Alastair asked, after being silent for a long while. "You get the feeling you were being taken?"

"No." Dar shook her head. "Lightning storms, floods, wild animals...no one had time to rig that. Some of the stuff at the beginning? The glass and all that? Eh." She lifted her hands up and let them back down. "We actually thought it was the punk who joined us making trouble for everyone he could."

"Right," Kerry said. "So after Doug didn't come back, and we ended up getting the raft to the pull out near the cabin, and Josh had started up to the ranger station, we decided to go follow Josh because with all the rain and people getting hurt right and left it didn't seem like a good idea to stay."

"As it turned out, would have been better if we'd stayed," Dar said. "But we didn't know that."

"No. So we grabbed all the stuff we could carry and started to hike out," Kerry continued. "We realized there was a big cat around after we found Josh's body."

There was an uncomfortable silence. "Wow," Alastair finally muttered. "Poor fella."

"Yeah, there wasn't much left." Dar acknowledged. "Went downhill pretty fast from that point."

"We were scared," Kerry said. "And it was raining, we were cold, and we were running out of supplies pretty fast."

"So at this point were you deciding all future vacations would be in a tent in the backyard?" Ceci asked.

"A tent?" Dar eyed her. "How about inside our bedroom?"

"Lord," Andrew chuckled briefly.

Ceci shook her head. "So then what?"

"The cat was tracking us, I guess, because it came after us that night, in the storm." Kerry paused. "We were under a little rock shelter and it jumped down and came at us." She glanced over at Dar. "So Dar jumped on it and started stabbing it with her pocketknife."

Another short silence. "See, Dar?" Kerry turned to her. "No one at this table even looked surprised when I said that." She lifted her hands in some small exasperation. "Not even your parents."

Ceci leaned forward. "Especially her parents, kiddo. We've known her longer than you have."

Alastair covered his eyes and shook his head.

"You're the one who told me we were the kind of people who would jump on a mountain lion and not let it eat us," Dar complained. "What in the hell was I supposed to do?"

"Xactly what you done," Andrew said. "Ah woulda done it. Something looking to kill you can not be run from." He smiled a little at Dar. "And you all do come from me."

Dar smiled back, and her body relaxed as she sat back, taking a moment to acknowledge the truth of all of that. She'd been fighting with herself for a month over the instinct to put herself out there, to get into scraps and defend others because it seldom ended to her advantage.

And yet, it was part of the person she was. Part of the heritage, of the lineage she came from, inbuilt and instilled and unquestioned from a long line of people like her father who regardless of moral compass had been uncompromising scrappers.

A long line of warriors for their own particular and often peculiar causes that weren't always right or wrong but often graded and shaded and personal.

She carried no weapon and served in no service but nonetheless she stood up for things she judged to be right just because that is who she was.

Crusader. Dar smiled self-deprecatingly. Yeah, maybe. Idiotically. She imagined she could hear the echo of a rich, deep, knowing laugh back in the shadows of her own psyche. "I do." She answered Andrew. "Thanks, Dad."

Andrew smiled again and winked a little bit at her. "G'wan, kumquat."

"So then came the avalanche," Kerry soldiered on. "And talk about going downhill from there."

"YA'LL WANT ME to drive this here, Kerry?"

Kerry settled into the driver's seat of the RV. "Nah, I got this, Dad," She fastened the seat belt and started up the engine. "Time to get going."

Behind her, Dar was filling the water dishes for the dogs, and Alastair and Ceci had settled onto the small couch across from the galley for the short drive back to the regional airport.

Andrew seated himself next to her in the cockpit, and extended his long legs out. "Ah do not think you all should drive all the way back home," he said. "All sorts of things might happen."

Kerry chuckled wryly. "We had an uneventful trip out," she reminded him. "It only got bad when we actually started the vacation part of our vacation."

"Hm." Andrew gave her a squinty eyed look, his rugged, scarred face with all its intense character displaying extreme skepticism.

Kerry smiled, though she kept her eyes on the road. "Thanks, Dad." She felt Chino's breath on her elbow as the dog came forward to peer through the window. "I'm really glad you knew what to do to help us."

Andy chuckled, a little. "Get a lot of practice," he said. "Ah did not think I would have to do this near as much as ah do now after coming out of the service."

"We just get in a lot of trouble," Kerry said. "I don't know why. We even picked the most sedate rafting trip we could. They even had some Barcaloungers on there."

Andy folded his arms over his broad chest. "Ah do wonder if that there bunch wasn't looking out for well off folks," he said. "For other reasons."

Kerry drew in a breath, then paused. "No one brought valuable stuff on the trip. Only thing I had was my camera."

"Coulda kidnapped you," Andrew said.

Kerry considered it. "Boy would they have been in trouble." She grinned a little. "But really, a lot of those guys weren't super rich I don't think. Except Todd maybe. We had some college kids who saved up, and some yuppies. No one was the silver spoon type."

"Could just kept their yap shut about it," Andrew said. "Nevah know, with people."

"Eh." Kerry looked both ways, and pulled out onto the road. "I don't think so." She thought about Sally and her sister, and PJ and the gang, and Rich and Dave, none of them seemed like anyone who might be a target. "They all seemed pretty mundane."

"Didn't mean them. Meant you," Andrew remarked. "You all kids might be interesting to bad guys."

Kerry blinked, then she checked the road ahead and looked quickly to her right. "Us?"

Andy looked surprised at her surprise. "Gov'mint," he said, as though that would explain everything.

Oh. The idea was not appealing. "I don't think so, Dad." Kerry's brows twitched. "I'd rather think it was just our WTF vortex."

"'Scuse me?"

THEY WATCHED THE plane take off from the airport, lifting quickly up into the sky and banking away, heading southeast into a clear, and cloudless sky.

"That took a lot of convincing," Dar said. "Thought they'd never take off."

"Well." Kerry slid her hand into Dar's hip pocket, her fingers unexpectedly encountering the smooth roundness of a stone inside. "They're your parents, hon." She drew out the rock and inspected it. "That's pretty."

"That's why I kept it," Dar said. "I know they're my parents but we're both grown-ups, Ker."

"Grown-ups who get into tons of trouble."

Dar sighed.

"So they're stopping in Birmingham?" Kerry changed the subject, as they watched the speck in the sky disappear.

"Yeah." Dar leaned against the front of the RV. "Dad promised Mom some real fried green tomatoes." She stifled a yawn. "I told them we'd keep in regular touch until we got back."

Kerry smiled, and patted her on the side. "They're cute," she said. "And your dad did get us saved, remember."

"I know." Dar pushed off and went to the door, opening it carefully to prevent the whining dogs from escaping. "I shouldn't sound so damn ungrateful especially since they flew out here to make sure we were okay."

Kerry followed her inside and they both sat down on the couch on the RV together. "So now what?" Kerry asked. "Get driving?"

Dar petted Chino's soft head. "Yeah. Don't want to stay around here. Let's get some distance. We can stop someplace tonight, and then go all day tomorrow."

"Okay." Kerry got up and went to the counter, opening the laptop sitting there. "Want to fire up the sat? Let me find us some nice anonymous place to sleep."

Dar went to the console and flipped the switches, then sat down and started up the engine. The air outside was starting to turn golden and she put the sun behind her as she started down the two-lane road away from the small regional airport.

She felt a little discomfited. "I don't like all that stuff about terrorists. I don't really think those people were doing anything, Ker."

"No, me either." Kerry had her eyes fastened on the screen. "It was kind of like when you told me about those pilots that flew you and Alastair back. They got taken away by the spooks, but it turned out okay."

"One of them went to the same flight school as the terrorists," Dar recalled. "And he was from India. Not the Middle East. That what you meant?" She asked. "Turned out to be nothing."

"Right. So maybe it's the same with these guys. Maybe they didn't know who those people were and they were just part-time help. I found a campground. How about we just park and plug." She looked up at Dar. "I'd rather stay in here with the dogs."

"Sounds good to me."

They drove for three hours down the highway, then turned

off onto a smaller two-lane road that had wooden post fencing on either side of it and by that time the sun was setting in earnest. They passed between a pair of impressive saguaro cactus and spotted the campground just past it.

It was gated. They pulled up and Kerry opened the window. "Hello."

"Hello there, young lady." The guard returned the greeting. "Looking for a hook up?" He smiled blandly at her. "We got that."

"Yep." Kerry ignored the smarmy comment. "Just overnight."

He studied a clipboard. "We only have two Class A slots, they're in the back, last row." He glanced up at her. "Need a credit card to activate the power."

Kerry handed hers over, and they waited for him to process it, catching the hint of wood smoke on the air. "What else is back there?"

He handed the paperwork over for her to sign. "Mini's place." He took the clipboard back. "She runs a little café and bar." He handed Kerry her receipt. "Have a nice night."

"Thanks." Kerry closed the window and they moved slowly on, down a boulder lined path interspersed with weathered wooden posts. At the end of the campground, as promised, were two larger parking spots and she picked the second one, with a nice view of the mountains.

The campsite was about half full, and there were a few people walking around, more gathered near a round, weathered fire pit with bottles and cups in their hands. There was music playing, vaguely new age sounding from someone's rig and various scents of barbecue were evident.

"I'll hook us up," Dar said. "Watch the dogs." She opened the door and hopped out, going around to the side of the RV.

Kerry went to the RV's control panel, pressed the keys that would activate the slide outs and went to the galley to ponder what to do about some dinner. Chino followed her and sat down next to her feet, tail sweeping the floor.

After the week they'd had, it was a stunning bit of normality. It was hard for her to comprehend that less than twenty-four hours earlier she was in a cold river, at the mercy of the rapids, not knowing what in the hell was going to happen to her.

In danger, feeling the chill start to grip her, Dar's arms around her and both of them knowing bad things could easily happen any moment.

Now? She reviewed what was in the pantry and decided on gyros, taking out a package of sliced lamb from the tiny freezer and putting it on the counter to start thawing.

Outside, she could hear the sounds of Dar connecting the RV; the thumps and bumps of the hoses and electrical and she pushed the window over the galley open to let the fresh air in.

Now it was almost as if it all had never happened. She shook her head and put some coffee on, hearing the ventilation kick on and seeing the flicker of the lights as they switched over from the RV's batteries to the campground connection.

Gyros, and coffee, and after that she had some easy bake cookies they could share.

"Hey, kids," she regarded their two pets. "We can go for a walk, how about that?" She saw both tails start to wag faster, and Chino stood up, looking at the door in anticipation. With a smile she got the leashes from their hook on the wall and fastened them to the dog's collars as the door opened and Dar's head appeared. "Hey hon. Kids want to go walk. We set?"

"All set." Dar took Mocha's leash and waited for Kerry to join her outside. "Nice and quiet." She closed the door and they started along the path that lead to the edge of the campground where people were gathered, watching the setting sun's pattern on the far canyon walls.

Their approach made some heads turn, but as they walked past Kerry could see the eyes focused on the two dogs, and she smiled a little, returning the brief waves.

On a small side path, they spotted the café, which had a patio that had a little crowd also watching the sunset with glasses in their hands and they could hear a soft buzz of conversation drifting over from it and the sound of a softly playing guitar.

The air was cool and dry. They found a weathered picnic table to perch on at the far edge of the property to watch the sun go down. Kerry exhaled, stifling a yawn. "This is an unusually quiet end to our little adventure, Dardar."

"Yeah," Dar said. "I will be damn glad to sleep in a bed tonight, with no rain, no snarky jackasses, and nothing to worry about." She shifted Chino's leash from her left hand to her right as the dog sat down on the concrete pad the table was set into.

"Me too." Kerry observed the sliding light, melding and changing and painting every surface it touched. "I'm glad we decided to drive home. Get a few days to decompress."

"Let's find some hot springs," Dar suggested. "I'm sure there have to be some between here and Miami."

"Mm." Kerry could feel the heat in her imagination soaking into her bones. "I'm sure there are. I'll check when we get back to the RV." She paused. "Wonder what the rest of them ending up doing?"

"Leaving. If they're smart." Dar concluded. "You could send them an e-mail."

"Meh," Kerry grunted softly. "Now that I said that I'm not sure that I want to know."

Dar watched the horizon benignly, content to leave the past in the past as well. She drew in a breath of the dry air and blinked a few times, suddenly wishing for the damp moisture of home, and the sound of the waves rolling up the shore; so different than the Colorado River they'd so recently left.

The last of the sun disappeared, leaving the air tinged with coral and lavender as behind them someone stirred the fire in the fire pit and the wood let out several solid pops as it cracked.

Life had gotten better again. Kerry took Dar's hand and squeezed it. "Maybe we can see stars again tonight."

"Bet we can."

AFTER DINNER, KERRY settled down in the comfortable chair in the RVs' little workspace and hooked her camera up to her laptop, watching the two devices sync up. Her photo program open to ingest the contents of her solid-state memory cards.

As they popped up on the screen, she propped her chin on her fist, watching Dar in her peripheral vision . She sprawled on the couch in a t-shirt and sweatpants, her bare feet extending past the edge of the furniture.

Kerry could still smell a hint of the stir-fried lamb from their dinner and a bit of the wood smoke, drifting through the screens of the open windows all around them.

She could hear voices, soft, indistinct and far off. A dog barked. Beside her, Chino's ears twitched and the Labrador lifted her head to listen, while Mocha jerked and whimpered in a doggy dream, curled up in his bed.

She turned her attention back to the screen, and started scrolling through the pictures. "Oh!" She zoomed into one, the picture of the owl landing on Dar's arm, her partner's eyes widened and vivid blue watching it.

"Oh, what?" Dar put down her book and rolled to her feet, coming over to where Kerry was seated. She looked over Kerry's shoulder. "Ah. My owl whispering moment."

Kerry flipped through the photos, pretty sunsets and rocks, and a bobcat's paw. "Glad I got that one."

"Me too," Dar smiled.

The river, and their companions. The rapids, the pools and slides and everyone enjoying themselves. Dar in her swimsuit stretched out fully in a dive from the cliff side, then one of her pushing herself up out of the water to go for another round, surrounded by a halo of sun splatted droplets.

Then the stars, outlined against the canyon walls. "That's nice," Dar commented. "You can really see the Milky Way."

"You can," Kerry said. "But here's the rain, so..."

"Downhill we go."

Then the caves. Dar's hand against the rock, outlined in sun.

Then more rain.

Then the somber outline of wet stone around tatters of cloth and bone. "So here we are." Kerry studied the photo, remembering the horror in her guts and how sick she'd felt on seeing this bundle of refuse that was once a person she'd known.

Sad and horrible. "He was so nice."

"He was," Dar said. "Good kid." She studied the screen. "You going to send these back to the cops?"

"When we get home, yeah." Kerry set the computer up to send the pictures to their storage system at the condo and leaned back, as Dar put her arms around her and gently nibbled at the nape of her neck. "Well, we can show our friends half our vacation, Dar."

Dar chuckled. "Better than our last one," she said. "I think that was what? One day good?"

"Maybe two."

"No. It was one, because we ran into the asshole after our first dive, remember?" Dar reminded her. "We got a few good days on this one."

Kerry went back to the beginning of the pictures and had to agree. She expanded one she'd taken with them halfway through a rapids, a curl of river water in beautiful clear green coming over the pontoons of the raft, sun blasting through it. "We did."

"Done for the day?" Dar bit the edge of her ear. "Looking forward to a good night's sleep."

The luxury of that sounded awesome and Kerry was happy to get up and join Dar. They walked to the cozy bedroom area of the RV, picked up the remote and turned off the lights except for the bedside ones that allowed a low level of amber glow.

Dar pulled her t-shirt off and Kerry untied the strings

holding up her sweatpants, as the buttons on her own shirt were undone, one at a time.

She looked up and saw Dar's smile. She leaned forward and planted a kiss on her collarbone, allowing her shirt to be pulled off and tossed gently onto the narrow dresser. She put her arms around Dar and they pressed together, skin on skin warmth contrasting the cool breeze from the windows in a pleasant way.

She could taste a bit of the chocolate from the cookies they'd shared on Dar's lips and they paused long enough to fall sideways onto the bed and roll into its center.

The covers were soft and from home. They smelled like their laundry soap comfortingly familiar and Kerry felt her body relax as Dar stretched out next to her and ran her fingertips along Kerry's ribcage.

She was tired, and not. The familiar burn started and she felt her attention sharpen as Dar's lips nuzzled her and a warm flush came over her skin.

Dar's long arm reached out and the lamps dimmed and they were in the dark together, knowing each other's body and needing no light to explore familiar sensitive spots as their breathing quickened in unison.

Far off, a coyote howled and they paused for a moment to listen.

Chino barked softly, a gruff, chuffing sound.

Then there was just the faint music from nearby and they went back to each other, secure in the safety of their rolling home.

THE SOUND OF footsteps outside made them both jerk awake in the same moment, and look at each other in the dim light. "Did you lock the door?" Kerry whispered.

"Yeah, I think so." Dar lifted herself out of bed as the dogs woke up and looked at her. "Let me check."

Kerry slipped out of the other side and went to the slimline closet. She opened it and reached inside for the shotgun she'd stored there.

Chino shook herself and trotted over to the front of the RV, sniffing the air. Then she barked, a loud and commanding sound that echoed inside the cabin. A moment later Mocha scrambled past her to the door and yapped excitedly.

Dar reached the control panel and checked, then relaxed. "It's locked." She said, glancing back to see Kerry next to the bed, naked, holding her shotgun. "Hey, you know we could sell calendars for the NRA if this whole tech thing doesn't work out for us."

"What?" Kerry stared at her, then looked down, and laughed. "Oh for Christ's sake, Dar."

They both turned as a knock came at the door and the chuckles ended. Dar grabbed her shirt and slipped it over her head then went over to the door, nudging aside the two Labradors and opening the small window. "Yes?"

There were two men outside in police uniforms and jackets. "Sorry to bother you ma'am," the nearest one said. "We're from the local police department."

Dar studied them. "And?"

"We're looking for some folks that was seen around here, and the gate said you folks were the last ones in," the man said. "We'd like to ask you some questions."

Dar blinked at them. "At two a.m.?"

"These folks are supposed to be dangerous."

Dar could see them outlined against the soft glow of the lamp post near the edge of the road and she watched their body language intently for a moment. "They're not in our camper," she stated flatly. "I don't know anything about any dangerous people around here."

Kerry had come up behind her and Dar glanced back briefly. She had the shotgun cradled in her hands and she'd taken the precaution of putting her shirt and jeans on.

"Ma'am, please," the nearer man said. "We just want to ask a few questions."

Dar took a step back and lifted her hands in question. Kerry shrugged, and went back to the bedroom, returning with Dar's shorts and handing them to her.

"Yap!" Mocha sat down and barked at the door. Chino was already between the living area and the cockpit, head a little down, tail straight.

Dar slid her shorts on and buttoned them, then got in front of the dogs and triggered the lock, waiting for it to retract. She stepped down out of the camper and stood in the way, as Kerry slid into the passenger seat behind her in the cockpit, the gun visible in her hands.

The man took a step back. "You want to go inside? I know we woke you ladies up."

"No," Dar responded calmly. "Ask your questions."

The second man stepped forward, extending two squares. "These are the people we're looking for."

Dar took the pictures and studied them, then she passed them back to Kerry. "I don't know them."

"Not seen them on the road, in a restaurant, nothing?" the man asked. "We know you came from the Canyon Rim. They told us."

"Nothing here." Kerry handed them back. "We only stopped at one place, there wasn't anyone like that there."

"Mind telling us where that was?"

"Big E Steakhouse," Kerry supplied. "We had lunch. They'll remember us for the dogs."

Dar looked at the pictures again, two men with dark skin and beards, wearing knit caps, walking past the camera with sideways, furtive looks. "No." She gave the pictures back. "They don't ring any bells. What are you looking for them for?"

"An active investigation," the first man said, with a tone of finality. "Here's my card. If you do see either of these men, will you call me and let me know?" He handed her a square of cardboard. "Which way are you ladies headed?"

"Florida," Dar said, noticing then that there were others in the campground, milling around the fire pit, watching the two men from afar. "You ask everyone else yet?"

"We did," he said. "Sorry to wake everyone up. We just can't be too careful." He stepped back. "Thank you. Have a good rest of your night." He and his partner turned and walked away, going past the fire pit and back toward the gate.

"Dar, that was weird." Kerry said, as she climbed onboard and shut the door.

"Meh." Dar locked the door and went back to the bed. "All relative when it comes to weird, Ker. All relative."

DAR IDLY WATCHED Chino and Mocha sniff around some scrub grass as she stood in a pool of early morning sunlight in the now very quiet campground.

The area was painted in coral and pink light. She could smell sage on the light breeze that ruffled her hair and fluttered the shirt against her skin.

The half-filled campground around her had mostly smaller campers, two of them pulled by a car, one a tiny teardrop model that looked very old and weathered.

Two silver Airstreams. The nearest one's door opened and a middle-aged woman got out, put down a step and looked around with a yawn. She saw Dar, and gave a friendly wave which Dar returned.

On the road leading from the gates a small pickup truck headed toward them, turned off at the café and parked behind it. Two men got out, one of them holding a cup of coffee and they went inside.

Dar headed back to their RV and as she reached the side of it the door opened and Kerry emerged. "Hey."

"Hey." Kerry pushed the door open to let the dogs enter. "Lets some grub and be on our way?"

Dar turned and pointed. "That joints opening up. Want to grab something there?"

Kerry shrugged. "Sure." She closed the door and joined Dar as they walked down the gravel road toward the café side by side. "Want to do me a favor?" she asked. "Drive for the morning? I did not want to wake up today." Her voice was a little husky.

"All day if you want." Dar was feeling fine. She woke refreshed and now looked forward to getting on their way home. "Snooze all you like." She added as they walked up to the small café window where two women were putting out some muffins. "Morning."

The nearest looked up and smiled. "Morning." She pushed the tray with the muffins forward. "Got fresh boysenberry today."

"Two, and coffee," Dar said.

"Right up," the woman said. "Coming or going?"

"Going." Kerry looked at the muffin with interest. "We were on a, um, tour."

The other woman was making them their coffee. "Yeah? Did you enjoy yourselves, ladies?"

Dar and Kerry exchanged looks. "Sure," Dar said after a brief pause. "Scenery is gorgeous."

The first woman beamed. "It is pretty here isn't it?" she said, proudly. "I love it here. Where you headed back to?"

"Miami." Kerry took both of their cups of coffee while Dar picked up the plate with two muffins and pushed a ten dollar bill over the counter.

"Oh! Miami," The coffee maker came to the counter. "I hear it's really crazy there."

"Has its moments." Dar shook her head at the proffered change.

"Thanks for the tip," the woman smiled at her. "Good thing you ladies weren't on that rafting trip that's all in the news. My goodness I heard everyone got arrested and they're in jail."

"That's right." The other woman agreed. "It's crazy!"

Dar and Kerry exchanged another look, as they walked backwards away from the café. "Yep, glad we missed that one." Kerry said. "Bye!"

The two women at the café waved, then turned to another customer who had stepped up.

"Ho boy." Kerry exhaled. "Let's get outta here." She hustled Dar back to the RV and they climbed inside. "We unhooked?"

"Yep." Dar put the muffins down and got into the driver's seat. "I'm going to get us rolling." She started the engine. "Before someone decides to try and chase us down."

Kerry settled a cup of the coffee in the holder next to Dar's seat and took a muffin, going back into the RV and taking a seat on the couch as Chino jumped up to join her. "Yeah. Be glad to get home."

Dar pulled out of the campground and back onto the road, pointing the vehicle southeast and settling into her seat for a long drive.

KERRY HADN'T NOTICED it. She picked up her cup from the holder and took a sip, glancing to either side of the RV as Dar came up and sat down next to her, with a faint grin on her face. "What?"

"We're home," Dar said.

"No we're not." Kerry gave Dar a perplexed look. "What are you talking about?"

"You can tell by the trees." Dar folded her hands over her stomach. "We just went from sub-tropical to tropical."

Kerry looked around at their surroundings, which seemed identical to the tree laden scenery they'd been subject to since hopping on the turnpike. "What?"

Dar chuckled, then cleared her throat a little. "Florida is mostly sub-tropical climate right up until our end of it, when it turns tropical. More palm trees, more sawgrass, more open space, less orange groves and deciduous."

Kerry's brows contracted as she looked at the lines of pine trees on either side of the road.

"Australian pines. Imported to hide the turnpike," Dar correctly interpreted the look. "We're in Palm Beach County now. Give it a few miles."

"Okay." Kerry eyed her with profound, if loving skepticism.

But as they drove she realized Dar was right, and that the

land she was driving through was changing to familiar outlines and from one moment to the next their trip was over. It was a matter of steering the RV to the rental center and picking up Dar's truck.

It was weird, yet definite and she increased their speed a little, sending an end, finally to their journey. Her mind was making that change, and while she'd been thinking of their adventures just a short while ago now she was thinking about getting home, and going to work, and all the things she had to do.

It felt like a relief. To be just thinking about meeting with new customers, and... "Hey Dar, can you check my phone? See if we got a text from the real estate agent?"

"Sure." Dar got back up and retrieved the device. "Think they found something?"

"Be nice if they did."

Dar paged through the texts. "Nothing yet. I'm going to call the folks so they know we're back and have the concierge service check the house." She wandered back into the body of the RV. "Want some coffee?"

"Tea," Kerry said, glancing briefly aside as Mocha came up and sat next to her knee. "Hey, little man. We're almost home."

"Yap." Mocha stood up and put his paws on the console, gazing out at the road. "Yap yap!"

"Yap yap yap," Kerry echoed him. "Bet you'll be glad to get back to our garden, won't you?"

Mocha's tongue emerged, vivid and pink against his dark fur and he lifted one paw up and waved it, making Kerry laugh, as she saw the exit that would take them seaward and already she imagined she could smell salt in the air and hear the rolling rush of the ocean.

"Next time, Moch, absolutely. we just stay home."

"Yap!"

"AHH," KERRY FLEXED her bare toes, looking around with new appreciation at their high ceilinged, peaceful condo. From the sea foam walls to the large windows that let in piles of South Florida sunshine, to the wrap around patio with its view of the sea. It was good to have that familiar comfort around them.

Dar was seated outside with both dogs in attendance, having a peanut butter and jelly sandwich and a tall glass of milk. She smiled indulgently at the white milk mustache she could just see on Dar's face.

With nothing more than dinner and some TV to look forward to, she climbed up the stairs and went into her home office, sitting down behind her desk and giving her trackball a spin to bring up the image on the large screen monitor.

She glanced at her mail, found nothing more than what she'd seen on her device and shifted her attention to their joint cloud storage, opening up the folder she'd stored the trip's pictures in. After a few more clicks the pictures started to load and she sat back to wait, leaned back in her leather chair and propped her knee up against the desk edge.

The spare room they'd converted for her office was painted in a light lavender gray, and the big bay window that looked out over the interior of the island had white wooden plantation shutters that admitted the late afternoon sun in sedate stripes.

Aside from her desk, there was a book case against one wall and a leather couch along the long wall that occasionally hosted her tall partner's form reading a book, or sometimes just the two of them talking as she worked.

The floors were covered in Berber carpet in a mixed pattern motif that rather effectively hid dog hair and Kerry wondered briefly how that would all translate when they moved.

To wherever it was they found to move. She glanced at the screen, which was about half full of pictures, painting slowly as they downloaded. She scooted her chair closer and started to review them, smiling a little as she clicked.

She sorted some of them, making copies and putting them in a folder to send to the group and another set to send to her family. There was one where Dar stood next to the horse she'd ridden and was tickling his nose, the big animal regarding her with benign affection.

They had been in the corral, and she went to edit it, cropping out some of the background that was just some random people walking behind the rails, heading toward the barn.

Then she paused, and zoomed the image. Two men were in the group, that she didn't remember, walking between Janet and Doug. There was something familiar about them.

She heard the sliding door open and close downstairs. "Hey, Dar?" she called out. "C'mon up here a minute."

Dar's bare footsteps on the carpeted stairs followed and then the doorway was filled with her tall form. She leaned on Kerry's desk, bringing the faint scent of salt air and peanut butter with her. "What's up?"

"Look at these guys in this picture." Kerry moved her

monitor so Dar could see it. "Dar, are they the guys those cops were looking for?"

Dar leaned over her and peered at the screen for a long moment in silence. Then she shook her head. "Can't tell. It could be, but it could also just be some of the workers there." She zoomed in a little more. "But they've got guns."

Kerry got her head next to Dar's. "In the back of their pants there?"

"Yeah."

Kerry was silent for a moment. "Dar, didn't they say they didn't like guns at that company? Did I imagine hearing that?"

"No, you didn't." Dar sat down on the edge of the desk. "I remember that too."

They sat in silence for a minute. "Should we send this to those cops? I kept their card." Kerry suggested. "Let me look through the rest of these shots and see if I caught them again."

Dar frowned. "I'm not sure it'll do any good. That was at the beginning of our trip. If they already knew they were there that wouldn't tell them anything new."

"True." Kerry admitted. "What the hell was really going on there, Dar?"

Dar leaned closer to the screen again. "I don't know. There's a lot of stories we'll probably never know the end of. But yeah. Send it. You never know."

"You never know."

DAR DROPPED INTO her chair in her office, the soft sounds of activity floating through her door and the faintest sound of a lawnmower from the open central space in the middle of their office building. She was in jeans and a polo shirt, and actually glad to be back at work.

Chino was curled up in her bed in the corner, and her tail wagged as Dar looked over at her. She could hear Kerry in her office next door, laughing into the phone.

Back to their normal world.

Maria entered, with a folder. "Good morning, Dar," she handed it over. "Here is the bank report for you."

"Thanks," Dar put the folder down. "I need to order more space at the datacenter and more bandwidth," she said. "I just checked the metrics those guys are chewing it up like cookies."

"I will call and get the proposal for you," Maria said. "I am glad you and Kerrisita are back."

Dar smiled. "Yeah, us too. No more vacations for us, Maria. We're just going to take weekends down at the cabin from now on."

"Terrible," Maria said, in a sympathetic tone. "But you did not get hurt, and those horrible people are in the jail, so it is good, no?"

Was it? Dar shrugged a little. "They weren't bad to us, Maria. We were all just stuck on the river together, helping each other."

Maria shook her head. "Terrible," she repeated, then waggled her fingers and danced out, to the faint Latin music coming from across the hall.

Dar sat back and rested her hands on her thighs, thinking for a moment back to their last night on the river. When it all went so terribly wrong and she dove into the water. Would it have mattered if some of the crew had been bad guys?

They hadn't done anything to either her or Kerry.

No, Dar decided as she opened the folder and reviewed the statement. It wouldn't have mattered. She looked up and smiled briefly. She was who she was.

Mocha came running in with something in his mouth.

"Hey, kiddo." Dar turned around to grab him. "Whatcha got there?" She removed the item from his teeth and held it up. "Where did you get this feather, huh?" She twirled the long, black feather in her fingertips, it's blued sheen reflecting the light. "Did you catch a crow?"

"Yap!" Mocha scrabbled up onto her lap, reaching for the feather. "Yap yap!"

Kerry entered, and came over to the desk. "What's that?"

"Present from Mocha." Dar handed it to her. "Pity the poor bird he got it from."

Kerry twirled it in her fingers, and smiled. "Hey, maybe I'll write a poem with it." She winked, and sauntered back to her office.

OTHER MELISSA GOOD TITLES

Tropical Storm

From bestselling author Melissa Good comes a tale of heartache, longing, family strife, lust for love, and redemption. *Tropical Storm* took the lesbian reading world by storm when it was first written...now read this exciting revised "author's cut" edition.

Dar Roberts, corporate raider for a multi-national tech company is cold, practical, and merciless. She does her job with a razor-sharp accuracy. Friends are a luxury she cannot allow herself, and love is something she knows she'll never attain.

Kerry Stuart left Michigan for Florida in an attempt to get away from her domineering politician father and the constraints of the overly conservative life her family forced upon her. After college she worked her way into supervision at a small tech company, only to have it taken over by Dar Roberts' organization. Her association with Dar begins in disbelief, hatred, and disappointment, but when Dar unexpectedly hires Kerry as her work assistant, the dynamics of their relationship change. Over time, a bond begins to form.

But can Dar overcome years of habit and conditioning to open herself up to the uncertainty of love? And will Kerry escape from the clutches of her powerful father in order to live a better life?

ISBN 978-1-932300-60-4
eISBN 978-1-935053-75-0

Hurricane Watch

In this sequel to *Tropical Storm*, Dar and Kerry are back and making their relationship permanent. But an ambitious new colleague threatens to divide them — and out them. He wants Dar's head and her job, and he's willing to use Kerry to do it. Can their home life survive the office power play?

Dar and Kerry are redefining themselves and their priorities to build a life and a family together. But with the scheming colleagues and old flames trying to drive them apart and bring them down, the two women must overcome fear, prejudice, and their own pasts to protect the company and each other. Does their relationship have enough trust to survive the storm?

ISBN 978-1-935053-00
eISBN 978-1-935053-76-7

Eye of the Storm

Eye of the Storm picks up the story of Dar Roberts and Kerry Stuart a few months after *Hurricane Watch* ends. At first it looks like they are settling into their lives together but, as readers of this series have learned, life is never simple around Dar and Kerry. Surrounded by endless corporate intrigue, Dar experiences personal discoveries that force her to deal with issues that she had buried long ago and Kerry finally faces the consequences of her own actions. As always, they help each other through these personal challenges that, in the end, strengthen them as individuals and as a couple.

ISBN 978-1-932300-13-0
eISBN 978-1-935053-77-4

Red Sky At Morning

A connection others don't understand...
A love that won't be denied...
Danger they can sense but cannot see...

Dar Roberts was always ruthless and single-minded...until she met Kerry Stuart.

Kerry was oppressed by her family's wealth and politics. But Dar saved her from that.

Now new dangers confront them from all sides. While traveling to Chicago, Kerry's plane is struck by lightning. Dar, in New York for a stockholders' meeting, senses Kerry is in trouble. They simultaneously experience feelings that are new, sensations that both are reluctant to admit when they are finally back together. Back in Miami, a cover-up of the worst kind, problems with the military, and unexpected betrayals will cause more danger. Can Kerry help as Dar has to examine her life and loyalties and call into question all she's believed in since childhood? Will their relationship deepen through it all? Or will it be destroyed?

ISBN 978-1-932300-80-2
eISBN 978-1-935053-71-2

Thicker Than Water

This fifth entry in the continuing saga of Dar Roberts and Kerry Stuart starts off with Kerry involved in mentoring a church group of girls. Kerry is forced to acknowledge her own feelings toward and experiences with her parents as she and Dar assist a teenager from the group who gets jailed because her parents tossed her out onto the streets when they found out she is gay. While trying to help the teenagers adjust to real world situations, Kerry gets a call concerning her father's health. Kerry flies to her family's side as her father dies, putting the family in crisis. Caught up in an international problem, Dar abandons the issue to go to Michigan, determined to support Kerry in the face of grief and hatred. Dar and Kerry face down Kerry's extended family with a little help from their own, and return home, where they decide to leave work and the world behind for a while for some time to themselves.

ISBN 978-1-932300-24-6
eISBN 978-1-935053-72-9

Terrors of the High Seas

After the stress of a long Navy project and Kerry's father's death, Dar and Kerry decide to take their first long vacation together. A cruise in the eastern Caribbean is just the nice, peaceful time they need—until they get involved in a family feud, an old murder, and come face to face with pirates as their vacation turns into a race to find the key to a decades old puzzle.

ISBN 978-1-932300-45-1
eISBN 978-1-935053-73-6

Tropical Convergence

There's trouble on the horizon for ILS when a rival challenges them head on, and their best weapons, Dar and Kerry, are distracted by life instead of focusing on the business. Add to that an old flame, and an aggressive entrepreneur throwing down the gauntlet and Dar at least is ready to throw in the towel. Is Kerry ready to follow suit, or will she decide to step out from behind Dar's shadow and step up to the challenges they both face?

ISBN 978-1-935053-18-7
eISBN 978-1-935053-74-3

Stormy Waters

As Kerry begins work on the cruise ship project, Dar is attempting to produce a program to stop the hackers she has been chasing through cyberspace. When it appears that one of their cruise ship project rivals is behind the attempts to gain access to their system, things get more stressful than ever. Add in an unrelenting reporter who stalks them for her own agenda, an employee who is being paid to steal data for a competitor, and Army intelligence becoming involved and Dar and Kerry feel more off balance than ever. As the situation heats up, they consider again whether they want to stay with ILS or strike out on their own, but they know they must first finish the ship project.

ISBN 978-1-61929-082-2
eISBN 978-1-61929-083-9

Moving Target

Dar and Kerry both feel the cruise ship project seems off somehow, but they can't quite grasp what is wrong with the whole scenario. Things continue to go wrong and their competitors still look to be the culprits behind the problems. Then new information leads them to discover a plot that everyone finds difficult to believe. Out of her comfort zone yet again, Dar refuses to lose and launches a new plan that will be a win-win, only to find another major twist thrown in her path. With everyone believing Dar can somehow win the day, can Dar and Kerry pull off another miracle finish? Do they want to?

ISBN 978-1-61929-150-8
eISBN 978-1-61929-151-5

Storm Surge

It's fall. Dar and Kerry are traveling—Dar overseas to clinch a deal with their new ship owner partners in England, and Kerry on a reluctant visit home for her high school reunion. In the midst of corporate deals and personal conflict, their world goes unexpectedly out of control when an early morning spurt of unusual alarms turns out to be the beginning of a shocking nightmare neither expected. Can they win the race against time to save their company and themselves?

Book One: ISBN 978-1-935053-28-6
eISBN 978-1-61929-000-6

Book Two: ISBN 978-1-935053-39-2
eISBN 978-1-61929-000-6

Winds of Change

After 9/11 the world has changed and Dar and Kerry have decided to change along with it. They have an orderly plan to resign and finally take their long delayed travelling vacation. But as always fate intervenes and they find themselves caught in a web of conflicting demands and they have to make choices they never anticipated.

Book One: ISBN 978-1-61929-194-2
eISBN 978-1-61929-193-5
Book Two: ISBN 978-1-61929-232-1
eISBN 978-1-61929-231-4

Partners

After a massive volcanic eruption puts earth into nuclear winter, the planet is cloaked in clouds and no sun penetrates. Seas cover most of the land areas except high elevations which exist as islands where the remaining humans have learned to make do with much less. People survive on what they can take from the sea and with foodstuffs supplemented from an orbiting set of space stations.

Jess Drake is an agent for Interforce, a small and exclusive special forces organization that still possesses access to technology. Her job is to protect and serve the citizens of the American continent who are in conflict with those left on the European continent. The struggle for resources is brutal, and when a rogue agent nearly destroys everything, Interforce decides to trust no one. They send Jess a biologically-created agent who has been artificially devised and given knowledge using specialized brain programming techniques.

Instead of the mindless automaton one might expect, Biological Alternative NM-Dev-1 proves to be human and attractive. Against all odds, Jess and the new agent are swept into a relationship neither expected. Can they survive in these strange circumstances? And will they even be able to stay alive in this bleak new world?

Book One: ISBN 978-1-61929-118-8
eISBN 978-1-61929-119-5

Book Two: ISBN 978-1-61929-190-4
eISBN 978-1-61929-189-8

Of Sea and Stars

Of Sea and Stars continues the saga of Interforce Agent Jess Drake and her Biological Alternative partner, NM-Dev-1, that began in Melissa Good's first two books in her Partners series.

This series chronicles what happens to human kind after a massive volcanic eruption puts earth into nuclear winter. The planet is cloaked in clouds and no sun penetrates. Seas cover most of the land areas except high elevations. These exist as islands where the remaining humans have learned to make do with much less. People survive on what they can take from the sea, and with foodstuffs supplemented from an orbiting set of space stations.

This new world is divided into two factions, and the struggle for resources between them is brutal, pitting one side against the other.

In Of Sea and Stars, Jess and Dev uncover a hidden cavern at Drakes Bay full of growing vegetables and fruit trees. There is evidence that the "other side" has been negotiating with Jess's brother, and with someone on the space station that created, Dev. This sends them on a quest into space to solve the mystery.

ISBN 978-1-61929-298-7
eISBN 978-1-61929-299-4

OTHER YELLOW ROSE PUBLICATIONS

Brenda Adcock	Soiled Dove	978-1-935053-35-4
Brenda Adcock	The Sea Hawk	978-1-935053-10-1
Brenda Adcock	The Other Mrs. Champion	978-1-935053-46-0
Brenda Adcock	Picking Up the Pieces	978-1-61929-120-1
Brenda Adcock	The Game of Denial	978-1-61929-130-0
Brenda Adcock	In the Midnight Hour	978-1-61929-188-1
Brenda Adcock	Untouchable	978-1-61929-210-9
Brenda Adcock	The Heart of the Mountain	978-1-61929-330-4
Janet Albert	Twenty-four Days	978-1-935053-16-3
Janet Albert	A Table for Two	978-1-935053-27-9
Janet Albert	Casa Parisi	978-1-61929-016-7
Georgia Beers	Thy Neighbor's Wife	1-932300-15-5
Georgia Beers	Turning the Page	978-1-932300-71-0
Lynnette Beers	Just Beyond the Shining River	
Carrie Carr	Destiny's Bridge	1-932300-11-2
Carrie Carr	Faith's Crossing	1-932300-12-0
Carrie Carr	Hope's Path	1-932300-40-6
Carrie Carr	Love's Journey	978-1-932300-65-9
Carrie Carr	Strength of the Heart	978-1-932300-81-9
Carrie Carr	The Way Things Should Be	978-1-932300-39-0
Carrie Carr	To Hold Forever	978-1-932300-21-5
Carrie Carr	Trust Our Tomorrows	978-1-61929-011-2
Carrie Carr	Piperton	978-1-935053-20-0
Carrie Carr	Something to Be Thankful For	1-932300-04-X
Carrie Carr	Diving Into the Turn	978-1-932300-54-3
Carrie Carr	Heart's Resolve	978-1-61929-051-8
Carrie Carr	Beyond Always	978-1-61929-160-7
Sharon G. Clark	A Majestic Affair	978-1-61929-177-5
Tonie Chacon	Struck! A Titanic Love Story	978-1-61929-226-0
Cooper and Novan	Madam President	978-1-61929-316-8
Cooper and Novan	First Lady	978-1-61929-318-2
Sky Croft	Amazonia	978-1-61929-067-9
Sky Croft	Amazonia: An Impossible Choice	978-1-61929-179-9
Sky Croft	Mountain Rescue: The Ascent	978-1-61929-099-0
Sky Croft	Mountain Rescue: On the Edge	978-1-61929-205-5
Cronin and Foster	Blue Collar Lesbian Erotica	978-1-935053-01-9
Cronin and Foster	Women in Uniform	978-1-935053-31-6
Cronin and Foster	Women in Sports	978-1-61929-278-9
Pat Cronin	Souls' Rescue	978-1-935053-30-9
Jane DiLucchio	A Change of Heart	978-1-61929-324-3
A. L. Duncan	The Gardener of Aria Manor	978-1-61929-159-1
A.L. Duncan	Secrets of Angels	978-1-61929-227-7
Verda Foster	The Gift	978-1-61929-029-7
Verda Foster	The Chosen	978-1-61929-027-3
Verda Foster	These Dreams	978-1-61929-025-9
Anna Furtado	The Heart's Desire	978-1-935053-81-1

Author	Title	ISBN
Anna Furtado	The Heart's Strength	978-1-935053-82-8
Anna Furtado	The Heart's Longing	978-1-935053-83-5
Pauline George	Jess	978-1-61929-139-3
Pauline George	199 Steps To Love	978-1-61929-213-0
Pauline George	The Actress and the Scrapyard Girl	978-1-61929-336-6
Melissa Good	Eye of the Storm	1-932300-13-9
Melissa Good	Hurricane Watch	978-1-935053-00-2
Melissa Good	Moving Target	978-1-61929-150-8
Melissa Good	Red Sky At Morning	978-1-932300-80-2
Melissa Good	Storm Surge: Book One	978-1-935053-28-6
Melissa Good	Storm Surge: Book Two	978-1-935053-39-2
Melissa Good	Stormy Waters	978-1-61929-082-2
Melissa Good	Thicker Than Water	1-932300-24-4
Melissa Good	Terrors of the High Seas	1-932300-45-7
Melissa Good	Tropical Storm	978-1-932300-60-4
Melissa Good	Tropical Convergence	978-1-935053-18-7
Melissa Good	Winds of Change Book One	978-1-61929-194-2
Melissa Good	Winds of Change Book Two	978-1-61929-232-1
Regina A. Hanel	Love Another Day	978-1-61929-033-4
Regina A. Hanel	WhiteDragon	978-1-61929-143-0
Regina A. Hanel	A Deeper Blue	978-1-61929-258-1
Jeanine Hoffman	Lights & Sirens	978-1-61929-115-7
Jeanine Hoffman	Strength in Numbers	978-1-61929-109-6
Jeanine Hoffman	Back Swing	978-1-61929-137-9
Jennifer Jackson	It's Elementary	978-1-61929-085-3
Jennifer Jackson	It's Elementary, Too	978-1-61929-217-8
Jennifer Jackson	Memory Hunters	978-1-61929-294-9
K. E. Lane	And, Playing the Role of Herself	978-1-932300-72-7
Kate McLachlan	Christmas Crush	978-1-61929-195-9
Lynne Norris	One Promise	978-1-932300-92-5
Lynne Norris	Sanctuary	978-1-61929-248-2
Lynne Norris	Second Chances (E)	978-1-61929-172-0
Lynne Norris	The Light of Day	978-1-61929-338-0
Paula Offutt	Butch Girls Can Fix Anything	978-1-932300-74-1
Surtees and Dunne	True Colours	978-1-61929-021-1
Surtees and Dunne	Many Roads to Travel	978-1-61929-022-8
Patty Schramm	Finding Gracie's Glory	978-1-61929-238-3

Be sure to check out our other imprints, Blue Beacon Books, Mystic Books, Quest Books, Silver Dragon Books, Troubadour Books, and Young Adult Books.

About the author

Melissa Good is an IT professional and network engineer who works and lives in South Florida with a skillion lizards and Mocha the dog.

VISIT US ONLINE AT
www.regalcrest.biz

At the Regal Crest Website You'll Find

- The latest news about forthcoming titles and new releases

- Our complete backlist of romance, mystery, thriller and adventure titles

- Information about your favorite authors

- Media tearsheets to print and take with you when you shop

- Which books are also available as eBooks.

Regal Crest print titles are available from all progressive booksellers including numerous sources online. Our distributors are Bella Distribution and Ingram.

Lightning Source UK Ltd.
Milton Keynes UK
UKHW02f0624250918
329480UK00016B/1509/P